UNHOLY ALLIANCE

A COUNTER-TERRORISM THRILLER

SIMEON HUGHES

AIRBORNE
PUBLISHING

For Suzanne & Scarlet

PROLOGUE

BELFAST, NORTHERN IRELAND

The flashing light of the ambulance sent a ghostly blue glow up into the grey, drizzle-laden sky of a cold Belfast night. Another emergency service vehicle turned into the approach road of the Odyssey Arena, sirens and lights blazing into the night.

A night out gone badly wrong for someone, thought the police constable as he exited his vehicle and approached the crowd of onlookers, ushering them back to give the medical team space and privacy as they worked.

The crowd were noisy and animated; probably another victim of the Ecstasy craze taking a hold on the Belfast club scene. The battle-hardened police officer couldn't get excited about these incidents, not in the same way as when he had worked in an actual war zone. He watched as the paramedic and doctor went to work on the man, his lifeless, near-naked body sprawled on a pavement strewn with the detritus of emergency medical intervention. Both were in deep concentration, bent over the body, frantically doing whatever they could to save a young man's life. Blue-gloved hands searched for items in the numerous red bags they had beside them.

For half an hour they tried to resuscitate the teenager. His party clothes had been cut off to enable the medics to do their work. The yellow pads of the defib loomed on his chest. Their regular convulsions took hold, forcing his unseeing eyes wide, staring into eternity. The officer had seen enough trauma in his time to know this was a serious situation. He looked away and turned to the crowd.

"Okay, everyone," he shouted, "the show's over. Can we make a move, please?"

Like reluctant sheep, the crowd dispersed down the long road leading out of the Arena.

Andy Carr went down to the front door of his office. The office had once been a hive of activity, but now it was a sleepy backwater as the 'Troubles' in Northern Ireland were becoming a distant memory. He used to love his work; now he was looking beyond the horizon. He had been given a new role as a Liaison Officer between MI5 and the Met Police; at least it got him away from the boredom of post-conflict Belfast. Andy pressed the electronic buzzer, and the door opened with a clunk. Professor Eaton stood in the ever-present rain. Andy noticed he dressed as something between a geography teacher and a spook. He ushered the professor into the building and led him purposefully to the secure briefing room.

They both took a seat. Professor Eaton paused, gathering his thoughts.

"Andy — may I call you Andy?" He had a slight stutter. Andy nodded. "I have a worrying situation," Eaton began, "and I really don't know what to do. Last weekend, a teenage boy was rushed to hospital after being treated at the Odyssey Arena. He died that same night. Cause of death: reaction to taking a substance we suspect he'd purchased in the night-club." Eaton paused for a moment, then continued. "My team has to analyse the findings of these drug deaths and submit a report, via the police, to Stormont. I have grave concerns that the police will try to cover this one up." Eaton again paused, staring into space for a while. After an uncomfortable silence, he said, "As you know, the paramilitary groups still play a very active role in the drug trade in this city and across the province."

"Yes, I fully understand the situation in the province." As the Senior Operations Officer for MI5, Andy knew this area intimately, though he was confused why this was a matter for his organisation, and not the police. "Professor, what relevance is this to MI5 Operations in Northern Ireland?"

"I'll explain, but I'm concerned the consequences of my findings may cause certain members of the police serious problems, and that they'll somehow try to interfere."

Andy realised that the professor was suggesting he didn't trust the police. He knew he had a point. Andy himself had witnessed the way the police colluded with various sectarian groups, supposedly at peace.

"We have tested the substance and the findings have been double-, even triple-checked if needed." Professor Eaton fiddled with his ear and exhaled. "This variety of drug is called Captagon, recognisable by the logo of two interlinking letter Cs." He produced a couple of photos from a jacket pocket and showed Andy. "They only produced this version in labs across Lebanon's Bekaa Valley, notorious for its legacy of drug production and smuggling. It's the drug of choice for ISIS and Jihadists all around the Middle East, and is known as the 'Potion of Terror.' These groups have sole distribution rights, and nobody messes with that. Furthermore, it has never been found in Europe, and especially not on the club scene."

Andy was listening intently now, the penny finally dropping why the professor wanted his organisation to be involved. "Let me be clear on this," Andy said. "What you're saying is, the drug of choice for Jihadists is being openly supplied to Belfast's club scene?" Andy wanted clarification from the professor as he realised the dire consequences if this were true.

Professor Eaton nodded. "Our colleagues in the States have analysed drugs lifted after raids on Al-Qaeda and Isis safe houses in Iraq and Syria, where large quantities were found. The toxicology tests are an exact match. That's why I asked to see you... I didn't know who else to turn to."

Andy thought the professor sounded nervous.

"Right, I'm going to have to send this up my chain of command. I'm warning you, this will go to the very top," Andy stated. "Pack a bag, Professor, you may need to fly to London today."

"Erm, okay. Any idea where?"

"Ten Downing Street. And make sure you have your facts straight. This could be massive."

Andy left the room and headed for the secure landline to London, struggling to comprehend what he had just been told. However, if he were honest with himself, Andy felt a growing excitement that things may be hotting up again.

Chapter 1

"Thank you, Professor."

The Prime Minister stood and shook the man's hand, then watched as he left the room. She sat down, giving those gathered around her time for the news they'd received to sink in. The PM was dressed smartly in a trouser suit and blue business shirt, giving her a corporate air. As always, her black hair was neatly trimmed and elegantly coiffured, though her good looks were showing signs of service, dark bags starting to appear around her intense brown eyes.

The atmosphere in the COBRA briefing room could be cut with a knife. The large monitor at the end of the room was blank, with only the COBRA logo visible. The oak table that ran the length of the room was neatly laid out with coffee cups and bottled water, a smattering of Moleskin notebooks, and Mont Blanc pens.

Sitting next to the Prime Minister were her close aides, her inner sanctum of politicians and advisors. At the far end of the table sat the Commissioner of the Met Police, the heads of MI6 and MI5, and the Director of UK Special Forces. Perched on the end of the row, looking as if he wasn't really supposed to be present, was Paul Allen, head of the newly-formed organisation, Phalanx. After studying them, the PM had named them the 'macho corner'. Due to the short notice they had received, most were dressed in casual clothes suited to a lazy Saturday, yet the service personnel, as ever, were smartly dressed in uniform.

"Gentlemen," she began forcibly, "I would say sorry to have called you out on a weekend, but frankly, I am not sorry. We have a situation which is a matter of utmost urgency. You all heard the brief. My question to you as a collective is, how the fuck can this have gone unnoticed?" The PM didn't normally approve of swearing, but she wanted to emphasise her annoyance. She looked around the room at the gathering of the most powerful people in the British hierarchy, maintaining eye contact while struggling to keep her cool. She continued. "What is obvious to me is this: this situation has caught us totally unaware. Can anyone explain to me how the situation in Belfast could have come as a total surprise? No intelligence — in fact, no bloody idea this was happening?" She again directed her glance towards the end of the table where the police and security services sat, ensuring they knew where she was placing the blame. "It took the tragic death of a young man to bring this to our attention, and if that professor hadn't been involved, we would still be in the dark." She slammed her fist into the table, surprised by the echo it sent resonating around the oak-panelled room. She paused to gather her thoughts. The effect seemed to work. Men of power seemed to shrink into their seats, she observed. "If, as is being suggested, Irish paramilitaries are engaged in drug-trafficking with as-yet-unknown jihadist groups, then we really have a major problem on our hands. In fact, our friends at Langley are correct; we are off the pace when it comes to global terrorism." She couldn't help but mention the opinion of the CIA on UK counterterrorism. The PM continued. "This is not a normal partnership in crime. In fact, it is pretty damn sinister, somewhat of an unholy alliance."

She gathered her thoughts and checked her notes on the desk in front of her. Others around the table took sips of water. No one uttered a word in the complete silence. The PM looked up from her notes. Her expression was intense, her gaze steady. The deep brown eyes offered no compromise. "What is clear to me is that this is a total intelligence failure. I have no option but to make this a Tier One national security situation. It is totally unacceptable that we don't know why these organisations have started to do their own unique, twisted business together. It's nothing short of a disgrace." Her gaze moved around the table. "We shall sit down again on Monday to progress this further, at which time I demand full updates from you all." She gestured to the macho corner.

A loud knock at the door gave the macho corner a slight reprieve, and an aide entered. The smartly-dressed young lady went directly to the PM, who took hold of the iPad she was offered. Her face initially showed surprise, which soon morphed into a look of horror. She continued staring at the iPad with intense concentration, then turned to the young woman.

"Can we get this on the live feed screen, please?" she said, handing back the iPad.

"Of course, ma'am."

The PM turned back to the table. "We have a serious situation happening, right now," she stated, as the main screen at the end of the conference room burst into life.

Chapter 2

The aftereffects of anaesthetic played crazy tricks on people. The nurse checked her patient with care and compassion, knowing well how the aftereffects of anaesthetic played crazy tricks on people. This man was one of her own, and he had a heart-breaking story he was yet to awake to. She placed the metal folder containing his post-operation observations on the end of his bed, and was about to leave the door when the man let out a loud groan — almost a cry. His eyes shot open, staring at the large fluorescent light above the bed.

Dominic Leigh had been admitted to the hospital after a long journey from the hills of south Wales via a hospital in the Welsh town of Brecon, close to the hills he was aiming to conquer in order to gain a place in the elite 22nd Air Service Regiment.

The surgeon who had put the ankle back together had briefed the pretty young nurse. It was a severe injury and, because of the nature of the wound, he may have an infection in the bone. She knew he would be in intense pain.

She walked back to the bed. "Hello. Take your time," she said, attempting to ease the man back into the real world.

"Where am I?' he asked, looking around the room but

falling back onto his pillow as pain from his ankle racked his lower body. "Fuck!" he blurted, then flushed, clearly embarrassed. "Sorry."

"No worries, I've heard a lot worse," the nurse replied. Her blonde hair was neatly tied in a bun beneath her army nurse's triangular head-dress. She was tall and slim. With the nature of a true carer, she moved closer to the prostrate man. "Fancy a brew, and maybe some toast?"

Dominic turned to her. "Yes, please," he muttered in a tired, hoarse voice. She left the room, leaving Dominic to his thoughts.

He glanced around the bare room. One dirty window offered a view to nowhere but the back of the next squat, redbrick building. Standard army hospital room: bland, Formica locker by his bed, plastic chair for the visitor he knew would never come, no flowers, no grapes... no nothing.

The nurse returned with a tray, two mugs of tea and some white toast loaded thick with butter.

"Mind if I join you?" She placed a mug on his locker and moved forward to help him shuffle up onto his pillow.

"Bollocks," he let out in a pained voice.

"I'll sort you some pain relief with the doctor. He'll be round shortly to see you." Dominic sensed an edge to her voice, as if something wasn't right.

They both sat in silence, drinking their teas and lost in thought, until she broke the uneasy quiet.

"You're 2 Para, aren't you?"

"Yeah, Patrols Platoon. I was on SAS selection when this happened," he said, indicating his lower leg, hidden beneath the mechanical frame that kept his army-issue sheets from putting pressure on the open wounds around the bolts inserted in his shattered ankle.

"Yes, we heard all about you before you arrived; walking on a broken leg. Typical Para." She laughed. "My other half is in the Parachute Signal Squadron. Rich Wood, do you know him?"

"No, don't recognise the name, but Sigs are good lads. Did some training with them prior to selection."

They both looked round in unison as the door burst open and in walked a tall, commanding figure in surgical scrubs, complete with white plastic croc-style shoes. It was obvious to them both this was the surgeon. The nurse stood at attention.

"Please." He motioned for her to sit back down.

"Sergeant Leigh," the Surgeon said, calling Dominic by his Army rank, "I'm Lieutenant Colonel Gillespie, head orthopaedic surgeon here at Cambridge Military Hospital." He paused, looking down at the broken man laid before him. Dominic noted an almost fatherly air to him. "Well, young man, you certainly gave me a tough end to my week." Again he paused, searching for words. "The good news is, I managed to place the metal work exactly where I wanted to, but you will be sore for a while. I shall make sure you have some powerful painkillers for the next twelve hours or so." He glanced at the nurse.

"So, what's the damage, sir? How long before I go back?" Dom asked.

The surgeon looked out the window for a second, stalling for time.

"Son, your ankle is badly damaged. It was touch-and-go whether you would lose your foot. I can't yet be sure of the extent of the long-lasting damage. How you managed to walk to safety is amazing — well done on that." He paused again. "This isn't easy to say, son, but your days of Special Forces are over. You may get back to fitness and return to your unit, but Hereford... I'm sorry, but that won't be possible."

Dom's mind was racing out of control. He couldn't really grasp what he had just heard.

"It's tough," the surgeon said, "but I have a duty of care for my patients. Please, don't underestimate your injury. Sergeant, you're a very lucky man not to have damaged yourself even more. I'm sorry, I truly am, to give you this bad news so soon after your operation." With that, he nodded to them both and left the room, closing the door behind him.

Dominic couldn't control himself. Tears streamed down his face. His chest heaved. He felt the nurse grab his hand. It felt warm, safe and caring.

"I'll call your wife. Is she in married quarters in Aldershot?"

"Good luck," Dominic replied with more venom than he meant. "She won't give a fuck. That's another disaster."

He laid back his head, still staring ahead, eyes fixed on the long lighting strips in the ceiling.

"Listen, I have my rounds to do, but I'm on duty tonight so I'll check on you later," she said, almost apologetically.

Dominic lay still in his bed, a prisoner to his injury and to his predicament. Special Forces Selection had been his dream, his chance to escape to pastures new. But that dream was now shattered into pieces, just like his ankle.

His wife never visited him. Dom was right, she couldn't give a fuck, and her aim was to ensure Ronnie, the daughter he doted on, didn't give a fuck either. Dominic knew, from the moment the surgeon had informed him his injury meant he would never serve with the SAS, that his life would never be the same.

Chapter 3

GORAZDE, YUGOSLAVIA

Gorazde was the front line for the Muslim BIH army. They numbered 80,000, but only had weapons for six and a half thousand. They were surrounded by the Serbian army who numbered 40,000 and were intent on capturing this strategic town. Almost certainly, a massacre would ensue. Ethnic cleansing had become the new weapon of terror in what was fast becoming the worst example of its kind since World War II.

"Hello, Zero. This is Bravo One Zero. Over."

The British Army Command radio net was being monitored by the duty watch-keeper. He was based at what was once the local school in the centre of Gorazde, hastily fortified with whatever the company of fusiliers could get their hands on. The ops room occupied what used to be the teachers' staff room, where some of the children's drawings of happier times still hung on the walls.

The duty watch-keeper sat overlooking the map boards, marked up in red with the various company locations and those of the Serb forces. The duty signaller sat monitoring the array of radios and specialist communication kit, which monitored the Serbian army based around the town.

"Zero send."

"One Zero, we have unusual activity up here: an unidentified male approaching us from the direction of Samiri Ridge down the track that runs parallel to our location. Roger so far, over."

"Zero Roger."

"One Zero, he will have come from the Serb lines, direction of Zepa, and we cannot verify if he is armed, however he looks in clip. Advise, over."

The call sign from Patrols Platoon based at Observation Post No. Three, the strategical high ground facing the Serb frontline to the northeast of the besieged town, were rightly concerned that this could be a trick by the Serbs to draw the team into an ambush. Call sign Bravo One Zero held a strategic advantage, and they wanted this ground. The once-pretty town of Gorazde, nestled in the valley, was a sitting duck for Serb artillery if they gained this ground off the British Army.

"Zero, monitor and keep us updated, do not let him into the patrol base. If he approaches, hold him short and await further instructions. Out."

The ops officer threw down the radio handset and turned to his signaller. He knew OC Patrols was a top bloke and wouldn't be blowing this out of proportion. Something wasn't right here.

"Get me the Serb LO on the phone. I need to speak to him, no fucking excuses."

The ops officer spoke with the LO, who tried to calm the young army captain down and kept repeating that they had no men dressed in civilian clothes trying to approach the British Army observation post, either on Simiri Ridge or anywhere else in their tactical area of responsibility.

Some time passed, then the radio sparked into life again.

"Zero, this is Bravo One Zero. Update, over."

"Zero, send."

"One Zero, we need medical assistance and an interpreter up to my location asap. Roger so far."

"Zero, confirm no friendly casualties, over?"

"One Zero, confirm no friendly casualties. The male we observed has collapsed short of our perimeter and we have secured him. He needs immediate casualty evacuation. Over."

The ops officer pressed the klaxon to signal a crash out; the soldiers lounging on camp beds or sat watching films on laptops in the fortified shell of the old gymnasium sprang into life, their helmets, body armour and SA-80 rifles never more than an arm's length away. It didn't take long for the battle-ready troops to get kitted up, all of them looking lean courtesy of the lack of fresh food and months living on army rations.

The lightly-armoured Land Rovers sat parked in line, primed and ready, their white UN paintwork now tainted from months of abuse and muddy roads. There was no mains water and little fresh water in this besieged town, so vehicle washing was impossible.

The OC's Land Rover vehicle group comprised three vehicles. One was a specialist communication vehicle manned by a member of the Royal Signals, while the other two vehicles held the OC and his interpreter, as well as the operations officer and two soldiers who acted as bodyguards for the group.

Everyone tensed up as they left the perimeter of the now-fortified school. The soldiers in the makeshift sandbag sangers kept their rifles at the ready in case anyone tried to have a go.

The vehicles turned left and started the drive over the river and up towards the high ground of OP3, overlooking the town from the north-east.

Blue lips. That's the one thing that had struck the reception team when they'd completed the drill to ensure the person wasn't armed or attempting a suicide attack. He stank of a strange deathly scent, and was dressed in light clothing, track suit and trainers.

He must be freezing, the OP Commander thought, and wrapped him in a warm jacket one lad had in his patrol day sack. The man's lips were blue, like someone made up for a casualty simulation exercise.

Where the fuck are the medics? Captain Cummins thought, though he kept it to himself, not wanting to phase his blokes about how serious this guy's condition was.

"Boss, he's trying to say something. Can't understand. It's in English, though."

Captain Cummins cradled the man in his arms, hugging him and putting his ear towards his mouth. He was so utterly worn out that his words were a mere whisper.

"All... gone," he murmured.

"Who, mate, who's all gone?" Cummins asked.

Another long pause. He was now drifting in and out of consciousness.

"The men and boys... my town... all gone."

Then came the word that would come to haunt the western world in the fullness of time.

He opened his eyes, staring into the very soul of the army captain in a way that spooked Cummins, who sensed almost hatred in them. With his blue and chapped lips close to Cummins' ears the man muttered, "Srebrenica." He coughed, summoning all his strength, "All the men and boys are gone... killed in my hometown." Tears were now streaming down his face.

The effort was too much as he collapsed into the British army officer's arms, convulsing uncontrollably from the cold and the physical hardships he must have endured.

Captain Cummins tried to make sense of what he had heard. He would need to brief the OC, who — from the radio he was monitoring via the small earpiece in his left ear — was five minutes away.

He passed the casualty over to his senior corporal, who was

constantly checking the vital signs of the casualty to ensure a rapid handover to the Army Medical Corps sergeant who formed part of the OC's group.

It can't be true, surely not? Cummins knew from the regular intelligence reports that the Serbs were making a push for Srebrenica, just as they were for the town he was helping to protect. But not a massacre, please? The Dutch held that zone. He also knew the SAS had teams in that area under the cover of being Joint Commission Observers, so they would have heard.

Three white vehicles, with "UN" emblazoned on the side, came slowly into view around the last bend in the steep track up onto the high ground. The wind was now bringing sheets of rain across open bleak hillside; *Not unlike Sennybridge*, thought Cummins as he pulled the zip up on his Softie duvet jacket, that had become the new must-have clothing item.

The OC got down from the passenger seat of the Land Rover, and with his SA-80 rifle held aggressively in his right hand, he made a beeline for Captain Cummins, flanked by two bodyguards who were constantly checking the area for any threats to their charge. As the medical team stabilised the casualty and made him ready for evacuation on a scoop stretcher, the OC received the update via his trusted Patrols Platoon OC. Both men stood silent, staring into space as they digested the severity of what had most probably happened in a town not forty kilometres from where they stood.

Safely back into the school, the medics, who gave him a drip with glucose and another with fluids to combat his severe dehydration, thoroughly assessed the casualty. He was then washed and placed into a new army sleeping bag and left to sleep in the med centre, monitored by the medical team.

Major Hickes sat deep in thought in the corner of the ops room, mulling over his next move. He had the responsibility of informing the UN Coalition that there had likely been an act of genocide right under their noses, and they had done nothing to stop it.

"Get me Sunray on the secure means, please." He was always polite, even under extreme pressure.

Luka Avdic had inherited his classic Slavic looks from his father, also called Luka — chiselled square jaw and jet-black hair, now slightly greying on top of his tall and athletic frame. It was obvious he kept in shape. His piercing blue eyes had a thousand-yard stare to them; a look of sadness, but also a glint of steel.

In his formative years he had two loves: his family — he had a brother and sister — and football. Like all his friends, all he'd wanted was to be a footballer. For some it was a pipe dream, but not Luka — he excelled at sport and was captain of his school team. He was even on the radar of the Bosnian Football Federation.

He had been a good, loyal son to his father and mother, both of whom had worked hard at the local factory and, in doing so had instilled a solid set of ethics into him. Not wanting to let his parents down, he went on to further education as a fallback in case his dream of pro football didn't come to fruition. He was close to his siblings, and as the eldest, was very protective of his sister. Luka was always the joker but with a serious, almost perfectionist edge. No one messed with Luka. He was tough, but a fair competitor, both on and off the field.

He worked hard at his studies and his faith, and was a regular visitor to the local mosque, where he upheld strong Islamic beliefs of fairness and justice. His work ultimately paid off. After graduating from college, his parents found the funding to send him to university. Their dream was for him to become a blue-collar worker at the motor car factory they had both worked at all their working lives.

Luka wanted more from life than what his parents had; after all, communism was long gone, and opportunities abounded. However, those dreams, along with any form of normal life, changed for Luka in that fateful summer of 1993, when events shaped his destiny and changed his moral compass for life.

He became one of the few military-age males to survive the Srebrenica massacre. Thanks to his athletic prowess and a stroke of luck, he'd escaped unharmed and spent two days on the run, with no food or water. He'd evaded countless minefields and Serbian patrols, until, near death, a British Army patrol from the Royal Welsh Fusiliers picked him up as he wandered deliriously on a forest track heading into Gorazde. It had been a walk of over seventy kilometres.

That day, he'd lost his father, brother and all the male relatives and friends he had. It took nearly eighteen months to find his mother and sister who had witnessed horrors and abuse not seen since World War II. His mother never really spoke again and died of a broken heart three years later, leaving Luka to bring up his sister alone.

From that day forth, his relentless focus was for revenge. It now contorted his strong Islamic faith into a radical belief that the perpetrators and those who stood by and watched should be punished and made to pay. Nothing and no one was going to stand in his way. He just needed to find that way, and he would leave no stone unturned in blazing that trail.

However, he needed to honour his parents and look after his younger sister. The guilt that he somehow hadn't protected her from the hell she had endured would never leave him. He took a job at that same car factory, though in the sales office, to provide a home of sorts for his still-traumatised sister.

But he never strayed off the path of his actual goal: Revenge.

Chapter 4

Luka Avdic liked his job. No single day was ever the same, and he liked variety in his life. He checked himself in the full-length mirror hanging on the back of the door. The hotel provided his expensive work clothes: smart black Hugo Boss suit, crisp white shirt and thin black tie. With his Slavic features, and athletic physique honed by time spent in the hotel gym, he was ever popular with the female customers who frequented this high-end London hotel.

Happy with his appearance, Luka left the small office he occupied deep in the bowels of this grand old hotel, making certain he had double-locked the heavy security door. Luka's office held the safe that housed various expensive jewellery items and envelopes containing many contraband items entrusted to him by the hotel's residents. He was respected, and this helped him feel safe in his legend as a normal man earning an honest living.

He emerged via a concealed door just behind the luxurious main reception desk. The hotel was buzzing with people; this time of day was popular with tourists hoping to get a table for the famous afternoon tea. Staff dressed in colonial-era, long-tailed red coats moved quickly through the crowds.

"All good?" Luka addressed the lump of a man who held the security post on the front entrance to the hotel, just off the Strand, the busy London Street connecting Fleet Street to Trafalgar Square.

'Yes, Boss. Busy, eh?' All Luka's security staff had been hand-picked by him, but none had any links to him or his homeland. He liked it that way.

"Okay, good. Yes, it will be busy. Keep me updated via the radio, please." Luka tapped the covert earpiece to reiterate the message. Luka didn't like to rely on mobile phones for communication. The mantra, "no comms–no job," had been drummed into him many years ago, and mobile phones often failed to connect.

Luka made to walk back into the large lobby area, then turned back to the man.

"Get a fresh shirt off me after work," Luka instructed. "That one's looking worn." Attention to detail was key. He never missed a trick.

Luka took his job as head of security seriously. He had worked his way up from the ground since getting the job via a charity that assisted displaced people. He'd never looked back.

He walked back across the lobby, observing the large hotel. It was a living organism, almost breathing for itself. He felt his iPhone vibrate in his pocket. His heart sank when he received texts — they usually brought bad news or more heartache. He left the phone in his pocket to check later when alone.

He was brought back to the present as the earpiece in his radio burst into life.

"That's call sign Papa One with a female friend into front lobby," the guy on the front entrance announced.

Luka had given certain guests of the hotel call signs; these guests were high profile and important in the eyes of Luka, who realistically controlled who got into the hotel. Once the message was passed, Luka ensured all the relevant departments could be told of the imminent arrival of important guests, and this one was very important to him.

George Taylor was a larger-than-life character, whose vast wealth had been amassed by dubious means. He was a big player in the London underworld, running under a legitimate demolition business. Born to Irish immigrant parents, George's formative years of true hardship had forged him, and made him as hard as the preverbal coffin nail. He had once been a champion amateur boxer in his beloved East End, and his face showed it. Early in his career at the hotel, Luka had alerted George to people in the bar asking questions about him, undercover police or members of a rival gang. It didn't matter to George. Luka had shown him loyalty, and he'd never forgotten it. The Rolex GMT 2 on Luka's wrist was a testament to that appreciation.

Luka always made sure he met the important clients at the entrance to the lobby. They often had packages for him to store in his safe, no questions asked. Luka was building up credit to cash in when he needed it.

George Taylor dressed well, with class and finesse, strange for a man from his background. The handmade, open-necked shirt and smart blue suit fitted his physique perfectly and anyone could tell he kept himself in good shape. No doubt the good-looking young blonde on his arm thought so, too, although she probably wasn't with him for his good looks. Luka had seen many women accompany George into the hotel. Other staff raised eyebrows, but Luka didn't care. It wasn't his place to pass judgement. All he knew was that this man could be relied on for favours, if and when he needed them.

"Luka, how are things?" George Taylor spoke with a broad Irish accent, not fake or put on.

"Mr Taylor, nice to see you." Luka was always polite to the guests when he needed to be, and he nodded a welcome to the as-yet-unknown lady on Taylor's arm.

"Luka, please meet Belinda. She's helping me with some research," Taylor said. The young lady started to blush.

"Very nice to meet you, Belinda. If there's anything we can do to make your stay comfortable, please let the team know." Luka kept eye contact with the good-looking young woman, holding it for a moment too long.

"Off to the Savoy Grill for a working lunch." Taylor's statement almost sounded like an excuse.

"I will keep an eye out, sir," Luka whispered, receiving a pat on the back from the gangster.

"A word." Taylor moved Luka aside. He reached into his suit pocket and pulled out a white envelope, passing it to Luka. "Could you send this for me?" He looked around the bustling foyer with its colonial feel, conscious of prying eyes, or worse.

"No problem, sir," Luka replied, taking the white envelope and discreetly planting it into his suit pocket.

Luka made his way behind the large reception desk and through a hidden door, one of many routes into the secret bowels of the hotel. He knew every inch of this hotel from top to bottom. He unlocked his office door and sealed it behind him. The large old-fashioned desk occupied the room, neat and tidy, with not an item out of place. He placed his large key bunch and his iPhone down on the leather blotter. Next he took off his jacket, and hung it on a hanger on the back of the heavy door. He pulled out the large leather office chair and flopped into the seat.

Luka stared at the black iPhone which lay face down in front of him, unwilling to check the message that had come in earlier. The bank of CCTV monitors above him on the wall flickered with the throng of guests and staff; no part of the hotel was unrecorded apart from toilets and Luka's office, a safe haven for so much and so many.

He reluctantly picked up the iPhone and opened the message. To his relief it wasn't from who he had feared.

"Hi, you free tonight? It's my night off xx."

It was from Sally Anne. Because of his strong Muslim faith, she was his secret girlfriend. She worked as the deputy manager of the Thames Foyer restaurant in the hotel.

It could actually be a pleasant end to the day, he thought, checking the restaurant on his battery of CCTV cameras. He spotted Mr Taylor, who seemed happy, taking a long swig from a flute of champagne.

Luka stood up and went over to his jacket to retrieve the envelope Taylor had given him. He eased open the flap and pulled out the contents. Settling back down into his seat, he viewed the official-looking documents. They were titled "Movement Order" and detailed a lorry, a heavy goods vehicle operated by a firm based in Dundalk. It was apparently arriving at Dover off a ferry, with a cargo of bananas. It had originated in southern Spain and requesting a "Green" service. It was addressed to a fax number only, with no other details. *Strange,* Luka thought, *who was this destined for?* No name, just a number. Must have been shady business — hence George wanting Luka to send it for him. Luckily, hotels still used fax machines, and he had one in his office.

He tapped in the number, listening for the dial tone, then the unique sound of the electronic handshake both machines made to each other. The two-page document was sucked into the machine. Luka ripped off the transmission report and placed it into the hotel envelope, complete with a large gold crest of the Savoy Hotel. He sealed the envelope, then wrote his initials over the flap as a fail-safe. He placed a copy of the document into a large A4 envelope and, tucking it safely under an enormous pile of official hotel correspondence in the safe, he carefully closed the door and spun the dial.

Chapter 5

CUSTOMS HOUSE, LONDON

Out in the real world, beyond the window where Dominic Leigh stood, he observed normal people passing by who lived and worked in London.His side of the window, the group assembled in this large old anteroom didn't really exist. The group now officially known as Project Omega physically existed alongside the normality of everyday life. But, instead, it occupied the dark parallel reality of the modern-day western world, the long shadows of jihadism sporadically crashing onto centre stage then disappearing before galvanising to appear again in murderous fury.

That was what Omega was supposed to stop, using modern technology and good old-fashioned hard graft. Project Omega was part of the specialist terrorist target team known as Phalanx, named after the group of heavily-armed infantry, formed in ranks and files, close and deep, with shields joined and long spears overlapping, and who dealt fear into the hearts of the enemies of ancient Greece. These were the spearhead of law enforcement, a radical new method of both recruitment and operating procedures.

It was nearly a year since Dominic had started the probation course that had taken him from the classrooms of Custom

House in London to the dusty plains of Texas, where the SEAL Team Six firearms centre was. Then it was back to UK for driving and surveillance courses, finally finishing up with the last exercise, which involved going undercover in some of the UK's most deprived areas. The Gurnos Estate in Merthyr, south Wales was considered the worst and most dangerous. This training ensured the teams could operate in the very areas where their targets lived and planned their barbaric regimes. Dominic had loved it and had gotten himself a name for being the lone wolf who wouldn't say "no" to any tasks, however dodgy. He was always trying to prove himself.

The atmosphere in the room was one of uneasy silence, but it also felt stuffy and hot, the air-conditioning not up to the job. No one said a word, deep in thought and quiet with anticipation. The old customs clock ticking high on the wall offered the only sound, other than the constant drone of traffic from the ever-busy Lower Thames St.

The large oak door creaked open. A man walked in, wearing a very expensive Savile Row suit that wasn't complemented by his frame. Years of intelligence work showed in his pasty demeanour, and even his thick glasses needed a good clean.

"Ladies and Gentlemen, I hope you're enjoying the weather. Unseasonably hot though — can a window or two be opened?" He paused, casting his eyes over the assembled group. "Very well done for getting this far, but now the work begins." He paused again for effect. "Over five thousand applied, and now we have you thirty-two." A further pause. "You are now Operations Team South. I'm sure you will agree the process was thorough, but you all deserve your place on the team. You've earned it." Yet another pause. He was a Master of Public speaking, Dominic observed. "Shortly, I will hand you over to begin your induction and kit issue. We shall all reconvene at four — sorry, sixteen-hundred hours."

Stifled laughter ushered from the group gathered around the hot room.

"We shall then have a meet-and-greet and social with your sister team, Project Alpha, the brains of the organisation. They are doing amazing work already, and we've programmed you in today to hear a brief from them." He glanced over to another man who had slipped in behind him, and who offered a nod. "Be careful with them," he said, "don't break them... they're a sensitive lot." This generated more laughter, and with that the man turned towards the door. Before he got there he spun around. "Sorry, forgive me — I never introduced myself. My name is Paul Allen, Director General of Phalanx. I'm your boss." Chuckling at his own joke, he closed the door.

The other suit now took his place in the centre of the room. An altogether different character, this man was lean, smartly dressed and sported a trimmed grey beard..

"Welcome. My name is Danny Haigh, Branch Commander Omega South. I will brief you fully on my role and the organisation within the group later — first, grab a brew." He pointed to a very well-stocked tea trolley. "Then I will outline how the day will pan out."

The room burst into conversation as the group all homed in on the tea and biscuits. Dominic grabbed himself a black coffee and went and stood by the enormous windows that overlooked the Thames and Tower Bridge, He spotted HMS Belfast guarding Tower Bridge, still standing proudly, though now somewhat tired and worn in appearance. The Thames was a mass of brown flowing out of town.

"Hi Dom, how was your leave?"

Dominic glanced around and made eye contact with Charley. They had worked together a lot during the probation phase and had struck up a rapport. He liked her; she was tough, professional and stunning, with a petite frame, and black hair cut into a bob. She had an athletic figure and loved cross fit training. It showed.

"Good mate, thanks. Yours?" Dom said, almost embarrassed.

"You were going to see your daughter, weren't you? Ronnie, isn't it?"

Dominic had never been that confident with women, and Charley was stunning. He struggled to elaborate on his car-crash of a personal life.

"Yeah, got her for a couple of days... took her to my mum's... not easy."

They lost eye contact as he glanced again out of the window, focusing on the river and some random barge taking landfill out to the Thames Estuary.

"She must love a bit of daddy time. Bet you're a great dad." She rubbed his arm in a tactile gesture.

Dominic was uncomfortable with his messed-up personal life, and not confident talking about it with a relative stranger. Charley seemed genuine though, and he liked her. In fact, he fancied her. It was the first time he had looked at someone in this way since his ex-wife, Carrie.

Charley had invaded that space in a way few got to do. Her thigh almost touched his, and he could feel the heat of her through his trousers. She was dressed in a neat black trouser suit that fitted her perfectly. Her pert bottom was the icing on a very nice cake.

"She certainly kept me busy, which meant I avoided the beer. What about you? Your partner must have missed you?"

He was unashamedly fishing for information.

"He went before the firearms phase. Didn't like me being on this gig. Captain in the Artillery."

Dominic missed his previous life so much. Second Battalion Parachute Regiment had been his life, and now it was gone. He had a huge void to fill. To make the hole even bigger, his attempts to join UK Special Forces had been cut short by injury, and it sliced him to the core.

They both laughed, and for the first-time eye contact was made, deep and full on, and lingered past a normal amount of time.

"Ladies and gents, we need to move on. Today will be an induction into the organisation and kit-issue day, followed by some beers. As the chief intimated, Project Alpha are different beasts to you, so basically screw the nut and don't get them hammered."

Definitely language from a Service background, thought Dominic. *This guy must be ex-MI5 or 6.*

"A lot has been made about your formation. You should all be Hereford or Met Police SO19 blah blah. However, the PM thought differently, hence you guys are here in front of me now." He paused, confident in his posture and clearly in charge. "My background is SIS, that's it. No CV or war stories. I won't be giving any, and warning... don't ask." The group shuffled collectively. "Phalanx is the brainchild of the PM. Research her at your leisure; impressive lady — as your ultimate boss, be aware, she is God-fearing and hard as nails." He surveyed the group now with a serious look, holding eye contact with those who maintained it. "The aim of Phalanx is to differ from conventional law enforcement. Our skill-set and tradecraft will be at a higher level. Our ability to operate in the relevant target area will be increased, and our compromise levels negated."

Branch Commander Haigh appraised the group. He had their full attention. *Good.*

"The police like to arrest quickly and remove the threat from the public. We, however, will defeat the problem, not by focusing on the foot soldiers, but on the infrastructure. With the aid of Project Alpha, we will light them up from the inside. We'll find and turn off their financial backing and recruiting procedures, infiltrate their ranks, and locate their command structure. Our task, in a nutshell, is to identify the beating heart of these organisations and stop them for good. So, ladies and gentlemen, for those who want to know, we have been formed for the sole purpose of taking the fight back to radical Muslim extremists who threaten our interests and population. They are our priority number one. Our targets will be all Tier 1. SO11 and MI5 have made up target packs for us. And later today we will give you your first job. It's decent, believe me." He paused for a moment, thoughtful and intense. "Okay. Project Alpha: your sister team, now operational for four months and doing some exceptional work."

No swearing or jargon. So must be MI6, Dominic reckoned.

"Once we finish our refreshments, we shall reconvene in the briefing room. It's the old tax collector's office, but it's had a bit of a makeover for us."

The tax collector's office overlooked the Thames. The furthest up the Thames the tall ships could get was Tower Bridge, so Customs House was established on the north bank next to the Tower of London, where ships' captains had to report in and pay the monarch a bit of tax, a form of import duty.

Inside, the room had been totally modernised. Seating was akin to a university lecture room or modern theatre. The half-circle had three levels, affording everyone an excellent view of the massive briefing screen proudly displaying the Phalanx emblem. In an open space to the rear of the room hung large screens above desks scattered with high-tech communications equipment. Dominic recognised the emblem he had seen on the induction letter all those months ago.

The walls were painted a clinical white with a variety of screens of different sizes mounted to provide more information. The smell of the place was a mixture of a new school term and a new-build house; unoccupied, new and ready. Everyone took their seats. The briefing room held many more than the thirty seated in there now, all with notebooks out and pens at the ready.

"Team, let me introduce my counterpart, Branch Head of Project Alpha, Andrew Lothian."

The two nodded as they passed on the podium. Lothian fumbled for the PowerPoint remote, initially going back a slide. He was a typical brainbox: no common sense, but a brain the size of a planet.

"Hello everyone. Welcome to our new briefing room. Nice, eh? No notes please. All info to be committed to the old grey matter."

Educated Scot, probably Edinburgh, Dominic deduced.

Lothian started the PowerPoint, which showed very busy slides. "Okay, well, erm," he said, fumbling for the relevant slide. "Ah, that's it." Another busy slide, with a mission statement and aims. "Project Alpha was formed to take the fight back to those who believe they can operate with impunity. Our aim is to blah blah... all a bit corporate this, for me... read it for yourselves."

The room filled with unease. It was clear Lothian was not confident in front of the group. He then turned to the next slide before everyone had read the last, and a collective shuffling took place. He was losing the audience.

"Project Alpha: who are we and, more importantly, what have we been doing since we formed over three months ago?" He again turned to the screen to find the correct slide.

He spent the next hour outlining in his own unique style, fleshing out the information on Project Alpha, explaining the methods and techniques they could employ and their enhanced capabilities in relevance to Omega's role.

"Ask any youngster, mine especially," he said, laughing at his own joke. "They love anything digital, and that's the beauty for us." Now he was confident. He was in his world, and he soon regained control of his audience. As the brief flowed, they became mesmerised. "A digital footprint, mobile number or IP address is all we need. You see, it's all out there in the air, all around us, free of charge, waiting to be swallowed and digested by us like one big itemised bill." He paused, no sign of unease now and fully on a roll.

Dominic looked around at each of his peers, all mesmerised, hanging on this guy's every word. It was impressive, like a Tom Clancy movie, but very real and in the here and the now.

"From that titbit, we can get you associate emails, phone numbers and text messages." He took a breath. "From that, our exceptional analysts will be able to find social media profiles, addresses and benefit records, even CRB if they've been naughty, vehicle details, movements, travel bookings... basically, the whole nine yards."

Classic joke. Dominic chuckled. He had warmed to this guy. If his team were all the same, how awesome would they be?

"We have by far the best telephone intercept and tracking capability, and great links with British Telecom's providers. In fact, even global telecoms providers. Some may be a little more reticent to divulge information than others, but with good old-fashioned British diplomacy, we get what we want. We can even turn on the microphone and cameras on their phones, to have a little peek — how bloody annoying for them." He moved from behind the briefing lectern and faced the audience. "So, that's us; but, as the actress said to the bishop, I've saved the best till last." Everyone laughed. He really had won them over. *A good start,* thought Danny Haigh. From the flank, it had started so fucking awfully.

"These types are sneaky bastards. You've all heard of the dark web, SilkRoad and all the other dens of inequity. They hang around in there, chatting and passing information at will, thinking they're safe. Well, we are there too, and they are far from safe. We have basically turned bush."

Another classic British Empire term. Dominic chuckled. *This guy harks back to the Great Game era.*

"We have accessed the dark web in a variety of guises, some less palatable than others, but we are there, operating and trusted, and if they are too, we will find them. I suppose we have hacked the hackers, out-thought all the clever geeks out there, because my geeks are better, more thorough and one step ahead." He turned, and the emblem of Phalanx flashed back onto the screen.

With that, he left the stage and the entire room burst into laughter and animated conversation.

"Okay, okay, yes, I know — a real character... but be under no illusion. He and his team are cutting-edge, breaking new ground in the cyber war daily. Right, let's move on; kit issue next." The chief highlighted what everyone was thinking. "Your weapons have all been brought back from the States and we have an armoury at our mounting base. Please review the weapons policy for carriage and use on mainland Britain and Northern Ireland. Next, it's kit. I will hand you over to the tech team department. They will issue your personal kit and go through some of the gear we have at our disposal, which is very impressive. After that, it's free time till 1630 for drinks. Oh yes, forgot to say–they have put the target brief back until tomorrow." There was a collective sigh. Everyone wanted to get into it. "Right listen," he said, gaining control again with a stern look around the room. "There is good reason: the PM wants to attend." And with that bombshell dropped, he turned to leave the room.

The afternoon passed in a whirlwind. Whilst not James Bond level, some of the gear on offer was amazing, and all bought off the shelf from the best in the business: CIA, MOSSAD, even some Russian gear. *Fuck knows how they got hold of that,* the room collectively thought.

A new man entered the door, pushing a tea trolley loaded with white boxes.

"Okay guys, last from us for the day: your job phone — but not as you might imagine it. Samsung Galaxy X5. Before you all start dripping, Android offer us more scope for — facilities, shall we say."

The group opened the plain boxes that contained their phones like children on Christmas Day, not caring for the wrapping, just eager to get to the wares.

"People, please don't use them yet. It will take a while to sync with our secure server."

The phones contained the latest technology available to any organisation. Everything hidden within the phone was on an innocuous application called *Client*. This app hid the full scope of this phone and was accessed via a security generator system, similar to a bank app and a thumb scan. Once inside this app, all the relevant operational information was available, from intelligence information, to live tracking of other operators and targets. It even gave live feeds and listening-in facilities in case of problems. It was more secure than any covert operations application on the market. But this one was not on the market; the technicians had designed and developed it at Project Alpha. Even the friends across the pond had nothing to match this. Ironically, the chief designer had virtually stolen the idea from an app designed for people having extramarital affairs but who didn't want to carry the signature "black ops" second phone, which ultimately gave the game away. The app never took off, and the person who first thought of the idea could have no idea of what it had now become: the ultimate tool in the murky world of organised crime and terrorism.

Chapter 6

The man with the nom de guerre of Redbeard sat cross-legged, staring at the dirty, white-washed wall in front of him. For once, he'd forgotten the pain in his lower body. He gripped the TV remote control, his mind racing uncontrollably with the news that was unfolding on the TV news channels he monitored almost hourly from his de facto home.

The pretty blonde news anchor from Fox News was speaking as scenes of carnage were being flashed onto the screen.

"The Head of US Forces in Iraq can confirm the death of Qasem Soleimani, head of the Iran terror group, the Al Quds Force, by a drone strike as his motorcade left Baghdad Airport." The newsreader turned back to the screen showing the attack, as body parts were pulled from the wrecked vehicles, the scene of carnage plain to see on the screen.

"What the fuck?" Redbeard said to no one. He was sitting alone in a room that felt more like a prison. *But this news could change everything,* he thought. He pressed the small syringe-like plunger clutched firmly in his hand, which would shoot a shot of morphine into his system and ease the pain permeating from his broken limbs. He had sustained these injuries whilst working for the man the Americans had just killed outside Baghdad Airport.

Since being injured in the southern Iraqi city of Basra, fighting with Iranian-backed militia, Zacarias Ali Agca, aka Redbeard, had been recovering as a guest of the Iranian Al Quds Force in Baqubah, fifty kilometres north of Baghdad. It was once a Sunni Muslim stronghold, but was now controlled by the Iranian-backed Shia militia that was raging havoc across Iraq. His medical treatment was of the highest order, and Soleimani, reputedly the most powerful terrorist leader in the modern world, had orchestrated it all.

Redbeard sat back on the red-checked cushions that formed a low-level seating area in the threadbare room, that had once been the main living room of this modest farmhouse. *What now?* he thought, the opiates sending his thought process into overdrive. As delusion overtook him, he fumbled under the cushions and found the Icom radio and pressed the buttons.

"Waleed, come to my room now," he shouted into the radio as if it made his words travel faster.

"Yes, boss," came the reply, the words spoken almost in a whisper.

Redbeard looked up to the ceiling as he heard footsteps crossing the roof above him. Waleed had been on watch on the roof of the building, watching for US Army patrols, listening for the familiar sound of a drone overhead.

The door opened and Waleed Mutar entered, Redbeard's aide-de-camp, and his carer.

"Look at this." Redbeard held up the TV remote control, pressing buttons furiously towards the large TV that sat precariously on an old cabinet. The screen burst into life. "Look. The infidel bastards have killed Qasem!" Redbeard shouted, his voice emotionally charged. The two men stood watching in silence as the TV displayed footage of Soleimani hours before being killed, speaking on Iranian state TV.

"Boss, this is serious. It could change everything," Waleed said nervously. "We are his guests in this country; he sanctioned your treatment and your safety."

"Do you think I give a fuck about those Iraqi amateurs? Without our help most of Iraq would have a McDonalds on every street corner," Redbeard replied, anger in his voice. "They dare not touch me," he stated.

Waleed had grounds for being worried — the Shia death squads were running riot over much of Iraq, unimpeded by the American occupying forces. Anyone they thought to be a threat was removed, including allies from other countries.

"I think we will need to relocate closer to the border." Waleed tried to reason with the now-enraged Redbeard who had slowly, painfully, got to his feet and stood awkwardly at a bizarre angle. He fixed his eyes on the TV as a limb was dragged from beneath the wreckage. It was a lower arm, the hand grotesquely stretched out. Redbeard was now transfixed; any doubt about whom the Americans claimed to have killed was gone in an instant. On a finger of the hand was a gold ring with a predominant eagle, the symbol of Al Quds' external security organisation, their international elite terror force. The ring was the only one of its kind and its owner was now dead: that owner was Qasem Soleimani.

The Americans were right. He was dead.

"Okay, I need to contact the cell.. they will know what to do. Get me my phone!" Redbeard shouted. Waleed passed the phone to Redbeard who struggled to hold on to it whilst supporting himself on the walking stick. "Fucking thing!" he grumbled, struggling to unlock the phone. Frustration raged in his mind. His body was wrecked and needed the daily dose of morphine to function, though he knew it was slowly messing up his thought process, which straddled the divide between realism and living nightmares. He pressed the *Telegram* icon, quickly scrolling down the list of contacts until he found the one he wanted.

He typed the message quickly, adept now at one-handed typing on his smartphone screen. *Have seen the tragic news. I request permission to activate a lily-white. We need to hit back fast.*

He pressed the send button; the message was gone in an instant.

"We need to prepare to move," he said to Waleed.

"A wise move, Boss. Where to? Karameh Border Crossing?"

Redbeard sat down, pain etched over his face, "Karameh?!" he screamed. "Don't be such a pussy! You're a fucking coward! We are not running to Jordan; we are going back to Basra. We need to avenge this murder. I need to get back to the Cell. Go now and get the team ready. We'll move out in two vehicles. Use the Land Cruisers — they have the range to make Basra."

Waleed left the room. Redbeard sat back down and took out his notebook. He wrote his request for the use of a lily-white agent, a lone wolf sent to live a normal life, with a normal job and even a normal family. These people were trained to a high standard, the pride of Al Quds. And Redbeard knew the exact lone wolf he wanted to use; he just didn't know the target yet.

He surveyed the room he was in, which had been his home for six months, a time of pain and nightmares. He could smell the burning flesh and taste the metallic blood in his nightmares. He had been lucky to escape alive; the ambush on his vehicle convoy had so nearly taken his life, and he'd often thought he may have been better off dead. However, now he had fresh reason to get back into the fight to re-join his brothers in arms.

Chapter 7

CUSTOM HOUSE, LONDON

The thirty fledgling members of Project Omega team south sat in quiet anticipation. Not only were they preparing for their first operational brief, but they were awaiting the arrival of the Prime Minister, who was due to join them. The room hummed with quiet, excited conversation.

Dominic took his place in the second row, feeling slightly rough around the edges courtesy of the previous night's social with their sister team Project Alpha, who had put to bed their geek reputation and, in fact, had led the way in the drinking stakes. As he glanced around the room at his colleagues and the professional grandeur of this facility, at least compared to those he had experienced in the military, he saw Charley laughing together with a colleague. She was looking as vibrant as always, her black hair in a neat bob and her complexion exuding health. No doubt she had trained at her beloved cross fit gym before coming to work; her sexy, athletic figure was hardly disguised by the casual attire clearly in vogue for this meeting. They had struck up a close bond whilst on the firearms package in the USA. He liked her strong, determined character — it reminded Dom of his soon-to-be ex-wife back in the days when they'd loved each other.

Charley glanced around the room, and they made eye contact; it lingered a little longer than usual, and then their attentions were taken by the announcement of the day's proceedings.

The central feature of the room, the huge LCD screen, burst into life with the shield and spear emblazoned with the symbols of alpha and omega, the Phalanx emblem. As the Director General took the stage, the briefing room's secure door buzzed open and the Prime Minister walked in, followed urgently and aggressively by her bodyguard. She was dressed casually in jeans and a Barbour jacket. She acknowledged the DG, then made her way to the back of the auditorium, climbing the steps with confident strides, then taking her seat at the rear and pulling out a Moleskin notebook and a Mont Blanc pen. The entire gathering followed her movements like a room full of new army recruits, and as she composed herself, they immediately did an eyes front to face the stage.

"Prime Minister, permission to start the brief?" the Director General asked.

The PM gave a nod and a polite wave as a signal to get the brief under way. It was the start of many, and the beginning of something no one present in the room could fathom.

"Thank you, Ma'am." Formal, respectful. "Ladies and gents, before I hand over to Danny who will commence proceedings, I would like to welcome you all to our first outing." Nervous laughter. "We are all here by merit, and you are all capable, so let's prove it. But we are all only as good as our last success; thus, no one will be allowed the privilege of coasting. Your feet won't touch the ground, believe me." She made eye contact with several of those around the room, and paused for effect. "Right, let's get this show on the road. Danny, over to you."

As the DG left the stage, Danny Haigh climbed onto the podium. With an air of quiet confidence and purpose, he picked up the PowerPoint remote and, without confirming his slide order, launched into the brief.

Impressive, thought Dominic. He had warmed to this man, displaying all the character traits h'd expected in his senior command. He was starting to feel as if this might be the outfit it had claimed to be.

"Team, welcome to Op Broken Arrow. Okay, our target is tier one-classified, and was handed to us by our colleagues over at MI5 A4."

Fuck, A4 handing over targets. Must be a good one, Dominic thought, his pulse pounding in his ears. The nagging thought of this being second best to a career in the SAS was almost ever-present with him, and he was desperate for his hypothesis to be proven wrong.

The operation name disappeared, and an image appeared on the screen; it looked as if they'd taken it at a gym or club of some sort, and not a surveillance photo. It was of a man in his late twenties, of North African origin, good-looking with thin, angular features and long, slicked-back black hair. His shoulders were muscular and he looked in fantastic physical shape.

"Let me introduce Abu Talib Haleem, born Paul Dixon to mixed parentage in Tottenham, Broadwater Farm to be exact. He became radicalised in prison, and since then it's believed he's been training with our friends in Iraq, AQIM. By all accounts, he fully acquainted himself with all their skill sets and has several US military kills to his name, so our friends over the pond also have an active interest in him. However, all this is unsubstantiated from a source the Company says is of limited use. They don't really consider him credible. However, since 9/11, nothing can be discounted, hence the reason we got the call. If this guy is the real deal, he is a danger and needs to be taken out." He took a deliberate drink of water from a glass beneath the lectern. "Our problem initially is housing him. He has been totally off radar for some time, not even claiming benefits, which is rare. For those of you in the room who have studied Islam, this individual has taken on the name of the Prophet's uncle, who, as folklore has it, raised him once his parents had died. This man is a true radical, and not a pleasant individual at all." He paused, and the room remained silent. The image of the man on the screen emanated evil and captivated the seated audience. He had something about him, murderous, almost ungodly, and devil-like aura. "Please open your briefing packs on your new phones; as per the government's directive, we are officially paperless."

A wry smile from the PM, who remained silent but attentive in her seat at the rear. She didn't miss a trick.

Almost in sync, the group activated their phones, and as the briefing packs appeared on their individual devices, the room fell silent. Everyone was absorbed in the information.

"Let's move on. Why has this target been given to us? Well, he has since reappeared. He is apparently active and considered a tier-one threat for this reason. We have intel that he and his group are actively seeking to lift off the street a member of A4, police, or a security service agent; kidnap, torture, then behead them on live feed. But, and this is a big *but*, it's all totally unsubstantiated, a shot in the dark, so to speak."

A new slide appeared: surveillance footage showing a grainy image of an industrial unit, taken from the roof of an adjoining building. Three men dressed in casual jeans and t-shirts stood observing the inside of the open unit. Rubbish strewn everywhere emphasised the rundown nature of the area.

"Getting control is the issue. He is very surveillance-aware and employs a range of tactics to avoid detection, which is why he is ours. If we are not on our game, he will blow us out of the water and go underground again. We don't have any technical on him, nor do we know if he has a phone — this is by association. So, any reporting and footage we take is crucial to us getting the green light to take him out. This was taken in the last forty-eight hours, and from intel gathered over the intercept lines, this is the location where they intend to take the snatched operator. SO19 has control of this and it is teched up, but we need control of Haleem, and only when the time is right. However, our problem is that we don't know where he is or where he lives. At present he is literally a ghost. All we know is where he has gone to pray in the past and that's it, but we need to be careful and protect our source within the mosque. Okay, our mission is to impose surveillance on Abu Talib Haleem in order to gain further evidence, which we'll use to facilitate arrest and removal of the threat to life he poses."

Never heard that mission statement, Dominic thought, though he was under no illusion that this was a search and destroy mission.

Chapter 8

The journey had been long and painful for Redbeard, his only companion the constant pain from his injuries, and the fear and anger of losing his mentor and leader to a US drone strike. The two Toyota Land Cruisers he and his protection team travelled in were ideal for this type of journey: no refuelling stops needed, just a quick halt for a toilet break. They carried no phones or communications kit, a lesson learned the hard way after the Bin Laden courier situation.

The motorway that ran virtually the length of Iraq was still in relatively good condition and the team made good time. He'd chosen not to take the usual route into Basra, past the large airport that was now operational, but also a hub for the foreign infidel invaders of the US and their British puppets. They took a road further south, a quieter option with less chance of being stopped by a random army checkpoint. He was still fearful of the Shia and Sunni death squads that had once roamed free, killing at will in the name of their own Allah.

The two vehicles sped into Baghdad past the infamous Abu Ghraib prison and on into the city as it awoke to another hot and hazy day. The entrance off the motorway was a mess, but nothing like the city itself: the air was heavy with the smells of oil, decaying rubbish and death; dogs and even donkeys lay rotting in the street where they had died, bloated by the sun, their bellies distended with the ferocious heat.

They passed a pack of dogs, that didn't give the two vehicles a second glance as they hungrily continued eating whatever they could scavenge off an enormous pile of rubbish on the side of the road. The two vehicles swerved past on the other side of the street. *No traffic cops here,* thought Redbeard as he took in the scene of total deprivation that unfolded in front of his eyes. *What the fuck has happened to this once thriving capital city?*

The drivers knew where they were going. Well-practised in anti-surveillance drills, they took an indirect route to the riverside villa where the meeting was to be held. The Icom radio burst into life as the passenger confirmed the two-vehicle convoy was clean of anyone or anything following them and requested the gate to be opened. The curt reply came, and the huge, rusty metal gate slid open and both vehicles sped through before abruptly coming to a halt in front of the large white villa. *This wouldn't look out of place on the riverfront in Miami*, mused Redbeard as he surveyed his surroundings. The place was heavily fortified, with barbed wire on top of all the external walls. The low roof to the side of the main structure was a mass of satellite dishes and radio antennas.

Redbeard exited the car. The oppressive heat hit him first — the overnight drive-in air-conditioned cars hadn't prepared him for this. The second thing was the stench. Human waste and diesel fumes hung heavy in the air like an invisible face covering. He waited, holding onto the door of the Land Cruiser for the blood to navigate down his twisted limbs to return some feeling.

"As-Salam-u-Alaikum," said a man as he approached from the front door of the villa. He wore dirty, threadbare khaki fatigues and combat-style boots that had all seen better days.

However, the American Armalite rifle M16 he carried with purpose in his left hand was pristine. *The well-maintained tool of a professional in his field, the field of violence,* Redbeard noted.

"Wa-alaikum As-salaam," replied Redbeard.

The man approached Redbeard, kissing him on the cheek. "My friend, you must be thirsty and hungry. Come, let's go inside." He used the term "friend", but Redbeard knew he was anything but a friend to this man. He was a member of the El Muz Palestinian Brigade. The black and white keffiyeh worn like a scarf proudly round his neck was the only clean item he wore.

They both entered the house, that had the musty air of somewhere that hadn't been properly lived in. Like everything in this part of the world, it had once been grand and opulent but was now in a state of decay and despair. A huge marble staircase that led upstairs dominated the large entrance. Large dirty marks on the walls showed where paintings and artifacts had long since been looted. *No doubt this housed one of Saddam's high ranking officials,* Redbeard surmised. *Why did the regime want everything white?* Walls, floor furniture... it would have been a sensory overload, but now it all looked unloved, unwashed.

They entered an enormous reception room in which the only furniture was a couple of white leather couches, and a huge dining table, which had an open laptop and a variety of radio equipment and other high-tech gadgets scattered over its surface. The house may have been in a state of disrepair, but the equipment on the table looked high-tech.

Redbeard gingerly sat on the couch facing the coffee table, watching the man pouring green tea into glasses from an ornate-looking silver pot with a long spout. The lady who had brought in the tea stood still, nervously looking at Ahmed Nidal, the leader of the Palestinian section of El Muz. He waved her away with a dismissive sweep of his hand. She sheepishly moved back towards the door, nodded without eye contact, and disappeared. *This man holds fear in people,* Redbeard recognised; his men also showed him the utmost respect. In this region, that respect was earned the hard way.

The man moved over to where Redbeard was sitting, passing him the glass of pale brown liquid. Redbeard took a sip; the green tea was delicious and sweet. Too hot to gulp, but he eagerly drank long swigs.

They both sat in silence; the only noise was the clanking of pans from what Redbeard presumed was the kitchen, and the muffled voices of the guards outside. Redbeard looked around the room. Large floor-to-ceiling windows dominated the space, no doubt with views over the river, but large dirty curtains hung to the ground, obscuring any views outside. It was eerily quiet. This area of Basra had little traffic nowadays. The diplomatic quarter — as it used to be — was long deserted by the mainly Arab nations who'd done business with Saddam and his regime.

"Why have you come? It is a substantial risk to travel now, and the occupiers have good surveillance. Why now, after all this time?" He paused, looking Redbeard up and down. "You are in no state to travel — what happens if you need to fight?" he said in a derogatory tone.

Redbeard felt his anger surge; who was this peasant to pass judgement on him? He took a deep breath, maintaining his composure. His analytical brain, when not swimming in opiates, was more than a match for this person. He arranged the script in his brain, using the silence.

"Friend," he started, pausing for a long sigh. "How long must we take this? We fought bravely, but for what? Our so-called allies forget not only Iraq, but our brothers in Syria." He paused again, but not for too long so he wasn't interrupted. "We cannot sit on our hands any longer. AQ did this and look what happened to them: ineffective, stale and finally taken over by a bloodthirsty bunch of criminals and rapists." Redbeard alluded to ISIS; no one in El Muz had any respect for them, and in fact, they saw them as the enemy of the cause. "We are being oppressed, used and forgotten. Take Syria. How many dead? How many families homeless? It isn't meant to be like this; we are meant to be free, not under these regimes. They are no better than the man who put his henchmen in houses like this whilst the population starved. No, it isn't meant to be like this," Redbeard said, maintaining eye contact with the other man.

The man opposite sat in quiet contemplation, staring down at the floor. Then he raised his head, gazing at the unseen horizon out the obscured windows that shielded them from the crazy world beyond.

Redbeard continued, gambling with his next move. "Take your homeland —"

"Fuck you, what do you know?" the man spat back, losing his cool at that one statement.

"I know your people are being murdered and killed, your children starving, as those behind the wire live in luxury, aided by the so-called free West."

"We have fought, and continue to fight, for our freedom. Never a day goes by without my brothers taking the fight back to the occupiers," he replied in full defence mode.

"And to what end? Has it changed? No, all I see are land grabs, there're no food or jobs, and you're being pushed ever further back to the sea. They are doing to you what it says in their Bible, and the world watches and does nothing. We need to react, to strike back at them. We are being forgotten, ignored and laughed at," Redbeard continued, perching painfully forward in his chair. He had to convince this man of his plan, as he was a direct link back to the war council now based back in Iran. "The great bastard infidel Trump thinks he can kill at will. They took out the shadow commander in Baghdad and no one cares. We all loved him. He was a true warrior and now he's gone, and if we are not careful, they will do to us as they did to Afghanistan, leave us to more of this shit civil war, with murder on every street. With our great leader Soleimani gone, we are seen as finished. My brother, they all eat from the same trough. We have no allies, so we must strike them hard, make them listen. 9/11 is a distant memory; the abuses in Bosnia, Palestine, here in Iraq, are all being tolerated to feed the fat bloated pig governments." Redbeard was animated now. He felt not only anger, but a strange longing, a desire to get back into action. He had been out of action far too long.

"What does it have to do with me? We have our job here in Baghdad."

Redbeard stifled a laugh.

"What, throwing a couple of rockets over the fence of an American base in the hope you hit something? That's not enough, and that's not why we are here, is it? All the training, all the deaths, and we have been brought down to this: hiding in expensive villas like a rich man's lover hidden from the world."

The man sat down, now looking deflated. The reality was that the jihadist ideological struggle had long since disappeared and had become more sectarian and criminal.

Redbeard needed to stand up; his legs had lost all feeling. He shuffled, his face unable to mask the pain. The man stood and offered him a hand, no words, only gestures, soldier to soldier, both with the indelible ink of the warrior creed on their hearts.

They both stood in silence. The man held Redbeard tightly by the arm. "Okay, how can I help? What can I do?"

"Speak to the Council, ask them to sanction a special mission using the lone wolf I have in London."

"Lone wolf?" the man questioned.

"I have several lone wolves, operators of the highest quality who have been sent back to live normal lives, but ready for the call. No attachments, no links to anyone."

"And what is it you have planned for this lone wolf?" The man's sarcastic tone had returned.

Redbeard reached under his shirt and opened the bum-bag firmly attached to his waist. It held his Glock 19 pistol and a small notebook — like one a journalist would use to scribble down the latest scoop. Yet this was far more than a mere scoop.

The man took the notebook and started to read. His face wore a look of confusion, not quite understanding what he was seeing on the paper.

He smiled, a wry sinister grin. "You are a truly murderous bastard".

Chapter 9

The two men sat opposite, silently facing each other across the oversized mahogany table. Identical grey beards gave them an elderly yet authoritative look. Both were smartly dressed in a shirt and tie. Their relationship went back many years. They'd both fleed the regime of Saddam Hussain, whose persecution of the Shia population drove them to fight for the Iranians during the bloody Iran-Iraq war.

The heat was oppressive. Another power cut in the city meant that there was no air-conditioning. Tension hung in the air. Sporadic gunfire echoed across this once thriving city. Fear permeated the stinking streets.

"We are facing uncertain times," said Mahmoud Al, head of the Iraq Intelligence Division, "but we must carry on. It is our duty to Allah to stop the Americans and their cronies residing here in our seat of power." He made an expansive circular gesture with his long arms.

"I appreciate that, but we are looking weak, so how do we take the fight back to them? They see Kataib as toothless." The man facing Mahmoud was a senior member of Iranian intelligence. He had taken temporary command of the militia group based in Iraq after the death of Qasem Soleimani, the Iranian leader of the Hezbollah-backed Shia militia. That group had been gaining power in Iraq until the fateful night outside Baghdad airport, when the silent kill of a drone strike had taken out two of the most powerful Shia leaders in the world.

"We have taken the fight to Daesh and destroyed them here in Iraq and Syria, but now we have done the infidel pigs' dirty work for them, they go ahead and do this."

The conversation paused, as both men sat staring quietly through the dusty window of the office with a commanding view over a wounded city. A dirty heat haze laid siege to the horizon. The revenge killings that swamped the void left by the removal of Saddam had left their indelible mark on the city, the population and the entire country. The atmosphere was caustic. Death hung in the air.

"Okay, down to business. Who is this man?" Mahmoud finally asked, picking up the battered brown envelope from the dusty desk.

"His nom de guerre is Redbeard; he trained in Bosnia, helping our brothers during the war, and he has seen action in Afghanistan and Iraq. He is highly respected."

Mahmoud raised a hand. "I've also heard he is not of sane mind, and somewhat volatile."

"Yes, I have also heard the rumours. The Americans badly injured him in a raid on his farmhouse and he is now semi-crippled and in constant pain."

"My point exactly — not of sane mind. Any action we take now has ramifications not only here, but back in Iran." Mahmoud was getting irritated.

"My job must be to carry on the work of the Popular Mobilisation Force. Since Abu was killed, it has been tough to get any sense back from Tehran. We are on the edge again. We cannot afford another civil war here in Baghdad and beyond."

"I appreciate this, but what will some futile gesture do for us here in Iraq? Since I returned to our beloved country, we have had a purpose. All the exiles from the Badr Corp came back to fight a common enemy, and by Allah, we will stop the Americans. But they are fuelling the war between us and the Sunnis."

The other man looked purposefully out the window as he let out a long, sustained breath. "Anything we do in this country will not have the required effect. We need to strike outside our borders."

"Exactly, we must prove ourselves capable of being a force once more."

"He has a plan that will involve awakening the sleeper cells we put in place in the UK."

"Why there? So far away, and a tough place to infiltrate. It is an island, after all."

"I know it is easier to use our old Belgian-French route, but we have a good man ready and waiting in Britain. In fact, in London."

"Tell me more." Mahmoud placed his elbows firmly on the table and crossed his hands. The large gold signet was ring like an extra knuckle.

Chapter 10

Whipp's Cross was the perfect location for the FOB, the old Territorial Army centre on the edge of Epping Forest with the main northern arterial routes out of London, especially if your target area was nearby Walthamstow.

The garages with silver rollover doors that used to house the Army Signal Squadron vehicles were modern and clean, but being encased in metal meant that the heat of the daytime sun didn't dissipate. Bright artificial light from the long fluorescent tubes cast an operating theatre-glow over the ten men, and the associated vehicles being prepared for a battle of sorts. It could have been a film set for some covert action Hollywood film, or *The Full Monty,* as the team got into their various legends; builders, workmen or businessmen in suits. But this was real life, and Dominic couldn't quite take it all in. The rollercoaster of life had finally let him off here within Project Omega, the latest attempt by Her Majesty's Government to fight terrorism on home soil.

Over the past twenty-four hours, the entire team had been in isolation, and given in-depth briefings and target recognition presentations, all designed to provide a total picture of exactly who the target was and what he was all about. They had given each member of the team personal briefs on their exact role, almost like a Premier League football player prior to a big game. There were situational awareness briefs to enable the team to operate in the harshest of areas. They were taught the language to use if approached, and how to hold oneself, how to blend into the background on these dangerous, deprived inner city London streets and estates; how to remain unseen and unheard amidst the shadows.

Dominic was busy struggling to fit his slim covert radio into a harness on his leg and didn't see Charley walk over.

"You sorted?" came the familiar female voice, alerting him to her presence.

"No, this fucking harness gets on my tits." He didn't look up, caught somewhat off guard by her appearance.

"Let me help."

She moved close to him; he could feel her warmth. He felt a strange sensation, like an electric shock when she touched his leg. She quickly secured the slimline radio into its covert hiding place and stood up. He glanced at her. Dressed in ripped jeans and converse pumps, she looked every bit like a mature student renting out cheap digs in the area, which would be the perfect reason to be there. She looked even more sexy dressed like that than when she was in formal gear. He found the way she adapted to this environment a real turn-on, the sort of woman he should have been with instead of the psycho he married. She turned around to face him and caught him almost engrossed in her. She flashed him a smile; the sort that lovers give each other after committed, passionate sex.

She broke off, turned around to observe the others, then touched him on the hand, though in a more meaningful manner than usual. "Be careful out there, and none of that hero bollocks. You promised to take me to watch Man City, remember? Okay." Her brown eyes transmitted a caring glow.

Fuck, he thought, *when did I promise to take her to Manchester? Must have been last night, courtesy of too many beers.*

Dominic was initially going to be the van man, but at the last minute, they changed his role. He was to be dressed as a tramp and would be the one with eyes on the Masjid e Umer Mosque. The role of a tramp for this task was crucial but not pleasant, as it required specific details, down to the stench of urine, dishevelled clothes and the rotten false teeth; no smack-head had pearly whites. The team had made them at the BBC props department; however, these teeth weren't destined for the set of "Poldark" but a ruthless urban jungle where one mistake could be fatal. Dom looked the part. Other surveillance teams used this legend, but with the advance training Omega Operators got, these guys could stay in a hostile environment for extended periods of time, even living with fellow homeless people. The ultimate weapon: people were cautious approaching a homeless person, especially one who stank of piss and had rotten teeth.

"Okay, everyone," said ?, breaking the silence. "Ops update five minutes."

The whole team wandered over to the corner of the hanger that had been setup as an operations centre. A large interactive map of London hung on the wall, the coloured spot codes positioned on each major junction giving it the look of a colour blindness test. The surveillance team would use these as a quick and accurate method of keeping ultimate control of the target by foot, car, bike or plane.

The operational team leader gave an updated brief on the target call sign: "Buzzard", as Abu Haleem would now be known. Images of him flashed up on the modern plasma screen and everyone in the room tried desperately to etch this person's face in to their brains.

Dominic focused on the picture. It looked as if it had been taken on a smartphone. *Where the fuck had they got that from?*

He made a mental note that there was an informant on this job. Such a person had sold his army unit out whilst in Belfast, and his trust for them was very diminished.

"Okay, the best place for us to get a hold of this man is at his mosque. Dominic is going to hold the trigger here." He pointed out the area using a laser pointer on the satellite image on the screen. The team leader carried on with his brief. "It's the edge of the graveyard, with good eyes on the door to the mosque and the sideroad option to the side. I know, it's not ideal; however, he is not like an ordinary punter and if he appears, I'm sure we can pick him out. As you can see, he is huge and his head is shaved, or so we believe."

The group in front of the screen muttered in quiet, positive tones.

"Okay. It's now 0330 hours. We go live in figures ten. Remember, guys, the weather is fucking baking, even at night, so beware of heat exhaustion. Especially you, Dom," he added, nodding in Dom's direction. "Call sign Falcon will deploy with one person to clear the route and confirm drop off is clear, then Pegasus will go again one-up to complete the drop off. Griffin and Eagle will form the quick reaction force until first light, when we go to conventional stake out. Remember, we have no air assets on this task, so stay switched on. If Dom is in trouble go in hard and go in fast. Surprise, speed and violence of action will win the day, team. Good luck: let's do this! Questions?"

None came. Danny stood up and waved them away, then turned back to the ops boards and live feeds from the area, talking in depth to the Project Alpha specialist, who was ensuring all the links were working. The ops officer knew how much hung on this job. His brain throbbed with the focus and determination needed to prove the detractors wrong.

"Pegasus check," came over the radio net loud and clear to all in the hanger, causing heads to turn to see the first Omega team to deploy in anger.

"You're good to me, Pegasus," came the quiet, calm response for the ops desk, manned by the operational team leader and a radio operator from Project Alpha.

"Fuck me, Dom, you stink," said the drop-off vehicle driver.

Dominic and Steve went to the rear of the vehicle to complete loading the kit into the clinically clean interior. They loaded med bags and bags of clothes in. This team would be constantly changing their disguises to enable them to remain on the job.

"Okay, Dom, let's do a three-sixty check of you."

Dom rotated around, letting Steve check him over for anything that would break his cover. They discreetly taped his radio to the base of his spine, and his battery was on an extension lead so he could change it when needed. His SIG Sauer 226 pistol was tucked firmly down the front of his piss-stained jeans. He reassuringly reached for the gnarled handgrip, his hand finding it first time — he hoped he could repeat this if the shit hit the fan out there tonight.

"Check on your covert radio mate: no comms, no job, remember?" Steve said.

"Sierra Four check," Dominic said as he checked his covert comms.

"Good to me, Sierra Four, two-minute warning," the ops desk warned them.

"Roger that," replied Steve, who quickly finished his prep and jumped into the van. "Good to go, mate."

"Yeah, and don't drive like a twat, mate."

"Trust me, I'm a Royal Marine," he said, giving him a wink and wry smile.

"That's the fucking problem, I don't trust you."

Steve jumped into the front seat and started the engine. The entire team turned to observe the first Omega team to deploy, giving waves or wanker signs, depending on their previous backgrounds.

"Pegasus, hold in area of Red Five two until Falcon gives the green light to begin drop off sequence."

"Roger. That's Pegasus mobile towards Red Four Nine."

"Roger towards Red Four Nine."

As Steve slowly but purposefully drove towards the target area, the other car was now in the area of the mosque, reporting back that the drop-off area was clear and the mosque was still closed. Call to prayer was still a way off at first light.

Steve approached the junction of Markhouse Road and Queens Road that started the drop-off circuit; a natural bend in the road by the cemetery would be the drop-off. The side door of the van was fitted with an automatic opening mechanism and the back of the van was blacked out, as were the van's brake lights. To anyone watching, the van would just be taking it slowly around a tight bend. In fact, Steve would be expertly using engine braking to slow the van down enough for Dominic in the back to literally dive out and into the shadows. Rural work was a lot more straightforward. So many things could affect or compromise a drop off in an urban environment.

"Pegasus at Red Five Zero and onto drop-off circuit."

"Roger onto drop off circuit."

The whole hanger was now silent, with everyone listening to the net. Waiting, listening.

"Pegasus approaching."

Everyone had eyes on the interactive maps in their vehicles or on their phones, looking at the bend in the road, picturing the dark, dangerous, hostile world one of their own was about to enter. It seemed like an age. Not only was the target a concern, but also the fact that only police and bad guys were on the streets at this time of the morning.

Dominic had his hand firmly on the side door of the van, which was specially fitted out with red and green lights, like those in a plane for parachuting. He felt the vehicle slowing down, his eyes fixated on the red light shining by the door. He checked himself one last time. The green light illuminated to signify the door opening. The streets lights pitched an orange cone towards the pavement. Dominic left the safety of the van and rushed for the shadows, his senses hyper alert.

"Pegasus drop-off complete and towards Red Five One," declared Steve over the radio. Dominic was now on his own.

The next phase was crucial. If the ground operator didn't establish comms within five minutes, the QRF would deploy to the area to find him and extract to safety or worse, begin search procedures.

The seconds ticked by.

"Sierra Four check."

"Sierra Four Lima Charlie."

Dominic moved quickly in the shadows through the gateway with its broken lock, and quickly settled down into his makeshift observation post. The weather was cool but clear, with a slight wind, which masked the sound of him pushing through the undergrowth to his preferred position. The paraphernalia of drug and alcohol abuse surrounded him, and it stank worse than he did. Many piss heads had forced holes in the cemetery's fence to go about their addictive actions. Needles and empty bottles of cheap cider were strewn all around him as he settled down under the bush nearest the gate to the cemetery, which gave him a good line of sight to the target, but also the all-important bolt route out of the area if the shit came down. The pre-arranged emergency RV was etched into his mind and was a little over two streets away. He wasn't alone; others were in the undergrowth. He could hear the snoring and living, tortured dreams some were having, but they were so far gone on their chemical journeys they wouldn't wake till mid-morning.

"Sierra Four good to me. I have eyes on Zulu Two."

The whole hanger burst into life, and the job was on. The

rest of the team went back to their cars and their kit, finalising their prep and ensuring they were ready to deploy: first light was coming soon.

"Sierra Four, that's one times male IC3 Longbeard black, light-coloured skull cap, black jacket, white kameez into Zulu Two."

"Okay, team," the ops officer shouted over the banter, "call to prayer is about to begin. Let's get ready to rock." The hanger turned into a hive of activity, verging on aggressive, like attack dogs about to be released from their leash.

"Sierra Four, that's lights on and the call going out." He could now make out the green dome on the roof of the building, taking mental note of the modern security cameras tucked into corners.

The team were now all ready to move. It was still too early to flood the streets with surveillance assets, but if they needed to they could deploy immediately. It was now a waiting game.

As the dawn light cast its shadows low across the streets, the area came into dull, slow life. Somewhere a metal shutter was raised, a local newsagent opening for early morning business. Dominic started to make observations of the target area. He noted the number of derelict and empty properties, looking for a suitable long-term observation post. He noted any vehicles, searching for a pattern. The only vehicles that came past him were a variety of vans bringing supplies to the local shops, mostly white vans, the drivers distant in their own worlds, not taking any notice of anything but the road in front of their misted windscreens. Counter-surveillance drills always formed a pattern to the trained eye. People arrived at the mosque, most on foot, but others dropped off by dutiful wives or even taxis.

Dominic lay in a foetal position, as if in a drunken stupor, resting his head on his outstretched arm, looking without moving. He listened intently to the radio traffic as his fellow teammates deployed into the area and took up their prearranged positions, all the time alert to third party attention: this was Op Trident terrain. The mosque was slowly filling up as the chanting continued over the tannoy. *The local non-Muslims must love this,* he mused. Just then, something caught his eye, out of place, hence why he gave it a second glance. Two IC3 males were walking past the mosque on the opposite side to his makeshift OP; they were dressed differently, in jeans, modern white trainers and stone island jackets. They acknowledged the man who seemed to be some form of improvised security on the mosque door; just a slight nod, but enough to confirm association. Without turning his head, Dom shifted his eyes until they almost popped out. His sixth sense didn't like this. He was hyper-alert and the unease and cramp brought on by his prone position was suddenly forgotten.

"Sierra Four check." The ops desk made a comms check; he dared not speak.

"Sierra Four, nothing heard," came the ops desk reply. He knew they would start lost comms procedure within five minutes, flooding the area with cars and blowing any chance of this job going down.

"Pegasus, standby for walk past of Sierra Four."

Dominic could not change his body position, but he moved his cramped arm up to get his covert switch to send a signal to base. When the two IC males appeared out of nowhere directly in front of him, the adrenalin rush surged through his body, hitting the top of his skull. His urge was to react, but he had to act as if drunk — being comatose could be the only thing that could stop this getting out of hand.

He felt the kick to his stomach. It forced the wind out of his lungs. He felt panic as he struggled to breathe, and knew he needed to stand to give his lungs a chance to re-inflate. He didn't see the next kick coming — they aimed at his head but caught him on the shoulder. He still couldn't breathe. They dragged him by his feet, the cleanest part of him, from his hide and out into the open.

"You fucking pig, kaffir bastard," one of them yelled, launching another kick to his stomach. "You stink."

"Why you here?" *East London accents,* Dominic noted as the blows rained down. He swallowed hard, the metallic taste of blood running into his mouth from his nose. Tears filled his eyes and blurred his vision.

The one leading the beating seemed to be the boss. Dominic was now worried his pistol, secured down the front of his jeans, would fall out; at least the large piss stain would deter any hands from searching that area. If they found the weapon that would be the end for him, no doubt. His hand was clamped on his covert pressel switch, and despite the attack he managed to press the tones button, sending out three long bleeps. Another kick to his back sent a spasm up his spine, bouncing off the top of his skull. Anymore, and he knew he was in trouble. The radio pressel switch slipped out of his filthy hands, blending into the detritus of his hiding place; he was now totally without a voice.

"Standby, standby," announced the desk. "Three tones, is that you, Sierra Four?"

The entire team was now focused on the next transmission, knowing something was wrong.

"Sierra Four check, Sierra Four, acknowledge." Silence. "All call signs, stand by. Standby for hard extraction of Sierra Four."

"Salim, leave him — he's just a drunk low life, he's not the Feds. You're going to fucking kill him, brother."

Dominic now had a name.

"Okay, okay. He's not worth messing my shoes on, Kaffir cunt," he growled, and spat squarely in Dominic's face.

Then the *coup de grace*.

"FUCKING SCUM!" A final kick to his groin finished the beating and, just as swiftly as they'd had arrived, they left him.

Dominic gathered himself: his whole body ached and his heart was pounding. His eyes watered from the smash to his nose. He quickly shifted through the bottles and litter, and found his pressel.

"Sierra four okay, had soft compromise but all good, I still have a trigger on Zulu two."

"Zero Roger." The entire team breathed a collective sigh of relief.

Dominic steadied himself. His ribs hurt and his nose was still bleeding, but no actual damage had been done. In truth, he actually felt good. He had been tested to the maximum and had got through a proper compromise.

"Sierra four, be aware counter team is out and active, two x IC3 males, med build, green on black, with white Nike trainers, they are aggressively sweeping the area around Zulu two."

"Zero Roger, call signs acknowledge. Sierra four, how long you got?"

"Still good."

"Zero Roger."

The first prayer of the day was coming to its end, the sermon reaching a rousing crescendo over the loudspeaker. It was now fully light, and traffic had built in the area. Early morning workers were sitting on buses, blankly staring out of windows on their way to some low-paid, mundane job, without a clue what was occurring in their backyard. Dominic monitored people as a steady flow left the mosque: young, old, dressed in traditional and less traditional attire. Some even wore suits, no doubt on their way to make money in the City. *Hypocrites*, he thought.

"Standby, standby. There's a good possible Buzzard outside Zulu Two."

"Ops copy."

"Sierra Four, I have Buzzard, now foxtrot away from Zulu Two, with two IC3 males, full description sent on other means."

Dominic quickly retrieved his job phone which had been taped to his inner thigh and, using the covert app, wrote full descriptions on each target. He was now more relaxed as the area to his front cleared. The radio messages in his ear relayed a hectic game of surveillance leapfrog as the teams struggled to follow the targets.

"Team, this is now a foot follow; the targets are all surveillance aware," Ops alerted the ground teams.

The team worked through the follow, each taking turns to follow the targets, keeping control and relaying their exact positions. As they made their way up Queens Road, all three were in deep conversation.

"That's Falcon, drive by for photographs of the targets."

"Roger, Falcon."

The targets took a left turn, walking with purpose down the small London side street; single pavement, with cars parked wherever they could, on or off the pavements. A total nightmare for a surveillance team.

The ops officer was scanning the map with intense concentration.

"Fuck." He grabbed the radio handset. "Ops, dropped them: do not follow. Bollocks, they're doing three sides of a square," he said, to no one in particular.

A classic counter-surveillance move, using three streets that formed three sides of an imaginary square, meaning anyone following them would either live in the street, or be a surveillance team.

"Griffin can take control at Red Five Four." A car team had a position outside a newsagent to take control of the targets. Charley, being one of the operators, got out of the car and went into the shop.

"Sierra One Zero into the shop for cover," she said as she went into the shop, giving them time to get in position.

"Griffin, that's Buzzard, plus two unknown males, at junction Red Five Four." The driver paused.

"That's them into the shop — Sierra One Zero, acknowledge."

"Bleep, bleep," came back over the airwaves.

Charley was now in the small newsagents with the targets. They were behind her as she casually put two cans of Red Bull and some tampons on the counter, the perfect deterrent for any male interest. Her heart was racing, but she never broke, keeping eye contact with the shop owner who accepted her ten-pound note whilst giving her a once over. Somebody said something from behind, and he reached down and pressed some form of electric release on a concealed door behind the rack of cigarettes. Buzzard bumped past her in the tight aisle between the value tins of beans and the rack of magazines; he never looked back. Only the last male gave her a stare, and she committed his face to memory. *Not a bad looker*, she thought, and with that they were gone.

She calmly walked back to the vehicle, jumped in, handed the Red Bull to her supposed boyfriend, and they entered the rush hour traffic at a steady pace.

"Stand down, stand down, RV back at WC."

The ops officer took off his headset and turned to the Alpha technician, who was working on his laptop. Images were flashing up on his screen from the Griffin drive-by.

"Anything?" he asked impatiently. The next call he would have to make would be to the branch commander.

"Bingo."

They both looked at the screen, and there was a perfect shot of the three of them in conversation. Buzzard's head turned to reveal his full profile.

"Perfect. Get this over to Alpha HQ. Let's hope he's flagged on the system."

The team leader picked up the radio handset from the now-cluttered ops desk, scattered with empty cups and paper after a busy night for all.

"Sierra Four and Sierra One Zero, if you're back on the manor can you both come to the ops desk?"

"Sierra Four copy, just getting cleaned up."

Thank fuck for that, thought the still-pristine ops officer.

Chapter 11

Since being given the go-ahead for his mission, Redbeard had been manically planning every detail. When not on a chemical high, he was a meticulous planner and left no stone unturned. His key problem would be getting the necessary equipment into place in London, ready for his team arriving. But he knew the exact people to call, and he knew what they needed to hear the most.

Redbeard waited for the link to connect. The beauty of using the dark web was that video calling was easily accessed and almost impossible to hack. That suited the creatures that inhabited this depraved world. The person on the other end of the link accepted the call and suddenly Redbeard's screen sprung to life. A man sat down behind the distant computer, his head coming into shot.

"Kevin, how are you?" Redbeard said in a matter-of-fact manner.

"I'm nay bad, though you look fucked, Zac," he replied in a guttural Belfast accent, crude and harsh.

Redbeard, known to Kevin Donaldson as Zac Banner, sat awkwardly on the hard floor of the villa, the constant pain he felt in his twisted limbs making him feel dizzy and sick.

"I've felt better, Kevin. Nice to see you again. It's been too long."

"Aye, you keeping busy?"

"Very, unlike your boys, by the look of it," Redbeard replied. "I need your help, Kevin. I have a job to do."

"What the fuck would yee cunts know about that?" Donaldson replied angrily, fully taking the bait. Regaining his composure, he carried on. "Why do yee need my help?"

"It's not help, it's a co-operative: call it an alliance. I need to get some hardware for a team of mine heading to London."

"Really? London? Listen to me, Zac. They tied London down, and police and spooks have eyes and dirty fookin' ears everywhere." Donaldson was animated now.

"Well, that's as maybe, but I have the go-ahead to mount a reprisal mission to avenge the killing of Soleimani."

Donaldson looked shocked. "You for real? And how the fook are you planning to manage that?"

Redbeard outlined the plan to Donaldson in as much detail as he wanted to give him, leaving out the really juicy bit: the actual spectacular they were going to mount.

"Well, Zac, I think that morphine — or whatever you're on — has fooked with your mind," Donaldson stated. "You're planning all this under the nose of Western intelligence, and you think it will work?"

"Yes, it will." Redbeard paused for effect. "Right, down to business. I need you to supply me with four AK-47s. Russian variants, no shit; and four pistols; four magazines for the AKs and two each for the pistols; a thousand rounds for the AKs, two hundred for the pistols. Decent gear, and I will want it tested by my UK agent."

"This all sounds very cloak-and-dagger. UK agent, indeed," Donaldson replied sarcastically.

"Don't take the piss. Here is the deal: you boys are broke, you need funds, you need cash." Redbeard was getting angry.

"Aye, you're not fooking wrong there."

"I have a proposition for you to take back to your leadership."

"Go on, I'm all ears," Donaldson replied, his entire head filling Redbeard's screen. His pockmarked face and broken nose gave him the appearance of a street fighter — which he was — his black glass eye gave added to his sinister appearance. He had lost the eye and got his face smashed up when a bomb he was assembling had gone off. Luckily for him, only the detonator had engaged. His squat face and thinning black hair, which was receding into a widow's peak, gave him a devil-like look. He oozed evil.

"I will trade weapons for a substance you can make a fortune with. It's new and unique; you boys will be in at the very start of a lucrative market."

"What you talking about? Not more shite counterfeit fags, as that won't cut it with my bosses."

"No, it's a drug called Captagon. I have attached an article in the chat box. Have a look."

The article flashed up on Donaldson's screen. *Le Captagon, la pilule qui rend fou.* The article had headlined in Vanity Fair:

Chapter 12

The story, which was in English after the headline, highlighted the use of the drug by the so-called soldiers of Islamic State, or Daesh, as they were known across the Middle East. Suicide bombers and suchlike widely used the drug, and because of its popularity it was being widely produced initially in the lawless Bekaa Valley region of Lebanon and, more recently, in Syria. It had similar effects to those experienced by Ecstasy users: euphoric highs and crushing lows. What made this even more interesting was the ready availability of this drug and the obvious lawlessness of the area they produced it in.

"As you can see, production is no problem, and transportation the same. We have well-established smuggling routes from Lebanon, through our old stomping ground in the Balkans. We also have links with friendlies in UK Customs who will ensure safe passage... for a price, of course."

"Why do you think we will be interested in drugs?" Donaldson inquired.

"Please, don't treat me like some sort of fool. It's common knowledge that you boys are mixed up in the drug business, as your loyalist enemies have been for years. It's all about a commodity your bosses need: money, hard fucking cash. This will give you the chance to make millions of pounds, ready to relaunch your war with the Brits."

Redbeard let it sink in. The silence was golden; he could see Donaldson carefully reading the article, his good eye scanning the pages whilst his glass eye stared straight ahead, keeping a ghostly lookout for danger. Redbeard broke the silence. "You know the security services and police will trace and seize any large amounts of cash being wired around the globe, regardless of how clever your bent accountants or bankers claim to be. It wouldn't work to use cash transfers, but drugs? That could work. And you have the foot soldiers to turn the little white pills into money easily. Believe you me, they're the real deal."

"So, if we go for it, what's the exchange? The hardware you want isn't cheap."

"A million pills, street value of ten quid a tablet,. If matched with an Ecstasy tablet, it gives you a return ten million pounds of untraceable cash, and the chance of this being a regular agreement if it goes to plan."

Redbeard monitored Donaldson; the man looked shocked, speechless. Redbeard knew it was a serious amount of cash for an organisation starved of funds and desperate to get back on a war footing.

"Okay, I'll take this back to my bosses. We'll need to know logistics and timescales."

"No problem. Once you get the green light, we can talk again."

Donaldson nodded at the screen, and without another word, the screen went blank.

Redbeard laid back onto the cushions. He hit the button and with an electronic buzz another shot of morphine surged into his body. The effect was almost instant, and his head slipped back as he drifted into unconsciousness. The dream would return and then wake him, to set the entire process in motion again. He knew he was addicted to the powerful painkillers, but he needed relief from the physical and mental torture he endured every waking hour. Before he awoke from his drug-induced coma, the Irish would come back to say the deal was on.

Chapter 13

Luka exited the tube station on the busy Mile End Road, expertly dodging the oncoming cars as he went about his now-addictive anti-surveillance routine; he knew anyone following him across this busy London Street would most probably be imposing surveillance on him. The feeling of paranoia never left him, even after such a long time away from his past and the training in his homeland. He often drifted off back to his youth and the happy times before the war had ripped his life apart; the nightmares never stopped. His girlfriend Sally Anne knew better than to ask questions.

He always relaxed as he entered Victoria Park, a vast expanse of green amid the urban deprivation that was the East End of London. Pockets of wealth, occupying the large Victorian townhouses that flanked the park, competed with the urban sprawl of old three-storey houses that had survived the blitz bombings of World War II and the now-decrepit square box flats that were built to replace them. Gang violence and drugs kept the police busy, which suited Luka.

The park was full of sunbathers and people playing games. Young children ran around in joyful play as their parents stretched out on the grass, taking in the evening sun at the end of another hot day.

Luka was thinking about dinner, and about whether he needed to stop at the small convenience store next to the bustling Tiger public house, where drinkers hogged the pavement engrossed in their beer and conversation. He felt his phone vibrate and quickly retrieved it from the pocket of his jacket, draped over his arm. He reckoned it would be Sally, asking him if he wanted her to bring a bottle of wine or something. She would be slightly behind him, as he had left work earlier than she had.

He unlocked the phone and scrolled down. His stomach turned to lead; he stopped, unsteady on his feet, and leaned against a large advertising hoarding promoting holidays to Spain. The *Telegraph* app had an unread message for his attention. He had never received any messages on this app — it was solely for use by his leader, a man who had picked him up from the gutter, who had taken him under his wing and got him into the training camp in his Bosnian homeland. Such a long time ago. *Why now? What do they want with me?* He stared at the large block of flats in front of him, bins piled high with rotting rubbish, daubed in the graffiti of the local gang, "London Fields Boys". Someone was painting LFB in these parts, but Luka didn't care about the deprivation in this area of London. More than ever he wanted the sanctuary of his own nearby flat.

He swiftly walked up the familiar threadbare carpet of the communal stairs, and let himself into the small flat in which he'd lived since they brought him to the UK as part of its mission to assist post-war Bosnian refugees. The flat was clinical, and everything had its place — a mirror of his life; or, at least, the lie he told of his life.

"Hello?" he said in a friendly voice, to check if he was alone.

Nothing, just the faint hum of his fridge in the small kitchen, and the ever-present road noise from outside his windows; being second floor, he usually left the windows slightly ajar to let in fresh air. He quickly poured himself a whiskey from the bottle on the small round table, the only piece of furniture in his living room, except the modest sofa he now sat on.

He stared down at the black screen of his slick iPhone, as immaculately clean as he himself was. He knew this message could herald the end of life as he knew it. A message via this means meant his handler required him, and that could only mean trouble.

He pressed the blue icon on his phone, then selected the message to open. It was the only one in the message frame and was from an unknown number. *No shocks,* he thought.

The message flashed onto the screen, stark against the white background.

Bosnian, it's been a long time. You have done well to stay hidden, but now is the time. I need you to help. More to follow, RB

Modern end-to-end encryption meant no more need for crude codes; they could now send everything with no fear of interception... or so they thought.

Luka threw the phone onto the brown leather sofa and crouched forward, then let out a long breath, his heart racing. He gulped down the golden liquid in the small glass, the contents biting at his throat. He had waited so long for this — maybe too long. Had he now gone over the edge? His wanton lust for retribution was now a smouldering ember.

The sound of a key in the door brought him back to the present. Sally pushed open the front door and placed her keys down with a loud rattle on the small table that barely fit in the tiny square hall. Luka grabbed his phone off the sofa and thrust it into his pocket.

Sally entered the living room. Sunlight sent beams of light across the room through the white net curtains.

She stared at him for a moment. "Luka, are you okay? You look like you've seen a ghost."

He didn't answer. Instead, he put his head back against the sofa, his mind awash. *Indeed*, he thought, *I have just seen a ghost, but this one will not disappear easily.*

The evening played out in a manner neither of them had wanted or envisioned. Luka spent the night pushing his dinner round his plate and not listening to any of Sally Anne's conversation. She eventually got fed up, leaving Luka on his own in the cramped kitchen, half a bottle of wine left on the table as his only companion. He poured himself a large glass and sat back, staring at the ceiling light. His mind wandered back to a time he wished he could forget but couldn't.

The smell of wood smoke was heavy in the thick, wintry morning air. He stood looking across the valley at a cluster of homes, scorch marks around each window, the roofs long gone, just the skeletons of homes long since empty. A few hard people remained looking after their cattle, smoke rising in steady lines from the fires they used to cook and keep warm.

Anger raged in him as he walked from the building that acted as his accommodation towards a tent that housed the kitchen, the letters "UN" emblazoned on the side, stolen from the now-empty Army camp down the road. UN Force. *He smirked inwardly.What* use had they been to his country when his people had been raped and murdered, displaced, forgotten?

They had taken this large farm complex over for a purpose that suited his mindset: revenge. He pulled back the large grey canvas flap and entered the kitchen. The smell of strong coffee was heavy, almost pungent — the Turkish coffee he had so loved to drink with his father and brothers.

He took a cup and poured himself some of the thick, treacle-like substance, putting two large spoons of sugar into it and stirring vigorously. He looked around. The room had long wooden tables arranged in rows with benches on either side. Groups of dishevelled-looking men hunkered down, talking in inaudible whispers. A mixed bunch, mujahideen from all over the world coming together to fight for a cause.

"Luka!" a voice boomed, and he turned around to see three men sat at the back of the tent. No-one sat near them: an invisible demarcation zone seemed to exist. Luka recognised Redbeard, the de facto leader of this camp. His reputation went before him, a true freedom fighter, a true warrior of the fight.

"Come, join us." He waved Luka over, heads turning all around the room. "Sit." He pointed to a space. "How are you doing?"

"Good, thanks." Luka wasn't sure what to say. His heart was racing.

Redbeard addressed the two other men. "Luka is a local boy."

"Is this the one you told us about, who survived the massacre?" They both set their eyes on him; it felt intimidating.

"Yes — what a story. He is one of our best students, a natural. Look at this." Redbeard slid a black clip folder over the table. The men opened it and turned the pages.

Luka sat like a naughty schoolboy, taking occasional sips from his now-cold coffee; the room had big industrial blow heaters, but they struggled against the intense cold of winter. These two men differed from other visitors he had seen in the camp. No ingrained dirt under their fingernails, and their clothing was clean and functional, not the ragtag attire he and his colleagues had to wear. Both wore shemags, but green and white, not the usual black and white.

The older of the two, who seemed the senior man, looked up at Luka. "Very impressive, young man. You have taken to the training well; you are a diligent student."

Redbeard smiled broadly, giving Luka an overindulgent pat on the back.

"Special one, my prodigy." Redbeard's English Home Counties accent felt somewhat out of place to Luka, but English was the language of choice for this camp.

"Indeed," the man answered, settling a steely eye on Luka. "Are you ready, boy?"

Luka didn't know how to reply — what could he say? Life had dealt him some shitty cards; he felt nothing other than emptiness and loss.

He steadied his eyes back on the man. "Yes. Yes, I'm ready."

"Luka? Luka!"

He opened his eyes with a start, and realised he was in his kitchen in Hackney, not some freezing cold hillside in Bosnia.

"Come to bed, it's late," Sally Anne said, a sympathetic edge to her voice.

Luka put the empty wineglass down on the table and slowly got up. He exited the small kitchen, turning round to turn off the lights. *The plates can wait till the morning; I have an appointment with the devil*, he mused. He slid between the sheets and Sally Anne pressed her head into his chest. He really wanted the freedom of sleep, but it never came. It hadn't for years.

Chapter 14

Project Alpha certainly are the business, thought Dominic. From a snatched photo, they had identified today's target. This was a big job, and the entire team was tense. Today's target was the only link to the ghost who was code name Buzzard.

Dominic sat alone in his vehicle. He'd been staring out of the windscreen for an eternity. His job was to alert the team, who were covertly placed around the target's house, to the target's first move. He'd been parked in the same place since well before first light, and his backside was going numb.

The radio burst into life, bringing him abruptly back into the present.

"That's Griffin, now static covering Blue Five Two."

Dominic mentally made a note of where the vehicle had moved to; *not dissimilar to a game of chess,* he thought. The communications went quiet again, and they left him to his own musings. It didn't take long to mentally drift back to his dysfunctional relationship with his daughter and soon-to-be ex-wife. He felt his anger rise as he thought of someone else taking his place as father and playing happy families where he had once been. He glanced at the clock, barely visible under the heaps of paper and old building paraphernalia amassed in the front of the vehicle to maintain the appearance of being a handyman's untidy old van, all for the benefit of any prying eyes.

It was quarter to eight; Ronnie, his daughter, would be getting ready for school, the house a pleasant form of chaos as she tried to eat toast and watch TV whilst getting into her school uniform. Lost in thought, he only just caught the back of the man who had left the target house and who was now walking with purpose away from the scene. Annoyed with himself for nearly missing the man leaving, he quickly pressed the pressel switch on his radio.

"That's a good possible Zulu One towards —" He paused, racking his brains to where his teammates were in this invisible bubble they held the target in. "That's towards you, Falcon," he finally confirmed.

Nothing — the comms net was quiet, and time stood still. Broadwater Farm estate was a labyrinth, and he was now worried they had lost control of him.

"Falcon, I have Zulu One; dressed black top, blue jeans, white trainers, carrying shoulder bag over left shoulder towards Tube. I am following."

Dominic breathed a long sigh of relief. He'd so nearly missed the person leaving, too deep in thought about his less-than-ideal personal life.

His mobile vibrated in his pocket. "Dom here," he answered.

"Fuck happened there on the lift off?" came the blunt question. It was the ops officer back in the operations cell, not too pleased with Dom's lack of notice for the rest of the team that the target was out of the premises.

"Sorry, boss, he was out in a second; could only trigger him from the rear," Dominic replied.

"Needs to be better." With that, he hung up.

"That's Zulu One Foxtrot towards Philip Lane; who can take

at the next option?" The surveillance operator on the target was keen to hand him over and not compromise himself.

Dominic knew he needed to get back into the follow. He edged the van out into the morning traffic and headed toward Seven Sisters Tube station; he was gambling on the target getting on the Tube.

"That's Zulu One at the junction of Old Well and the Main, and towards Seven Sisters Tube."

Dominic's gamble had paid off, and he was now in an excellent position to take control of the target from the safety of his van. He watched the crowds approaching the Tube. It was peak time, and the hordes were descending into the station.

"That's Zulu One halfway to the Tube, right-hand side," the surveillance operator in covert control of the target said, giving the team as much detail as possible.

Dominic knew the target would approach the entrance to Seven Sisters Tube and he could direct the foot team to the correct platform from his vantage point. He watched the crowds, secure in his cover: just a builder having a brew and a bacon roll and catching up with the sports news in the paper. He caught sight of the target.

"Hercules has Zulu One towards Tube entrance one." Dominic focused on the target. The man stopped just short of the tube entrance, checking his phone and looking around. *He seems to be waiting for someone,* Dominic thought. "That's Zulu One now stopped outside entrance one, on his phone."

The radio went quiet as the team silently moved into position to take the target onto the next leg of his journey. The people carrier — call sign Trojan — was parked to the rear of the Tube, with four operators ready to deploy on foot. Dominic knew he had to be on the ball, as public transport surveillance follows were the most difficult to do and the easiest to fuck up.

"All call signs from Zero. We have it from Alpha he is

waiting for a friend." The message from the Ops Room was via Alpha Projects, who were monitoring his phone.

Dominic watched him intently; he seemed uneasy. Was he suspicious? Had he spotted something? Surveillance operators were inherently suspicious of their targets. The target looked up and waved at someone; Dominic didn't see who. A white Ford Fiesta pulled in just in front of Dominic. The target crossed the road and jumped in.

Fuck. All Dominic could do was send out a quick warning on the radio and start his engine. He would have to begin the mobile follow.

"Standby, standby, that's Zulu One into a white Ford Fiesta mobile towards Blue Fifty-Two."

Dominic moved into the heavy rush hour traffic. He had a car covering him from the target vehicle but only had a partial registration.

"Hercules has the white Fiesta two up mobile towards Blue Five One. Partial reg Alpha Whiskey five seven."

"Zero roger, wait out."

"Falcon backing you, Hercules." The car behind Dominic was in support. *Great,* he thought, *this is game on–a chance to redeem myself.*

The surveillance team covertly followed the car, handing control over at various natural positions. The two people in the white Fiesta appeared none the wiser as they made their way through the rush hour traffic.

"Zero, we have the vehicle registered to a Leroy Sante. Nothing on him, he's clean." The ops room confirmed the driver of the vehicle was not known to the authorities.

The vehicle made slow progress through the London traffic, eventually turning off the A102 and heading towards Hackney and the enormous expanse of Victoria Park.

"That's off. Off and towards Red One Nine." The lead surveillance car kept control of the white car.

"Indicating right, into — wait..." The radio went silent as the operator scanned for a road name. "That's the target complete Brookfield Road and — stop, stop." The vehicle had turned into a small side street.

"I'm forced past; who can take the trigger?" The follow car had to drive on and hand over control of the target vehicle. Dominic had ensured he was always in the follow after his initial mistake, and quickly got on the net.

"Pegasus can," Dominic said as he entered the small one-way east London Street, looking for a parking place to keep watch on the now-stationary vehicle. "That's Pegasus complete. Brookfield Road, with the trigger." Dominic settled into his seat, feeling better now that he was back in the chase again.

Chapter 15

Luka rarely stayed at his flat on Brookfield Road, preferring to stay at Sally Anne's place in Pimlico with its fringe benefits. However, he needed time and a place to put his operation order down on paper for the all-important authorisation from Redbeard. Things had moved on quickly since his initial contact; he was now told to produce a detailed plan of what he wanted and his intended target, and had been given a new method of communicating.

He got up from the desk in the tiny living room and moved to the large window, absentmindedly observing the world outside. This city was never silent; the sirens and traffic noise so far removed from his home as his mind wandered back to his early years in Bosnia and his once-happy family life. His gaze was soft and distant, his mind awash with loss and grief, and the burning desire to seek retribution. Whether it was a sixth sense or just the constant fear of being watched, his eyes rested on a white car parked directly outside of his flat, in the spot usually occupied by the old lady with the disabled car sticker. He moved back from the window; the small bedroom next door had net curtains, so he moved to perch on the bed in the shadows and watch.

The car windows were open, the occupants smoking and occasionally glancing up towards his flat... or was he just being paranoid? He needed to find out. He grabbed his coat and left his flat, exiting through the communal front door and turning left towards the row of shops at the end of the road. His senses were straining, but he needed to look normal, as if he were just getting milk. He heard a car door bang shut behind him but didn't look round, just kept walking. It took no time for him to reach the shop, with its offers of cheap booze and two-for-one deals. He entered quickly, which enabled him to observe the street. Sure enough, on the opposite side of the road, a man stood, watching the shop doorway.

Luka felt the dread hit the pit of his stomach. He had kept himself clean for years and now someone knew where he lived and was watching him. The only saving grace was that they were not good at their trade. *Who the fuck were these people?*

"THAT'S passenger door open and one male, black on blue, white trainers, foxtrot towards the main," Dominic announced over the net. Sitting in his vehicle, he could watch the person for a good fifty metres without having to show himself. The man had no purpose to his walk. *Strange,* Dominic thought. "That's him, stood left-hand pavement, halfway down Brookfield, phone out." The man had left the Ford Fiesta and was aimlessly walking whilst talking into his phone. Dominic attempted to give as much information as possible; paint the picture, as he had been told in training.

Minutes passed. The man stood his ground, looking furtive; somewhat bothered, observed Dominic. Other pedestrians were going about their business up and down the road. Nothing strange, people with shopping bags, a normal morning.

"That's the man back in the car, door shut. Stand by."

Dominic paused in case the vehicle went mobile. "That's situation no change; white Ford Fiesta two up, half up Brookfield on the left, Pegasus has the trigger." Dominic felt his phone vibrate. He pulled it out of the pocket of his paint-stained cargo pants.

"You okay? Happy with your position?" the ops officer inquired.

"Yes, boss, happy no one paying me a blind bit of notice," Dominic replied.

"Good. Any idea what that was all about?"

"Not a clue, boss. Strange, though, seemed to be looking for someone, maybe waiting to pick someone up, I think."

"Okay. Don't burn yourself, rotate with the team and don't get tired." With that, he hung up.

LUKA MADE a point of fumbling for his keys and then dropping them; it afforded him a chance to glance around. He heard the car door slam shut. The man had returned to the same vehicle. His heart was thudding in his chest as he entered his flat. He pulled the door behind him and put the security chain on. The modern, minimalist flat now seemed even smaller as he contemplated his options. Second floor flats in this area of London didn't have the luxury of fire escapes; too far to jump, so it trapped him — his only route out was the front door. He caught himself in the mirror. *Am I overreacting?* he wondered. He looked at the cheap laptop that Matrix had sorted him with. He needed to get the message into the draft box of the Hotmail account, and then he could plan his next move.

He found the *Telegram* message with the login details, clicked on the new message icon and typed his message, ever fearful of a knock at the door or worse. His fingers sped across the keys like a spider on acid. Happily, he posted it into drafts and logged out. *Great idea,* he thought. *This way the message wouldn't be sent, just sat in drafts, unseen, unknown, apart from those who needed it.*

He hastened over to the window. The street was now quiet, the early morning rush over and just the occasional black taxi or delivery van using the road as a cut through. The white car was in the same spot it had occupied since earlier in the morning; he knew this place was now compromised. He quickly grabbed a few items he didn't want to fall into the wrong hands. Whosoever hands those were. His home was sanitised out of habit, so nothing in the flat would incriminate him if the police raided it. He scanned the living room last and walked over to the shelf above the TV and grabbed the photo of his family — the last one ever taken — and placed it into the laptop bag. He locked the door to his flat, carefully placing a small piece of transparent plastic into the door by the hinge, a tell-tale that would alert him if anyone had been into his flat, should he ever decide to return.

He exited the building, laptop bag over his shoulder; a normal look for a less-than-normal person and situation. His plan was to walk into the park as if heading towards Mile End Tube and hopefully lose them on the Tube. He reckoned they weren't very good at surveillance, so a follow on the Tube would be well out of their grasp. He used the road crossing as a chance to glance back, and noticed both men were exiting the car, obviously flustered. Luka quickly passed through the gate and into the wide green expanse of Victoria Park.

His mind was running fast, trying to make sense of the situation. They didn't appear to be a professional organisation and until now their skills had been poor and predictable, but why were they both out of the vehicle? He walked along the tree-lined avenue, heading along the natural route to the Tube station, maintaining the appearance that he was unaware of their presence. Luka's mind was racing now; were they going to harm him? Was he being paranoid? His thoughts galloped, his heart starting to beat faster, and he sensed the start of a panic he hadn't felt since the worst days all those years ago. This made up his mind: no one was allowed to make him feel this way. That was the promise he'd made to his dying mother. Now, Luka made a plan.

He knew the park well, quickly taking a right turn towards the bowling green and the public toilet. Luka entered the old red-brick building that housed the toilets — the smell of urine stung his eyes, but it was perfect for his ambush. He stood around the corner where the cubicles were situated. He heard running footsteps, and heated talking; they stopped outside. Luka readied himself, remaining calm. He used the bank of mirrors by the row of dirty sinks to keep watch over the door.

Footsteps approached the doorway to the toilet, then stopped, followed by whispered discussion. Luka sensed both men had entered the building and that he would have to act swiftly. He spotted the first man, the one who had followed him to the shop, edging around towards the bank of cubicles. Luka sped forward, hitting the man fully in the throat with force. The man dropped like a stone, and as quick as a flash Luka sprang forward, head-butting the second man flush on the nose. He felt it shift to the left with a crack, blood spurting out of the open wound that was once his nose. He kept hold of the man by the collar of his black hoodie, the only part that wasn't covered in snot and blood. Luka placed his hand menacingly over the man's mouth to prevent him screaming.

"Shut the fuck up!" snarled Luka. "Who are you? Who sent you? Why are you watching me?" he asked coldly, slowly.

The man stayed silent, desperately trying to breathe through his destroyed nose. Luka, quick as a flash, grabbed the man's nose and pressed hard; the man screamed in agony, retching loudly as the pain took hold.

"Again, who sent you?" Luka kept up the pressure on the man's nose, bone on bone, the crepitus echoing around the empty toilets. Luka didn't have time to waste. The man's knees gave way, and he fell to the floor, his face now a bloodied mess.

"Brother, I can't tell you, he'll kill me."

"So will I, you motherfucker. Now fucking tell me!" Luka screamed, his anger eating into his rationale.

The first man started to murmur as he regained consciousness. Luka quickly glanced back as the man was slowly scrambled to his knees. Holding his throat, he was struggling to breathe, his windpipe crushed by the force of Luka's initial strike, his jacket and jeans covered in piss. Luka assessed the scene: both men were badly injured and the amount of pain he had inflicted on the man with the broken nose was intense, yet he still wouldn't talk. He would have to really work on him, but he didn't have time. He heard footsteps outside. He couldn't do any more. Luka stepped over the prostrate figure and left the stinking building.

He walked away, the smell of the pungent public toilets finally leaving his nostrils as he mentally replayed the disturbing events of the past few hours. One thing had his attention more than anything else. Why had the man called him "brother"?

Chapter 16

BAGHDAD, IRAQ

Redbeard turned away from the laptop he had opened on the coffee table in front of him. The large villa, with its opulent living rooms, had once housed a senior member of Sadaam's Bath Party; all the expensive items, paintings and furniture had long since been looted, a tatty pair of armchairs and a large, flat-screen TV remaining the only items of luxury.

The email he had received from the UK had not made for good reading. His mood deepened. He wasn't happy with the situation in London. His protégé had proven his worth; he had easily detected and negated the people following him, but now was aware and suspicious. This annoyed Redbeard and placed him in a predicament. He would have to reach out to Luka to appease him. The mission needed his skill; after the mission... that was another matter, he mused.

"Waleed!" he shouted.

He heard the rush of footsteps emerging down the long marble corridor followed by a curt knock on the door.

"Yes, boss?" The man tentatively approached his boss, who was awkwardly sitting on the edge of the square of cushions arranged on the floor, laptop open.

"We have a problem in London. The people we put on

Avdic to check he was still loyal were no good. He got onto them almost immediately and hospitalised them both. My man is truly special." He paused. "We need to arrange a meeting between him and the cell commander, but we must be careful. I don't trust the system in the UK; too many spies." He looked back at his screen, moving his thumb across the track pad, concentrating.

Redbeard made notes on his laptop of exactly what he needed his lone wolf to facilitate; there was a lot to do, not least the provision of the hardware required for the task. He mulled over this problem. Europe was easy. He knew this from past examples, but mainland UK was a totally different matter. Most of the weapons available were via gangland quartermasters who had guns for hire. But they had neither the capacity nor the equipment he needed.

"Sir, can I get you tea, or water? It is very hot today," Waleed asked his boss, looking awkward.

"Yes, tea, and check the air-con, it's unbearable in here." Redbeard was feeling the oppressive heat more than ever.

He kept mulling over the problem in his head, which was pounding from a mixture of the medication and the heat, the intensity made worse by the white-walled courtyard and building he was living in.

The man returned with the tea tray and set it down next to Redbeard. He poured a glass of straw-coloured liquid and mixed in two teaspoons of sugar. Redbeard accepted the glass without looking up from the screen.

"Waleed, we have worked together on many jobs."

"Yes, boss, we have."

"So, how the fuck can I do this? Maybe I acted in haste, but now the council has backed my plans and I cannot turn back."

Waleed took this as a cue to sit down on the red-cushioned square, close but not too close to his boss. He was a man of intelligence, having served as a senior figure in the Iranian

Army during the Iran/Iraq war. An Iraqi fighting against his own — but they weren't his own, they were the Sunni elite who had persecuted his Shia brothers brutally for years.

"Okay, sir, let's have a look at the concept of operations," he said, reverting happily back to his army days.

"Okay, we need a plan — then we need to brief Avdic."

"Agreed, boss. May I ask how the team's preparations are going?" Waleed knew a handpicked team of fighters currently in Syria had been chosen for the mission in England.

Redbeard was still engrossed, looking at something that now had his complete attention. "Yes, yes, they're fine," he snapped back, not engaged in anything but his laptop. He closed it shut with purpose, laying it down next to him, almost as you would handle a baby, "Okay, Waleed, let's get to work on this plan. I need to update the council soon."

Chapter 17

EAST LONDON

Dominic entered the briefing room with the ops officer. He could sense the anticipation in the room; the last few hours had been bizarre, to say the least. The chatter subsided and the ops officer addressed the seated group, still dressed in the various legends of a surveillance team.

"Okay team, the last few hours have been somewhat confused, and we are still trying to get a handle on it. I will hand over to Dom, who will take you through the incident that he stumbled on and why we had to lift off." He motioned to Dominic.

Dominic stood up and addressed the team, going through the scene he had found: two men badly beaten, one seriously injured, his airway badly damaged and the other requiring reconstruction of his face, his nose barely hanging on. He paused, ready for questions.

"Dom, you were first behind them; were they following anyone?"

"Not sure. No-one was in sight when I got in the follow, just the two of them," Dom replied.

"Are we saying it's a meet gone wrong?" another asked.

"No idea, but they were smashed to bits by hand, no knives

or weapons, so I doubt it's gang-related." Dom aired the view shared by most of the team. The situation made little sense. "I administered first aid and got onto the police, then left. In my view, we're not compromised. Both men were treated by London Ambulance Service on the scene and the police are not aware of our presence on the ground either." Dominic paused, looking at the ops officer for confirmation.

"Has Halbeem... sorry, I mean Buzzard, dropped his phone?" one of the assembled group asked.

The ops officer cut in. "No, still active; at present both men are in-patients at the Royal London Hospital under police guard because of the severity of their beating. Local police are concerned its gang-related."

The briefing room erupted into chatter as the ops officer took a call on his mobile.

"Okay, listen in," the ops officer said, raising his voice to gain control of the assembled group. "Our friends at Alpha have again come up trumps, with a CCTV image of a man leaving the area of the public toilets where the assault happened, five minutes after our two targets entered." He checked his phone. Behind him, the plasma screen burst into life and an image appeared of a white male, smartly dressed, carrying a laptop bag over his shoulder. The image was slightly out of focus, but he was square-jawed and black-haired.

Dom looked at the picture, racking his brain; he must have seen this man, as he was in the same area of the park at the same time, but he couldn't recollect him. He was concerned the team was somehow blaming him for this apparent lapse of control. He couldn't help thinking he'd had a bad day. He knew he was trying too hard, his desire to prove himself putting stumbling blocks in his way.

The team were told to get a brew whilst the ops officer spoke to Control about the next move. Dominic moved away to the back of the large, sterile briefing room, looking out of the window.

"Mate, you look down." Charley had moved next to him.

"Shit day, not happy," Dom replied.

"Don't worry, you did well — saved one of their lives, I'm told." She rubbed his arm in a comforting way.

Dominic tensed up. His nose filled with the scent of her; he sure as hell fancied her but also knew that would be him off the team if they had a fling. It didn't stop his feelings, though. They carried on the idle banter, and she somehow raised his mood. She always seemed to make him feel good.

The door from the control room opened. The screens and radio were busy with chatter as the ops officer strutted in with purpose. He moved to the front of the briefing podium.

"Okay team, phase two. As you're aware, our main priority is to gain control of Buzzard. Tarek, one of the injured men, is our only link, and he is lying in bed with severe facial injuries. Thoughts are, he may make a visit to his boys — we're not sure, but they may have been on some sort of business for him." He paused. "The local police cannot be trusted, so we're going to have to stake out the Royal London."

Chapter 18

Luka entered Sally Anne's flat, flustered, but happy he'd not been followed. He had sanitised his route several times. He went into the smart, clinically-clean kitchen and got himself a glass of water, but as he filled the glass under the tap, he noticed the damage to his hand: the skin had been stripped off his knuckles and bruises were appearing. He carefully washed his hands, the hot water providing some relief.

He walked into the living room. The adrenaline had now worn off, and he was feeling tired... niggly tired. He pulled out his phone and placed it on the small glass coffee table, treating it as if it were somehow contaminated. For the first time since 1995 he felt scared. *Who the fuck were those two goons?* Amateurish, but they knew where he lived and what he looked like. He sat back, resting his head on the comfy leather sofa, his mind awash with images and thoughts, none of them going in the direction he wanted. His head was full of doom.

What could he do? He didn't have long to come up with a plan. He'd been careful, yet they had found him, and maybe this flat was compromised too. His mind raced to his sister, safely based in a women's refuge in the Kent countryside. Or was she? Did they know about her as well?

"Fucking get a grip," he said out loud to himself. *How could anyone know what I'm about?* His mind raced; had the CIA or Security Service somehow got into the El Muz? His eyes rested on the large sash window and, below it on the desk, the iMac computer. *I have to get in touch to tell them I'm compromised.* He felt deflated. HLuka never thought it would come to this: running scared, and from fuck knows who.

He moved into the hall, deadlocked the front door, and put on the security chain. Moving back into the lounge, he quickly sat behind the iMac, logging in via Sally's profile. He found the TOR browser icon which he had hidden, and then opened under Thunderbird, using the shared login he had been given.

When Thunderbird opened, he looked into drafts, and the message he'd left there had gone. They had read it. He typed a new message outlining the events of the day and paused when he came to the part he never thought he would have to ask: what to do next? He checked the message over, then posted it into the drafts box and logged out. Now it was a waiting game.

He made himself a cup of tea, then sat back on the sofa and made a mental checklist of what he needed to do; nothing would be recorded on paper or anywhere else. He could leave his flat, as there was nothing there of importance. Luka's primary concern was his sister. She was happy in her school and was starting to come out of herself, talking freely for the first time in years. He would have to get her to his relations in Dubai. That plan was in place, but it should have been before his holy war had started, and not like this.

His phone vibrating on the table brought Luka back to the present. He reluctantly picked up the phone and, using thumbprint recognition, he unlocked it. Scrolling down, he came to the *Telegram app* where he saw a message. His finger hesitated over the message; he drew a deep breath and pressed to open it.

Go to early morning prayer... you will be met.

Luka was concerned. What did this mean? Was he being withdrawn from the frontline, his lone wolf status lost, or worse?

He spent the rest of the night with Sally. She'd cooked an enjoyable meal, engaged in small talk and tried to instigate sex, but to no avail. Luka's mind was elsewhere; in fact, he was out of his mind — all the years of waiting, the promises he had given to his mother, all could be gone in a heartbeat. Compromised by two idiots. He now regretted his actions. He didn't want to alert Sally to his problems, but he sensed her unease as they spent a sleepless night in bed together, both still awake as the alarm went off at 0400. As they sipped early morning tea in bed, he explained his mood. He was worrying about his sister, and he needed to pray to Allah for her, hence his early morning trip across London to the mosque.

LUKA HAD an uneventful ride across London on the early morning bus. He got off a stop early and walked the rest of the way to the mosque along the quiet streets lined with terraced houses. Most people were still in bed at this hour. Happy he wasn't being followed, he approached the mosque door. Call to prayer hadn't yet started, but the door was unlocked. He opened the door and walked into the cavernous interior, his footsteps echoing on the tiled floor. The place smelled musty. A large carpet stretched out in front of him. Lights were on in a room to the rear of the building, a place only the chosen few could enter. The door opened, and a man dressed in casual clothes emerged and signalled to Luka.

Luka entered the room, and the man motioned to him to sit down. No chairs, just a large red-checked carpet and a smattering of cushions. They did not offer Luka one. He sat down, and as time passed slowly, he became more and more concerned. Was this the end? Was he going to be killed, his body never found? He knew it happened; he felt the back of his shirt wet with a cold sweat. The silence was almost unbearable, until suddenly the call to prayer broke it, which made Luka jump. The door behind him opened, and he tensed. He felt someone walking behind him.

Please, no, not now.

A small man appeared in front of Luka, dressed in an immaculate white shalwar kameez with a neat, crocheted skull-cap. His thin, pointy features and wispy black beard gave his appearance a sinister edge. He stared at Luka.

"Hello, Luka. I would ask how you are, but I know you've not had the best twenty-four hours," the man said.

Luka was surprised. *How the fuck does this man know who I am? He must be linked to Redbeard somehow, but how did they know?* Confused, he offered no response.

"Well, you certainly did a job on the two brothers yesterday. Somewhat extreme; both are very badly injured."

Luka thought he sensed a well-educated man.

"I was concerned; they knew where I lived, and they followed me, too obvious to be the infidels."

"Our security cell sent them to check you out, to ensure you were safe," the man lied, his voice raised, though remaining cold, calculated and controlled. "And you put them in hospital. Is that how you *Bosnians* treat fellow Muj?" His voice was back to normal, unnervingly controlled.

Luka now was certain Redbeard had arranged this meeting — too much information, and now his old *nom de guerre*.

"I reacted... I just wanted to get on with my mission —"

"Shut up, Bosnian!" the man yelled, cutting Luka off. The man was angry now. "Because of the situation you have gotten yourself into, the cell leader is thinking you're unhinged." The man paused just long enough to make it uncomfortable for Luka. "So, you need to behave and do as you're told."

The call to prayer was coming to an end, and outside the

room the mosque sounded packed. Without a word, the man got up and walked towards the door.

"Check the account tonight."

The door closed, and with that, he was gone.

"Fuck," Luka muttered. *This is serious.*

Chapter 19

Dominic was fully clock-watching now. The endless stream of people heading to smoke or visit the in-house Costa Coffee was petering out. Dominic knew he would have to lift off for cover soon, as he'd been in position for two hours. Many people had come and gone onto the ward through the entrance door Dominic was observing, but none of them had resembled codename "Buzzard". All comms with the team were via the work secure message app, as no radios were allowed in the hospital. Dominic had passed a handover of sorts to the person relieving him and now sat waiting for the anonymous handover, a seamless drill he'd practised many times.

Dominic clocked his teammate as he left the Costa next to the ward and took a seat outside the door. Dominic got up, placed his rubbish in the bin and left the now-empty waiting room, heading for the staff staircase. They had been given access passes in case they needed to move in an emergency.

Dominic swiped the keypad with his fob; a red flashing light and a beep signalled the door was unlocked. He moved down the first flight of stairs, taking them two at a time in a hurry to get some fresh air and stretch his legs. He wasn't looking as a man crashed straight into him in a full rugby-style shoulder charge.

"Fuckin' hell, mate!" Dominic looked at the person, initially pissed-off, before a rush of adrenalin surged around the top of his skull. It was Buzzard; even the grainy image they had been shown and the prison mugshot from years ago couldn't hide this distinctive person, his huge physic bulging out of his traditional dress.

"Yeah, sorry man, but look where the fuck you're going, innit," the man said in a London street accent. With that he carried on rapidly up the stairs

Once he was safely clear, Dominic reached for his phone and pressed the talk button. His heart pounded.

"Stand by, stand by, that's a good possible Buzzard on the staff stairs heading towards our ward; any call sign, acknowledge," Dominic blurted out. There was no reply. *Fuck,* he thought, *someone fucking acknowledge.*

"Roger, good possible Buzzard, entering the ward now," Mac reported.

"Ops, copy that. Mate, can you hold trigger on the ward — and other call signs, prepare for the follow. Any call signs get a vehicle?"

"Negative, only triggered him on the stairs," Dominic replied.

"I have the trigger," Mac announced.

"Okay team, this could be a foot or mobile follow, so get ready." The ops officer's voice was tense.

Dominic raced back to his van, jumping into the back to get into his legend workman gear. He joined in the game of surveillance chess as the team manoeuvred around the hospital grounds, trying to keep a secret eye and silent follow on Buzzard.

Again, the waiting began; the tension was tangible as the team waited for the call.

The streetlights around the steadily emptying carpark flickered on as the chorus of confused bird song grew louder. People dressed in blue NHS uniforms walked by, hump-backed, checking smartphones as they headed out of the hospital complex and away. *Any longer and we're going to show out.* The latest call of another car almost echoed Dominic's thoughts as he moved into position, everyone feeling exposed in the twilight zone of a near-empty hospital car park.

"Stand by, stand by," Mac whispered. "That's Buzzard out of the ward and towards the stairs."

"Roger, he is now call sign X-ray One," the ops desk replied.

"That's X-ray One exited the ward and down the staff stairs and unsighted to me." Mac's voice was now tense.

"Roger; anyone got a trigger on the staircase?" The ops officer was now on the net.

"Griffin is parked with trigger on the entrance to the staff stairs and can give direction but not take."

"Roger, Griffin," ops replied.

"That's X-ray One foxtrot towards the main, black jacket, blue jeans and white trainers," said the operator in call sign Griffin, giving the team direction.

"I have X-ray One foxtrot left-hand pavement just short of the main... wait —" The operator paused. "That's left, left towards White One."

Dominic was checking the mapping on his tablet; all the team's cars and operators foxtrot were live tracked and he saw that the foot follow was well manned. As he zoomed in, Holborn Tube station caught his attention. He wanted a piece of this follow, so he gunned up the engine and headed onto the back streets at speed, guessing that X-ray One was heading for the Tube.

"That's Xray One, five zero short of the junction," announced a new female voice.

Dominic recognised Charley. She was now in control of the target and as cool and professional as ever.

Dominic locked the van door, quickly checking nothing was left out, then checked his pistol was safely holstered and headed off towards the tube station. He had a daypack and was dressed in paint-covered overalls. He picked up a copy of the *Evening Standard,* then entered the busy concourse of Holborn Tube station.

"That's X-ray One entering Holborn Tube station — who can?" Charley offered the target as she didn't want to follow him into the Tube.

"Pete can; that X-ray One did a one-eighty and back onto the main."

Dominic and the rest now knew this guy was implementing some counter-surveillance tactics. *We need to be on our game.*

"That's X-ray One at the kiosk and back towards the Tube." A different member of the team had control now.

"That's X-ray One through the barrier, heading for the Piccadilly line, and unsighted to me," the operator reported.

Dominic stood on the platform. He knew from the chatter over the net that two other members of the team were behind X-ray One on the escalator. He nonchalantly read his *Evening Standard*, looking every inch the painter and decorator, tired after a long day's work. He glanced at the board: a train was due in two minutes. He would have to get on it in case a counter-surveillance team was being employed. He knew he had to act normally, and not getting on trains when they arrived at rush hour wasn't normal.

"That's X-ray One, north-bound platform."

Dominic glanced up and saw the distinctive build and hair of the target. The train approached. Dominic immediately got on, surveying the target. The target got on, then turned around and got off.

Fuck, that's me out of it, Dominic thought. X-ray One stood on the platform, checking, then at the last minute he jumped on, having to prise the doors open with his large hands. *This guy's sharp*, thought Dominic, using classic overt counter-surveillance that would have forced a less well-trained team to drop him. Dominic was now firmly in the follow.

"I have X-ray One, carriage two of four, heading north-bound; next stop, Russell Square," Dominic said, using his iPhone earphones to make it look like he was singing to himself. They hammered it into the team in training that covertly using comms was an art, and only surveillance operators or mad men appear to talk to themselves.

Because of problems at the busy station entrance, Dominic was the only member of the team who got onto the train. Ideally, another member of the team who hadn't been directly behind Buzzard would have joined them, but that wasn't an option. The benefit of the new Tube trains and their long, cavernous design was that he could maintain good observations on the target from three carriages down. Those standing, and there were many, kept Dominic hidden as they aimlessly swung from the straps hanging down from the carriage roof. Next stop, Caledonian Road; the tube was heading towards High Barnet, the end of the Northern line.

As the Tube slowed aggressively into the station, Dominic nonchalantly moved towards the door, shielded by the many others pushing to be first off the stifling hot train, all no doubt wishing the summer heatwave would come to an end. Dominic felt the sweat trickling down his back; he also noted Buzzard making a move towards the door, three carriages down, his impressive bulk standing out against the other commuters. Dominic had to make a choice; he couldn't hang around, but if he committed to leaving the train, there was no going back. Buzzard could use this stop to see if anyone was indeed onto him.

The doors opened with their monotone warning to "mind

the gap" and the throngs literally carried Dominic out onto the packed platform. The race was now on as he scanned the cram of humanity heading like sheep to the stairs. Dominic felt dread fill his stomach. *Surely not another loss?* He felt his reputation was on the line after the missed lift-off at Broadwater Farm. As he moved closer to the stairs, the crowds naturally slowed down, and he spotted the familiar, unmistakable figure high up the staircase and quickly alerted the team above ground. They had been following the Tube as it made its way across London in the baking hot tunnels.

"That's off, off, off at Caledonian Road; I have control," Dominic alerted the team, not caring if anyone heard him. No one would understand anyway, over the noise of a rush hour Tube station.

"Copy that; all call signs, let's get into position to take at the exit," Control ordered.

Dominic made his way aggressively through the crowds, attempting to get closer to Buzzard — now called X-ray One for brevity and ease of communications. He was now three banks of people back from him, and he was relieved to see that Buzzard had dropped his hypersensitive alert state. Since leaving the Tube, he hadn't looked back once.

Daylight crept down the staircase as the crowd spewed onto the pavement out the front. Dominic kept Buzzard under covert control, conscious that he could have a counter-surveillance team watching his back, looking for the likes of Dominic and his team. He had to act normally.

"That's X-ray One at the exit, and he's gone right, and unsighted to me," Dominic alerted the rest of the team.

The silence seemed to go on for an eternity. Dominic naturally turned left and onto the baking hot street, heading for his covert pickup, just as he thought it was all lost.

"I have X-ray One, right-hand side toward the junction of Edge Road and the main," Charley stated.

"Copy," Control replied. The sense of relief was almost tangible over the airwaves as the team collectively regrouped.

Buzzard made no attempt at anti-surveillance and walked nonchalantly up the busy street, with the huge Victorian complex of Pentonville Prison dominating the skyline. He turned right into a nondescript road, a mixture of new, local authority two-storey boxed maisonettes and Victorian red-brick semi-detached houses made into cheap flat rentals. The entire area had an air of degeneration.

"That's X-ray One gone right into a small gated area; I'm forced past." The surveillance operator couldn't risk following the target into such a confined area. "Looks like a small lockup type building; that's me unsighted," he said.

"Copy; anyone got eyes on?" Control asked, raised voices audible in the background.

"I have X-ray One — he's speaking into an intercom… and that's him, inside the building," Charley stated.

"We need an address, team, for fuck's sake." Control was now feeling the pressure.

"I'm into the area, going off comms. Wait out," Charley said.

Dominic was nervous. Charley had a lot of exposure to the target, and this could be an ambush.

His unease didn't go unnoticed in the car that picked him up. "Don't worry, Dom," the driver said sarcastically.

"X-ray One is into the building — the address is Safe Haven, Downland Cold Storage Depot; wait out," Charley stated.

The vehicle Dominic was in moved into position on an adjacent street to collect the female foot operative. She entered the rear of the vehicle and readily took the proffered bottle of water.

"What the fuck?" she said aloud. "It's a fucking homeless shelter." She picked up her secure mobile phone and called in to control. "Hi, it's Sierra Zero Seven — is the boss there?" She paused, making eye contact with Dominic. "Boss — yes, I housed him. Yes, I saw him enter," she replied. "Boss, it's a homeless shelter." Her voice raised by a few octaves. "Yes, I'm sure; it's called Safe Haven."

Chapter 20

Dominic felt that outwardly he was showing signs of embarrassment, but inside he was buzzing; the glowing debrief he had just received for his surveillance foot-follow on the Buzzard target had eased the insecurity that was always just below the surface. Yesterday's mission had been the most successful yet for the fledgling Project Omega. The hi-tech briefing room was alive with conversation as the team digested the latest updates from the Project Alpha intelligence team.

HDom'sis eyes briefly locked onto Charley — or at least the rear of her head — the female team operative who he not-so-secretly liked a lot. She was sitting in front of him, alert to the screens depicting yesterday's follow on a high-tech GPS display, whereas he was transfixed on the neat flower tattoo situated slightly behind her left ear, visible where her hair was raised into a messy bun atop her head. *Still stunning*, he thought, but quickly reverted his eyes back to the screen, that now showed a recent photo image of the homeless shelter to where they had followed Buzzard the previous evening.

The room fell back into silence with the opening of the door and the entry of the operations officer, flanked by someone Dominic didn't recognise. She was dressed smartly in a long black trouser suit, and had an air of Britishness — maybe Foreign Office — about her. Dom thought she also possessed a sinister look. She had been good-looking in her day, graceful but stern, giving her the edge of a John le Carre character. *Not to be messed with,* \ Dominic mused.

"Team — again, well done on last night's serial. The chief has briefed the PM on our success and we impressed her, to say the least." The ops officer paused, casting his steely blue eyes on the assembled team. "In all seriousness team, well done. This guy" — he motioned to one of the large plasma screens on the wall showing the mugshot photo of the target — "is a Tier One target and very surveillance-aware." Again he paused, seemingly to gather his thoughts. "Okay, let me introduce Julia Picton, head of Branch Eighteen. She wants to discuss our next move on this target." The ops officer moved back and took a seat behind the tall, elegant-looking figure.

Strange way to put it, thought Dominic. *What the fuck does "our next move" mean?* Was the team about to lose this target to "The Firm"? He sensed the entire team thinking exactly that as they sat collectively, staring at the tall figure on the briefing podium.

"I want to echo your boss and say to you all, very well done," the woman said, addressing the room with confidence. "Buzzard — aka Abu Talib Haleem — has been a priority target of ours for some time, and, as someone briefed you previously, he seemed to be a ghost until yesterday." She glanced around the room, making eye contact with as many operators as she could. "This level of Tier One target never usually leaves our organisation, but you guys have certainly proved me wrong." She paused again, searching for her next words. "May I remind you of your level of security clearance, and what that entails, before I carry on," she said condescendingly, then turned to the screen. A picture of Buzzard appeared, higher quality and certainly more recent. "As we initially briefed you all, Abu Talib Haleem was born Paul Dixon, of mixed Arab-English parentage. He had a normal upbringing; shone little at school, to be honest — bit average, but he excelled at boxing. However, he fell in with the wrong crowd when his boxing career was cut short by injury and by all accounts, he became a bit of an enforcer." Picton paused. "He ended up in Belmarsh Prison for aggravated burglary, which we believe was more a case of reclaiming goods back for his bosses, drugs and weapons. At this time, he wasn't showing any signs of radicalisation, just the normal small-time criminal thug. All this intel came from the local CID." She again turned to the screen on the wall, which was now displaying another picture of Buzzard; he had the wispy black beard and Kufi Topi prayer hat, making it clear he was now a devoted Muslim. "They took this in Belmarsh before his release. He adopted the Muslim faith within the prison. Then he was paroled. That is where the trail goes cold. This man literally became a ghost. Until yesterday, we only had our suspicions he was back in the UK."

How much more have they not told us? Dominic wondered.

"Back from where?" interjected the ops officer with clear annoyance.

"That I cannot tell you, Danny, I'm sorry. May I?" Picton replied, obviously irritated by the interruption, nodding at the screen to intimate she had more. "I will be honest with you all, I had my reservations about handing Haleem across to you. The PM overruled me, so you have friends in high places." A wry smile spread across her face as she carried on. "What is of utmost importance now is that we have control of him, and we must maintain it. We know from our sources that he has been abroad and trained in several camps, and unconfirmed intel states he is back to form a so-called crocodile cell, awaiting orders from on high. We believe this man has been trained and is proficient in the construction and deployment of high spec

Improvised Explosive Devices, and is planning an attack on UK soil."

"On high"? What the fuck does that mean? How much are we not being told here? mused Dominic. *This lot are playing us. They know more, so why aren't they sharing it?*

The ops officer and Picton moved to the back of the room and entered a heated conversation. At this the entire room erupted into chatter, Haleem's evil face staring down at them. Dominic sat there, looking at the screen. He had been upfront and personal with this man, and could understand why this whole task was getting messy.

"Okay, quiet." Danny, the ops officer, brought the room back to order. "Can everyone leave us alone for a minute? Go to the Interest room and get yourselves a brew." He turned back to Picton.

Dominic stood up and moved towards the door, deep in thought. He never saw the ops officer move from behind the briefing podium.

"Dom, a word please."

"Boss?" Dominic replied and waited for the room to empty.

Danny and Picton ended their conversation and moved forward and proffered an empty chair for Dominic.

"Dominic," Picton began, "I have been speaking to Danny about you, and your past in the army." Dominic felt uneasy — where was this heading? Surely he wasn't being taken off the task; it was his worst fear. "You have been trained in resistance to interrogation... correct?" Picton carried on.

"Yes," Dominic answered, wondering where the fuck this was going.

"Normally we would use trained undercover operators for this task, but again the PM has insisted that Phalanx execute this operation." Picton paused.

So that explains the sarcastic comment about friends in high places, Dominic reckoned.

Picton glanced at the Omega ops officer, then turned to Dominic — icy stare, piercing blue eyes. "With your background and training we've decided that you are the best candidate." Dominic listened intently, observing the woman's once-pretty face, with elegant, high cheekbones and perfect skin that now showed signs of aging. Her neat, bobbed black hair was tinged with hints of grey. "We want you to go undercover into the shelter where Haleem is living. We need someone in there watching what he's up to." Picton maintained eye contact.

"Dom, it's a volunteer serial and you cannot be forced, but —" Danny didn't have time to finish.

"Yeah, I'm up for it, too right. What I joined this unit for." Dominic's heart was racing. He didn't need to think about it; he hadn't felt a surge of adrenaline like this since he had started his ill-fated Special Forces course, and since then everything had seemed second best. This was a real chance, a proper job, the ultimate chance to prove himself worthy.

"Thank you." Picton held out a hand. "You will have a provable legend, so if questioned, the reason you have ended up in a hostel will be legitimate."

Dominic sensed some unease amongst the group of three, huddled together in the deserted Ops room. Danny shuffling awkwardly in his seat only emphasised this.

"I don't understand how you can ensure it's provable," Dominic said.

Picton glanced at the ops officer, then turned her focus to Dominic. "Well, before you decided to leave the Army you had — shall we say, an altercation in the sergeants' mess with another soldier." She paused.

Dominic sensed the anger seeping up through his legs, reaching his chest, his heart pounding. *This woman was definitely out of a spy novel. How on earth has that become common knowledge?*

"What the fuck?" he blurted, his voice raised.

Danny held up a hand to calm him down, while the sinister Picton sat poker-faced.

"May I carry on?" she asked, with no sign of emotion. "Yes, you had a set-to, and they documented that the person involved wanted to take action against you."

The tension in the room was now palpable. the temperature of the boiling streets outside in the continuing heat of the hot baking summer the UK was experiencing. "However, Dom — can I call you Dom?" Her tone was again condescending.

"Yes," came his blunt reply.

"You too have friends in high places. Your CO swept it under the carpet as your career was, excuse the language, fucked, and you were on Ed's radar," Picton said. Noticing Dominic's lost expression, she continued. "Ed Walker, Brigadier Five Airborne Brigade; we go back a long way to when he commanded D-Squadron 22 SAS in Bosnia during that awful war." Picton stared at Dom, pausing as the three fell into silence.

Dominic's mind was now in overdrive. He'd never learned that tosser had tried to press charges against him; it was a time when he hadn't been in a good place, with his wife wanting a divorce and his SF career over. He had turned to his only solace — the bottle.

"So how are you going to manipulate this, then?" Dominic asked aggressively, his annoyance plain to see.

"Dom, we have nurtured you since you first applied. This is the perfect cover for you — we have put in place that they discharged you due to this lack of discipline and are now basically on the bones of your arse, unable to find work." Picton waited to let the message sink in.

"You fucking what?" Dom raged. "This is bollocks." He looked to his ops officer for support. Danny offered none and instead just turned to Picton as she carried on.

"Listen," Picton said, now also raising her voice, "you volunteered for this organisation."

"Yes, but not to have my entire past put into turmoil. My ex-wife will fucking love this."

"You in or out?" Picton asked flatly as Dominic stared back at her. "Since your inception on this course you have been off everyone's radar, including your now ex-wife. Yes, she has tried to find out what you're doing — her new boyfriend has recently joined the SAS." Picton carried on, twisting the knife with every word. "So, no one really knows who or where you are now."

"Perfect."

Picton cracked a smile that Dominic really wanted to wipe off her face.

"So, we have managed to use our connections to get you a place at the hostel. I have a briefing pack here on your legend and what the backstory is... all provable and will stand up to the scrutiny of anyone checking you out." Picton passed the briefing pack to Dominic, who opened it with a sense of trepidation.

He flicked through the briefing pack. It contained discharge papers, psychiatric reports on his mental health, DSS registration, and a letter from the local authorities registering his homeless state. It was mind-blowing. He stared out of the window at the blue sky and the so-called normal world outside; he felt like a fucking alien.

"So basically, you left the Army under a cloud, couldn't find employment, and have fallen on hard times — hence your being in the shelter." *Simple for you to say,* thought Dominic as Picton carried on. "Listen, I know this has come as a tremendous surprise to you, but this is the chance you have been waiting for. It's obvious you've been trying to prove yourself since you failed to get into the Regiment."

"I got injured, broke my fucking leg. I didn't *fail*," Dominic grumbled.

"Yeah, yeah," replied Picton, waving an arm as if to brush aside Dominic's comments. *This woman really is a heartless cunt*, realised Dominic. "Well, whatever, but this is a chance not even Hereford could have given you; going UC without training is unprecedented, and yours for the taking." Picton stopped and stared at Dominic with a different look to her now, somehow more motherly.

Danny, who had sat in silence, shuffled round to face Dominic, eye-to-eye, person-to-person.

"Dom, as Julia said, this is a chance in a million, totally off the wall. It's a fucking big ask, but you're the man. I've seen you operate. You're a maverick, different to the rest: a real risk-taker."

Dominic pushed his chair away and navigated his way towards the window. East London was going about its afternoon business, unaware of the world Dominic was about to enter. His heart was racing but in truth, he was elated; at last, a chance to put the failures of the past to bed, to prove he really was a special operator. He turned back to Picton and Danny who sat in silence.

"I'm in," he simply replied.

"Okay, good," Picton said in a matter-of-fact way. "We have contacts within the local authority who will place you in the shelter. Your cover story will be given to you, and we shall hold you in isolation to practice, just in case you get compromised. I will leave you in Danny's capable hands to carry on the process. Questions?" She looked him straight in the eye, holding the stare, searching for a weakness. Finally, she looked away, nodded her head in tacit appreciation, and slid back her chair and stood up to leave. At the door she paused. "One more thing; it's all deniable, so if you fuck up or go rogue, you're on your own." She kept eye contact with Dominic for just a little too long, confirming the ramifications of that last statement. It sounded almost like a challenge, a gauntlet, throw down.

Dominic nodded and turned to look out the window. *What a total cunt,* he thought.

Picton left the room without another word, her tight grey trouser suit not showing a single crease; *rather like her emotion,* thought Dominic. She was probably the most heartless and ruthless women he had ever met. *Apart from my ex-wife, but that's another battle.*

"Mate, sorry about that; she totally ambushed me on that one."

"Not a problem, Boss. She's a real piece of work. Who is she?"

"A career MI6 officer, now heading up a specialist cell aimed at recruiting high-level covert human intel sources; stops at nothing for a result. Never married, nobody has a clue about her life outside of her office at Vauxhall. She is directly overseeing this task, PM has authorised it, bit pissed off with it. I can't argue; at least they haven't taken this target off us."

"No pressure, then." Dominic let out a stifled laugh.

"Yeah, mate, no idea as to why she's taking such a keen interest. No doubt we'll find out. Right, we need to get the wheels moving. Alpha are working on your legend, sticking to a military theme and broken marriage; injured ex-serviceman, now homeless."

"Fucking made for me then," Dominic replied, a sad irony to his voice.

"Right, we need to brief up the team. She wants you going live on this asap."

"Boss, how am I getting into the shelter with my legend intact?"

"Alpha are working on it now; you'll go in as a proper case with a social worker, obviously one of ours, but it will be all watertight."

Chapter 21

Dom paused at the electric entry gate, gathering his thoughts, and trying to tame his inner chimp. The dating game was new to him, and he felt uncomfortable and out of touch, especially as Charley was the most sought-after woman on the team, and *he'd* been invited for dinner.

The summer continued to be a scorcher and saw no signs of abating. Dominic was sweating after the short walk from nearby Tower Hill tube station, not helped by the lingering lazy heat of the long, endless summer days. His polo shirt was stuck to his back.

He pressed the buzzer on the electric entry system and waited. The block of flats was modern and afforded a view over the River Thames to the south bank.

The intercom burst into life.

"Oh, hi! Come on up, flat nine."

The gate lock clunked open, and he entered the complex, where neat flower beds led the way into the communal door and the lifts. His heart was racing.

He exited the lift, checking which way the numbers led, and turned right. The plush carpets and decor highlighted the expense of this complex, all paid for by the Phalanx group. His new employers certainly had a budget to match their ambitions.

He took a deep breath and pushed the brass doorbell on the centre of the wooden door. He heard footsteps and a chain being released; the door opened.

Silence is golden, but not now, he thought. Charley stood in the door, her athletic figure complemented by a tight t-shirt and skinny jeans, her dark hair messily tied in a bun with sexy curls descending around her ears. Her brown eyes would melt the hardest heart.

"You coming in, or just hanging on my doorstep?" she said jokingly.

"Sorry, yes," Dom blustered, almost thrusting the bottle of red wine he carried into her hand.

"Thank you, very nice." She observed the label. "Didn't have you down as a wine expert. Château neuf-du-Pape? Wow, thanks."

They entered the open-plan kitchen, the smell of food pervading. He glanced around the functional space. Amongst the usual kitchen utensils was an area of protein powder pots and creatine supplements. *You don't get a figure like that at Weight Watchers.* He smiled inwardly. They both shared a passion for fitness, and both loved cross fit.

"My old boss in the Army got me into wine. Said, if in doubt, default to this one."

"Well, he was a man of taste; it's a lovely drop and will go well with dinner." She paused to check the oven which contained a large casserole dish. "I've made a Spanish dish, kind of a beef stew; plenty of protein," she said, chuckling to herself.

"Smells lovely," Dom replied, struggling to add to the conversation.

She opened the fridge and pulled out two bottles of Moretti. "Save the wine for the food," she said, handing him the beer and moving into the lounge area. The balcony doors were open. The view stretched over the tops of the nearby houses and out across the Thames, the sun glinting on the water as it dropped below the horizon far out to the west of London.

They both stood in silence on the balcony, soaking in the end of a day. Adele was playing quietly in the background. This time, silence *was* golden.

"Thanks for the invite, I... I'm honoured," Dom said after a long silence.

"It's good to get you on your own. You've intrigued me since Texas. You're a complex man, Dominic Leigh," she said before turning to him with wide eyes. "Hey, I'm worried about you. They've really dropped you in at the deep end on this one."

"Bit strange, the whole situation. Some shadowy woman from MI6. In fact, she's driving this job."

"Really? She must have some interest in our target or something," Charley replied.

A bleeper sounded in the kitchen.

"That's dinner ready. Can you open the wine?" Charley asked.

They took their seats at the round glass dinner table, a minimalist setting with a solitary breadbasket and two place settings laid.

They both ate in silence, barring the odd compliment from Dom.

Dinner was finished quickly; both were hungry, and the food was good.

"So, Mr Leigh, why are you so insular? You intrigue me." Her eyes were flirtatious.

"What do you mean?" Dom replied cagily. It felt like a game of chess.

"Well, the team doesn't know how to take you."

"What's that mean?" Dom replied, starting to feel annoyed.

"No, no... I'm not saying they don't like you — you're one of the main players, but..."

"But what?" he snapped back.

"You're deep. But in a nice way."

"Well, it's complex. My life is a fucking car crash," Dom said. He pushed back from the table slightly, eyes fixed on the ceiling; he could feel the emotions of the past years flooding back. He felt tears coming. *For fuck's sake, get a grip. A date with the hottest girl on the team and you're starting to fucking cry.*

Charley must have sensed the raw nerve she'd tugged.

"Hey, sorry... forgive me, it's not my place to pry."

"I'm lost," he blurted. "My life doesn't mean much anymore. I've lost my career, my daughter, and the woman I truly loved is intent on destroying me." His eyes were filling with tears.

"That's crazy. How many applied for Phalanx? Two thousand, or more, and thirty-two of us passed," she replied.

"It means nothing to me; second-best dream chasing."

"To what?" Charley asked, intrigued.

Dom's mind took him back to a Welsh mountain, where his life had changed forever. Life had been brutal.

The sheep track rose steadily uphill away from the Claerwen Dam, a line cutting through the heather and tussock grass unique to this part of Wales. Sergeant Dom Leigh adjusted the straps on his heavily-laden Bergen rucksack, trying to ease the pain in his shoulders, and took an unorthodox single-handed hold on his rifle, leaving him a free hand to carry his map and compass. The climb away from the checkpoint was steep, but the track gave him good traction and he soon got back into his tabbing (fast marching pace) rhythm again. The vehicle checkpoint at the base of the huge Victorian dam starting to be obscured by the mist and rain.

Elan Valley was a tough environment, a sombre, moody, barren moorland with little or no human habitation, just the odd farm etching out a living sheep farming; months spent in constant low cloud and rain, which was why the Special Air Service had used it as part of their brutal endurance testing process since the inception of the modern-day Regiment back in World War II.

Nearing the end of the second week, Dom Leigh, of Second Battalion Parachute Regiment, was feeling strong and pleased he hadn't succumbed to blisters or niggling minor injuries. All those days spent on the hills covering the ground, sacrificing any form of social life to be sure he was up to the challenge, was paying off; his dysfunctional personal life was a different matter. If he kept up this pace he would get inside the time again; test week was a mere two days away.

His mind wandered back to the cosy married quarters in Aldershot where his wife Carrie would be keeping his daughter, Veronica, entertained. He always got a smile on his face thinking of this curly blonde-haired bundle of untainted joy; he could smell the freshly shampooed hair of his daughter as he read her a bedtime story. He feared the happy family life with a supportive wife had gone forever. The constant time away training like a professional athlete had taken a toll on the once-ideal family life.

The fierce wind and heavy rain hit him full in the face, bringing him back to the present. His legs were pumping like well-oiled pistons as he gained height onto the bleak moorland.

As he crested the hill, he spotted the two old mine chimneys, long-since disused, on the horizon; he rechecked the bearings and picked out his next navigation point in case the mist descended again. The chimneys were from the bygone era of lead mining and now provided a navigation waypoint for potential SAS candidates. Just below that point, at a track junction, was the next checkpoint, the last on today's twenty-six kilometre march.

If I pass today, I'm two days from test week, *he thought, and the dream he had carried since childhood was a step closer to fruition. Once he was a badged member of Britain's elite special forces and settled into a new house in Hereford, he could knit his family life back together. He had prayed for this frequently since Carrie had told him it was over.*

The visibility was getting obscured by the now-horizontal rain that was being blown across this lunar landscape by near gale force winds. It would take at least an hour and the going underfoot was tough. Better watch my step. *Pulling his woolly hat down to shield his ears from the wind, he upped his pace; four kilometres an hour sounded easy, but it was up hill and down dale, and was far from easy.*

In that instant his life changed forever. His leading foot slipped on an ice patch left over from the recent snow, sending him into a pirouette with the weight of his Bergen spinning him forcefully to his left. His rear foot, stuck solid between the grass tussocks, stayed put and with the inertia produced his ankle didn't stand a chance.

"Fuck!' he shouted in a long, drawn-out pained voice. He crumbled into a heap, the snapping sound of his tibia permeating deeply into his brain. This is serious, *he immediately knew.*

He lay there for a while. There was no immediate pain, but he could feel his clothes getting soaked as he lay in the heather and peat. Hypothermia would become a real problem very soon — he had to act rapidly.

He needed to get on his feet, as he was already feeling the cold through his now-soaked combat clothing. He struggled out of his Bergen straps and gingerly rose to his feet, not putting the damaged leg down. Right, *he thought,* if I can put weight on it, I can make my way back to the last checkpoint.

He gently put his damaged leg down and pain shot up his leg as if he had been hit by a bullet. Any type of weight-bearing was out of the question. Survival mode soon kicked in: he opened his Bergen and found his medical kit and his duvet jacket. He took off his smock, put on his warm jacket then replaced his smock; he soon felt the warmth.

Now for his leg. He got out two "SAM" splints, and moulded them to the front and back of his leg and round the ankle and, using two

Velcro straps, he tightened the splint to make a makeshift support for his ruined leg.

He could at least hobble like this. The only way back was to throw or roll his Bergen as far in front as he could then hobble to it and start the process again. His weapon was glued to his right hand: it was more than his life was worth to lose that.

"Bollocks, I can't believe this," he said out loud as he slowly made his way back off the hill to the checkpoint and, he knew, away from SAS selection, his dreams shattered.

It took nearly four hours to get back to the checkpoint. The last five-hundred metres, came courtesy of a lift on the back of a farmer's quad bike, sprawled next to his trusty sheepdog. He could make out, through the burgeoning darkness and mist, the headlights of the vehicles where he had left them some six hours ago in what was a very different life. The area was bathed in a subdued glow, the mist giving the area a ghostly hue.

The directing staff had just been about to launch a search operation and register him missing. He was soon in the back of the Army ambulance parked next to the four-tonne truck which housed the DS and the candidates, eagerly awaiting the return to camp for a warm meal and bed.

There were voices outside, speaking in loud whispers that he could hear, outlining his potential injuries and his withdrawal from the course. For the first time in years, he cried; tears of anguish, not physical pain. He had gambled on this being his escape to a better life.

His despair was interrupted as the back door of the ambulance swung open and a member of the DS poked his head in, dressed in a civilian duvet jacket.

"Mate; bad luck, but you're finished on this course. But you put in a top effort to get yourself off the hill." His tone was friendly and genuine, but brutally to the point. "Did you know you walked almost four kilometres on a broken leg? Sort of bloke we want in the Special Forces, so get yourself fit again and reapply. Don't bother with the

usual bollocks, ring us direct. I'm on the training team for another two years, so we'll fast track you and stop your unit blocking your application."

"Thanks," Dom replied, taking a sip of the brew he was proffered. No instructor v candidate bravado here.

"Parachute Regiment, aren't you?"

"Yes, Two Para."

"Even better. Get back asap, mate, we need a maroon mafia back." He laughed and with that the door closed. What Dom didn't know was the door was closing permanently on this phase of his life.

The next few hours went by in a blur. He was whisked away to Abergavenny Hospital and admitted; the damage to his leg became fully apparent: the tibia was broken just below the knee but worse was the damage to his ankle. A rotation fracture with a potential dislocation.

Once he had been seen by the on-call doctor, they informed him that he was being transferred back to Aldershot Military Hospital; a place he knew well, his daughter having been born there five years ago. To add insult to injury, he had to go into an isolation ward, as Abergavenny Hospital was not declared as being free of MRSA and they were taking no chances.

In an isolation ward — now truly alone to his thoughts and the demons in his head — his predicament hit him hard. This time no-one interrupted his tears. The life he had planned for himself, and his family, was gone; the sacrifice of all his family time and enjoyment to train like a pro had all been in vain. Alone with only the voices in his head, Dominic had never felt more vulnerable and lost. The tough paratrooper, who eighteen hours ago had been on the cusp of proving himself fit enough to serve with Special Forces, was now broken and alone in a hospital bed with no-one by his side and no idea what he would do.

His estranged wife Carrie and beautiful young daughter Ronnie never visited him in hospital, making his feeling of ultimate loss and failure stronger than ever. He doubted Carrie had even told his lovely daughter that daddy was home — and broken.

"HEY." Charley put her hand on his shoulder. She had cleared away dinner whilst Dom had drifted on a boulevard of broken dreams.

"Sorry. I'm so sorry, I didn't mean to make a tit of myself."

"Hey, it's my fault for being a nosey bitch." Charley laughed at herself. She poured him more wine and sat back down, now facing him, holding a long look into his eyes. *Boy, her eyes,* he thought. "I love your vulnerability; tough guys like you don't show their soft underbelly and end up fucked in the head."

"Thanks," Dom muttered, shocked that in two hours this girl had unwrapped years of hurt and left him totally vulnerable and open. But he trusted her: something he thought he had lost the ability to do.

They spoke long into the night. Dom explained about his ex-wife: his true love, Carrie the city girl, a high-flying management consultant who had loved her bit of rough. The hardest loss was not being able to see his five-year-old daughter, Ronnie, whose blonde hair and blue eyes could melt any heart. He explained the void left in him by not getting into Special Forces; and the eventual breakdown of his marriage and leaving his beloved Parachute Regiment. They spent three hours on a journey down the river of his life, the whole nine yards. It went by in a heartbeat.

"Wow, it's three a.m.," Charley said, checking her watch.

"Shit, sorry. What a shit night, you playing agony aunt."

"It was a pleasure," she said, moving over to him. She placed her lips on his, but not as a goodbye; it was a full-on, passionate kiss. They melted into each other's arms. "Don't go... please stay," she whispered into his ear.

They moved into the bedroom. Her SIG Sauer P226 in the

quick-draw holster was on her bedside table. *Not the usual bedside items for a good-looking girl*, Dom mused as she pulled the shirt over his head, revealing his toned chest and Para tattoo proudly adhering to his left pectoral muscle. She bent down and kissed his chest.

Chapter 22

Dominic stood for a moment taking in his new home. The factory unit that housed the shelter had certainly seen better days, and the loading area he had to cross to get to the entrance had given up the battle against weeds long ago. He approached the door to the left of the roller shutter and rang the bell. His heart was racing as he pressed the buzzer; he sensed he was being watched as he he heard the magnetic door clasp release, and the heavy metal door opened.

He entered into a makeshift reception area, the old Army daypack slung over his shoulder. It held the few items that he was allowed to keep in line with his legend. The lady who had let him in sat behind an untidy desk that formed a makeshift barrier from the outside world into the womb of the shelter.

"You must be Dominic." She held out a hand. Dominic shook it, looking down at the floor, not wanting to make eye contact.

"Hi," he replied quietly.

"Let's grab a cup of tea, then we can get you checked in and sort you out a bed. Showers are hot at this time of day, before the mad rush," she continued.

They moved into the main area of the rundown converted

factory unit. The communal area had an array of decrepit sofas facing a large TV, and further into the building was an area that must have been the dining area, surmised Dominic as he tried to observe as much as he could. Several round tables made up the dining area, each covered with a garish plastic tablecloth depicting fruits or flowers.

The woman made two cups of tea from the large silver water boiler that was chugging away like a steam train. She directed Dominic to a table, and they both sat down.

The first thing that hit Dominic as he got to know his new home was the smell: a mixture of unwashed bodies, food and cheap disinfectant. As he glanced around, everyone seemed to have the same hopeless expression on their faces. They sat either mindlessly watching daytime TV or staring into space; most, if not all, had a phone in their hands, but were paying little attention to them. It suddenly dawned on him that this job would not be glamorous in any way — this was a trip into abject misery and despair.

"So, Dominic, we will need to do some paperwork; did you bring your 'fit to attend certificate'?" she asked matter-of-factly.

Dominic nodded and reached into his old khaki-coloured Army daypack, removing the suitably crumpled manila envelope that held the doctor's report and toxicology results.

She accepted it with a smile and immediately opened it, pulling out the A4 report. She seemed to know exactly what she was looking for and, nodding with approval, slid the paper back in the envelope.

They both sat in awkward silence, sipping their drinks. Dominic took the opportunity to scan the rest of the room, the sunlight arcing through the large skylights giving the area an opaque glow. A Dell desktop computer was perched on a table in the far corner of the room and an elderly man sat stooped at it, aimlessly scrolling down the pages of an online newspaper.

Dominic knew he would have to gain access to the computer's search history as soon as he could.

"So, Dominic," she said, breaking the silence, "my name is Sophie, and I'm one of the permanent staff members. I shall be your caseworker. I'm here to help you and our aim is to get you somewhere permanent to live, and into employment."

Dominic couldn't help feeling for these poor bastards in the rundown industrial unit that made up this de facto shelter. No wonder people turned to drugs and booze to ease the reality of life in this place.

They remained in an uneasy silence until both had finished their drinks, finally putting down their chipped and stained cups on the plastic tablecloth. "Right then, let's give you the grand tour."

They spent the next few minutes looking around the shelter; it didn't take long. The most important area for Dominic was the sleeping area. To his relief the males shared one long dormitory, with the females sharing another, in two long purpose-built wings to the rear of the factory.

Having been given his bed space Sophie left him to his own devices, not sure why he had been given thirty minutes to settle in. He had fuck all to unpack but he made the token gesture of arranging his paltry life belongings on the bedside cabinet next to his unmade bed. He was relieved that the temporary residents weren't in bunk beds, as it afforded him more chance to observe his target: Buzzard. Dominic had ensured he was totally sanitised before he entered the shelter; a member of his team, basically acting as a guardian angel, checked every item of his kit to ensure his legend lived up to the harshest of scrutiny. Still, he checked once more that nothing would blow his cover.

Once he was organised and happy with his surroundings, he noted fire exits in case he needed to get out quickly; the people he was up against wouldn't think twice about killing him if they even sniffed out who he was. Luckily, the plug sockets for charging mobile phones were in one area and there was a row of various chargers situated near the computer. This was a stroke of luck, since one of his key tasks was to install spyware on Buzzard's mobile.

Happy with his covert recce, he went back out to the main area where the smell in the air suggested it was lunchtime.

He hung around, truly not knowing what to do next. Sophie was nowhere to be seen, and the place was now a hive of people all forming a line behind some shutters which reminded Dominic of his school canteen. As if on cue he heard metal clunk as the shutter was unlocked, and it was pushed up, clattering noisily and revealing a commercial-style kitchen and two women in striped aprons, fussing over a large pot of what appeared to be steaming soup and plates of bread rolls with various fillings.

Once he received his soup and a roll, he meandered over to the collection of tables with their gaudy-coloured tablecloths, not quite sure what to do. A young kid, not much more than a teenager, intimated to Dominic that he could sit next to him at a free table tucked into the corner of the dining area. The young kid offered his hand.

"New here, bro?" he asked, with a gangster rapper twang to his London accent.

"Yes, mate, just arrived," replied Dominic, unable to not stare at the kid's dress sense: a mixture of cheap, unmatched tracksuit bottoms and tops. Still, he thought he was cool, so Dominic played along with the kid.

"You watch out man, know wat I mean? Some bad-ass dudes in 'ere. Name's Addict, man." The kid paused. Dominic just carried on eating his soup greedily, keeping up the image of a hungry homeless man. "Not 'cos am into the gear or any shit pills or that bro, 'cos I'm a Charlton fan." The kid named

Addict returned to his own food, noisily slurping at his soup, his hands and fingers covered in homemade tattoos.

Really? thought Dominic. *No drugs?* He observed the line of vivid puncture holes, now healed, on the forearms of this young Londoner. "Dominic, that's my name. Don't take the piss. My mum had some fucked-up reason for it." They both laughed in unison and then returned to their food. "What did you mean, mate, about geezers in here being bad dudes?" Dominic asked after a suitable period of silence.

"You kna, normally we just get skank heads or old-dude black blokes down on their luck, but more recently we're getting these nasty Muslim dudes; nasty, man..." Addict's sentence tailed off as a young, slim man walked past the table and sat adjacent to them. Addict now spoke in a low whisper. "Him, innit, bad man, always out in the smoking area with a big black dude, proper hench man, lethal bro," Addict continued in his gangster rap mode, but he now had Dominic's ear. Because, the guy he was describing could only be Buzzard, and from the sounds of it, he had an accomplice in the shelter.

The arrival of the man dressed in full shalwar kameez and skull cap had stopped Addict in his tracks. No more small talk; he simply finished his dinner, got up without a word, and headed to the dormitory, leaving the rest to *a mundane daytime programme* blaring out from the large-but-cheap flat-screen TV mounted on the wall next to the serving hatch.

The afternoon continued at a monotonous pace, with more briefings on rules and regulations to follow, the timings of his regular checks to see if he had broken his abstention from drugs, and timings for meals and showers.

After that they left him on his own. Dominic settled onto his bed, staring at the stained and cracked ceiling, the fluorescent light cover filled with dead and dying bugs. The whole placed made his hair literally itch, it was that desperate.

The afternoon slid by very slowly. Dominic observed a

number of men coming and going, none of whom raised his pulse at all. They all had that defeated air about them as they made the regular walk out of the fire escape at the end of the dorm to the smoking area. Dominic mulled over the fact he was a non-smoker.

He went through the list of rules for the shelter; he had read with interest the curfew which was set for 1930 hours every night. Breaking this curfew could signal the end of your tenure and after entering, no one was allowed out again. Apparently, volunteers worked in the shelter at night and could deny entry. *Good luck,* he mused.

The evening meal passed without any sight of Buzzard. Dominic sat nursing a cup of tea, pretending to watch the communal TV that had now moved onto the evening news. He hoped to get a sight of the man he was in here to track, but eventually people started to drift off to their respective dorm rooms.

Dominic watched as the night staff cleared up the remnants of the evening meal and the mess the guests had left. The volunteers looked to be from a variety of backgrounds: some had arrived in suits from their desk jobs; others wore dresses, jeans, and Converse trainers, more in line with the nearby residents of Camden. He couldn't help thinking that these volunteers were no match for a hardened jihadist like Buzzard.

Dominic's attention was caught by the latest news on the heatwave the UK was experiencing and he listened intently as the newsreader laid bare the dire situation the country could face if there was insufficient rain. That's when he heard raised voices from behind the door that led out to the shelter's main entrance.

With a crash, the internal door was pushed open with such force that it nearly came off its hinges. The few watching TV turned around in unison. Dominic also looked towards the noise and, to his amazement, directly in front of him was

Buzzard, arguing loudly with a male member of the volunteer team.

"I know the rules, man, don't treat me like a child," Buzzard said.

"But Abu, I have to mark you down as late," the suited man said, "it's the shelter rules."

"FUCK THE SHELTER!" shouted Buzzard, showing signs of his extreme temper, his eyes glaring with evil intent.

Dominic hoped the "Suit" would back down, or this task would be over before it began as he couldn't let this poor, do-gooding volunteer get a kicking. Luckily for all, Buzzard dismissed any other attempt to admit his lateness. He strode past the man, kicking one of the chairs as he passed the dining area and slamming the door to the men's dormitory with a bang. The group around the television simply returned to their robotic TV-watching and the Suit disappeared into the makeshift office, no doubt to enter a report on Buzzard.

Dominic returned to his position, pretending to watch the television, but he was in fact using a special visualisation technique, taught to him on his probation course, to make paperless notes of large volumes of detail. He was committing to memory an accurate description of Buzzard: his non-conventional clothes, which consisted of black Nike tracksuit, white trainers, and a man-bag. He would certainly blend in with his surroundings in this area of London. Dominic would detail this when he dropped off his first situation report in the dead letter box he would use whilst working undercover.

First, he would have to go to bed. His heart was racing as he entered the dorm with the line of beds covered in a variety of old, faded quilt covers which shrouded occupants in various stages of undress. Some slept, some lay staring at the ceiling, whilst others stared intently at the screens of their smartphones. Dominic let his gaze follow the line of beds to the door, where, speaking intently, was Buzzard. He still looked annoyed, and when he spotted Dominic, he said something to the man and they both gave Dominic the once-over. The stare was held for slightly too long, in an aggressive — not inquisitive — manner. Dominic broke the stare and turned to climb on his bed. Behind him he heard the fire door bang shut, and when he turned over on his bed both men were gone, no doubt into the safety of the smoking area.

Dominic made a mental note to request a listening device to be installed to cover that dead spot, and with that he got under his old but clean quilt and, still fully clothed, fell fast asleep. The first day of his undercover career was a success.

Chapter 23

Luka ensured he was early. It was a bizarre location for a meeting; the small shop was only up the road from his mosque, and he knew the area well. He made sure he did several procedures in order to check, as much as possible, for anything to suggest he was being set up. Quite what that would look like, he didn't know.

The first procedure was a drive-by, but on a bus. He'd gotten on the number 30, close to his flat in Hackney, and the journey was relatively short. He sat at the back with an excellent view of who got on and off the bus, and more importantly, who came to sit close to him.

The bus made slow progress, stopping every few minutes to let people on and off, all going about their daily lives with no idea what was about to happen in the city they called home. The bus stopped just short of the convenience store he had been told to report to. He looked down at it from his elevated position. The shop had a single glass door which was open, and a large window advertising the various deals they had running, mainly cheap alcohol. A variety of fruits and vegetables were randomly stacked on boxes outside the store, catering to the wide ethnic community that inhabited this part of east London.

Luka stayed on for two more stops further up the road, then pressed the buzzer to signal to the driver that he wanted to get off at the next stop. He felt his heart beating faster as he exited the bus onto the dirty pavement, the heat of the day making the car exhaust fumes thick and pungent. The bus pulled away in a large plume of diesel smoke as Luka casually checked around him; he was happy — for now. He crossed the busy road, making sure he jumped between passing cars. A dangerous move, but it would force anyone following him to do the same. Once on the other side of the road, he placed his headphones into his ears and turned on the voice recorder on his iPhone. To any passer-by, he was simply talking on his phone. What he was actually doing was making a commentary about the surrounding area, noting everything. It was an old skill he had learned many years ago, before mobile phones when people used small Dictaphones. The procedure worked, and he felt a sense of security doing it.

He was now level with the shop and glanced across. The upstairs windows had dirty net curtains hanging loosely, with the windows wide open in a futile attempt to let in fresh air. Even if someone *was* watching, he couldn't be certain; he noted this. People came and went from the door in quick succession, and it was a busy place.

He'd been told to go into the store bang on 3.00 p.m. He had five minutes, so he quickly checked Google Maps; as he'd thought, a road ran to the rear of the shop and it looked like it had a small loading bay with a battered white van parked lazily at an angle. The rear of the building was obscured by a fence of sorts, but it had a large new lock on it. *Strange*, he thought, *and why go to those lengths?*

At exactly three minutes to three, Luka turned back onto the main road and made his way to the shop. Without pausing, he entered through the open door and made his way towards the counter down the central aisle, stacked with tins and packets of cheap food. The three other people in the shop took no notice of the smartly-dressed, chisel-jawed man, who looked distinctly out of place. Before he got to the counter, a large man of Arabian origin, slightly overweight and wearing a dirty brown shirt and jeans, signalled to Luka with his eyes and a slight move of the head, motioning to a door behind the counter. He lifted the counter hatch to let Luka through, then reached under to press a hidden button. With a loud clunk the hidden door sprang open enough for Luka to push through. The weight of it surprised him; *must be armoured,* he thought. Wondering exactly what he was about to enter made his heart race, but his external demeanour remained cool and controlled.

It took Luka by surprise: an enormous table dominated the inside of the room; magazines grouped in piles; large photocopiers occupied the rear wall, and other walls were adorned with Arabic writing and posters depicting men in camouflage clothing, all carrying modern assault rifles.

Three men occupied the room, all of whom appeared to be British. None were wearing an immaculate white shalwar kameez, but instead were dressed in trendy jeans and Nike trainers. The man sitting directly in front of Luka broke the silence; he spoke in English, but Luka couldn't place the accent. He had a light sheen to his coffee-coloured skin; he was tall and muscular with dark, empty, soulless eyes above a neatly-trimmed beard. Neat gelled hair completed the look.

"Avdic, take a seat," he said with menace. Before Luka knew it, one of the other men came from behind and jammed him into a chair. His forearms were as thick as most people's legs. Luka could feel this man's raw power. "You have upset our leaders, and they are not happy with you."

"You think you're some sort of hard man, eh?" Luka said

"Well, those boys were careless. It won't happen again, be sure of that." The man paused. Luka wasn't sure if this were a threat or simply a reassurance that he was being protected. From the look of these men the threat was more likely.

Silence filled the room as all three men stared at Luka. He knew this intimidation tactic from his days of being trained to withstand situations exactly like this. He went on the offensive. "Do I not get an introduction to who exactly you are?"

This seemed to rattle the leader and spokesman of the group. "No, you fucking don't. You're fucking nobody." The veins in the man's neck were bulging now, his eyes popping out of his head. "You're lucky we've been told not to fucking hurt you. Those brothers you put in hospital are my boys and I don't like people hurting my boys. SO SHUT THE FUCK UP, AND LISTEN!" he screamed.

He reached down and picked up a laptop, a MacBook Pro. He opened it and started to tap away, concentrating on the screen, his eyes darting back and forth. He seemed to be checking something. He grabbed the laptop which was on a chatroom site. Luka scanned the screen for any clues.

The room on the screen was empty, the microphone was unmuted, and he could hear noises: busy chatter, car revving, then the unmistakable sound of a helicopter passing over.

Sunlight burst into the room on the screen as someone entered and sat down, his form filling Luka's view of the distant room.

Luka's heart missed a beat; he couldn't believe it.

"Hello, Bosnian, it's been a long time," Redbeard said, opening the conversation.

Luka didn't reply. He didn't know what to say; he was speechless. The last time he had seen this man was many years ago in that godforsaken farm complex where Redbeard had become a huge part of Luka's life. The last thing he had given him was his new passport.

"Hello, Leader," Luka replied.

"Bosnian, how are you?" the man with a long unruly beard said in a conversational tone, no signs of menace or anger.

"Fine, Leader, thanks. You look tired," Luka said with genuine concern; the man looked ill, he thought.

"I'm fine. I got smashed up pretty bad last year, but as God willed it I survived, and am now ready for action again. How's your sister, Luka?"

"She's good. Doing okay, but still can't handle life outside the home."

"That truly is a shame, my boy, but you have a chance to avenge all this now." He paused.

"Yes, Boss," Luka replied, not really knowing what else to say.

"I appreciate that the situation the other day got the better of you, but you cannot act like that. They could have been agents of the infidels, and once they get you to a black site you will not be able to hold out for long, believe me."

"I understand, Boss, truly I do, but after all these years, I thought the worst."

"Okay, enough." He raised a hand.

The hand was damaged, Luka noted, deformed. It looked almost melted. Redbeard looked ill; his eyes were glazed, nor was his speech as clear and precise as Luka remembered. He seemed drunk.

"Bosnian, I'm officially activating you, under authority of the Revolutionary Guard War Council. It's your time, my boy." Redbeard went into a brief that he read from a modern, hand-held tablet. "At this very moment we have four brothers, warriors in the final stages of preparation. Once ready, they will start the long journey to England. We are using established smuggling routes; details will be shown to you by Abu." He paused, checking his electronic notes. "Once in London, you are to assist them in our initial safe house, then the team will move to a more suitable location to finalise themselves for the mission." He paused again. "Absolutely no one outside this room knows about this mission. I have cleared it at the highest level but the detail even they don't know, for operational security reasons. There are kefir spies all over us. I am controlling this one myself. I have operational control, fully and totally; do you understand, Bosnian? If you step out of line again, we will kill you." He said it so matter-of-factly that Luka almost missed it. "Abu will be the cell commander in London, and you will take orders off him; do not underestimate him." Redbeard was throwing out a warning here, Luka knew. This whole situation had sinister undertones, and for the first time Luka felt a sense of foreboding. "Well, Bosnian, it's nice to see you again. You have kept yourself well and you seem to have settled into a pleasant life. I just hope you haven't gone soft on us. Oh, before I go, send my regards to that pretty little girlfriend of yours... No doubt we shall speak again soon."

With that, the screen went blank. Luka sat back in his chair, staring into space, his mind struggling to take it all in. *How the fuck did they know about Sally?* He had been careless, and now it was apparent Redbeard was laying down barely-veiled threats in case Luka stepped out of line.

"So, this is what's going to happen next." The man he now knew as Abu broke the silence. "You will take ten days off work — say it's a family issue — then you're to sanitise your flat and under no circumstances are you to see your bitch." He almost spat the words out.

Luka didn't like this and he felt his temper going. Abu could sense this too and flung himself across the table, grabbing Luka by the lapels of his Hugo Boss suit jacket. It ripped; the man was a brute. He pulled his face close to Luka's, his eyes full of hate, sinister and dark.

"You piece of Bosnian shit. Your kind are dirty." Luka felt the spittle showering his face. "If you fuck with me, I will break you, and finish the job on that little sister of yours."

Luka reacted; the headbutt landed straight on Abu's nose. It surprised him, but not for long. The onslaught was as savage as it was quick. Luka was picked off his feet and thrown across the table, hitting it before landing on the floor, smashing the back of his head as he landed. Abu was round the table with surprising speed, hauling Luka up. He pulled him off his feet, holding him eye-to-eye so Luka couldn't touch the floor; this man had immense strength.

"You're lucky that I have my orders not to mark you; we need that pretty boy face fresh," he said, smirking as he let Luka's feet touch the ground. He pushed him away. Luka stumbled, just managing to keep his balance. The three men burst out laughing. "Fuck off, and I'll be in touch," Abu said before turning his back on Luka and speaking quietly to his two goons.

Luka pressed the large red button on the security door and exited into the shop. No one was any wiser to what had just gone on in the back room of this east London convenience store. As Luka exited the shop and headed towards the nearby Tube station, he knew one thing for certain: he would kill Abu, or Abu would no doubt kill him. Worse still, the only two people on the earth he cared about were now also at risk. The shit had just got a whole lot deeper.

Luka was told he would have to provide support for an active service unit coming into the country via a known people-smuggling route. A four-man active service unit was currently being prepared somewhere in Syria, and once en route, Luka would be updated.

They gave him an address on Broadwater Farm Estate and the brief to prepare it, with internet, food and satellite TV — including the Al Jazeera channel.

Chapter 24

Dominic breathed deeply, the fresh morning air filling his lungs with lightness. His first few days in the shelter had passed without incident, but it was slow progress. Buzzard was very surveillance-aware and did no talking in public. Dominic had observed and made a mental note of the technical help he needed.

Dom walked with purpose along a route he had already planned to use. He was en route to meet one of his team, his only link to them. Every forty-eight hours he would make the RV. Today's RV was in the nearby Highbury Fields Park, a small green enclave in the middle of the roughest part of north London.

Dominic entered the park first, relieved to be out in the fresh air and enjoying the warm sunshine on his face. *It's going to be another baking hot day,* he mused. He knew the exact park bench he would sit on and the signs that the meet was on or off. He felt secure, knowing his full team would be out imposing an invisible protective screen around this meet.

Dominic sat down on the bench, carefully placing the *Metro* newspaper next to him. He sat observing the park, which was getting busy with families fresh from the school run, the grass parched brown with the relentless summer heat. Small children were running around, playing loudly as their mothers stood or sat drinking out of their familiar red takeaway cups from a nearby Costa Coffee. None of them gave the down-on-his-luck figure Dominic presented to the world a second glance.

A man wearing a retro Arsenal football shirt walked in through the far gate and made his way nonchalantly through the park; he was carrying a Tesco supermarket plastic bag — this was the sign Dominic had been looking out for. These were old-school espionage tactics, honed and perfected during the Cold War. He had no mobile phone, no tracker and no internet, just good old-fashioned human intelligence.

He sat deep in his own thoughts and waited. It didn't take long until he sensed and then heard somebody approach him from behind. Dominic sat facing forward, and the man took a seat at the opposite end of the park bench, placed his coffee cup on the floor between his legs and took out a newspaper, which he began to flick through.

"How's it going?" the man said, breaking the silence. Dominic gave him a quick glance, but he wasn't part of his Omega team; it was an older man, longish hair, and looked like an ageing rocker, a perfect appearance for this part of Islington.

"I'm in, I have eyes on Buzzard, in the same dorm." Dominic paused, observing his front. "He is mega aware, never talks in public, and has one or two associates in there with him, I think."

The man sat at the end of the bench, poker-faced, reading his *Guardian* newspaper. "Think or know?"

"I'm sure he holds meets in the smoking area at the back of my dorm. I've drawn you a plan, enough for a close target recce for a technical solution to go in." Dominic broke off again.

"Not much. Is that it?" the man said bluntly.

"What the fuck do you expect?" Dominic snapped back, feeling his pulse raise at this barbed comment.

"Well, we need his phone number. That is the hashtag number one task."

Dominic knew the drill. He would have to get Buzzard's phone and tap in a collection of numbers. Then, if the phone was connected to 4G or Wi-Fi, it would give Project Alpha control and access to Buzzard's all-important mobile.

"Okay," Dominic snapped back. "CTR report is inside." For the first time, Dominic shifted his gaze to the paper laying between them.

"Forty-eight hours, same location. Phone: sort it," the man stated coldly, and with that he picked up the paper Dominic had placed on the bench, leaving his *Guardian* paper in its place, and walked off.

Dominic sat, letting his temper slowly simmer. The man had really pissed him off. He didn't know what the fuck it was like to be in such a shithole. He sat in his own world, feeling really alone. He missed Charley. He had no doubt that he was falling in love with her and it scared him. His daughter would have forgotten he even existed. This only made his feelings of isolation more intense as he slowly got up off the bench and made his way out of the park, past the kids still loudly playing on the swings, mothers pushing absentmindedly them while deep in conversation.

Dominic left the way he had come; he knew the surveillance team would watch his back, ensuring he wasn't being followed. Once he got to the main traffic lights on the high street, he knew he was clean. He headed down the busy street lined with trees, the houses a mixture of privately owned and rented; *and you can tell which are which,* thought Dominic.

The route back to the shelter wasn't far. He crossed the road, looking behind him; *the coast is clear.* This final cut-through was the last part of his counter-surveillance route and led him down a small alleyway at the rear of a row of downbeat shops, mostly closed. Only the Spar shop was lively, a haunt for the underage local youths to buy cheap cider and get pissed.

He entered the alleyway. It was strewn with the debris of bins ransacked by foxes and stunk of piss and decay. He heard the commotion before he saw it: a group of white kids, dressed in the norm of grey and black tracksuit and white expensive trainers, had a man pinned to the floor. The man was dressed in a black shalwar kameez and sickening kicks were raining down on his head.

"Paki cunt! Fuck off back to where you came from," the ringleader shouted as he aimed a kick at the prostrate figure's torso.

"Where's your jihad now?" another shouted.

Dominic acted without thinking. Years in the military had given him an inbuilt hatred of bullies. Warlord, soldier or street kid, it didn't matter: bullies were bullies, and the oppressed were in need of help. This man was outnumbered and in serious danger of being badly hurt.

As he approached, he took a mental note of his target: of the five youths, one was the ringleader, and he would need to be taken out first. In his head he remembered his training back in the Paras — speed, surprise and violence of action, to achieve the edge against your enemy.

He didn't change his pace; he simply walked down the alley, grabbing the ringleader by his hair and pulling him backwards. The kid swung round to face him and quick as a flash Dom struck the kid fully in the throat with a hard jab. He dropped like a stone, fighting for breath. *One down.*

Two of the others turned to face Dominic.

"Oi, cunt, who the fuck—?" The one speaking didn't have time to finish. Dominic launched himself with speed across the metre or so divide between them, landing his forehead right on the kid's nose. He heard the loud crack as his nose collapsed. It erupted with a spurt of blood, and he fell away squealing with the pain. The remaining three took a glance at their two fallen comrades and another glance at the wild-eyed figure of Dominic, whose face was splattered in blood, giving him a devil-like look. They didn't hang around; grabbing their two fallen comrades, they ran off, not looking back or saying a word.

Dominic knelt down. The man in the black shalwar had turned his back to his aggressors and had curled into a foetal position facing the wall.

"Mate, it's alright, they've fucked off; you're safe now," Dominic said.

The man groaned; he was hurt. Dominic didn't know how badly. He needed to turn him over to do a first aid primary survey. He helped the man roll over onto his back slowly; the last thing to move was his head.

Dominic felt the realisation hit him like a bullet; he could not believe what he was seeing. The battered face staring up at him was Buzzard's. Dominic sensed recognition in the man's eyes. The man he had saved was the target they had put him in the shelter to watch.

"Mate, don't worry — I'll sort you out," Dominic said quickly, checking his limbs and chest for damage.

"Thank you, man. I'm fucked-up bad, think they done my ribs, bro," Buzzard whispered. It surprised Dominic to hear a Birmingham accent.

"Hey, no drama mate. I fucking hate bullies, fucking creatures." Dominic emphasised his words. "Let me check."

Pulling up Buzzard's shirt revealed a vivid purple bruise to his lower rib cage. He ran an expert hand over the rib cage to check for lumps or unnatural movement, telling Buzzard to take some deep breaths.

"No dibble, man," Buzzard said.

"Okay, okay — but I'm not sure you don't need to see a doctor."

"Just get me back to the shelter man. You're in there too, aren't you?" he quizzed.

"Yeah, dude, no dramas," Dominic replied, gently easing Buzzard to his feet and putting an arm around his shoulder. He started to slowly move towards the ironically named Safe Haven.

The man weakly held out his hand to shake Dominic's. "Thanks man, you saved me then. The name's Abu," Buzzard said, struggling to speak due to the pain in his chest.

"Hey, mate, it's cool. I'm Dominic." They started slowly walking back towards the shelter. Dominic hoped they didn't bump into the police on the short walk back; it would take some explaining why he was carrying a badly beaten and wanted jihadist, whilst he himself was covered in blood. However, he doubted that those feral youths would have gone to the police; their street cred would be in tatters anyhow after a down-and-out had given the two ringleaders a kicking.

Chapter 25

Luka sat nursing his coffee, staring out the window, not taking any notice of the hordes of people passing by, all going about their daily lives and suffering as the heatwave that had gripped London and the rest of the UK showed no sign of abating. The cafe was located on a thoroughfare from Covent Garden to the busy Charing Cross station. In better days he had sat people-watching and used this coffee shop as a place of contemplation and reflection. His life had certainly taken a turn for the worse over the past few days.

Since the meeting in the rear of the shop, he had struggled with what he had been instructed to do by the shadowy leader of the fledgling jihadist group, the El Muj front. He knew he had to be careful; to totally disregard his orders would be fatal and negate the chance for him to ever gain the revenge he so craved for his murdered family.

He now had so much to organise and prepare; the team of mujahideen that Redbeard was sending were en route to the UK. Not only did he have the issue of being given such a potentially deadly attack against innocent people, but he would also now have to nursemaid a group of battle-hardened fighters fresh off the murderous battlefields of Syria. How on earth could he do this?

They were currently en route, and they wouldn't be landing at an airport or using any form of recognisable route in from that part of the world. Instead, they would be using tried and tested people-smuggling routes. Once in the UK they would simply disappear into the urban web of people living in the twilight zone, not appearing on anyone's radar; virtual ghosts, but these men would be very nasty ghosts. *Worse still*, mused Luka, *I have to house and administer these ruthless bastards*. He felt the enormity of his predicament well up in his chest.

The man he knew as Abu had a look about him, his eyes with the deep-seated evil stare he had given back to Luka. It also brought back dreadful nightmare memories of the Serb Militia who had overtaken his hometown and murdered the menfolk; they too had a variety of tattoos on their hands and necks that enhanced their devil-like appearance. He wanted nothing to do with global jihad, he just wanted revenge for his family. He was in no doubt that this man was a truly nasty individual, and no doubt the ones arriving soon would be even worse.

He mulled over the white espresso cup sitting empty in front of him. He needed to distance himself from Sally; he couldn't guarantee her safety. These ruthless bastards would stop at nothing to get their deadly mission done. He had arranged to see Sally this evening. He had started to miss her; emotions he didn't want to feel, but she was a welcome relief from the realisation that he was now in deep with a lethal terrorist attack in the very heart of London, against thousands of innocent people. He had formed a plan of sorts, but he hadn't been updated of the progress of the group or where they would infiltrate the mainland UK.

He unlocked his iPhone and typed Sally a message. She was working at the hotel until early evening.

I will cook tonight at yours, meet you there xxx

He then drafted an email on his phone to the hotel duty manager to request some time off for family problems; he hated doing it, but he used his sister as the excuse. He pressed send.

"Hey Luciano, another coffee please."

"No problem, my friend," replied the big Italian in an immaculate white shirt, and in a loud voice. The cafe was empty. No doubt he was glad of the business, but he loved to talk. "You okay? Look like you have the world on your shoulders," he carried on.

"I'm fine — just got woman trouble," Luka replied.

The man roared with laughter. "Plenty more fish in that sea, my friend."

The large silver machine behind the counter burst into life, the smell of coffee filling the small cafe.

Luka accepted the cup with a smile and returned to his thoughts. The most important thing was to ensure his sister was safe. The facility she was in had been brilliant for her, but the mental scars etched into her brain ran deep. He had been advised not to expect miracles, but time had dragged on. He needed to move her somewhere safe, somewhere these bastards could not get to her.

Luka finished his coffee, said his goodbyes and made the now regular journey by bus from the Strand out towards Victoria Station and onto Pimlico. He liked the bus, always the top deck and near the rear; this gave him a view of anyone getting on. He surveyed the world going about its business and started to appreciate the magnitude of what he was about to do. The heatwave that had gripped the UK was brutal, and the entire city was melting and baking before everyone's very eyes.

He got off at the bus stop, past the one nearest Sally's flat, and then began a very slick anti-surveillance route back to the flat. As he entered and silenced the alarm, he felt happy no-one was on his tail.

LUKA SAT in his own world during dinner with Sally. He had cooked a favourite dish of grilled trout. It was a dish that reminded him of home, and that didn't help his mood. He didn't want to get involved with global jihad anymore; he felt as if life was moving on, but his hands seemed tied at the present.

"Luka, Luka." Sally looked at him, incredulous. "Where are you tonight?" she asked, her tone now more caring than angry. "Not with me, that's for sure." She looked down at her food, letting her fork fall loudly onto her plate and pushed the half-eaten dish of food away from her.

They both sat in awkward silence, neither wishing to break it, both dealing with their own fears and insecurities.

"Listen, Sally." She looked at him with sadness in her eyes. "I think we should stop seeing each other." Sally's eyes filled with tears. She shook her head, slowly at first. "It's for the best, believe me," he said in a compassionate, low voice. Sally sobbed, her whole upper body bobbing up and down violently. Her stare made Luka feel worthless: *how many more lies will I have to tell?*

Without a word she got up. "Best if you left then," she said in a cold, sterile tone before disappearing into the bedroom.

Feeling thoroughly pissed off, Luka collected his keys off the small table by the door, then quietly opened the door and left the flat. He descended the creaky, threadbare-carpeted stairs and opened the communal front door. The night was warm; the surrounding buildings seemed to emanate the heat of the day, giving it back when everyone wanted cool night air.

Luka sat in the twilight of his empty, cold living room, deep in thought. The streetlights were the only illumination he wanted; they mirrored his mood. He'd got an Uber back from

Sally's flat. He sat nursing a whiskey as he thought about his next move. Given his current predicament, Luka decided to take a tremendous gamble: he needed people he could trust watching his back, especially now the Syrian gang was about to arrive in mainland UK.

The only person Luka would trust was his lifelong friend, Ardian; they'd made a pact when they had left Bosnia to claim revenge for their murdered fathers and friends, but not like this — this wasn't revenge, it was the mass murder of more innocent people.

Chapter 26

The train journey from London went past in a blur. As the InterCity eased back on its speed, the conductor announced that the next station would be Macclesfield. Luka had been briefed to leave the train at this station and find a car in the small car park to the front of the concourse.

He exited the small station, rain coming down as the town spread out in front of him. A market town famous for its silk, the mills had long-since closed and you could tell by the town's drab appearance that the good times had left. It added to Luka's mood. He didn't know what this journey was all about, just the vague brief and keys to a car left in space number twelve. It made him anxious; he'd entered a world of blind obedience.

Checking the key fob, he noted the Toyota logo and walked down the few steps into the car park. There were only a handful of cars. Pressing the buttons on the fob made the car in the far corner flash its indicators. He approached the car with caution, checking the interior: nothing seemed out of place. He reasoned that checking under the vehicle would look suspicious. Whilst maybe that was what he should do, he didn't want anyone to become interested in him and why he was in these parts.

He got into the car, a blue Toyota Avensis that smelled of unwashed bodies. The upholstery was stained, and the interior had a general air of untidiness about it. On the passenger seat was a blank white envelope. Luka picked it up and slid his thumb along the flap to open it; inside was a single sheet of A4 folded in half. The note was type-written and simple.

Go to SK11 0NY and wait by the gate. You will be met by a man dressed in blue on brown carrying a black daypack.

What the fuck is this all about? he thought. He was in the north of England, with no brief other than to meet someone by a gate. He understood the other parts of his brief, but this was strange.

He got out his iPhone and typed in the postcode. Zooming in on the location he noted it was a huge, forested area to the east of the town. On the train he had noticed the hills that abruptly halted at the flat Cheshire Plain. He eased the car out of the small car park and onto the damp road as a bus driver generously flashed him out with a smile. *Bit different to London,* he mused.

On the way out of town, he did some anti-surveillance drills, basic ones, but it seemed he was alone. The satnav took him onto the A537, with signs proudly announcing it was the gateway to the Peak District National Park. The route took him out of the old mill town and almost immediately he started climbing. He was soon out amongst the beautiful scenery, which he would have enjoyed if he weren't on some form of wild goose chase. He drove past farms and endless fields with traditional dry-stone walling. He kept checking his rearview mirror but was alone on the road; in fact, nothing had been in his mirrors since he had left the outskirts of Macclesfield.

The car radio was tuned to the local station and the female presenter was animated about the wildfires now rampant across the national park. The rain was a welcome respite from the oppressive heat of London. He indicated off the main road and onto a single-track, a signpost pointing to Standing Stone Car Park. It seemed from the satnav that this was to be his final destination.

The road was narrow. He didn't like roads like these: too easy to block people in, or worse. If he'd planned the route, it would have avoided this. He rounded a corner to the announcement that he had reached his destination. It was a small car park tucked away beneath some trees. He turned into it, the gravel crunching under his tyres. He parked in the corner of the car park, nose-first, adjusting his rearview mirror and door mirrors to give him some sort of awareness. He turned off the engine, the rain immediately obscuring the view out of the front windscreen as the wipers ceased.

He waited; his phone had full signal thankfully, as this was his only means of communication. Ironic though — who would he call? He tried as best as he could to orientate himself. Various well-trodden paths led into the dense pine forest to his front. It must have been the rain keeping people away. Looking at the overflowing rubbish bins, he knew this was a popular spot.

Luka kept activating the tired windscreen wipers of the Toyota that arced slowly over the dirty windscreen. Just then a figure emerged from a small track and turned onto the main path, walking purposely towards the car park. *Towards me,* thought Luka. His heart started to beat faster as the person got closer. He was wearing a blue waterproof jacket and wore brown walking trousers. He turned to check behind him and Luka noted the black rucksack. It must be the person he was meant to meet. *Why the fuck am I here?* thought Luka, *middle of a fucking forest just south of Manchester, with no rhyme nor reason.*

Brazenly, the man walked straight to Luka's window and tapped on it with a ringed finger. Luka grabbed the window handle, and it came off in his hand; an out-of-place comedy moment. Luka was forced to break the secure seal he had inside the battered Toyota. The door opened with a creak. Luka was set for violence, every sinew and nerve awake. The man stepped back to let Luka out; he pulled back his hood, glancing up at the persistent rain.

He then steadied his focus on Luka. "Top of the morning to ye," the man said in a sarcastic Irish voice.

Luka studied the man, squat, smaller than himself, a bullish face pockmarked with days of stubble, a large broken nose and tight lips. A sinister glass eye dominated his entire face, weeping out of a damaged eye socket. Luka noticed further damage and scarring on the man's face. This man had been in a war, or something like it.

He fixed his good eye on Luka, who could not shift his own gaze off the glass eye of the man standing opposite; it seemed to have a life of its own. Dark, deep, unforgiving and like a shark.

"I see ye come prepared," he said to Luka, his deep accent guttural Irish.

Luka looked the man up and down; he was wearing waterproof clothing and sturdy walking boots; he looked sodden and unkempt. *Had he been out in this weather all night?* Luka pondered.

"What do you mean? Not sure what you're getting at. Prepared for what, exactly?" Luka replied, irritated.

"For a good hike in the rain. Didn't they tell you we've got a good five miles to get to our cache up and over that?" He pointed to a distant peak that looked like a shark's fin jutting out of the dense forest.

Luka felt anger welling up inside him. This whole situation was getting out of hand. What was this delinquent-looking Irishman doing up here, and why did Luka need to go with him to a cache? *A cache of what?*

"Well, Bosnian..." The man noted Luka's reaction. "Oh, I know ye from way back when, my son," the man replied, keeping his one good eye fixed on Luka.

"How the fuck do you know me? And what the fuck is this all about?" Luka replied angrily.

"Listen, I'm here just as you are: under fookin' orders. So calm yerself, boy." The man had a sinister look to him and no doubt wasn't a nice person if crossed. "Ye got the gear?" the man asked.

Luka snagged the large manila envelope out of his inside pocket and handed it to the man. "One thousand tabs, as agreed." Luka relayed the message he'd been given.

"Champion," the man said and placed the envelope into his daypack. "We need to get moving. For fook's sake, take a look at ye." Luka stood like a naughty schoolboy dressed in the wrong sports kit. He had jeans, white Nike trainers and a thin Hugo Boss jacket, clearly not enough to keep this northern rain out. "Right, yeh, let's sort this bag o' bollocks out." The man took off his daypack; it seemed heavy. He opened the lid and pulled out a red jacket. "This should do ye, for the nu." He handed Luka the jacket.

"Thanks." Luka slid the jacket over his now-sodden clothes.

"Can't de fook-all with your dabs," the man said, pointing to Luka's trainers, "just have to get on with it. Phone: turn it off and leave it in the car." Luka started to say no but didn't get far. "Just dee as ay sat, that's a good boy," he said forcibly. "Reet let's fook off. I'm Kevin... Donaldson," the man said to Luka, before turning and setting off down the track, making no effort to miss the large puddles. Luka had no choice but to follow suit; this would be a long day. The smell of wet pine and moss filled his nose, serving as an unwelcome reminder of home.

Donaldson set a relentless pace and Luka was soon struggling to keep up. The wind was howling down the tree line of the pine forest. The rain stung his eyes. They exited the forest onto open moorland where the ground was boggy and Luka struggled to keep his soaking wet trainers on his feet.

The man in front turned, shouting over the wind. "That

beauty is called Shuttlings Low; our base is over that and down into that valley." He pointed into the distance, then turned and set off. Luka had plenty of time to look at the man from the rear, trying to analyse what he was. He was certainly hill-fit, he kept up a decent pace given his age, and he looked agile bouncing over the moss tussocks with ease. Luka couldn't be sure, but he thought he could see the outline of some form of rifle in the black daypack he wore; it looked heavy enough.

After four hours and with Luka's feet totally trashed, they arrived at what looked like a makeshift camp. The rain had eased and now the midges came out. Luka observed his surroundings — after descending off the high ground they had hand-railed a river.

The river was about five hundred metres away, swollen by the rain rushing downhill into the valley below them. They were tucked into a small re-entrant about fifty metres across, invisible to anyone walking on the footpaths that crossed the moors. *Great hiding place,* Luka thought, *but what the fuck am I doing here?*

There was a large green tent tucked into the side of the clearing, covered from the sky by overhead trees. The man called Kevin appeared carrying two plastic beakers full of steaming liquid.

"Here you go, boy, warm thee sen up."

They both stood in silence drinking the hot sweet tea and looking around at their new home.

Luka broke the quiet. "Kevin, can I ask what the fuck this is all about?"

Kevin took a last noisy slurp from his orange beaker and threw the dregs onto a nearby clump of bracken. He turned and looked at Luka, his good eye a little less piercing now. "Ye clearly have nay fooking clue, da ye?" Kevin replied.

"No, exactly."

"You're here to test the gear, ensure it's all as ordered."

"What gear?" Luka was exasperated now.

"Guns, you crazy wee fooker. AK-47 original Russian variants and pistols."

"You serious? Fucking weapons?"

"Boy, you're mixed up with some nasty wee bastards," Donaldson stated.

A man appeared, making his way down the side of the re-entrant, slipping down the bracken. He was wearing heavy blue coveralls that were covered in oil. He carried a shovel and what looked like a metal detector. He looked as if he'd not slept or washed for weeks.

Donaldson turned and approached the man, then they began talking in whispers. Luka for the first time had a chance to check his surroundings. The camp consisted of a large, green family-style tent and, pushed further under the trees, were three small dome-style camping tents. Luka realised he was here for the night. His feet ached and he was wet through; what else could possibly go wrong?

The two men finished their conversation, then the younger man headed into the large tent. He appeared a lot younger than Donaldson but definitely had a certain look about him. Luka had seen it before, and he neither liked nor trusted it.

"Okay, Bosnian, we have the goods ready. We shall get some food then wait until dark before testing them."

How the fuck can I test an assault rifle here? he thought. *Are these men fucking mad? We might be in the butt-fuck middle of nowhere, but a farmer or walker could raise the alarm and then we're right in the shit.* Luka was feeling thoroughly miserable when Donaldson appeared next to him with a mug of sweet tea.

"Dinner will be ready soon," he said, placing a cigarette between his scarred lips, expertly lighting it and taking a long drag. "You're in this up to your wee foocken' neck, Bosnian, I hope you know this."

"I have no choice, as they have me in a corner." Both men

fell silent, each analysing their respective predicaments: neither looked good.

Dinner was a rudimentary affair but it was hot, a form of stew with some pasta and chunks of once-fresh bread. The three men sat in silence, eating hungrily. The cool of the night was pleasant.

Dinner finished, Donaldson had another cigarette and yet another cup of tea. When he'd finished, he got up off his camping chair and walked out of the tent. Darkness had set in. He wandered back in, having changed into a dark boiler suit and green Wellington boots. He threw a set at Luka, complete with the boots. Luka looked back at Donaldson.

"Why do I need to change into these?" he asked, looking at the old stinking coverall.

"Bosnian, ye need to start fookin' trusting me; firstly, once we've done the test, we burn all this gear. Round here are some caves that them crazy wee fookers go down into and that's our cover story in case someone finds us. Okay, let's go." Donaldson picked up his daysack and what looked like a gaming console. He must have noted Luka's interest. "It's a Drone Jammer. The feds are out to get us and will use anything to succeed." Donaldson spat out the words.

Donaldson led the way, pulling a set of modern night vision googles down over his eyes. Luka noted that the third man, who hadn't said a single word and was bringing up the rear, also had NVGs on, a ring of green light illuminating his cheeks, giving him an alien look. His head kept roving left and right, constantly checking, though for what, Luka had no clue.

They followed a narrow sheep track for about thirty minutes. Luka could still hear the river, far to his left. They were on open moorland, not a sound, seeing only the far away light of a small farm. A dog barked in the distance, but a long way off. Luka felt very vulnerable. He looked up into the star-filled mass of black above him, the silently flashing lights of a plane high above them.

Donaldson stopped and got down on one knee. Luka followed suit. These guys were well-drilled, almost military in their field craft. Donaldson roughly pulled Luka close as he put his mouth to Luka's ear.

"Right, we're here." Luka strained his eyes, but couldn't see a thing. There was no ambient light out here. "There's a small group of trees." He grabbed Luka and pointed him towards the small copse. Luka's eyes started to get used to the dark and he could make out a few trees almost in a circle about fifty metres away. Luka sensed tension in the air. Donaldson checked the drone scanner; once happy, he grabbed Luka by the arm and almost frog-marched him into the cluster of trees. He nearly tripped over a pile of stones that had once been a dry-stone wall.

The other man got into a prone position at the entrance of the copse and to Luka's surprise had a weapon out and in the aim. It was long, possibly a sniper rifle. His heart pounded; Luka knew he was balls deep now.

Again, Donaldson put his mouth to Luka's ear; whispers carried at night. This was a tactic used by the military worldwide.

"To our front we have a sample of the goods, an AK, brand-new Russian variant, and a pistol: Browning Hi-Power, ex British Army. You're going to check them, and then test fire."

Luka grabbed Donaldson. "Are you fucking crazy? This is ridiculous: one burst of the AK and the whole fucking hillside will come alive!"

Donaldson moved with the speed of a lightweight boxer, grabbing Luka by the throat. His NVGs gave him a sinister look. Menace oozed from the man. "I'm no fookin amateur. LIKE I SAID, TRUST ME." Losing his cool, he pushed Luka back.

He moved further into the darkness and Luka joined him.

On the floor was a large green tarp. Luka could make out two long rifles and two pistols.

Donaldson got down on his knees; Luka joined him. Donaldson started to breakdown the AK-47 expertly, swiftly. He then pointed out the distinguishing marks highlighting this weapon as a true Russian-made AK-47. He then swiftly reassembled it; *darkness is no problem,* noted Luka. He did the same with the pistols. "Browning Hi-Power: dated but fucking reliable and deadly." Donaldson grinned. "Okay, here we go." He handed Luka an AK. He hadn't felt the cold metal of one of these for many years and he didn't particularly like the reacquaintance. "It's as requested, the airborne version with folding stock." Donaldson demonstrated how to use the metal feature.

Donaldson pointed out the characteristics of the AKMS, a simplified, lighter version of the AK-47, made from stamped and riveted sheet metal. A slanted muzzle device had been added to counter climb in automatic fire.

"Your boys are worried we're going to see them off with some Type 56 shit."

"What?" Luka asked, unsure of what Donaldson meant.

"Chinese copies of the AK, known as Type 56. Load of old shit, believe me. We had them until Gadaffi squared us away with the real deal. Fookin awesome piece of kit; never fails, never." *Donaldson's got a passion for his deadly trade*, thought Luka. "Happy?" Luka nodded. "Okay, follow me," he ordered and led them further into the woods. The darkness was enveloping Luka now; without NVGs he was blind.

Donaldson stopped and Luka could make out what looked like a large drainage pipe jutting out of a low bank, lying on a sandbag. Donaldson inserted the distinctive curved magazine into the weapon's body and pulled back the cocking handle, releasing it with a metallic clunk.

"Okay, Bosnian." He handed the weapon to Luka. Donaldson lay down and Luka joined him. "This is a makeshift pipe range; it will muffle the noise. You're to fire a full magazine through this weapon, auto and single shot. You know where the change lever is?"

"Yes," Luka replied, an irritated edge to his voice.

"Stop." Donaldson placed an arm to hold Luka back. He was listening to his radio. "Okay, go on."

Luka pulled the butt of the weapon into his shoulder. It felt familiar. He took up the pressure on the trigger.

He fired the first round; the noise was loud but muffled by the pipe; the weapon barrel was half inside it. The muzzle flash illuminated the pipe. Luka smelled the cordite from the bullet. The smell made him sick to his stomach, taking him back to hell.

Luka tested and fired both AKs and both pistols: they worked perfectly. Both smelled of heavy-duty grease; the years stuck in the hide hadn't affected them at all. Luka knew from his training all those years ago how difficult it was to hide weapons for a short period, never mind the years these had been hidden.

"Happy, Bosnian?" Donaldson whispered. Luka gave him the thumbs up: they had worked perfectly.

Donaldson got a small plastic freezer bag out of his coveralls pocket. "We must collect every round. You fired sixty out of the AKs and five rounds in each Browning; you had no stoppages?" he asked.

"No," Luka replied. Donaldson went about collecting the spent cases using an infrared torch. Luka felt, as was becoming the norm, that he was literally being left in the dark.

It had been a long day. Luka was tired and his brain was fucked with everything that had gone on over the last few days. He was glad to spot out the makeshift camp below them. A fourth man appeared. Luka hadn't seen him until now, but he must have been guarding the camp. The weapons they carried had now disappeared; they didn't seem bothered about lights now either. The simple kitchen was illuminated, and a band of light flashed across the ground as the three men went inside. Luka stopped outside, looking up at the stars; he had never felt so alone as he did now. *What the fuck have I been forced into?*

"Bosnian, take all the kit off and leave it in this bag, then get a brew." Luka looked down towards the tent. Donaldson had his head half out of the tent, his glass eye sparkling in the neon light. Luka did as he was ordered, and once back in his soaking wet jeans and kit, he entered. The three men sat around the table; cans of Tennants lager and a bottle of Bushmills took pride of place.

They offered Luka a beer; he refused and instead grabbed a Coke.

"I'm shattered, so where am I sleeping?" Luka asked, not wanting to really know the reply. "We've set you up in the last tent, the blue one, you'll find a sleeping bag in there."

"Thanks," Luka replied and made to leave for the tent, but something had been niggling him. "Donaldson?"

"Aye?" he replied.

"At the car park you said you knew me — how?" Luka inquired.

Donaldson laughed loudly, never taking his one good eye off Luka. "How the fuck do you think I got like this?" he intimated to his scarred and battered face. "I'm the best bomb maker around and I taught you fuckers how to build your own." Luka looked bewildered. "Yes, Bosnian, I was in that shitty farm with you. Freezing, wasn't it? That fookin smell of shit and wood smoke never left me." Luka was dumbstruck. "Bosnian, I remember you as a fucked-up kid; them cunts fucked you up, but Zac saw through the bollocks and knew you were good — in fact, a top student in that wee training camp. That's why you're here Bosnian; you're the best they have."

Luka took a deep breath, trying to make sense of all this. It was so long ago, and it was never meant to be like this: he simply wanted to avenge his family, not get involved with a group of jihadist psychos.

"Who's Zac?" Luka inquired, trying to make sense of it all.

"Zac, the boss man, big dude with a ginger beard."

Luka ducked out of the tent and made his way to the third tent, which he unzipped and scrambled in. Once inside, he took off his shoes; his feet were in a bad way, but nowhere near as bad as his mental state. He was into something he could not leave without risking the ones he loved. He needed a plan; he had to get out of this, and fast.

Chapter 27

Dominic ate his breakfast in silence. As he ate the hand-me-down croissants a large sandwich firm had donated to the shelter, he contemplated what had happened yesterday. He had made a friend of Buzzard, who he now knew was called Abu. It may not have been his real name, but it was a start. Of more concern was his predicament within the shelter. The shelter had a zero-violence policy, both internal and when out and about, and because of the state Buzzard had been in, it couldn't be kept a secret when they had both returned. The staff had helped to patch him up and recommended an A&E visit, but he had declined.

All Dominic could do was sit and wait to learn his fate. The shelter management had arrived and were sat behind a closed door in the tiny makeshift office located just off the main entrance.

He sat there, staring into his tea in his own world, when his attention was brought back by a tap on his shoulder. He looked up; it was Addict, his new best mate.

"Join you, man?" he asked.

"Crack on," replied Dominic, not taking his eyes off his brew.

Addict took a seat next to Dominic and noisily started to eat his breakfast, slurping the gloppy mixture off his spoon. Dominic knew what was coming next, and after a long silence between them, Addict opened up the dialogue. "Got in some drama, man, eh; you okay?" Addict threw out the question, fishing for gossip, not really interested in Dominic's health, he surmised.

"What the fuck you on about?" Dominic replied, hoping his aggressive manner would deter Addict's probing, but no.

"You getting in aggro with that big nasty dude. You look okay, but man, they batter him proper. You some tough bad-ass dude, eh?" Addict said in his pseudo-gangster slang, laughing at his own joke.

Dominic surveyed the interior of the shelter. The sunlight casting rods of light through the dirty skylight windows gave the interior of this building a shadowy, cold feel. This was exactly where his life was right now: dark, dirty and in the shadows. This was tough, and he knew it would probably get worse, especially if he was kicked out of the shelter.

"He needed help; would do it for anyone," Dominic said.

"Innit," Addict replied. What that meant, Dominic did not know.

They both returned to silence, the shelter slowly emptying as people drifted off to local parks or libraries to escape the heat of the summer.

"That's me done, I'll catch you later." Dominic excused himself, escaping the inquisitive Addict and leaving him to his Tourette's and stale cornflakes; *what a mix*, thought Dominic ironically.

As he put his cup in the large industrial dishwasher, he observed Buzzard entering the office, the flimsy Perspex door rattling on its hinges as it was slammed shut. It wasn't long before raised voices could be heard, the loudest being Buzzard's.

Dominic decided to go back to the dormitory. He entered the long, narrow room, the rows of bunk beds now predominantly empty, with only a few poor souls on their beds, staring into space and no doubt finding nothing. Dominic tidied the small area around his bed that he could call his own, his cheap Primark jeans on the floor where he had dropped them last night. Smatterings of blood and snot covered the jean legs, and his t-shirt. He was placing the items in a "bag for life" from Waitrose, which each of the guests — as they were known — were given to place their laundry in, which the volunteers would wash and dry for them.

His attention was brought back to the present by the door of the dormitory opening and Buzzard storming in, his face fixed with rage. Without acknowledging anyone in the room, he went to his own area of the dorm, noisily kicking a bin out of the way. Dominic observed him pick up his phone and, opening the fire door, he exited to the smoking area. Dominic hoped that the technical team had managed to covertly place the listening device he had requested; he could check this out tomorrow when he had his dead letter box meeting with his handler.

Dominic finished his housework, and having placed his laundry next to the washer, he made himself a brew and returned to his bed space; whilst it was quiet, he wanted to mentally prepare his brief as he committed nothing to paper when in the hostel. He had to avoid any form of soft compromise; his trade craft had to be as good as, if not better than, the guys he was in the hostel to spy on.

The fire door opened once more and a visibly rattled Buzzard walked in, one eye nearly closed and his face swollen; he wore the look of a second-best heavyweight boxing contender. He glanced up; noticing Dominic, he nodded, acknowledging him. Dominic went about his impromptu cleaning spree, deciding to change his bedding. As he was wrestling with his quilt cover, he felt a presence and turned around to find Buzzard towering over him, his wounds worse than Dominic had first thought.

"Man, thank you again. I'm sure they would have killed me if you'd not got involved," Buzzard said, his Birmingham accent more evident than ever.

"Listen, I would have done it for anyone. I hate cunts like that; fucking bully boys, not as hard as they think," Dominic replied.

"Well, they certainly had me. I was toast for a minute," Buzzard replied, his face breaking into a painful smile.

Dominic noted a change in his language; he was speaking in an almost normal middle class accent, not the gangster slang he had previously used. It appeared to Dominic that this man was not off the streets.

"You getting grief?" Dominic intimated outside the dorm.

"Yeah, threatening to kick me out for breaking the rules," he said.

"Listen, mate, I can tell them exactly what went on. You were the victim," Dominic said.

Buzzard held up a hand. "No need, man, all cool for now, but thanks. Fancy going out for a coffee? I have some money left; they didn't look down my sock."

"Why not? Be nice to get some fresh air, this place depresses me."

THEY TOOK a seat outside the street-side cafe, the unusually hot summer showing no signs of cooling down. Buzzard went inside, and soon returned from the cafe with two large mugs of milky coffee. Placing them down, he took his seat at the small plastic table that had been placed out on the busy street, to the annoyance of the throngs of pedestrians who had to side-step their way past them. Dominic noticed Buzzard had chosen the table that had the best field of view; was that good trade craft, or just street survival?

They both sat in silence watching the world go by, deep in thought. Buzzard broke the quiet.

"So where did you learn how to fight like that?" he enquired.

"I suppose my time in the Army taught me a few things," Dominic replied.

It was apparent Buzzard hadn't been expecting this. Dominic felt his stare boring into the side of his head as he turned his attention to his coffee.

"Army? Who did you serve with?" Buzzard asked, still maintaining his steely gaze on Dominic.

"Paras, but it all went wrong. Got thrown out for hitting someone," Dominic explained. "Gave a bully a kicking and they decided to back him and discharge me. Fuck 'em, ruined my life; got fuck all now, lost my family, my home, got no money and no job, and the way I feel at the moment, no hope," Dominic said, playing overly dejected.

Another long silence ensued. Buzzard looked deep in thought. Sat in his shalwar kameez and skullcap, he got a lot of second glances from the people passing by, especially with his bruised and battered face. He still had a certain look to him, an almost sinister look, Dominic thought.

He suddenly got up. "Come with me," he gestured, and walked off with purpose.

They entered a nearby park, sparsely occupied with workers enjoying a lunchtime break in the sun.

Buzzard lay face down on the ground; he gestured for Dominic to join him, face to face, hardly a gap between them both — Dominic could have almost kissed him. But he knew this was a tactic to defeat anyone listening in to their conversation with either a high-power microphone or by lip-reading. *Another example of this man's training,* he recognised.

"I hate the infidel armies — they have murdered so many of my brothers and sisters," Buzzard said with purpose, catching Dominic off-guard with his matter-of-fact opinion.

"You, however, I owe a big favour to, so I will not hold your past against you. Believe me, I should. I have seen so much slaughter in the name of the greatest infidel, America," he muttered, almost to himself.

Dominic wiped the sweat off his forehead, now running into his eyes. He was busy mentally logging all this: this man must be who the security services had said he was. It was obvious he had been abroad to fight or train and had that in-bred hatred for the West for their war on terror. Dominic wanted to keep this meeting going for as long as possible; he had gained so much useful intelligence for his team.

"Listen, I'm no fan of this country playing fiddle with the yanks. Many of my mates have come back smashed to bits, and for what?" Dominic countered, almost treating this conversation like a game of chess.

Buzzard flashed him a glance, checking himself. Dominic didn't know if he was about to kick off or was lost for words — after all, being rescued by a soldier was a shock for any potential jihadist.

"I have business to do in London; I obviously need protection." He paused, staring hard at Dominic. "I would like you to help me if I think I need it. Not all the time, only on certain business matters. I will pay you for your time," Buzzard finished, with the offer of money.

Dominic lay on the warm, parched ground, gobsmacked. *How the fuck had he managed this?* From a stroke of luck by happening upon a fight, he was now being asked to act as a minder for a Tier One security service target. The management, or Headshed, as they were known, would cream themselves when he got this update out there, he reckoned.

"Don't suppose I have much else on my cards, and I

certainly need money, that's a fact," he said, then laughed. Buzzard also laughed, and they both lay there, laughing, like in some bizarre love scene. Buzzard offered him his hand; Dominic took it, both men maintaining eye contact for just long enough for Dominic to sense menace behind the large almond eyes staring back at him.

With that, Buzzard got up and walked off; not in the shelter's direction, observed Dominic, who stayed on the ground, in a bit of a trance. He would have to call a proper debrief; he had too much to tell for the usual dead letter box meet.

Chapter 28

Dominic wasn't too happy that he was meeting his handler in the same location, but he needed to pass on the intelligence update he hoped his team would be actively working on.

He enjoyed the morning air; the smell of freshly-cut grass from the nearby park he was heading to made a pleasant change from the smog and vehicle fumes that were making everyone feel asthmatic. Dominic liked being out of the claustrophobic atmosphere of the shelter.

He crossed the road by a row of shops which were getting ready for a busy day, and paused to look at the newspapers laid out neatly. This also gave him the chance to check whether or not he was being tailed. He read the headlines, a mixture of political debate and warning of the hot summer and the impending hose pipe bans. *It really was a hot one,* he thought as he crossed the road and headed towards the park entrance, a pleasant street, tree-lined, with the park on one side.

Call it sixth sense or paranoia, Dominic felt as if something didn't seem right. He strode out, desperate to get into the safety of the park where no one would touch him amid all the families and small children.

His heart rate rose, and he turned to see a white, nondescript van approaching from the rear. It was going too slowly, but he left it too late to run; the van pulled level and as he glanced over his shoulder, he noticed the side door was open. In a flash two men wearing balaclavas jumped out and roughly threw him into the rear of the van. He had no chance, and the van sped up as the door was slammed shut.

Dominic tried to calm down his senses down, that were in overload. They laid him on his front where he had landed, and he tasted the metallic tint of the blood in his mouth from his nose, that had taken an enormous hit on the metal floor of the transit. He tensed up for the inevitable kicking, and his mind was racing. Nothing. He waited. All he could hear was the engine noise, which strangely had slowed to a normal level, neither racing nor screaming away.

He steadied himself, not knowing whether he would face a gun to his head or a fist he rolled slowly and non-aggressively onto his back. Through his moist eyes, courtesy of his bruised nose, he saw the two men who'd grabbed him, still wearing the balaclavas, jeans and jackets, not the shalwar kameez he was expecting.

Something didn't add up. One man moved his hand and Dominic expected to see a pistol or kosh, but he simply pulled off his balaclava.

"What the fuck?! You bastards!" Dominic blurted as he recognised his captor as one of his fellow Omega Operators. The other guy did the same. He too was from the team.

All three burst into laughter, shaking hands and hugging. Dominic had been out of the loop undercover. They gave him water and some food out of a bag that must have been specially prepared for him.

"Why have I been withdrawn?" Dominic asked. Both men looked at Dominic with surprise.

"Mate, you haven't. The Headshed just want you in for a proper debrief."

"What the fuck? I could be compromised if anyone from the shelter has seen me," Dominic said.

"Our brief was to give you a slap so your cover could be a drug dealer wanting his money back."

"But my legend isn't a druggy."

"No, but you can still be a dealer for money," the other observed.

"Suppose so. Anyway, you've done a job, I'm in clip," Dominic said, touching his swollen nose.

They all laughed, then sat in silence for a while

"Where're we going?" Dominic asked.

"Back to the FOB. We're still there, mate, chasing fucking shadows at the moment but busy."

"Cool, could do with a good scoff and a decent fucking brew. The tea in that place is shit."

The vehicle slowed and turned off the main road. From the muffled voices and the sound of a metal garage door being opened, Dominic reckoned they had entered the Forward Operating Base. He felt a sense of excitement at seeing his old team, but most of all he was looking forward to seeing his covert girlfriend, Charley; he was unsure of where he stood with her, as they hadn't spoken since the other night in her flat.

The transit's side door slid open, and Dominic jumped out into the garage that housed his covert operations team. A loud cheer went up as the team, en masse, made their way over to Dominic to say hello and take the piss; he had missed this banter.

People shook his hand and patted him on the back, offering him brews; it was all a bit of a gang fuck. He noticed his team leader enter the garage through the operations room door and behind him walked Charley; his heart started to beat faster.

"Dom, welcome." The ops officer shook his hand.

"Hi, Dom," Charley said and gave him a business-like peck on the cheek, but covertly, she grabbed his hand and gave it a huge squeeze. *Mega,* Dom thought, his heart skipping a beat.

"We needed a proper debrief, mate. Sorry for the cloak-and-dagger pick up, but we can't be too careful." Dominic nodded in agreement, touching his painful nose for effect. "Let's go for the debrief first, then you can have scoff with the team and chew the fat. And by the way, Charley's running this job. We're calling it Op Diablos, which is Greek for the devil; quite fitting, as you'll see from our updated target packs."

Dominic couldn't believe what he'd just heard. Charley was running the job that he was acting undercover on. *How much more complicated could this gig get?* he thought, annoyed but somehow excited and equally driven by it.

The three of them entered the operations room. As usual it was a hive of activity, the enormous TV screens adorning the walls showing an array of interactive maps and live feeds from cameras and drones covertly stalking high above in the London skies. The radios were a constant chatter as teams worked on the ground.

They moved to the large oblong briefing desk and sat down. Dominic noticed several classified files neatly placed in front of Charley, the front adorned with the Phalanx symbol and "Top Secret" in red on the top and bottom of the files: *this is serious shit,* thought Dominic.

The ops officer took a deep breath, then turned to Dominic. "Okay, mate, from the top: all you have. We need some leads. We are chasing fucking shadows, and the Headshed is getting impatient."

Dominic looked at them both in turn, paused, and passed on everything he could about his time in close proximity with the Buzzard.

As he outlined what had gone on and his bizarre relationship with Buzzard, the other two sat back, showing in a mixture of awe and shock.

"So, you're saying he's asked you to be his minder?"

Dom laughed, but it was a nervous, uncomfortable laugh. "Yes, Boss. Like I said, I didn't realise it was him getting the kicking, I just went to help."

"And?" the ops officer prompted.

"Well, I basically managed to get the others to back off."

"Gave them a kicking, then?" Charley butted in, laughing.

"Sort of; but he was in a bad way, and now he trusts me."

"Does he, though?" cut in the ops officer. He perused his notes for a minute.

"Listen, boss, I think we may be able to get a foothold."

"Carry on," the ops officer replied, seizing interest again.

"Remember that brief we got off the Alpha Geeks? The one from some random university professor in Israel re cyber warfare, and their technology for Trojan-horsing phones via replacement screens? Is that technology available to us?" Dominic posed the question.

"I remember," Charley cut in.

"I don't know about that technology, but why are you suggesting it?"

"Well, Buzzard's mobile got fucked in the fight and he's finding it hard to use."

"So?" the ops officer asked, looking slightly lost.

"If I can persuade him to let me fix it, we may get one of those screens fitted."

"Okay, right — his phone is vital, and we need him on the lines. You say it's a Samsung, and the screen is trashed?"

"Correct, totally fucked, and he can hardly use it."

"And this is his primary comms?"

"I reckon; never seen him with a burner, always going to the smoking area to talk."

"Um — yes, indeed, but I'm still awaiting authority on that

technical solution. Seems homeless shelters created issues with our Snoopers' Charter people."

The ops officer excused himself to make some calls in his office, leaving Dominic and Charley alone.

"How have you been?" she asked, moving forward and lightly touching his hand.

"Good, mate; place is a shit hole. Felt really sorry for the poor fuckers who call it home, but our man is a different beast. He exudes menace, a real psycho."

They both paused and gazed at one another.

"I've really missed you," she said, surprising him. He'd never expected an outward sign of affection from her, but he liked it.

"Me too; it's my turn for dinner next."

"Cheeky," she said, and laughed as she gripping his hand. They both returned to silence, pondering; thinking not about work, but about their feelings for each other... or at least that's what Dominic was doing, and he hoped she was too.

"Mate, have you taken the lead on this job because of me?" Dominic asked.

She paused, looking at the ground. "Yes, I put myself forward. I wanted to be in the best place to make sure you are being looked after," she muttered. Dominic sensed tears weren't far away. "Dom, listen; last thing I wanted was to fall for anyone on the job. This was my chance to make something of myself, not being held back," she finished, looking first into his eyes then down at the floor again.

Dominic knew she was referring to her old Army boyfriend, who had not liked her being involved with Project Omega. He gave her hand a reassuring squeeze, then let it drop quickly as the door to the briefing room flew open and the ops officer returned, chatting into his mobile, animated, not taking a breath as he sat back down. He finished the call.

"Right..." He paused. "We need that phone. Alpha projects

have a friendly guy; well, basically a plant who does jobs for the organisation. You're both right, the Israelis have developed the technology and once our guy fits a new screen, we will have control of the phone." He paused again, looking into the distance. He returned to the present. "We need a break, guys. We are near, and yet so far from anything tangible to put up the chain."

"Okay; so if I can persuade him somehow to get his phone fixed, what do I do to get it to our guy?" Dominic asked.

"He works at a mobile phone repair shop just outside Victoria Station; shit-hole, but that will help with the cover. The shop sells dodgy phones and all that vaping crap." The ops officer looked at his mobile and brought up a map, proffering it to Dominic.

'Yeah, got it. So how will I know who the correct guy is in the shop?" Dominic asked.

"You can't miss him, proper anarchist type dude, goes by the name of 'Matrix'. Security service tapped into him a while ago — big into cryptocurrency, and apparently he's loaded." He showed the pair a picture of Matrix.

"See what you mean — needs a good wash... and check out that hair." Dominic continued to look at the image, processing it to memory.

"Okay, you know what you need to do. This is our biggest chance yet. Good luck, mate, and well done." The ops officer offered his hand and shook it vigorously. "I'll leave you two to carry on." With that he turned and left.

Dominic looked at Charley. "Was that aimed at us?"

"Stop being paranoid. I'm running this op, that's all he meant by it. Do you fancy some food? Lunch is on soon, then we'll drop you back off to your new best mate."

"Can't fucking wait," Dom said sarcastically.

Chapter 29

Luka hated this journey more than any other. It dragged memories and guilt up from the sewer of humanity. He knew he didn't make the journey enough, and that hurt him. It broke the promise he had made to his mother on her deathbed.

He parked the car in the centre of the small village of Westerham. When he was visiting his sister, he had a routine that helped him cope. He went to the local independent bookstore, The Grasshopper, where he bought any books on flora and fauna he could find, then went to Costa Coffee and bought two large black Americanos — extra shot — and two blueberry muffins. It cut to the quick how false this was, and how his parents would be so disappointed with him, and that hurt more than anything else he had been through.

He drove the short distance from the town to the CWABW (Centre for Women Affected By War) based in an old stately home close to Chartwell House, wartime home of Winston Churchill.

The reception area was functional and tidy, akin to a public-school reception, Luka thought as he sat waiting for Merjem's case officer. He refused the offer of coffee, his Costa takeaway plain to see. He sat with the clicking of the enormous clock as his companion, alongside the guilt etched into his very heart for what had happened to his sister.

The door opened and out walked Dr Lyons, an attractive, elegant lady. Luka placed her in her mid-fifties, but she gave off a wholesome sex appeal; she had long, dark, ginger hair and an impressive figure.

"Mr Avdic, how nice to see you after so long." *Bollocking taken.* Luka knew he avoided the place. "Merjem is doing really well; totally dedicated to her studies and her love for anything to do with botany. She really loves it, and it helps the process of forgiveness. But I must say, she has been a little subdued and acting out of character recently — we're not sure why. Maybe you will find out."

"Forgiveness for what?" Luka inquired somewhat angrily.

"My dear, what your sister was subjected to and experienced: she totally blames herself. It's all part of the process, and it takes years." Dr Lyons paused. Luka avoided eye contact, and stared out of the window, his mind awash. "Let's go. She's in the garden, as it's a beautiful day." They walked down the corridor and out into the large, well-kept gardens. Luka immediately recognised his baby sister; she looked well, with her long black hair tied in a messy bun on her head, and wearing baggy t-shirt and denim shorts. She looked like any other young woman from these privileged parts of the world.

"Merjem, you have a visitor," Dr Lyons announced.

Merjem continued arranging the pot plants; Luka knew the drill. Eventually she turned. Her face was the image of their mother; it hit Luka like a sledgehammer every time he came, hence why he avoided it so much.

She ran into his arms, sobbing angrily. "Where have you been?" she cried.

"It's alright, *Draga*, I'm here now. It's alright, you're safe," Luka reassured her, using the term she would have heard lots from her parents.

They walked through the gardens; she was so proud of them. Luka looked around; they were beautiful. He hugged his sister tightly.

"Let's eat." He showed her the red Costa bag. They sat down on a wooden bench with a lovely view across the Sevenoaks Weald. Luka noted she hadn't said a word. The blueberry muffin, her favourite, stayed in the bag.

Luka sat for a while looking out at the view, enjoying the cool breeze on his face. He felt it first, then saw the tears.

"Hey, it's alright," he tried.

"IT WILL NEVER BE ALRIGHT... NEVER!" she screamed.

Luka was lost; she was angry, angrier than he had ever seen. "What? Why will it never be alright? You're doing well here, and it's a great place to live." Luka motioned towards the beautiful views.

"Because I will never escape my past." Tears ran down her cheeks in volleys. Luka grabbed her close, and she melted into him, sobbing loudly.

She eased out of his cuddle and fumbled in her pocket, pulling out a dog-eared paper cutting, a yellow tinge to the paper. "I found this in the weekend's *Financial Times*. I always read that edition, just like Papa did. I'm sorry, Luka, I cannot bear the fact she is alive."

Luka opened the large pull-out, his eyes scanning the content of the story and accompanying photograph. His heart sank — it felt like his world was falling apart. His sister took the turn of consoler now.

The tactics, routines and habits of a career diplomat — Julia Picton, a role model for career women.

Luka turned to his sister. "How is this bitch still alive?" he said.

"I hate her, Luka, and what she did to us was unforgivable. She broke Papa's heart."

Luka read and re-read the double-page story which went

through the career history of Julia Picton. The picture showed her as a good-looking woman, attractive, elegant in a corporate way. She didn't deserve this glory. A big part of the story was missing; her real identity as an MI6 agent. For what she had done to Luka's family back in his homeland, she must be made to pay.

Chapter 30

Luka opened the window of the old Ford Mondeo he'd been a passenger in for the brief journey to the service station. The electric window was well past its best; letting the window down was hard work. Fresh air filled the car, it was much needed, as his companion was a chain smoker, made all the worse by the warm muggy night. It seemed this summer was heading to be the hottest on record.

Ardian Memic had survived the massacre that took eight thousand of his fellow menfolk because he was away visiting his grandparents. He, like Luka, had never returned.

"You smoke too much," Luka said, more in observation than direct speech as he stared out the half-open car window at the ranks of lorries parked up for the night.

"You moan too much," replied Ardian.

They both returned to silence, staring out of the window. Luka mulled over the predicament he found himself in. His mentor and handler Redbeard had given him this mission, with the proviso that if it went well, he would sanction Luka to act on his revenge mission; he now had a tangible target in mind.

Within the next hour or so a group of battle-hardened

jihadists fresh from the apocalyptic battlefield that was Syria would exit the lorry that had carried them across the smuggling routes of the Balkans and into Europe. Luka was amazed by how the organisation had infiltrated the various law enforcement agencies and Customs Officers that then afforded these men safe passage.

"He is here: parked up at the rear of the lorry park by the row of trees. Got boys covering the exits; if any heat is around, we will know," Ardian said, not lifting his eyes from his phone screen. Row after row of articulated lorries were parked up neatly for the night, registration plates highlighting the enormous variety of countries the lorries originated from.

The van in which the men would be decamped for onward transportation into London had been provided by Ardian's fellow tobacco smugglers, who all knew these motorway services well, using them as unloading points for the fake cigarettes that flooded the capital's pubs and bars.

"Did you brief them to keep their mouths shut?" Luka said through a scowl, annoyed at his friend's lack of attention.

"Yes, yes, Luka, they're my top boys. Done jobs here for years, know all the rat runs off these services; that's why we use these shitty services," Ardian stated. "Look, shit-hole, all these foreign trucks use this place to shit and shag. Place fucking stinks," he continued, still transfixed on his phone.

Luka's own phone vibrated, rattling on the dashboard.

"Finished at drive through en route home be 60 mins," the message read. It simply meant that the group were safely through the UK Border Agency checks at Dover and en route up the M20 towards the M25 service station.

Luka sat in deep contemplation, dread filling his stomach. He was under no doubt that these guys were on a suicide mission. And in under an hour they would become Luka's problem. His orders from Redbeard were concise and to the point: help them do their mission and put El Muj firmly on the jihadist map.

He suddenly needed fresh air as the car had become too claustrophobic. He walked away, further into the huge lorry park, the ever-present hum of generators keeping the refrigeration trucks cool in the baking heat now filling his ears. Row after row of trucks, with their drivers catching sleep before moving up the motorway or heading into London for early deliveries. His gaze settled above the trees, the lights of the nearby town of Sevenoaks filling his view. He had an urge to run, to leave this impending nightmare behind. For a fleeting moment, he considered it, but for the first time in many years the images of that fateful day came spinning back into his head, the glow of Sevenoaks now morphed into the fires of his burning town, as the hum of the lorries all around him became the sound of the coaches that carried the menfolk of his town to their impending deaths.

"Fuck!" he screamed.

"Luka! Luka, what's the matter? Are you okay? For fuck's sake, keep it down." Ardian was out of the car.

The two men stood looking at each other. Ardian looked concerned, Luka noticed.

"I'm fine, I'm okay; just a flashback."

Ardian reached out, patting him lightly on the shoulder. "It will never leave us, brother, never," he said, almost in defeat.

Luka turned to walk back towards the car. He knew the memories wouldn't leave, and this was why he had to do what Redbeard ordered. He had to banish these ghosts once and for all.

They both sat in silence, staring into space out through the grimy, fly-splattered car windscreen. Time took on a new meaning when waiting for impending doom; it grew a life of its own.

The phone vibrated on the dash of the old Mondeo.

"Approaching." Luka read it and turned to his friend. "Here we go, they're here."

They both sat and observed the large articulated lorry pull into the lorry park, non-descriptive markings on the side, modern and not at all what Luka had expected. It duly headed to the rear of the park and reversed neatly into a space next to the white Mercedes Sprinter van.

Luka and Ardian both sat there, tense, eyes on stalks for the ever-present police or security services team to appear out of the shadows. Ardian had gotten some of his tobacco smuggling colleagues to keep watch, but Luka had ensured they were nowhere near this part of the lorry park to see the human cargo being unloaded.

Luka turned to his friend who knew what he had to do. He picked up the small radio that had been perched between his legs.

"Sitrep," he ordered.

"Clear. No-one followed the lorry in, no sign of heat, we are good to go," came the reply.

"Okay: get the van ready, this has to be sharp; we need to get out of here fast," Luka ordered.

Ardian picked up the radio and called the van team. "Open the back doors and stand by; two of us are approaching you on foot from the direction of the entrance."

The two men approached the rear of the articulated trailer, pushing up the locking levers, trying not to make as little sound as possible. The door creaked open and the smell hit Luka full in the face. It was primeval, like they had transported animals in the back. It was the unmistakable smell of human excrement and sweat.

Luka whispered the predetermined code word; "Nou Camp."

"Messi," came back the reply and from the shadows came

the first of the team. Luka immediately recognised him as the leader, who looked and smelled like shit. He gently jumped down off the lorry. The journey had certainly taken its toll on him, and he looked bedraggled. To anyone watching, this was a people-smuggling gang unloading their unfortunate cargo for onward transportation.

"Quick!" Luka barked and gestured to the rear of the Sprinter van. "There is food and drink in there for you, but hurry!" Luka commanded. Luka offered him a hand down off the back of the trailer. "Here, give me your bag." Luka made a grab for the khaki man-bag.

"Don't fucking touch my gear," Ibro replied aggressively.

The two men came face to face, almost in a standoff. No love was lost, and the tension was palpable. Luka's dislike for the man deepened.

"Hello, Ibro," Luka said without emotion.

The man stepped closer to Luka, invading his space; he stank.

"I need a piss, Bosnian. Out of my way." He pushed past Luka and moved to the nearby hedge, into the shadows to relieve himself. The others were doing the same.

Once they had all relieved themselves, they assembled in a huddle at the rear of the van. Ibro was obviously in charge of the bunch; he spoke fast, and it was obvious to Luka he was briefing the team on the next phase. He turned to Luka.

"Weapons?"

"Not yet," Luka replied.

"Not yet? The fuck does that mean? They promised us weapons once we reached here. We are, as you say, sitting fucking ducks," Ibro barked back, his temper barely under control.

"Listen, we're sorting them, just not yet. Now let's get going, we need to move," Luka stated.

The men, stiff from weeks of being cooped up, gingerly got

into yet another confined space and greedily went about getting themselves drinks and food. Luka grabbed the door to close it, looking into the dark rear of the van. Ibro sat drinking out of a plastic water bottle, his eyes never leaving Luka's, like a death stare. It sent a shiver down Luka's spine; this man was an evil force, and he was now Luka's responsibility.

The dirty white van finally left its parking space and headed for the entrance and onto the M25. Luka and Ardian followed at a distance, keeping a watch as the vehicle made its way into London; it was now early morning but the roads were already getting busy. Both men were looking for the tell-tale signs of a surveillance team: a motorbike speeding down the road for no reason, usually given away by a large bum bag on the petrol tank hiding the covert radio; easy pickings, if you knew what to look for.

They eventually entered central London through the Blackwall Tunnel and into the urban jungle of the East End. Only Luka, Ardian, and the van driver knew the location, and as they approached the general area Ardian picked up his radio.

"Boys, stand down. Thanks for your help tonight."

"Copy, cheers," came the reply, as the counter-surveillance team stood down.

Luka wanted to maintain the highest level of operational security on where these people were going to be hidden; this job had been sanctioned at the highest level of operational Al Quds Force Command. Redbeard was a powerful man, and his reach was omnipresent. Luka had to do a good job of hiding this murderous bunch away in preparation for their purpose: a truly twisted plot to hurt the Western world and put AQ back on the map.

Finally, they turned off the main road and into the huge concrete jungle of Broadwater Farm, the London estate made famous by the riots and social unrest of the 1980s and now a self-governing, virtually lawless part of inner London. The safe house these men were destined to use was perfect to hide in virtual plain sight; this community had a common hate for anything to do with the 'establishment' and the police. Perfect, as long as these mercenaries behaved themselves.

The van turned into a parking area at the rear of some houses. Dawn was fast emerging, but the shadows cast by the large block of flats made it a perfect drop-off. The van reversed into a bay and the driver turned off the engine. Luka and Ardian had pulled into a parking space at the approach to the estate; now it was a waiting game to see if they were being followed. A surveillance team would have to enter the estate by car or by foot. They waited. Thirty minutes passed; nothing. Luka was happy they were clean.

They parked the battered Mondeo next to the van and went to the rear, unlocking the door and opening the it only as far as needed for these guys to exit.

"About fucking time," growled Ibro, pushing past Luka.

This man is a real heartless fucker, thought Luka, but he had a job to do. "Follow me," he said.

He led the men along the rear of a row of maisonettes and into the back of a small garden; the back door of the house was open, and the men rapidly entered. The door closed silently behind them.

Luka turned to the group huddled into the small kitchen of this scruffy, unloved council flat.

"This will be your home for the first phase. Welcome. Showers are hot, and I have clothes for you to change into. The TV has all the channels that were requested." Luka paused, observing the belligerent attitude of Ibro, smirking as he looked around his new home. "Please place the clothes you have on into this bin bag, and I will dispose of them," Luka said and threw down a bin bag onto the floor. "You will be well looked after here and once you have gotten some sleep, we will meet in here to discuss the next phase. Please don't attempt to leave this house, as it won't be safe for you." Luka surveyed the rag-tag bunch; they looked like they smelled, but apart from the murderous leader Ibro, Luka felt for them; life at home made people do extreme things, as he well knew. "Make yourself at home."

Chapter 31

EAST LONDON

Luka hadn't slept well, the dread of what lay ahead only getting stronger as he went about mentally configuring a day he'd never wanted to have. He checked his normal phone, hoping to see a message from Sally, but found nothing, which worsened his mood. As he made coffee in the small kitchen, he caught a reflection of himself in the cupboard glass: his face looked haggard, and he was unshaven and un-showered.

Since breaking cover and contacting Ardian, his boyhood friend, he had enjoyed his company. They had kept quiet for all those years, hoping the call would come for their own mission, not babysitting these Syrian nutters. But it had to be done, and he knew Ardian would have his back.

The doorbell rang to the communal outside door. Luka moved to the large sash window of his Victorian east London flat. Safe behind his lace curtains, he observed the person buzzing his house number; his sense of paranoia was normally bad, but after recent events, it was all consuming.

It was Ardian, he confirmed, whilst checking up and down the street from his vantage point for any interest or surveillance teams. He buzzed his friend into the small, minimalist flat.

Ardian entered; it was the first time he had ever been in this flat. "When're you going to buy some furniture?" Ardian asked as he looked around the sparsely-furnished space.

"When I can be bothered. It suits me like this," Luka retorted.

"Same old Luka, hey? No ties, nothing you can't leave at a moment's notice. When're you going to settle?" Ardian continued.

"When I want to. Now leave it," Luka snapped, trying not to think about Sally. Luka turned and walked into the small kitchen. Like the rest of the flat it was sparse, but a large Moka coffee pot sat atop the cooker.

"Coffee?" Luka asked, picking up the silver coffeepot and getting a plain white mug off the tree of cups.

They both stood in silence in the tiny kitchen, drinking their strong Turkish-style coffee. Luka was deep in thought, mentally rehearsing the tough day ahead.

"Right, today's plan." Luka brought the moment back to the here and now. "We go to the house and ensure those fuckers have got what they want. We then need to arrange a meeting with my Irish contact, to get the produce to them, and sort the weapons and other kit to be available for us." Luka held his friend's stare. "Ardian, I didn't want to put you in danger, you know that, but once I was given this task I needed help; someone I can trust, as those warmongers I certainly do not," Luka said.

Ardian nodded. "Of course, I understand, you cannot do this alone. But why has this been given to you to do?" he asked with concern.

Luka continued to outline the entire story, starting from the training camp back home just after the war.

"So, you arrange to trade drugs for weapons? That's not like you, Luka," his friend said, very matter-of-factly.

"Well, we have to work with what we have, and this shit sandwich is ours now," Luka said, downbeat.

They both retreated back to their own worlds, quietly drinking the dregs of their coffee.

Luka once again turned it back to the present. “Okay, time to go. You get the shopping?” Luka asked.

“Yeah, all in the car. My guys have had a look around the estate; no signs of any unwanted attention.” Ardian was using his tobacco-smuggling cronies again to do some rudimentary anti-surveillance, none the wiser of who they were keeping safe.

Luka deadlocked his front door, and they both made their way down the tight staircase and to the communal front entrance. Luka checked his mail slot, noticing a handwritten note which he placed in his pocket.

The old, battered Mondeo smelled no better observed Luka as they set off, Ardian driving, lighting up a cigarette having not been allowed to smoke in Luka’s flat. Ardian dragged deeply on the cigarette, exhaling two plumes of smoke out of his nostrils. Luka opened the window to let in some much-needed fresh air. He watched the world go by as they made their way down the crowded streets of east London, heading for the A102 and the concrete monstrosity that was Broadwater Farm estate. The rush hour traffic had abated and they made good progress, both sitting in stony silence.

Luka pondered what the next steps would be. He had heard nothing yet of the team’s intentions, but he knew the outline plan. It was twisted on the verge of perversion, but he expected nothing different from these types of people. All Luka wanted was to avenge his town’s slain men; however, the people he was about to meet had no other focus than to create as much bloodshed as possible, all in the name of Allah.

Luka sensed the heightened tension in the car as they turned off The Avenue onto Willan Road and entered the concrete monolith of architectural obscurity that was Broadwater Farm. Concrete boxes piled on top of each other, housing families who no doubt felt the same: it was a truly awful design. Very much like the large La Castellane estate in Marseille, which Luka knew these men had passed through on their tortuous journey to the UK from Syria. He knew it well, as he had done the same journey to get out to the training camp he'd attended in Bosnia shortly after the war finished.

They drove round the back of the row of double-storey maisonettes that housed the team. It was a scene of decay, observed Luka, old cars, some on bricks, dirty footpaths and large wheelie bins overflowing with decaying rubbish. It seemed that the trash lorries left this part of north London alone. They parked the car next to a newish-looking BMW with tinted windows — no doubt the local drug dealer, Luka thought, taking a mental note of the registration. The old Mondeo fitted in with the urban decay, but the BMW didn't. This proved that little or no police activity happened on these estates, and it was obvious to all that these drug lords didn't feel the need to hide their wealth in an otherwise poverty-stricken place.

They approached in the same direction down the back alley, which stank of urine and was covered in dog shit. Each maisonette had its own back gate and small courtyard. The walls were high enough to stop people from seeing into the courtyards and some of the walls were adorned with broken glass to deter any unwanted guests. *Classy*, mused Luka as he unlocked the back gate and made his way to the back door. Ardian followed, a tactical bound behind to ensure they were clean of surveillance.

Luka sensed he was being watched as he knocked sharply on the back door; he heard the heavy chain taken off and the key being inserted into the three deadlocks. *Over the top,* thought Luka, but he was glad of the enhanced security. More for who it was keeping in than keeping out.

As the door opened, Luka was met by Ibro who aggressively

grabbed him, dragging him into the small kitchen and placing a hand over his mouth. Luka felt anger and a slight amount of panic surging through his body, unsure of what it was all about. Ibro grabbed him by the face and turned him to face another member of the gang, who held an A4 pad in his hands. Luka noticed writing on it; nobody had uttered a word. Ibro pointed to the pad, then to Luka's eyes. *He wants me to read what's on the pad,* Luka thought.

'Has this house been swept?' Luka read.

He nodded, confirming that the property was swept for listening devices and cameras prior to the team taking residence. The page was turned over and Luka read on.

'Do you know the neighbours?'

Again, Luka nodded and was relieved when Ibro released his powerful grip on his mouth and let him go.

"What the fuck was that about?" Luka said through gritted teeth, attempting to regain a certain amount of kudos.

Ibro stood staring at Luka with disdain, glancing at the door as Ardian knocked to gain access after having ensured no one was paying interest to them or the house. Ardian entered the kitchen, observing the standoff between the two main players in the scene.

"And who is this, another fucking Bosnian?" Ibro spat.

This got Luka's back up, but he had to maintain his cool. "He's working with me on this task. The Leader has agreed it."

Ibro smirked and walked into the small lounge that connected to the kitchen. Luka stood still for a while, unsure what to do as he surveyed the state of the kitchen: the place was a tip already. The remains of the food they had eaten on arrival last night was still on the plates, which were still on the table. The other members of the team must have been upstairs. The team member who held up the pad must be Ibro's deputy, also not to be trusted.

Luka needed to regain some control of this situation. He

glanced at Ardian; a glance that suggested he remained alert and ready to react. Luka entered the small lounge, with its fake leather sofa and chairs in a gaudy red. The flimsy curtains firmly closed. The room stank of body odour and cigarette smoke. Ibro was transfixed on the large plasma TV that sat covering the wall of the lounge, a foreign news channel beaming back pictures of some war-damaged town, no doubt in Syria. The way Ibro was concentrating, he must have been acquainted with it. As he leaned forward to grab the TV remote, Luka noticed the modern pistol, probably a Glock 19, tucked down the back of his grimy combat-style pants. Luka let his anger beat him this time and he reacted.

"What the fuck is that?" Luka said with menace.

Ibro turned and with that smirk on his face again, replied, "Bosnian, do you think for one minute I trust you and your ragtag bunch of losers?"

It tempted Luka to smack this cunt right in the face, but he kept his control. "You know the deal: we will sort the gear for your job once you're in county and on task," Luka said.

"Fuck you, I am not leaving myself open at your mercy. The Leader fully sanctions my actions. He also doesn't trust you by the way," Ibro said spitefully.

"Listen, I need the test batch to give to my contacts; if we delay, then we will be delayed getting the weapons and kit you need," Luka said.

Ibro laughed a condescending, menacing laugh. Dismissing Luka by turning back to the TV, he continued. "We need to get going. I have a meeting with the planning cell at the Sharia Law centre in Walthamstow. Do you know it?"

"Yes," Luka said, now confused. He thought he was to be the go-between, but this put a whole new spin on things. He couldn't risk these bloodthirsty nutters running free on the streets of London. He took a seat across from Ibro.

His mind raced. They must have some form of communication with the outside world: this wasn't safe. GCHQ would be all over the airwaves scanning for new mobile phones hitting the networks, especially one that had listed the Middle East, Africa and France in the past few days. The situation was getting out of control.

"Ibro, if you are using your own phones or IT, that's not a good idea; the security services are all over it now —"

Luka didn't get the chance to finish before Ibro cut him off, aggressively, his eyes wide open, his manner now totally changed. "You know fuck all. I have been fighting these pigs for years. Never try to dictate to me," Ibro growled, rising from his seat and towering over Luka. "I tell you what to do and you fucking do it, no question," Ibro carried on. "So, get this first fucking meet setup. It's for this afternoon. Go there at 1200 and they will meet you."

With that Ibro returned to the TV, which seemed to signal the end of this first fateful meeting.

"Listen," Luka said harshly, "I need the test batch to give to my contacts. If we delay, then they will delay us getting the weapons and kit you need."

"Don't take that tone with me; once this meeting is set up you will get your drugs," Ibro spat back.

LUKA SAT IN SILENCE, staring out the window of the battered Mondeo, watching without interest as the terraced houses flashed by, people heading about their normal, everyday lives. Luka's life was anything but that.

He broke the silence. "We're in trouble, Ardian," he announced, looking at his friend intently, who, between keeping his eyes on the road, kept eye contact with his now-distressed friend. "Far from us controlling them, they are taking the upper hand."

"How... what the fuck does that mean?" Ardian replied.

"They are communicating with people and arranging meetings, and they are armed."

"You fucking what?" Ardian shouted.

"Yeah, I know. This is turning into a gang fuck. It seems that the Leader is somehow not happy with me," Luka said.

"Don't let them get to you, Luka. He is *trying* to get to you. You know he has a screw loose," replied his friend.

Luka once more turned his attention to the busy London streets as he contemplated what he had to do. He had to contact the Irishman and arrange for the exchange of Captagon and the weapons. But Ibro was playing hardball and not giving him the drugs to exchange; without them, he couldn't organise the exchange and the entire operation would be delayed.

"Okay, we're here," Ardian alerted Luka.

Luka glanced around at the nondescript building on a residential side street just off Leyton High Street.

As they both sat observing the house, a gate to the side of the property opened and a man dressed in casual clothes approached the vehicle and tapped on the window. Luka slowly wound down the window, unsure of what was going on. The man handed him a piece of untidy paper, ripped from a notebook. Without a word he turned away and walked back through the gate, disappearing from view.

Luka opened the folded piece of paper. Written on it was an address on a nearby street and directions to a phone box. The handwritten message simply stated, "happy endings".

"This is getting out of hand. What the fuck does all this mean?" Luka grumbled. He was totally deflated; it was apparent he would be anything but in charge of this itinerant bunch.

It took ten minutes to find the phone box tucked away just outside Leytonstone tube station. The area was packed with a mixture of mums cajoling hyperactive, out-of-school children, and people simply heading underground, going about their days.

"Pull in here," Luka instructed Ardian. They sat in the car, using the mirrors to watch the phone box for any signs of ambush — or worse. Luka's mind was racing. *What is all this about? Are they trying to somehow set me up? Have they set me up with the police?* Nothing made sense anymore. He knew he had to enter the phone box. Unsure of whether he would be getting back in the car with his friend, he looked at him, holding eye contact. His boyhood mate knew that if Luka was compromised, he would have no option but to bug out, leave the scene and ultimately, leave his friend to whatever fate awaited him.

Luka entered the phone box. It stank so strongly of piss it almost burned his eyes. He stood there for a moment surrounded by the debris of hopelessness. As he scanned the inside of the phone booth, he saw the usual graffiti and a few calling cards for prostitutes of both genders. There, right in front of him, front and centre, was a black business card with a silver hologram image of a dancing girl. The card read: "Tink Tong Services". Luka surveyed the car. At the bottom next to the phone number, in tiny lettering, it read, "Happy Endings guaranteed".

The message on the piece of paper had stated "happy endings". Luka took the card down and examined it. As he turned it over, he noticed a number had been written on the back. His heart raced; this must be the contact number. He picked up the receiver. *Thank fuck this phone booth hasn't been vandalised.* He placed a pound coin into the slot and as it clunked into place, he heard a dial tone.

He quickly punched in the number; it went through, and only rang twice.

"Look down," the voice on the other end said.

Luka looked down; all he could see was the shelf below the phone and the piss-stained concrete below.

"Okay," Luka replied.

"Reach beneath the shelf."

As Luka reached under the shelf, he first felt the used chewing gum people had deposited there. Then, as he ran his hand further back, he felt a small package taped to the underneath of the shelf.

"I've got something here," Luka said.

"Take it."

"Got it." Luka replied.

With that, the phone went dead. Luka stood there, phone to his ear and with the small envelope in his hand. He kept up the pretence that he was making a call and opened the small plastic envelope. Inside was a small SD card.

"Mega," Luka sarcastically said out loud.

He quickly glanced around outside the phone booth. No one was paying him a blind bit of notice. He exited the phone booth, thankful for the fresh air, even though the summer heatwave still raged on, and made his way slowly back to the old Mondeo, ever vigilant.

"Well, this gets fucking better," Luka said as he jumped back into the car. "We now have to look at what's on this fucking SD card."

"Seriously?" Ardian felt things were getting ridiculous.

"Yes, I'm fucking serious. Let's get back to mine and see what the hell is on this card."

Chapter 32

The journey from London hadn't taken long. Being late at night, all the rush hour traffic had gone, and the motorways were quiet. An hour and a half after setting out, they had turned off the motorway and had made their way down ever-narrowing roads and sparsely-occupied villages. They eeventually found themselves at the gate to the location the shadowy people in London had given via the SD card. It had outlined how Luka needed to prepare this old migrant workers' camp ready for the Syrian team to use as a forward mounting base. The list was extensive. He'd also been given the location within the camp where cash had been hidden so he wouldn't have to use any form of electronic payments.

Luka sat staring out of the grimy windscreen of the old Ford, the headlights illuminating what seemed like a rundown holiday camp. Four rows of Portakabins occupied the main part of the small farmyard, next to a large dilapidated hay barn. Each cabin had a large Calor gas container placed by it.

"What the fucking hell is this place?" Ardian posed the pertinent question to his friend.

Luka turned to his mate. "It's a migrant worker camp, used by the local farmers for poor people who pick fruit for a living, or that's what the locals think." He paused, then turned to his friend. "It's actually a people-smuggling staging post, a stop-off from Dover. From here the poor fuckers get moved on by smaller vans to god knows where." He continued to observe what lay in front of him, staring out of the windscreen; these sorts of places brought back raw memories.

Luka exited the vehicle and trudged to the gate. The small farmer's yard was nestled close to the Kent North Downs. He immediately noticed the silence; nothing but the odd barking dog, and no road noise, just stillness; *so close to London, yet so remote,* he thought. *No wonder this place has been used as a sinister stopover*. The night had finally engulfed the area, casting shadows in all the wrong places: ideal places to hide in and watch from. Luka felt ill at ease here and didn't know why, but something wasn't right.

The gate was old and rusty. A sign with peeling paint announcing the site's name as "Bon Fleur" — *highly ironic*, thought Luka. He fumbled in his pockets for the keys, and pulling out his phone, he used the torch to illuminate the padlock, which, in contrast to the gate and sign, was new, robust and high quality. The key slotted in and the lock duly opened. He pulled the chain that was wrapped around the gates and with a metallic clunk, the chain fell and the gates creaked open. The sound echoed in the silence of rural Kent. Luka froze, his senses straining for any sign he was being watched or set up.

Surprisingly given its state, the old gate opened without an issue; a sign this place had been occupied recently. Luka approached the first cabin in the row of four; he tried the handle — it was open. Hesitantly, he entered the building. It was dark inside; the windows had all been blocked out using newspaper, ensuring no one could look in. *Or,* thought Luka, *was it to ensure no one looked out?* The place stunk of desperation, a smell he immediately recognised from his homeland back in the war days. The place was wrong on every level. He sensed the desperation of those brought here under false pretences.

"This place freaks me out." Ardian brought Luka back to the present with a start. "Whatever we need to do, let's crack on. First light is 0400. I want to be long gone by then."

Luka had a job to do here, so he started. He needed to ready this place for the arrival of the psycho and his band of mercenaries. Once he knew what he needed to buy, he could leave. He checked each room systematically, each one the same layout, each with a smattering of discarded clothes, which he gathered into bin bags.

"One room left," he said to himself as he stepped into the last cabin. Ardian was already in there, the torch on his phone casting dim light into the interior.

"Luka, check this out." Luka sensed emotion in his friend's voice. He moved to the end of the large cabin, to the last of the metal-framed beds with its filthy, stained mattress, just like the rest. "Look." Ardian pointed to the wall, low down. "I wouldn't have seen it but I was checking under the bed."

There was a message scrawled on the wall.

Someone please help me, they won't let me go, I miss my family I don't want to do this +387 7909 260389

"Luka, what is this place? I'm getting a bad vibe."

"You and me both. That's a Bosnian area code; they must use this place to farm the poor kids out, most probably young girls to those Albanian cunts in London."

With that, Luka signalled for them to leave. He had a list of what was needed but an even bigger list of questions. He needed to get back in touch with Redbeard: this was fast running out of control.

Chapter 33

The pain never abated; it was constant and was taking its toll. Redbeard sat cross-legged on the floor, his MacBook, an ever-present friend, lying open next to him. He stared at nothing in particular, his mind awash, fuddled by the opiates permeating his brain. He couldn't even see out of the windows as they were so dirty, and the desert dust, blown on the hot winds that blasted the rundown farm complex he called home, stained the blast curtains a light brown colour.

He picked up his iPhone, tapping on the *Telegram* icon, and with intent he scrolled down the message once again.

His rage bubbled over as he screamed for his trusted chief of staff and almost full-time carer. "Waleed, Waleed, where the fuck are you?! I need you in here... now!" he bellowed, straining to rotate the upper half of his torso to view the door.

He heard scampering footsteps coming across the ceiling and racing down the stairs. The door swung open and Waleed, the older man of the two, entered the room, his shalwar kameez — which hadn't been white for years — stained with sweat, and grim from the daily toil in the Iraqi desert.

"Yes, sir, what is wrong — you sound so annoyed?" Waleed asked, trying his hardest to calm his leader down.

"Fucking read this." He threw the iPhone at his aide, who almost dropped it. Silence overtook the room again as Waleed read the contents of the message. "Not even encoded. Has the Bosnian lost his fucking mind?" Waleed didn't comment, he just kept scrolling down the message. Redbeard observing his expression. "See — I told you he's out of fucking control... totally."

"Boss, the Syrian team you sent to me are out of control. They don't listen to me and I believe they have changed the mission to one you have not sanctioned. I'm asking you to exfiltrate them at the earliest opportunity. This could compromise the whole lone wolf operation. I'm not happy working with them anymore."

Waleed put the phone down carefully next to the cross-legged figure and exhaled loudly. "What do we do?" Waleed asked.

"You know this is important for us to get back on the map. We have been too quiet for too long and I don't want anyone to get in the way. Ibro is a warrior, and he will bring glory back to El Muz." Redbeard paused, his eyes fixed on an invisible horizon. The following silence went on for slightly too long, as he hit the button on his pain-killing machine. The reaction was instant and he slumped forward slightly. Minutes passed. "Okay." His voice was raised, angry. "We remove the Bosnian, and everyone linked to him, no trace." He paused again, noticing the look on his aide's face.

"Sir, I don't agree; we certainly need him, at least for now. Our friends in Belgium have been infiltrated and France is a no-go zone at present. Our only chance is to use Avdic and his contacts, especially with the first consignment of Captagon crossing the Balkans now."

When needed, Redbeard's mind was still clinical, even with all the chemicals helping him with the pain.

"Okay, okay," he mused, looking at his chief of staff, a smile spreading over his face. "I know what to do." He looked up at Waleed, a twisted grin spreading over his face.

Broadwater Farm, London

Luka opened the creaky door of the Mondeo and slammed it closed with more power than he had intended. His rage hadn't abated during the journey back. He wanted answers, and needed to know exactly what this motley crew intended to do. What was their mission?

The estate was quiet. Most people were asleep, and none of the surrounding maisonettes had lights on; only foxes and the ever-present smell of cannabis accompanied him on the streets at this hour. He opened the rear gate to the premises and made his way to the back door of the safe house. He put his ear to the glass and heard voices, or maybe the TV. He strained his senses, trying to see if anyone was active downstairs.

With speed and aggression, the back door swung open and Luka was grabbed by the hair and neck and catapulted into the kitchen. He was suddenly face down on the filthy kitchen floor. No one spoke. He felt the unmistakable cold pressure of a pistol being pressed into his neck. Not a word. After what seemed like an age, a familiar voice said, "Turn over, Bosnian."

Luka rolled over, a boot pressed firmly into his chest to keep him down. A pistol in the hands of one of the gang was pointed directly between Luka's eyes.

"Did you think you could creep up on us?" Ibro had a sarcastic edge to his voice. "We are not new to this game," he added.

Luka felt a rush of anger. Indignant at his treatment, he replied with venom. "I need to know what's happening. That place in the country — what the fuck used to happen there? This is not how we are meant to be." Luka strained his neck, angry with the boot pressed hard in his chest.

"Let him up," Ibro said to his colleague.

Luka felt the heel of the man's boot press into his chest as a last petulant act before the fucker put his pistol away and moved to the living room, leaving Ibro and Luka alone.

Luka stood up, trying not to let his anger and embarrassment show to his nemesis. Ibro stood on the other side of the kitchen, his shirt unbuttoned, showing the toned body of a man used to hardship and action.

"Bosnian, you need to relax a little. The Boss wants us to work together, you know that," Ibro said condescendingly. Luka observed him as he took a filthy glass out of the overflowing sink and filled it with water; he admired the glass before downing it. The khaki man-bag was over his shoulder; if the situation had been different, Luka may have questioned him about the contents, but now wasn't the time. "You people don't know how lucky you are," Ibro said. "We spent years drinking filthy water, our children dying of illness, and the so-called superpowers stood by and watched." He spat the words out, his eyes dark and sinister.

"I want to know your mission," Luka said.

"Why?" Ibro smirked.

Luka was raging and wasn't in the mood to let this go. "I need to understand what you're doing here. I am trying to help you, and if I don't know —"

Ibro cut in. "If you don't know what?" he said, his voice now raised.

"I don't know if what you're planning is worthy of the cause."

"Cause? What cause? You stand there thinking you're helping our brothers and sisters, yet look at you. You speak, dress and even fucking smell like them."

"Them?" Luka said with an inquisitive slant to his question.

Ibro paused, his eyes taking on a shark-like stare, deep and piercing. The silence went on, too long, creating a tension that neither person wanted to break; that would be a sign of weakness.

Ibro moved closer to Luka, like two boxers staring each other out, face-to-face, noses nearly touching. Luka could smell his breath. It was fetid. Body odour escaped from every pore of this man's body. No doubt he'd forgotten the luxury of a shower, long ago back in that far-away, war-torn hell hole.

"*TAGHUT*." Ibro spat out the words, speckles of phlegm shooting from his mouth. "You're a filthy *TAGHUT*," he said again, slow and menacing.

Luka flinched, not from physical fear but from something worse; these words invaded his very soul. Luka knew only too well what a *Taghut* was: it meant this bunch reckoned he'd lost the faith, had turned his back on Allah. Luka had heard the word so often in the camps back in his homeland. This man — a Syrian freedom fighter, in this country to wage war with the great Satan's cousin, the USA — thinking Luka was *Taghut* wasn't a good omen. Luka knew a man of his psychopathic character would only want one solution to this; to rid the great caliphate of this person. Luka knew that in Ibro's eyes, he was a dead man walking.

Luka pondered his predicament for a moment; maybe too long, as Ibro seemed to sense he had the upper hand and a smirk spread across his tanned, lean face. He knew he had to leave, and pushed past Ibro, brusquely but aggressively, leaving through the kitchen door and out into the relative safety of Broadwater Farm.

DOMINIC COULD SENSE THE ANGER. He trailed in the wake of his big companion as he pushed aside the bewildered pedestrians, any second looks receiving a death stare as people thought better of tackling this brute. It was as if the waves were parting, as people let through this angry-looking man in full shalweer kameez and crocheted skull cap.

He followed Buzzard into Caledonian Road tube station. It

was packed, and by the look of it the heat was still pissing everyone off. In any other city the Tube would be empty, but London so relied on its Tube system that even though it was claustrophobically hot, commuters still persevered. Dominic hated the closed-air environment, a far cry from his fresh air days in the Army.

They squeezed into a packed carriage. Dominic did his best to balance without having to reach up and grab a handrail. He knew he stank and didn't want the pretty office girl, smartly dressed in a crisp white shirt, having his armpit in her face. He glanced at the headline on the front of the paper:

Heatwave hits sixty days, Emergency Services stretched to breaking point.

He knew it had been a hot summer, but hadn't quite realised just how hot. Their train entered the next station with a metallic whine and the screech of rapid deceleration as the wheels on the hot metal tracks struggled for traction.

"We're off," Buzzard grunted as he pushed his way aggressively through the throng of people waiting patiently to board the train.

Dominic caught him up on the stairs; the escalator was broken and Buzzard puffed his way up the sixty steps towards the daylight ahead. Dominic pulled level with him. He needed to find out what was wrong; he just hoped Project Alpha still had control of his phone.

"Mate, what's up? You okay?" Dominic asked.

Buzzard flashed him a look, then seemed to think better of it. "Wait until the park," Buzzard replied and hurried through the barrier and out into the sunshine.

Dominic had kept track of the Tube route and now, above ground, he was out into the welcome open air on the Mile End Road in the heart of the East End. *Kray twin territory,* he mused. *What the fuck are we doing here?*

They entered the large green expanse of Victoria Park

together, an open space which had changed little since Queen Victoria had donated it to the local population. The grass was parched and bare, more dirt than grass, and the park was full of people escaping the heat, finding shade under the large trees scattered around the edge of the enormous park.

Buzzard found a shaded spot under a large oak tree and intimated to Dominic to lie down. Dominic immediately knew what to do, and lay down facing the prone Buzzard, heads almost touching as they lay face-to-face on the ground. No chance of an eavesdropper or lip-reader finding out what they were talking about.

"Bro, I need to follow someone; a man, a dangerous man, in fact. He's the fucking devil man, he bashed up two of my brothers over there in them toilets." Dominic nodded, not saying a word. He was sweating. Even in the shade the heat was unbearable. "So, my boss wants to see what he is up to; and also we need to know where he is at certain times as we have a little job to do."

"What job?" Dominic questioned, his mind racing now. *What fucking boss?* he thought.

Buzzard's demeanour changed in an instant. "I don't like questions."

Dominic sensed how dangerous this man could be; he may have been beaten up by a gang of white youths, but he had a very hard edge to him. "Okay," he started again, the anger abated slightly.

He rustled inside his baggy shalwar kameez and pulled out his mobile phone. He swiped away at the screen until he seemed to find what he wanted, then passed Dominic his phone. The large screen had an image on it that looked very similar to a surveillance target photo. Someone had obviously taken it without the person knowing. Dominic took hold of the phone and looked at the picture. The man in the picture wasn't what he'd been expecting, although he knew better than to ask questions again.

Dominic was getting nervous: the last thing he wanted was to be considered part of a hit team. He knew he would have to get a meeting organised to brief his unit, but he now had a new friend to worry about, and by the sound of them they weren't the tip-of-the-spear types.

"So, bro, my boy has a vehicle you can use, and he will be your driver. This dude, we think he lives just off the park. I will text you the address." Buzzard got up swiftly, dusting down his white trousers and baggy shirt and ensuring his crochet skull-cap was in place. He paused, placing a heavy hand on Dominic's shoulder in what Dominic felt was an almost fatherly way. "Brother, this is important to me. I will owe you big time," Buzzard said. Dominic smiled, his best coy smile, but his mind was racing. *One day you won't be so impressed with me*, he mused. "Come on, we will go and meet your driver," he said, laughing as he turned and walked between the prostrate figures soaking up the sun in the vast park and made for the gate and the busy road beyond.

Chapter 34

Dominic entered the room to muted cheers and a variety of piss-taking about his appearance and dress sense. Welcomed by the ops officer and Charley, they showed him into the large briefing room. The room was cool, he noticed, and had been enhanced with banks of monitors showing live feeds from streets in the capital and target boards with photos and lines linking them together, forming a tangled web. The hum of radio chatter formed a background soundtrack that filled the room.

Dominic approached the main board and studied it, following the lines linking the various images of the surveillance photos; it was a chance to get updated on his task. He took the proffered cup of coffee from Charley who moved close to him; in fact, too close for comfort. She smelled amazing, her perfume filling his nostrils with desire and lust.

He followed a line from the photo of his target, Buzzard, across the board and the underlying map of London, down to a photo labelled "Unknown Male".

Dominic turned; scanning the room, he noticed the ops officer talking to a group looking as if they had just returned off the street, still in surveillance gear, sweaty and animated, weapons still to hand. Max the surveillance dog barked for attention from his handler.

"Boss!" Dominic shouted, and as the ops officer looked up Dominic motioned him over to the ops board. He turned to the board, tapping the image. "This guy: Charley tells me you got this image off Buzzard's phone."

"Yes," replied the boss.

"Boss, this is the reason I have called this meet. Buzzard has given me a job to follow this guy with one of his goons." The ops officer looked at Dominic with a quizzical expression. "Boss, I've no idea where or how this person fits in, but I think this is serious. Buzzard has been acting strange for a while now."

The ops officer looked towards the screens on the wall. He paused, turning to Dominic. "Any idea why?"

"No, Boss, came out the blue. Not a clue where this guy fits into the organisation."

The ops officer sat down at his desk with its commanding view of the operations boards and monitors. He went into deep thought mode, his blue eyes fixated on nothing in particular.

Minutes passed.

"Right, let's fucking do this," he said. "I'm off to brief the boss and Picton, and get their authorisation for this to run. Dom, you happy to go with this?"

TWENTY MINUTES FLEW BY. Dominic enjoyed working with Charley; *we make a great team as well as great lovers*, he thought.

"You ready?" she asked.

"Yeah, let's do this," he replied, buzzing with anticipation.

The ops officer brought the room to attention. He had recently returned from briefing his superiors and had a serious look about him.

The team obediently took their seats facing the trio, the ops officer taking the lead, arranging his papers on the lectern.

"Okay team, we have a real-time Tier One task. Dominic will brief you up on the target, then Charley will give a tactical brief; normal routine target packs will be sent to your phones, so, no notes, and pay attention." The ops officer reiterated the paperless environment the team operated within.

Dominic enjoyed briefing the team; it took him back to his days in the Army. He missed those times, where he had a lead role, and he sometimes struggled to accept that he was just a foot soldier again, bottom rung of the leadership ladder.

He outlined Buzzard's routine and his regular trips to Broadwater Farm, and his trade craft being of the highest order. The team sat animated and at the end, the questions came thick and fast. Everyone on Project Omega seemed to sense that this game of ghost-chasing was stepping up a level.

The ops officer took to the lectern, pausing slightly to steady himself. Silence permeated the room. Dominic sensed the excitement and tension.

"Okay, listen, I don't want to steal Charley's thunder, but I think you all need to be made aware of the situation." He paused. "What Dominic has brushed on is of vital importance to this organisation. I have just gained the authority necessary to run Dominic in his role, knowing he will be live on this surveillance task given to him by Buzzard. Our job is to mount surveillance on Dom in order to gain control of this unknown target, to house him and gain any relevant intel we can give to Project Alpha to work their magic." He paused, looking around the room. "This could go wrong fast, and we need to be in a position to react and protect Dom; we all need to be on our game. If he is put into a position — to be blunt, a kill option — then we have to exfil him, quickly and aggressively, because if we don't it could get fucking serious." He finished talking and took time to look at each member of Project Omega, eye-to-eye.

The room again fell silent. The whole team looked stunned. Dominic stood with Charley as she delivered the tactical brief, but he wasn't listening. His mind was elsewhere, on those dirty, hot London streets that had become his de facto home; his new stomping ground.

The brief finished and the team dispersed to start their battle preparation on their new task; to follow one of their own. A strange atmosphere drifted through the room. Dominic sat down at one of the ops planning desks and picked up the First Sight Intelligence file, flicking aimlessly through the pages which laid out all the relevant intelligence that the various organisations had gathered over the past week, including Project Omega. However, he wasn't really paying attention to the content of those pages. He was deep in his own troubled mind. This new task was ground-breaking, but he had genuine concerns: was the team up to getting him out of the shit, untried and untested? It made him think. In his Army days he had trusted his companions in the Paras with his life. He didn't with his new team; the same old feelings of this being a second-best option to being in the Special Air Service returned with a vengeance. He realised that he was truly worried, bordering on scared.

Danny, the ops officer, wandered back over and pulled up a chair facing Dominic.

"Listen, you don't have to do this, and we can pull the plug now."

"Boss, I'm good," Dominic replied... but maybe his tone didn't seem to agree.

"You sure?" he asked again. Dominic nodded, looking down at his Samsung job phone, fiddling with it. "Okay, let's get on with this. I'll get the duty technician from Alpha to check your phone. He's going to put on a new piece of software given to us by the Firm, to be used if you're in the shit. Also, ensure your *Trojan Horse* app is working... then we'll get you back onto the manor." He patted Dominic on the knee, father-like, then got up and walked back over to the operations cells and picked up the phone on his desk.

The blonde-haired ex-Royal Marine approached Dominic, spitting out the usual banter about Paras and Marines. "Let me know when you're ready, mate, as we're dropping you back off. Using the small van; less conspicuous."

"Big words for a Royal. Who educated you?"

"Fuck off, Pongo. Hurry up or we'll miss scran," he replied.

"Typical Royal, food first."

"Yes, mate — and you look like shit, by the way."

Dominic took a moment to observe himself in the reflection of the computer screen. His hair was unkempt and his eyes were sunken and dark. His face was lean, bordering on skinny.

"Dom." Dom looked up; it was Charley. "Minute?" she said with authority and walked towards the door at the rear of the large garage.

They exited the garage into a hot summer's afternoon. The trees that surrounded the grounds of the centre offered some much-needed shade.

She turned to him and forcibly kissed him, hard and passionate. The kiss was more than just a physical gesture; it was of longing, love and fear. They carried on, totally immersed in each other. When the kiss finally finished, she looked up in tears, big pearls of water making pathways down her pretty face.

"Stay safe, please," she pleaded.

"Hey, come on — it's fine. You guys have my back and it's probably nothing. They're just looking to scare the opposition," he said. But deep down, he *was* worried. *What if they intend to kill this guy?*

She snuggled her head into his chest, sobbing quietly.

Dominic felt himself welling up; he fought back the tears, unable to speak as he knew his voice would break. "Come on, let's get back in, we'll be missed," Dominic said, finally breaking the awkward silence, conscious of not being caught in a relationship with a fellow team member.

They entered back into the bustle of the operational area. Charley got back into boss mode, barking orders at people and getting the teams ready to deploy.

Dominic noticed the look the ops officer gave them as they re-entered the room — it lingered a little too long: he knew about them. *Bollocks,* thought Dominic.

Dominic got the brief off the Project Alpha technician highlighting all the functions of his job android phone. He reiterated the panic facility and the button that switched to the listening mode.

"Okay, Dom, anything else?"

"No mate, thanks, all good."

"Good luck. Takes balls to do a job like this so early on. You know, with the team untested..." the tech said with meaning.

This just reinforced his thoughts, a feeling akin to the minutes before a parachute jump: fear and trepidation, but ultimately a perverse sense of excitement. He knew he was long past the point of no return now.

Chapter 35

Danny Haigh slipped his card down the electronic device on the airlock doors that led to the corridor that could only be described as "the Kremlin". The corridor housed all the high-ranking officials within Her Majesty's Revenue and Customs, and was also a covert home to the head of Phalanx. Hiding away in this historic building made sense, as it kept Paul Allen away from all the predators from other covert agencies. He felt they were now circling for the kill, as the fledgling organisation with the bloated budget had failed to get any tangible results on the job given to them under duress by MI5.

Danny kept the iPad he was carrying close to his chest, away from prying eyes. No classic manila folders here; Omega Project was nothing if not hi-tech and he was keen to avoid any gossip in the old school canteens and bars. He knew Omega was an unwanted lodger in this building and old boy networks were working to put more nails in the coffin lid. It was already closing, he thought.

He knocked on the heavy, old oak door, and glanced up and down the corridor: nothing but the highly-polished floor and walls lined with pictures of the past triumphs of HMRC.

"Come in."

Danny entered the room where Paul Evans was sitting behind his desk. The room had the feel that it was only on loan, and the fact his view was of Lower Thames Street, not the River Thames situated to the rear of this building, emphasised this. Normally a man of Paul Allen's standing would have the choice of the offices, but not here.

"So, we have some news." Paul intimated for Danny to take a seat on the large sofa pushed up against the old bookcase, long-since emptied, adding to the air of temporary residence.

Danny sat down; he paused, looking at his reflection in the blank screen of the iPad he was holding in his lap. His reflection was haggard, and he felt how he looked. This dream job was fast becoming a nightmare, and he had burnt all his bridges by leaving MI5, taking with him years of counter-terrorism experience, which they resented. The recent lack of cooperation with his once-close colleagues backed up his theory; everyone in the dusty corridors of British Intelligence wanted these new boys on the block to fail, and fail big.

Paul Allen glumly sat down and positioned himself facing Danny on the large sofa. The director wasn't the fittest man, and the incessant heat of the endless summer was putting an extra strain on his system, observed Danny. *Last thing we need is for the boss to go off sick.* He was the only thing holding this project together — but even his deep-rooted contacts along the corridors of power were waning.

He let out a long sigh. "So, Danny, what have we got?"

"Boss, we have a possible ID on the unknown IC1 male linked to our main target. Codename Buzzard has given our operator in the shelter a job."

"That's Abu Haleem?" the director said, seeking clarification.

"Yes, correct. He wants this guy followed and all the usual 'pattern of life' information gained."

"Go on," prompted the director, a quizzical look on his face.

"Buzzard has gone missing, and this guy is our only link. Dominic Leigh is with one of Buzzard's low-level team members following this guy around. We have his name and home details, but need the authority to mount a team on him to see why the interest, and whether it leads back into the main players, and what their game is. We haven't really got much support via the usual channels — apparently our RIPA applications were sketchy, and I'm sure they do have information for us, but they're delaying it." Danny swiped the screen of the secure iPad. "Here we go." He passed the screen over to the director. "So, we have a guy on our payroll I brought across with me from A4; he was on my old team's books, but the branch head didn't see the benefit in him and cut off funding." He paused, letting the director read the CHIS biography on the asset.

"Danny, are you sure about this guy?" the director quizzed.

"I am, Boss, one hundred percent. He got stitched with a rogue deal, losing a tremendous amount of Bitcoin; he claims it was organised Russian mafia linked to Putin, but who knows. But, he is the best hacker we've ever seen and he is our link into the seedy world of the dark web."

The director nodded. "He's not trying to get revenge via us, is he?"

"No Boss, he's actually a decent guy who just wanted to stop the Russians and Chinese from taking over the web. That's his whole life, and he's a total geek. The rest of his story is in the bio and I'll leave it with you to read. Interesting how good these hackers are, Boss: make Alpha Projects look like amateurs."

"Yes, yes, carry on, please."

"Well, he runs the shop that puts on moody screens on phones out of a vaping shop in Victoria, so we set up Dominic to take Buzzard's phone in there — hence how we got control of it." The director nodded approval, now listening intently. "So, when he put on the new screen and got us control of it and sucked out the contents, he recognised one image, claims he knows the guy really well."

"Really?" The director gave Danny a curious look.

"Gave us a name and place of work. I need your sign-off to check this out."

"Okay, but I need more; overriding the system has risks, especially if this is a wild goose chase. Our friends in the silks and wigs would chop our balls off, believe you me," the director said.

"His name is Luka Avdic; he works at the Savoy hotel as the night manager. He is of Bosnian origin, came to the UK after the war in ninety-seven or ninety-eight. Apparently he helped Matrix out with a situation when he got refused entry."

"Who the fuck is Matrix?"

"Sorry, Boss, that's the source's *nom de guerre*."

Danny sat back, flicking through the images on the iPad, ensuring he had missed nothing. The room fell silent, just the noise of the traffic on the busy London Street outside, and the sound of the expensive Mont Blanc fountain pen moving quickly across the quality headed notepaper the director had just plucked off the large printer behind his desk.

The Director of Phalanx moved back around his desk with an official-looking A4 document, the watermark of the Phalanx symbol clear to see as the hazy sunlight caught it as it was passed over.

"Right, you have total directed surveillance approval. This bypasses RIPA so you have free range. It's for forty-eight hours after that. I will have to let Picton know, and Danny, my balls are on the block with this one. This type of authority is only normally used at times of specific threat to the nation, so any fuck-ups will be cataclysmic for all." The room fell silent again, as both men stood awkwardly facing each other. "Danny, we need something to take back to Picton, or we could all be out of a job."

The pair shook hands, and Danny turned towards the door. He paused, turning around. "Boss, thanks for this," he said, lifting the envelope containing the authority letter. "I know the gamble you've taken and the team and I appreciate it. I so want this project to fucking work, Boss," Danny said with total authenticity; men like Paul Allen were being retired and replaced by faceless suits who answered to spreadsheets and budgets rather than body counts or bomb attacks.

The director nodded his appreciation. He seemed to have aged by some years in the last thirty minutes; his entire career and pension rested on the next forty-eight hours.

Danny left the room and got out his phone.

"Charley, it's Danny. He's given us forty-eight hours. Get the team back in, we need to brief and deploy asap." He hung up and proceeded down the corridor with steely purpose.

This was game on for Project Omega.

Danny Haigh entered the room slightly behind his boss, the Director of Phalanx, Paul Allen. Both men wore suits, and this had made for an uncomfortable journey across baking hot London on the packed rush hour Tube. Danny's shirt was fused to his back, soaked through with sweat, making him feel even more uncomfortable, as if being summoned for a meeting with Julia Picton wasn't bad enough. Picton was head of Branch 18: the so-called deniable operations directorate of MI6. Her character was as sinister as her department's role.

The pressure on these two men had intensified over the past months as the fledgling Phalanx organisation chased shadows, desperately trying to get a foothold on the investigation into this alleged link between Irish paramilitaries and jihadists from the Middle East.

The room was deliciously cool. Julia Picton occupied a large office with a heavy colonial atmosphere; floor-to-ceiling bookshelves, neatly laid out desk framed by a large window, and, unlike a corporate office, her desk faced outwards, giving her a view of the River Thames. She sat with her back to them, tentatively viewing a manila file on her neat desk; silent, almost ghost-like.

Without turning around, she pointed to a group of comfy chairs placed around an ornate coffee table. Both men took this as their cue to take a seat, almost like naughty boys in the headmaster's office. Danny glanced around this relic of a colonial past; *typical MI6,* he mused. He was brought back to the present as Picton purposefully slid her chair back and turned to face the two men.

"Afternoon, Paul, thanks for coming over at such short notice." She looked at Danny. "Have we met?" she asked, *at* him more than *to* him.

"Yes, Ma'am, we have. At the Project Omega launch."

"Oh yes, you're the ops officer. I remember now." She sat down to face them both. "So, you have an update for me. Not before time," she added in a chastening tone.

"Yes, Julia, we do. I'll let Danny update you fully."

She turned to face Danny as he removed the folder from his bag and passed it over to her. She opened it and leafed through its contents.

"So, we've had a major breakthrough. My operator, Dominic Leigh, the guy you sanctioned to go undercover into the homeless shelter to keep a handle on codename Buzzard."

She nodded, not raising her eyes from the file. "Yes, the ex-Para."

"Correct; so, to cut a long story short, Dominic managed to befriend Buzzard and as a result, persuaded him to get his broken smartphone fixed using one of our shops where we fitted a unique screen that has given Project Alpha control of the phone." Danny paused, noticing the attention she was paying to the file's contents. It took a moment for her to notice he had stopped talking.

"Yes, yes, please carry on." She waved a hand in his direction.

"Ma'am, a great deal of the information on the phone are messages in code. OTP — that's One Times Pad."

"I know what OTP is," she snapped.

Danny carried on. "But of interest is a group of photographs of an unknown male which I have printed off and are in the file. It seems Buzzard has been watching this man. Again, we don't know why, but as you can see from the amount of images, he has taken a lot of interest." Danny paused, awaiting an acknowledgement. She looked up and Danny took this as his cue to carry on. "We first got control of Buzzard at a hospital where we had mounted a surveillance serial on two foot-soldiers, who had been badly beaten in a park in Hackney's Victoria Park. Prior to this we had nothing really tangible on Buzzard, but this led us to house Dominic in the shelter."

"And?" she replied, her tone harsh.

"Well, photographs show this as-yet-unknown male, leaving a flat on Brookfield Road, most probably his place of residence given the time he regularly exited and returned and how he's dressed."

"Where is this preamble leading?" she asked, her voice now showing irritation.

"We think this man attacked the two men, and he is extremely violent and dangerous but in a controlled way," he said, pointing to the image he had pulled from his own folder.

"Controlled way, meaning?" she inquired.

"The violence and injuries inflicted on the two men suggest the perpetrator has been trained in self-defence to a high level; it was no random act of violence." Another pause, the room falling silent bar the ticking of a large old-fashioned grandmother clock mounted high on the wall between the bookcases. "We believe this links Buzzard's organisation to him in some way." Danny waited.

Picton sat staring at the picture for long moments; her face blank, but showing an interest Danny couldn't fathom.

Danny looked at his boss, raising an eyebrow to show his surprise. Paul Allen, his jovial round face now stern, had also noticed a change in the woman's demeanour. She spent a few moments looking at each image, and then, like a true ice maiden, she returned to normal and closed the folder, placing it on the coffee table.

"So, gentlemen, not exactly a breakthrough but more questions, really. You need to get on this unknown male and find out who the fuck he is." Her voice rose just enough to hammer the point home. She then stood up and returned to her desk, placing the Phalanx folder in her top drawer. Danny noticed and thought this strange — why hide it?

"Julia, we shall be in touch," Paul Allen said to alert the woman they were leaving her office. She remained staring out the window at the river and Thames House beyond.

Danny closed the door and they walked down the polished corridor towards the security desk and into the steamy London afternoon. They both remained silent as they made their way down the Embankment, with the lucky ones drinking cool beers in the riverside bars, enjoying the breeze that blew down the river. His experience in the Head of Branch 18 office confused and somewhat bothered Danny.

"Boss — what the fuck was all that about?" Danny asked.

"Don't know," Paul replied.

"So you sensed something too? She was more than pissed off with our lack of progress, wasn't she?"

"It seems so. I'm as confused as you are by her reaction. She's a cold fish and a bloody seasoned case officer, which makes it so strange," Paul replied. "Fancy a beer?"

After three pints of cold lager both men felt somewhat refreshed and the conversation had returned to Picton, and Paul Allen, his tongue loosened by the beers, outlined her career path. It did not surprise Danny at the places she had cut her teeth in the service as a young head of station; she had basically been involved in the war on terror since before 9/11. She'd seen service in Bosnia, escaping just before her station got overrun by the Serbs, then into Pakistan and Afghan before numerous visits to Iraq. She was the real deal, and Danny now had a genuine interest in her. He wanted to find out more.

"Right, time for me to get back to Mrs A. She'll be fuming." Danny's boss stood up unsteadily, proffered a sweaty hand then, with what looked like extreme concentration, made his way through the throngs of people, all happily drinking on the deck of the large ship that served as a popular bar beneath Waterloo bridge.

Danny got himself another beer and returned to his seat. The night was now cooling down as his thoughts drifted to his operation. He knew his teams would be out on the streets working hard to gain control of the various targets they had. But he felt unease; things on this operation weren't stacking up. He'd spent years in MI5, and had a sixth sense for things, and his senses were tingling — or maybe it was the beer. He sat back, admiring the talent stood and sat around him. Summer in London was great; the office girls certainly knew how to flaunt it. He smiled to himself. Always the poacher, never the gamekeeper, in both work and play.

JULIA PICTON SAT STARING at the manila envelope on her desk. The two men from Phalanx had long gone, and she was alone with her thoughts; they were deep and dark. She got up and moved round her desk to the bookcase that stretched the length of her generous office. She poured herself a large tumbler of whiskey and took a sip.

She sat back in the chesterfield armchair, staring into space, her mind on a path going back a long way. The smoky aroma of the quality whiskey she was drinking took her back to a time in her life when she thought she might have found love. He came into her mind's eye: dark-haired, tall and athletic, with a ready smile and deep blue eyes. So gentle, so humble. So utterly nice. She started to cry, large globes of tears making tracks down her face.

She could smell the fish, fresh trout caught from a nearby lake, cooked on an open fire as they both lay arm in arm by the lake shore. Truly happy days for the young Julia Picton; but as always, Her Majesty's Government came calling at her door and she duly did what she knew she must: she vanished. And, the only man she'd truly loved was gone forever — until now. Thirty minutes ago, he'd reappeared: the same eyes, hair, dark, handsome looks, Slavic cheekbones, white teeth. But this wasn't him; this was the son. A boy full of hurt, fuelled by revenge and trained by the best. She hadn't seen him since being a guest at his birthday party; she couldn't remember what age, fifteen or sixteen? She'd brought cake and chocolate, commodities scarce in war-torn Bosnia. The young Luka and his sister had finally accepted Julia and she became a regular visitor, often spending the night. She made their father happy and since the tragic death of their mother, happiness had evaded the four walls they lived in.

They'd meet whilst she was working out of the MI6 station in downtown Banja Luka, houses rented from their owners for a huge fee and used as bases for spying. Luka Senior had been her interpreter and they worked closely every day. Love had blossomed in that balmy summer; initially it had been hastily-grabbed moments, but the romance blossomed and got deeper and more intense. When the situation got worse, she had promised to help the small family to escape the impending brutal onslaught, resulting in the infamous massacre.

She had shut the whole situation away in a deep, dark box she called guilt at the back of her mind. It only came out on the odd occasion; normally in the middle of the night and accompanied her through until dawn when she could don her running gear and literally run herself into the ground. She never thought the ghost would return in this form and embroil itself in the most sensitive case she had ever been involved in. *In fact, it's all mine*, she realised, *the whole shooting match is my work*.

She picked up the file; he was the very image of his father. He looked evil in the grainy image of him leaving the toilet where he'd beaten the living daylights out of those poor blokes. They had no intel on the guy at all: she'd thought he'd perished along with the men of his village, but clearly not. Now he'd popped up out of nowhere like a spirit, involved with some thoroughly nasty people.

She reached behind her for the iPad on her desk, pouring herself another drink. She opened up the tablet and inputted the second password to access the secure memory and the files that were stored only on her iPad. She viewed the content; it was high level, the envy of many larger intelligence agencies, but it was dirty work. She paused, deep in thought. She knew she had to act. Picton rose from the sofa and walked around the large mahogany desk. She pulled her seat back and opened the larger slimline drawer just below the lip of the desk. She pulled out a small pencil case-type bag — a Faraday bag, a gift from a fellow spook in the CIA back in the day in Iraq. She opened it and extracted the contents; a small mobile phone, a Laalpoor 300. She remembered buying it in Pakistan and it had been her trusted servant, a vital tool in her dark life. She turned it on and went back to her comfy sofa.

She typed the concise message and sent it, immediately turning off the mobile phone and placing it back into the Faraday bag.

Chapter 36

Luka entered the back gate to the house; the square block style houses, so loved by the London authorities, were now decrepit and in need of attention. *Much like my life,* Luka mused as he entered the rear garden, or what was once a rear garden. He glanced around the small courtyard garden feeling despair. He knew it would fall on him to tidy up after these creatures. He stood observing the piles of rubbish, rotting food, bin bags overflowing where foxes had ripped at them. Perched up against the wall was a once-white mattress, a huge red stain visible in the centre. Had these idiots been fighting with each other? Whoever had lost that much blood must have been given a proper kicking. *Fuck 'em,* he thought, as he pushed open the back door and entered the small kitchen.

"Ardian, it's me, Luka." He heard footsteps move across the room above and start noisily down the stairs. Ardian entered the kitchen; straightaway, Luka knew something was badly wrong. His friend's face was pale and sweat had soaked through his dark polo shirt. "What the fuck is wrong?" Luka asked, concern flooding into his mind.

Ardian took a deep breath. "Upstairs, it's... they have fucked her up, bad."

"Who? What… she…?" Luka stuttered.

"Upstairs," Ardian intimated; he turned and took the stairs two at a time. Luka followed.

The small landing led into three bedrooms and a bathroom. The whole place was a mess. The stench of deranged humanity filled Luka's nostrils, his senses struggling to make sense of the way these people had been living.

"In here." Ardian walked into the room, standing to one side as Luka walked in.

"Fucking hell," Luka blurted, his brain unable to understand what lay before him.

"She's alive. I checked, but she fucked-up," Ardian said with a shaky voice. "I covered her with a blanket — She's half-fucking-naked, man."

Luka approached the prostrate figure of a girl lying vulnerable on the threadbare red-squared carpet. Her filthy, manky blonde hair was matted to the back of her head, and was the only visible part of her, the rest covered by the duvet cover. Her breathing was troubled, shallow, and quick. Luka pulled back the stinking duvet cover. The girl was curled up in the foetal position, naked from the waist down, her pale white legs tucked up tight to her stomach. Luka reached down and touched her gently on the shoulder. The girl let out a whimper and made a pathetic attempt to struggle, her spindly legs kicking out at Luka.

"Hey, shh. Calm down, I'm here to help you. It will be okay," Luka said. The girl was so weak she flopped back down, back into a defensive position. Her visible buttocks were scrawny and marked. "Are they fucking bite marks?" Luka pointed at the girl. Her buttocks were a mass of marks, raised, angry red welts. Luka bent back down and placed his hand on the girl's shoulder. All the fight had drained out of her. He rolled her onto her back, and her eyes rolled back into her head. Her breath had a strange, sweet smell to it. Luka was no expert, but this poor specimen was a drug user and she was loaded full of some shit at the moment. Her arms showed the signs of needle marks, some of which were infected. The girl was a mess. Even worse for Luka, all he could think of was his vulnerable sister, all those years ago when incarcerated by the Serb militia.

He checked down her body: her arms were skinny, her skin was almost opaque, and devoid of fluids. Dehydration was stretching her skin, giving her the look of an deranged doll from a fucked-up horror movie. She was naked from the waist down, her pubic hair an unkempt smattering of dark against her pale white body. Her nakedness enhanced her vulnerability.

Her mouth started to move. Luka bent forward, moving in closer to listen; her eyes, which would once have been a beautiful sky blue, were now sunk into her head, the whites yellow, with dark puffy rings surrounding them.

"Shush," Luka said a little less patiently, holding a finger to his lips.

The girl spoke, barely audible but enough to cut deep. "Help me, please. He's an animal — please, don't let him hurt me anymore," she whispered, big pearl drop tears dribbling down her filthy cheeks.

"She's been fucking tortured by them cunts, they've used her and left her for dead," Ardian blurted. "Look," he said, pointing.

Luka hadn't seen the inside of her thighs where, stretching down from between her legs, spreading out to the back of her thighs, were thick streaks of dried blood.

"Oh, fucking hell!"

Luka felt his anger surging again as he turned to look out the window. The concrete jungle stretched out into the distance. The noise of children kicking a ball against a nearby garage brought some sense of normality to the macabre proceedings.

"What the fuck have they done to her?" Ardian's words rattled into Luka's head.

Before Luka could answer, the girl started to fit. Her eyes rolled back into her head, her whole body contorting with the power of the convulsions as her bowels gave way. All Luka could do was look on in pity. She was just a girl. She thrashed around in violent, fitful movements in her own filth.

"Fuck it!" Luka yelled. He knew he needed to act, and fast. "Call a fucking ambulance now, she's fucking dying." He couldn't hang around the house; he needed to get the fuck away. He could just leave her, possibly the most sensible thing to do, but he just couldn't. He had to help her. It went against everything he stood for to leave the innocent to a horrible, unprovoked fate. It was too close to home for him, especially now. "Right, I need to know exactly... what the fuck did that bastard Ibro say to you?"

"Nothing; told me he had a driver and for me to go and sort out the house — no mention of this poor fuck up," Ardian said, pointing to the girl.

"Driver? What fucking driver?" Luka snapped.

"Some big, hard-looking guy, wearing full rig including the funny little lace hat thing."

So, they have got others helping them. Luka realised he was being used as a disposable asset. He needed to stay a step ahead of these people before they turned on him when he ceased being of any use.

They both turned back to the girl, who was muttering under her breath; haunting words, crying for help, her body continuing to spasm.

Luka was no expert, but he could see the effects of the last fix were wearing off and she was getting agitated and noisy; she needed to be moved, and quickly.

Ardian had put a call into 999, and in the distance, they heard the tell-tale sound of an emergency service vehicle.

Luka let out a long breath, turning to his friend. "Ardian, we need to go. She'll be fine."

"Okay. The place is clean. I checked downstairs before I found her, but the rubbish outside — I don't know if that is clear."

Turning to look out through the dirty bedroom window, Luka spoke with slow and deliberate words. "I'm going to sort out this fucking mess. And then I'm going to kill Ibro."

As Luka was driving off the estate, an ambulance careened down the road with a police car following. Not a normal police car, but what looked like an armed response team, Luka thought. This part of London was dangerous for the emergency services, but he knew the police would now pay attention to the house, its contents, and whatever Ibro and his cronies had left behind.

Chapter 37

Dominic sat in the communal dining area nursing a cup of tasteless, cheap instant coffee whilst other residents of the shelter went about their daily routines, which didn't really add up to much. He sat observing the surrounding scene; life could be so fucking tough sometimes. He hadn't left the hostel for a couple of long days, as Buzzard hadn't been seen in there for over two days. *This isn't good*, thought Dominic. If he didn't arrive back tonight by the cut off time, then as per the house rules, he would lose his space at the shelter and wouldn't be allowed access. Dominic would have to tell Omega Projects that he no longer had control over Buzzard, and would be told to leave the shelter and his undercover role. A shame, as he enjoyed the escape from reality. Time spent cooped up in the hostel had given him time to analyse his own life.

He hadn't seen his daughter for months and his ex, Carrie, was making everything difficult, including extortionate maintenance payment demands. Even if he could see his daughter, he had little cash to do anything nice with her. The situation wasn't made easier as Carrie was now in a relationship with an old nemesis from his former Army days, who had passed the Special Forces course he had been injured on. He sat staring up at the dirty skylight, that was filtering tainted sunlight into the room. Life outside of this escapism wasn't good. His ex-wife now had exactly what he had wanted: a family life in Hereford. It hurt Dominic that someone else would be playing dad to his daughter, who was now becoming old enough to be brainwashed about what a fuck up her real dad was.

His phone vibrated on the table, bringing him back to the present. He checked he was alone and then read the message. It was from Operational Control at Omega Projects: he was being called in for a Category One meeting. *Must be serious; something was wrong — must be about Buzzard*, he thought.

He took his cup over to the washing up area, casting a nonchalant glance around the dining room. No one took any notice as he went back into his dormitory to prepare for the meeting. He sorted his meagre possessions; life for the residents of these shelters was basic, to say the least. He pulled on a baseball cap and the old, battered Adidas Gazelle trainers. Flip-flops were not a good idea, as Omega exfil procedures tended to hurt the toes.

DOMINIC CLIMBED out the back of the battered Ford Transit van that had picked him up. Picks were now less dramatic, and he sensed a tension in the air. The journey back to the HQ had been silent, with none of the usual banter and piss-taking. He glanced around the outside of the large garages; it looked like the entire team was off the streets. Operational cars were being unloaded and repacked; even medical bags and oxygen cylinders were out getting checked by the team. Dominic sensed an increase in tempo.

He entered the garages and made his way through to the operations control centre. The room was a hive of activity. Project Alpha technicians were beavering away. The large screens on the wall were displaying maps and live CCTV feeds, intermittently going blank, then displaying prompts as they received updates. He exchanged pleasantries with the technicians as he pushed his way to the front of the room, where Danny and Charley stood in conversation next to the target vector board.

"Boss. Charley. How's it going?" Dominic attracted their attention.

"Dom — how's it going with you?" Danny replied.

"Hi," Charley said, not turning from the board she was updating with new photos.

"Right mate, to business: that bloke you've been following, we have a positive ID on him and the okay to impose full surveillance on him." Danny handed something to Charley, who kept her attention on the board.

"Okay, but why are we changing direction, Boss? Buzzard is our main target," Dominic said.

"That he may be, but to be frank, we have fuck all on him, apart from what you've told us. The Headshed are putting pressure on the director; in fact, if we don't get something tangible soon, we may all be out of a job."

"What?" Dominic said, surprised.

"Yeah, the old guard, the dusty corridors of power have the ears of the powerful and they are putting pressure on us for results. Give me a sitrep before you brief the team, please."

Dominic outlined the change in Buzzard's behaviour and demeanour, and that he seemed to be preoccupied. Leaving the best until last, he outlined the fact that Buzzard hadn't been seen for forty-eight hours, and if he didn't show up at the shelter tonight, he would be forced to leave.

"Fuck, so this makes this man" — he pointed to the image of Luka on the target board — "our only real link in the chain if Buzzard goes missing." The under-pressure ops officer sat down heavily, removing his reading glasses to rub his tired-looking eyes.

He sat pondering for a while, staring into space. Dominic moved over to the vector board next to Charley; he watched her as her eyes darted over the board, making sure all the detail was accurate.

"You okay?' Dominic asked quietly.

She turned to look at him; she looked tired and drawn; long hours and too much caffeine, no doubt.

"Good, bit tired, but okay," she said and returned to the board.

The ops officer got up and moved to the board to join them. The three of them stood looking at the board; a mass of information, photos, intelligence briefs and brightly-coloured maps.

"Right, Dom, from the top: let's go back over the whole Buzzard serial."

Dominic went over his time in the hostel with Buzzard in finite detail.

Once he'd finished they sat in silence, all three sat staring at the board and wishing the vector lines connected the people on the board and gave them at least some form of investigation to go on.

"Why the girlfriend? Is she linked?" Danny said out loud.

"None of this adds up, for fuck's sake," he said, his frustration apparent mixed with slight desperation. "At the moment we have the square root of fuck all really, so this guy is our lifeline."

"What about the boys at Alpha?" Dominic asked. "Can they put a ping on his phone?".

"He's disabled it. More than likely took the battery out, or it's in a Faraday bag of sorts, but no, that avenue's closed to us at present," Charley replied.

"Okay, let's go. You pair ready to brief up again? Becoming a regular team, you two," Danny joked.

Dominic gave Charley a sideways glance; she remained focused on her iPad screen.

The entire team sat quietly as Charley wrapped up the extended briefing. Silence fell on the room; no questions, just concerned faces. Charley sat back down to the rear of the lectern and Danny stood up; he cast his eyes over the team sat before him.

"Guys, this is the first time we have all been together for a while. This organisation is my life and I believe in it wholeheartedly, but there are people in those antiquated corridors of power who dislike us and want us gone." He paused. "I appreciate that this is not how it should be, but this is where we are, so I ask you all to give this task against Buzzard your full focus." Danny kept the doomsday scenario to himself. But he knew this could very well be the end before they even began.

Chapter 38

Tesco's carpark was manic, with people shopping in the morning's cool before the temperature rose and the day once more became unbearable. The large white-and-glass store was new to the area, and Hackney's variety ethnic groups was evident, a range of colours and variety in dress and appearance. The team was spread around the carpark, silently, stealthily keeping control of the target vehicle and its two occupants. One had gone into the store, while Dom remained in the vehicle. He was waiting for a text message declaring that the other man was in the shop and out of view, meaning Dominic was clear to move.

"Clear." The simple text flashed onto the large screen of his android device.

He quickly opened the door and placed a device the size of a matchbox underneath the car, on the metal subframe of the battered old Ford Fiesta he had been a passenger in. The older cars were easy to lump; Dom was relieved it had gone into place straightaway. He would conceal it better when given the opportunity, but this temporary fix ensured the Project Alpha team had a fix on the vehicle at all times.

The man returned to the car with a bag full of shopping, which he placed it onto the rear passenger seat.

"All set," Dominic said sarcastically; the humour passed straight over the guy's head.

"Yeah, bro, can't be too careful. Need to move quick, eh?"

Dominic nodded, looking out the passenger window and stifling a laugh. *This guy is thick as mince; is this the best surveillance bloke Buzzard has? Or is he relying on me?* he pondered.

"Let's go, mate — be dinnertime before we get on plot," Dominic said, attempting to get some form of urgency into the proceedings.

"Stand by, stand by. That's vehicle manoeuvring reversing light on." The Omega Operations net sprang into life.

"Roger, manoeuvring," the voice in Control said, always calm and level.

"That's Bravo One towards the exit."

"Pegasus has, intending left."

"That's Bravo One, white Ford Fiesta; VRN: Charlie Foxtrot fifty-one, Mike Oscar Hotel, towards Blue Fifty-Two."

"Bravo One slowed in traffic, speed fifteen; who can at Blue Fifty-Two?"

"Falcon backing."

"Roger; Falcon is backing you, Pegasus."

"Roger that."

The surveillance team went into the well-practised game of chess that was modern covert surveillance. Four cars and a motorbike would follow this car and its every move, without the occupants suspecting a thing. It was high-octane and potentially high risk. The whole group knew this job was important for their survival as a team.

The operators manning the desk had the benefit of large interactive maps and street images from literally thousands of

CCTV cameras. The ops room was quiet apart from the radio chatter.

The operator turned to Danny. "Boss, it looks like they're heading to his home address. Should I forward mount a call sign to be in place?"

"Yes, mate, good idea," Danny replied, his concentration focused on his iPad screen.

"Hawk, can you forward mount to Broadswords HA and plot up with eyes on?"

"Hawk, roger." The increase in engine noise could be heard over the operator's voice as he gunned the car down alternate back streets to get ahead of the follow.

The surveillance team was well spaced out behind the target, crawling in the morning traffic. The road led towards the large Victoria Park and the main A102 north to south arterial road.

"That's Bravo One at Blue Five One, indicating right."

"Bravo One indicating right."

"That's a stop, stop, stop. At Blue Five One, looks like a breakdown, and I'm forced past."

The follow vehicle had no option but to drive past the stricken vehicle; it sat in the right turn lane and the driver was out of the vehicle now.

Dominic had no clue what was going on, desperately trying to get a handle on the situation. The bonnet was slammed shut and the driver got back in. Gunning the engine, he jumped the red light, causing oncoming vehicles to move out of the way. All Dominic could hear was a cacophony of horns and angry shouts.

"What the fuck's all this about?" Dom inquired angrily.

"Keep quiet, you'll find out soon enough," the driver replied with menace.

The surveillance team following the car was now in trouble.

"That's Bravo One jumped the lights onto the main towards Red Five."

The ops room was in a panic now, people scanning maps and trying to gain back control.

"That's Bravo One onto the main and out of sight to me," the driver of call sign Griffin announced over the night. "I'm stuck in traffic, is anyone in a position to take?"

"Pegasus on alternate." The engine noise rose audibly over the radio. Call sign Pegasus was gunning down back streets adjacent to the main A102.

The ops officer got on the net. "Is anyone in a position to take Bravo One?"

No replies came back.

"Fuck." He knew that in every second, the car was getting further away. He turned to the operator manning the desk.

"How many options are there off the main until they hit the Blackwall Tunnel?"

"Two, Boss. Pegasus is heading down the one to the east, the other option leads into the city."

"Mega," Danny said. "Any updates off Dom?"

"None."

Danny grabbed the radio handset. He had to declare the target was lost at present. "Team, we are unsighted at Blue Five One; Kilo, can you check south on the main towards? Hawk, can you lift off and check to the north."

"Hawk, roger."

"Kilo checking toward Red Five." A rush of wind was audible in the microphone as the motorbike got onto the A102 to sweep the route for Bravo One and Dom, who was now in grave danger.

Danny slumped back into his chair. The radio operator next to him continued the radio conversation as the team tried desperately to get back control of the target. He looked at the large interactive map of east London above him on the wall with its little flashing, coloured dots moving around the electronic map like a video game. Danny knew this was anything but a game now. *The tracker is only good if it has a view of the sky or mobile data. Let's hope we don't lose that as well.* "Do you reckon that was all planned to lose us?"

The radio operator turned around to face his boss. "If it was, Boss, and it looked prearranged to me, we're in the shit, because they know we're onto them. And maybe Dom is compromised."

"Exactly," Danny replied. He looked at the map; the motorbike — call sign Kilo — was nearly at the Blackwall Tunnel, which took the A102 under the Thames and into south London, then onto the M25 orbital motorway.

"That's Kilo at Red Five, no sign of Bravo One."

"Roger. Kilo, lift off and wait for RV location." Danny turned to the desk. "Okay, we need to find a secure RV for the teams and just hope we can get a ping off the tracker — though but we don't know if he posted it," Danny said to no one in particular.

The phone on the desk rang. "Omega Ops," came the regimented reply. The desk operator listened intently to the person on the other end of the line, nodding and looking up at the large interactive map on the wall to his front. "Okay, thanks; I'll update the boss. Keep us updated, and we'll have the team on standby. Cheers, mate, bye." The man placed the phone down, turning to Danny. "Boss, it looks like Dom placed the tracker, but it's only working intermittently."

"For fuck's sake, was it not tested?"

"The boys at Alpha reckon it may be where he placed it, as it works off GPS and mobile phone signal, but they have a few fixes."

"Okay, good — where?"

"They have the car on the A102, then nothing until another

ping suggests they came off at the first option, onto the A11 heading west."

Danny sat down at his desk. The room was eerily quiet now that the radio was silent. He stared at the map on the wall, trying to make sense of what was going on. Why had the plan changed? Why didn't Dom make contact? Why did the lump not work? Something wasn't right.

The ops room desk phone rang. "Omega Ops." The operator sat listening intently to the call. "Okay, yeah, understood; yeah, will pass it on. Boss?" Danny wandered over to the desk "That was Alpha projects; the telephone intercept people had a panic alert from Dom's phone."

"Fuck. Okay, do we have a location? Is it on? Do we have a live mic?"

"Boss, the phone's been dumped, it hasn't moved. They have a tech team en route to the area now to try to retrieve it."

Danny stood in silence. He had to think fast to get his head around this situation. But he would also have to let his superiors know that it couldn't have gone any worse. Or could it?

Chapter 39

Dom sat in the passenger seat of the battered Ford Fiesta as the driver gunned the vehicle in front of the oncoming traffic, leaving behind them screeching tyres and blaring horns.

"What the fuck is all this about?!" Dominic shouted above the chaotic sounds.

The driver accelerated onto the A102, cutting up cars to get into the outside lane.

"Be careful, for fuck's sake," Dominic growled, exasperated, as the car just missed the vehicle in front as the driver swerved back into the nearside lane. Then, without signalling, he shot up the exit slip road onto the A11.

"Shut up, say nothing," the driver said coldly. "And give me your mobile." He put out a hand.

"What's happening? Who changed the plan? Abu will be raging." Dominic said.

"Phone, now, and shut the fuck up."

Dom reached into his jeans pocket. He double tapped the home button, which he knew would turn the microphone on and send out an emergency message with a location fix. He felt the vibration to confirm the alert had gone. He passed the phone to the driver, who took the phone and without pause, he threw it out the window.

"Oh, you cunt — what you doing?!" Dom shouted, now both angry and scared.

"Shut it." The driver turned and looked at Dominic with an icy, aggressive stare, different from the character he'd met this morning. The man must have sensed Dom's doubts. "We can all act, eh?" he said, a sick smile spreading over his face.

Dom had to do a regain. He knew the situation had changed, and he been compromised. He analysed everything he could to try to find some sense of what was happening.

The car slowed; Dom was desperately trying to get lock-ins to confirm where he was. He noticed a Tube station: *Devons Road — right, we're on the B140, heading into the City*.

The car slowed again; the driver seemed confused. *Probably not been here before,* thought Dominic. If the vehicle slowed again, he would try to exit the car. He moved for his seat belt.

"Hands on your lap where I can see them," the driver ordered. Dominic looked at the driver, making eye contact. Evilness came back. This man had certainly put on a good act over the previous days. He now took on the demeanour of a cold-blooded gang type. To confirm this, he pulled out a pistol from the litter-filled side pocket of the shabby vehicle.

Oh fuck, I'm in trouble now. He needed to keep his mind and situational awareness. *Okay*, he thought, *it looks like we're turning left.*

"Put this on." The driver threw him a crude hood made of black material.

"For fuck's sake, what's going on?"

"Put the fucking hood on now!"

Dominic slid the hood over his head; it was double-lined, the only light came from the opening below his neck.

Now he was in the shit for sure. He felt the vehicle turn left — the road seemed quiet, like a back road. They hit two speed humps. He heard the car indicator clicking, then another left turn and the vehicle slowed. The acoustics suddenly changed — was he now inside? The car came to a stop. Dominic heard the unmistakable sound of a metal shutter being closed.

The car door opened, and he was yanked out by at least two sets of hands and frogmarched a short distance. Bright light emanated from the grey floor that he could see out of the base of his hood.

The hood was yanked off. Dominic's eyes adjusted to the bright lights. He was inside a small, modern industrial unit, which smelled of paint, not oil and grease; obviously it had never been used before. Abu Haleem stood in front of him with three other men. All looked of Middle Eastern origin. Big, tough-looking men, tight t-shirts and bulging biceps. They all stared at Dominic with hard eyes. The silence was definitely not golden.

"You," Abu said deliberately, "have disappointed me. I thought you didn't add up." He walked forward. He was so close to Dominic, Dom could feel his breath. He knew that to react was futile; he was outnumbered and outgunned. "I knew you were no street boy — too clean. We street boys get a smell about us. You never wash it off." He was now in Dom's face. "BUT YOU AIN'T NO BROTHER!" Abu shouted, spittle hitting Dom in the face.

Abu turned and walked back towards the three brutes, and they started speaking in hushed, animated tones.

Dominic took the chance to assess his surroundings; as long as the hood stayed off, he would make a mental note of his location and look for escape routes.

"Abu!" a man's voice shouted from behind Dom.

Abu looked around. "What is it?"

"Dunno, but it isn't part of the car." The driver of the car walked over to Abu, handing him what he had found.

Abu looked at the small black metal box, then looked up at

Dom, his face contorted into rage. "It's a fucking tracking device."

He marched up to Dominic, who was still standing with his arms pinned behind his back. Abu covered the distance swiftly, and with the ease of a middleweight, smashed Dom with a perfect right hand.

Dominic didn't see the blow coming until it was too late, the enormous fist connecting perfectly with his nose. The pain was immediate and intense, and his eyes filled with tears; he managed to remain standing, but only just. The shockwave bouncing his brain off the inside of his skull put Dominic into a virtual universe for a moment, his sensory perception gone. He felt blood trickling down his nose, the metallic taste of it entering his mouth. He needed to spit the blood out, but Abu stayed in front of him. His breathing was fast, angry, his whole body oozing aggression and menace.

"So, you are a fucking fed," he shouted.

He back-handed Dom on the side of his head and this time he went down, hitting the floor hard. He felt blackness closing in.

Chapter 40

The operations room was silent. All the teams had returned to a holding area at Old Street police station. Danny sat in silence, his mind awash with what had happened in the last few hours.

The phone on his desk rang.

"Danny, what's going on? Why aren't we on the ground looking for Dom?" It was Charley.

"I know as much as you at the moment," Danny replied, losing his cool and noting the glances he was getting from the operational staff; tension was certainly in the air. "Listen, I appreciate your concern, but don't mix business with pleasure. I will call you on the live ops video link with an update when I have it." He paused, listening to the reply. "Okay, bye." He threw his mobile down onto the desk, leaning back and looking at the ceiling, exhaling a long breath. Danny looked down at his iPad. He had made some notes prior to his live link call to the team. He hadn't found much to go on. "Okay guys, can we get the link live to the team at Old Street?"

"Stand by, Boss, going live now." The big video on the screen flickered into life. "Okay, Boss, it's secure," the desk operator said, confirming the live video link was over a secure link.

Danny turned to address the team. “Okay, everyone, I know today has been a strange, if not a *bad* day. I haven’t yet got any answers, just the facts.” He paused. The team on the other end of the link looked withdrawn and shocked, Danny thought. “So basically, somehow they have compromised Dom; his phone was dumped. However, he got an alert off, so we have that location as the last certified lock-on.” He waited as the team at the holding base erupted into animated conversation. Then Danny continued. “The tracker only worked intermittently but we have a police helicopter up with an Alpha Projects technician onboard trying to reactivate the tracker via the interrogation feature. We await any update from the telephone intercept team. As of one hour ago, Buzzard’s phone was untraceable, which leads us to assume they know something or at least suspect something.”

“Boss?” Danny looked up at the screen. “Why aren’t we out on the ground trying to sort this mess out?”

Danny looked down at his iPad, searching for an answer, but he knew he couldn’t give them a suitable reply. The flood gates now opened.

“Surely we can start a profiled search of the area?” another member of the team said, all of them now animated.

Danny felt the tingling in his calves as blood surged to his brain and anger swept in. “Listen, I’m doing my best. We need to be patient; if we go in gung-ho it could fuck it all up and make this situation worse.”

“Can it get any worse?” Charley stated, the assembled group around her nodding in agreement. Danny felt his anger raging; he expected better from the girl he had put in charge.

“Right, we’re awaiting CCTV footage of the area to try and trace the vehicle and see if we can house it; the helicopter is up as we speak, and we’re waiting for updates. So, sit tight and be ready to react,” Danny finished, in no mood for questions. He turned to the operator on the desk, signalling him to terminate the link. The screen went blank. The room fell to awkward silence.

Paul Allen checked himself in the large floor-to-ceiling mirror in the steel lift heading for the top floor of the old colonial building, perched on the edge of the Thames with its back to the city. Custom House afforded panoramic views of the River Thames and the huge grey beast of HMS Belfast, permanently docked opposite the building that housed Her Majesty's Revenue and Customs. Allen wasn't interested in or receptive to the view; the meeting he was about to attend was not something he was looking forward to. The sun was high in the sky and the building cast a shadow over the Thames. Allen stopped, took a minute to focus his mind, then gave the door a sharp knock.

"Yes, Paul, please come in and take a seat," Picton said, surprisingly polite. Allen knew it wouldn't last.

"Thank you, Julia, and I'm sorry to call a meeting so soon after our last. I appreciate you're busy." He motioned towards her desk, which was piled high with official brown files. Neat but functional, as was her dress. Business shirt open at the neck and tailored trouser suit complementing her figure.

"Paul, it's not a problem. I'm glad to be of assistance. How can I help?"

"Operation Diablos."

"Yes," she said. "The Omega Project's job with that ex-Para lad going undercover." She paused, offering him a cup of tea from a tray on her desk. He took it and took a sip, then placed the cup carefully back on the saucer.

"Exactly that. So, this morning Leigh was accompanying one of the target Codename Buzzard's men to mount surveillance on Avdic — or so we thought."

"Luka Avdic, the Bosnian man," she confirmed.

"Yes, that's correct."

"Sorry, Paul, remind me of the outline of this task again."

"Okay, from the top: Phalanx was given Abu Haleem — known as Buzzard — as a target. He had been of interest to American Intelligence for some time and had been active in Iraq and, we believe, Syria. He then disappeared off radar and our friends over the pond were getting a little irate about it. He is a Tier One target and given to us as a high-level source: claimed he was planning a spectacular here on mainland UK, most probably London. But the trail went cold; we got the job, and made significant progress, tracing Haleem, who is or was living in a homeless shelter."

"How apt," Picton added sarcastically.

"Leigh managed to gain Buzzard's trust after helping him out of a beating by some local yobs. He then asked Leigh to be his de facto minder, and that's when we approached yourself for permission to let him run."

"Okay, got it: so what's the problem?" she asked.

Allen hesitated, looking out of the large glass window behind Picton, the various shapes of the tall buildings that made up the city of London dominating the view.

"The situation is this: we believe they have compromised Leigh. The surveillance team lost the target vehicle after it completed a very rudimentary anti-surveillance procedure." He paused, but to his surprise Picton stayed quiet. "The team tried to regain control of the target vehicle; unfortunately, it slipped through the net."

"Slipped through the net? Not really what I need to hear from my so-called premier surveillance asset, is it, Paul?" she said calmly.

"Well, it actually gets worse. Leigh's Omega Project phone was dumped out of the vehicle. He got an alarm off, so we have a last lock-on, but as it stands now Leigh is missing, presumed kidnapped or worse." He inwardly waiting for the abuse to start.

Picton stood up and walked over to the window offering a panoramic view over the River Thames and south London. The Shard building looked like a large, God-sent glass spike to her left. She stood silent for longer than felt comfortable to Allen, the only sound in the room the large antique clock ticking.

Allen sat back in his chair, finishing his tea and silently awaiting his fate. The job could not have gone more awry; it was looking like Phalanx would be finished before it had really begun.

She turned and returned to her seat and, with grace, sat down, ensuring her dignity was kept intact. She ran a hand down the expensive pencil skirt, deep in thought before she looked up.

"Okay, this is what's going to happen: eighteen hours, Paul. I'm giving you until the morning to sort this shit out. If it's situation 'no change', we will have to go live and take it to the PM." She maintained eye contact with Allen like a poker player.

"Julia, we are running checks on all the CCTV in the area, and Project Alpha technicians are up in the air trying to get a fix off a tracker we believe Leigh deployed."

"That's all very well, but I don't need bits of paper and metaphors. I need men on the ground and this poor soul found before he gets killed. The Hereford counter-terrorist team are at Regent's Park Barracks and deployable on my say so if needed," she continued.

"Understood. I will be at the helm from now on." He got up and made his way to the immaculately-clean glass door to exit the office. The entire building looked and smelled clinical, he thought, very much like the people who inhabited it.

"Paul?" He turned to face her. "Don't be like the captain of the *Titanic*; the iceberg is already in sight, remember."

"Yes, Julia." He nodded, opened the door, and exited into

the corridor. Its walls were bare of any pictures or decorations; sterile, like the person it housed.

Paul took out his mobile, scrolling one-handed to find the number he wanted. What was the *Titanic* comment about?

"Danny — I'll be with you in thirty minutes. We have until morning."

Chapter 41

The drive down to the training base in deepest Kent gave Luka a chance to clear his head. His anger at Ibro was still smouldering, but he had to make sure no one suspected his change of heart. The Irish would have weapons ready for delivery soon. In return, they needed the second, larger consignment of Captagon. He needed to keep the Irish on side as he knew they could be equally useful, but also dangerous.

The small villages he passed through, with their picture-postcard, chocolate-box cottages, were quiet, the heat the previous baking day taking its toll on people, no doubt struggling to sleep. Bedroom windows were wide open, only the odd fox sharing the night with Luka. He made the final turn into the Bon Fleur camp; apple trees surrounded the long, single-track road, while potholes in the road kept his speed down, until finally the headlights eliminated the dilapidated sign marking the entrance to the migrant worker camp.

He turned off the ignition and exited the vehicle. The still night air was uncomfortably warm. In the distance a dog barked. He struggled against the encompassing silence to hear anything else. The Portakabin building on the far side of the large parking area was in darkness. He checked his watch: a little after midnight. Maybe they were all in bed. Then, out of nowhere, Luka was hit with surprise aggression at great speed. Before he knew what was happening, he was face down in the dirt with a foot on the back of his neck, no chance to move.

"It's me, Luka. You fucking idiots," Luka whispered angrily.

"Silence." There were two men by the sound of it; one of them was talking in whispers, most probably on a radio. "Up." Luka got back to his feet as the lock on the gate was removed by one of the men. "Leave the car, we will move it later."

Luka didn't like his car being taken; it was his lifeline. He followed on, tiptoeing across the large parking area and as he got closer, he could make out light emanating from under the door of the largest Portakabin. He heard voices clearly now, heated voices by the sound of it.

"Stay here." The man left Luka and entered the building; the light was intense as the man opened the door and stepped into the room. Luka took stock of his surroundings: in the dark he could make out chinks of light coming from at least two of the buildings, which meant there must be more than just the four members of the Syrian Active Service Unit.

"In." A head emerged around the door.

Luka entered the room. It was surprisingly cool; they must have sorted some form of air con. The room was thick with smoke and the smell of coffee. A bank of CCTV monitors sat mounted on a desk. The room had maps and photos pinned up on a large wall, and a flat-screen TV playing some Middle Eastern news channel.

Luka noticed Ibro with his back to him, sitting on a tatty sofa in animated conversation with a large lump of a bloke, with stocky bulging biceps and a thick neck, and he wore a long shalwar kameez. Whatever they were speaking of was apparently of tremendous interest. The man who met Luka at the gate went up to Ibro and bent down to whisper in his ear. Ibro looked around at Luka; his eyes, cold and piercing, seemed more deadly than ever. He got up slowly and deliberately, and Luka noted the Glock 19 pistol tucked down the front of his waistband. The other three men followed close behind.

"Why do you need to see me?" Luka demanded.

Ibro stood in silence. The largest of the three men whispered into his ear, then pushed past Luka and left the building, followed by the other two. Luka noted they were dressed casually in jeans and white Nike trainers.

"I need to ensure you're focused on the task. The Leader thinks you have lost your direction."

"That is not the case. I have done everything you asked of me —" Luka broke off mid-sentence as he heard a commotion outside; slamming doors and raised voices. Ibro smiled at Luka and looked towards the door. Luka turned to look. The door burst open and in came the group of three, frogmarching someone who was hooded and wearing an oversized blue overall. Luka was confused. *Who the fuck is this?* he thought. They roughly forced the figure to stand up straight. Ibro turned to Luka.

"We need an insurance policy, to ensure you don't fuck us about again." Ibro spat out the words.

"What do you —" Luka was interrupted by Ibro who grabbed the hood and yanked it swiftly off the person's head.

Luka could not take it in. Standing in front of him was Sally Anne. The girl he had left to keep safe was now here, a prisoner of these savages.

"You cunt!" Luka moved towards Ibro but the man was too quick; he had the Glock pistol out and forcibly under Luka's chin.

"Back off, Bosnian, or I will blow your shit for brains all over your lovely piece of skirt."

"Luka, no!" Sally shouted. Luka looked at her; she looked like shit. She had been crying, her eyes puffy and dark. She was visibly shaking, yet she mouthed to him she was okay.

"How sweet," Ibro mocked.

"If you hurt her, I will fucking kill you." Luka felt the pistol pushed further up under his chin. Ibro's eyes glazed over for a moment.

"It is up to you how this ends. You do exactly as we tell you, and she will walk away unharmed; but if you don't, then I will give her to my boys." Ibro turned to the group assembled in the room and they burst into laughter.

Luka felt anger surge through him like molten metal in his veins, but the more tense he got the harder the pistol was pushed up. Luka knew he was in no position to fight back.

"Okay, okay, you have my word."

"Your word means fuck all to me, but it matters to this lovely lady," Ibro said, grabbing Sally's cheeks and squeezing them together, puckering her face up. "Take her back," Ibro ordered the man holding Sally. The hood was roughly forced on her head, and they frogmarched her back out the door.

Ibro replaced the pistol back in his waistband and walked over to the desk where all the CCTV monitors were stacked. Maps and photos were scattered all over it.

"Bosnian, here," Ibro ordered. "Right, this is what I need to happen." Ibro turned to face the large map of London pinned to the wall.

Chapter 42

Paul Allen walked into the operations room of Project Omega. The atmosphere was sombre and quiet. The radios were silent as the team was still holding off at Old Street police station.

Danny Haigh was sitting at his desk in quiet contemplation, staring aimlessly at the large interactive map on the wall. A large flashing gold dot marked the last known location of Dominic Leigh: his phone, found by an Alpha Projects Technician in the gutter, was luckily intact.

"Danny, how you doing?" Paul opened the dialogue.

"Not good, Boss, to be honest," Danny replied, almost defeatist.

"Okay, well, let's see where we are, shall we?" Paul said, positively pulling up a seat. "Right, so, from the top."

Danny relayed the entire story, from the sudden change of direction and loss of the target vehicle, to sending the alert. Paul Allen sat taking it all in thoughtfully.

"As per the map, that's Dom's last know location. Unfortunately, CCTV in that area is not the best and we're still awaiting the Alpha boys to interrogate the system fully. We had Heli 147 up with a sweep team trying to wake up the tracker we believe

Dom managed to deploy. It worked intermittently but then went dead in the area marked on the map with the white geo-fence." Danny pointed to the map. Both men moved closer to the board. "The area has some new factory units and is a mix of residential and reclaimed land being put up for development, hence the lack of CCTV or security cameras."

Behind them, the phone rang. "Boss, it's Alpha Projects."

Danny walked over to the phone. "Danny Haigh speaking." He listened to the animated voice on the other end of the line, taking notes on his iPad with a long electronic pencil. "Okay, understood. I will await the update," he replaced the receiver. "That was Alpha. They have an update of sorts, they're still awaiting some of the CCTV footage from the area of interest. A slight plus is that the tracker managed to ping intermittent locations, so it was working; but because of the small streets and all the brick and metal buildings it wasn't functioning enough to give live updates." Danny paused to look at the map. "They cannot be sure, but they reckon the device is now inside a building or storage facility that is blocking the signal."

"Meaning?" Paul questioned.

"It could be a building with shields installed to negate any form of electronic surveillance. It would almost be like insulating a building but with RFID material, almost like a huge Faraday bag," Danny explained.

"It's a tactic I've seen used in Syria, especially Aleppo, by the anti-Assad opposing forces. It proved very effective. Danny, it seems we are up against something a lot more than a lone wolf jihadist with interest from 'The Firm'." Paul continued, "So the boys at Alpha seem to think our man could be, or was, somewhere inside this geo-fence?"

"I presume so," Danny replied with a lack of conviction.

"Well, we need to take this as at least a starting point. Can we deploy a team into the area to commence a sweep?" Both men moved closer to the map board.

"Boss, I want the team to remain on immediate standby to move. We can get Alpha Projects out in the area with a Liaison Officer to coordinate; they have a variety of technical vehicles with good legends."

"Yes, yes, I'm aware of their capabilities." It seemed to the rest of the ops team, going about their business at their desks, that Paul was getting annoyed. "Danny, I want you on this one. Get out with them and ensure we sweep this entire area. The next move is to get back onto Avdic. He's our only tangible asset at the moment to lead us back to Haleem." He paused. "Okay Danny, let's go. Get the boys back onto the ground."

"Yes, Boss."

"Great; right, I'm going to base myself here. Can I grab somewhere to work?"

"Use my desk. I won't be here for a while."

"Great, thanks." He immediately pulled out his laptop and opened it, punching the keys with intensity.

Danny wandered back to the large interactive screen and initiated a video call to the team at Old Street.

Chapter 43

The intercom buzzing brought Luka back to the present, his mind now awash with guilt and dread.

Luka let Ardian into the flat. His friend seemed troubled by his appearance. "Luka, you look like shit my friend."

Luka went into the kitchen, switching on the kettle. Turning to his friend, he said, "They have Sally."

"What?"

"They summoned me down to that fucking camp and she was there. She looked okay, but scared, obviously."

"Why? For what?" his friend said, exasperated.

"They don't trust me to deliver. I'm being stitched up here. Don't know what has gone back to the Leader, but you know how dangerous those fuckers are." Ardian looked shocked. Luka handed him a coffee, and they both sat down at the small table. "I need your help. We have to go and collect something of importance and take it down to that fucking place."

"Yeah, sure — when?"

"Now; we need to do it under cover of darkness," Luka stated. "Where's the car?"

"Christie Road."

They both finished their coffees in silence, Luka looking out of his second-floor flat window across the rooftops. "Not much darkness left. We need to crack on."

"Ready? Okay, let's go."

"STAND BY, STAND BY." The ops room brought the silence to an end. "That's two males out of Alpha One, gone right towards the main."

Charley checked her map. "It would seem they're heading towards Charlie One, but they must confirm."

"Mike, I have Bravo One plus unknown male heading north on Cassland Road." The operator, standing as if waiting for an early morning bus, had control of the targets. Early morning workers were now on the streets.

"Bravo One gone left at first option and unsighted to me."

"Griffin, I have Bravo One plus unknown male towards Christie Road."

"Falcon has Bravo One towards Charlie One. Wait... That's Charlie One mobile, and towards the main."

Right, Charley thought, *that's the easy bit; we need to keep him under control.* Lessons learned from Dom's scenario meant they had cars available to leapfrog and get out in the front.

Charley got back onto Danny. "Boss, can we get Heli 147 up? We have our man mobile with an unknown male; bit of a strange hour to go mobile."

"Yes, will take it now. Take about twenty mins to get from Redhill into the area."

Luckily for the team, the morning traffic helped them blend in, and with the arrival of Heli 147 on target, the cars could distance themselves.

"Heli 147, that's off, off, off at Blue Five Two," came reassuring words of the helicopter over the radio waves.

The surveillance team closed in as the vehicle exited the

large dual carriageway. Four cars, plus a motorbike, all involved in the follow.

"Team, this is close to the area of Dom's last known location," the desk announced.

"Falcon, I have Bravo One indicating left... wait... Gone left into Violet Road."

"Okay, team, we need to keep control." The tension was palpable over the airwaves.

"Hawk, I'm static in Tesco Express car park and have Bravo One towards me."

"Hawk, that's Bravo One slowing, indicating left... that's a stop, stop, stop."

The surveillance team automatically started to impose an invisible box around the target vehicle, moving around the local area unseen, unheard. Charley was monitoring the situation, the dots moving around her head-up display on her vehicle windscreen. It took mere seconds, a well-practiced drill.

"Hawk, that's Bravo One mobile, indicating left... wait... gone left, and unsighted to me."

"All call signs, that's an industrial estate, do not follow... Heli 147, can you take?"

"Heli 147, we are on optics, about three clicks north; he's unsighted to us... moving closer."

Charley pulled into a side street of residential houses, most still asleep, the square block maisonettes all uniform apart from the balconies, some tidy, some piled with boxes. She pulled out her phone.

"Charley, hi."

"Boss, this is more than a coincidence, surely," she stated.

"That's what I'm thinking, but again we need to know which unit they have gone into." Danny knew what Charley wanted, but he had Paul Allen next to him who had different ideas.

"Griffin, Heli 147: you're obvious to us, you need to pull

back." The operator in Griffin alerted the helicopter that he was audible to them on the ground.

"Danny, we have call sign Steel on the ground holding off; we can send them in to sweep the estate," Charley suggested to Danny.

"Okay, send them in — but any heat at all, then abort."

Charley got on the net to call sign Steel, a small tipper truck in the livery of a cover company; it could go into the industrial estate no problem, she thought. "Steel moved into the target area."

As time passed the roads got busier. As London awoke, it would become easier to move closer to the targets but harder to keep control, as traffic became an issue.

"Steel approaching." The operator paused. "Steel, the entrance is gated on a keypad. It handrails the railway tracks; no way in without buzzing for entry."

Charley was cut off before she could speak.

"Steel, lift off immediately," Danny ordered.

Charley was now incredulous with rage: her thought pattern was definitely being affected by her feelings for Dom. She reached for her phone.

"Yes?" came the curt reply.

"Boss, what the fuck? We could at least bluff our case," she said with a little too much attitude.

"Charley, you're letting your judgement be clouded on this. Think who we are: a covert surveillance asset. We don't ring fucking bells and announce we're here, do we?" he said, his voice raised, then the line went down.

"Bollocks," Charley said out loud, realising she had fucked up big time. "Steel, there is only one way out of this estate. We can hold on the main and give direction."

"Copy, Steel holding trigger and can give direction," the desk operator relayed in a monotone, calm voice.

. . .

Danny put down the phone and turned to Paul Allen, who was transfixed on the map board and the interactive game of chess that was ever evolving around the location.

"Paul, I think we have an issue."

"Go on." Paul turned to look at Danny, now fully engaged.

"Charley, the girl running this operation, she's one of our best new recruits, destined for big things... but..."

"Sounds ominous."

"I think — well, I'm almost certain — she's in a relationship or the start of one with Dominic Leigh."

"Well, we're all grown-ups — but if it clouds her judgement in making operationally sound decisions, then remove her." Paul turned back to the map. "The clock is ticking for us all, believe me."

Chapter 44

"This is it," Luka said as he turned to his mate, "but I haven't got a clue what we're collecting."

He got out of the car and approached the metal entrance gate with its shiny new keypad. A morning tube passed by on the train line, momentarily above ground before descending back into the bowels of London. Luka gave it a momentary glance; it was already full of commuters heading for the nearby financial district of Canary Wharf.

The code worked and the gate opened automatically. They drove the length of the narrow road to the last unit. It looked brand new; up-and-over metal shutters and a small door to an office. Luka noted lights on in the office. The other units still had "To Let" signs on them. *Strange choice for this ragtag bunch, but who knows anymore.* He approached the door, but it opened before he could knock. Two men were in the office; they certainly weren't the Syrians, but fitted the bill for the London part of this organisation. African origin, short, cropped hair, piercing eyes and bulging muscles. He hated that Sally was at the mercy of thugs like these.

"Alright?" Luka broke the silence. They both nodded, then

one of the men left the office through another door to make a call on the mobile in his hand.

"You alone?"

Luka turned to the man. "No, I have a driver," he replied.

"Why?" the man enquired aggressively.

"Because I have no fucking idea what I'm collecting and I may need some help." Luka was getting angry now with the whole situation.

"Tell him to clear the boot out, need loads of space."

The other man returned, whispered something to his mate then turned to Luka. "Get your man to reverse in." Luka went out to Ardian. The shutter doors opened automatically, and Luka got a first sight of the inside of the industrial unit. It was larger than he thought, and a car was parked at the end in a small shipping container. As Luka followed the reversing Ford Mondeo into the unit, the doors closed behind him. Bright strip lights illuminated the place. Apart from the car the place was empty other than some large rolls of plastic sheeting stacked neatly by some empty shelving. Luka took a mental note of this place, including any exits in case it all went wrong.

Ardian approached him after sorting out the boot of his battered Mondeo. He laughed. "First clean out that's had in some years."

Luka was not up for humour. A commotion behind them broke the tension, and they both turned. The two men were dragging a man — was it a body? — towards the car. The man struggled — he wasn't dead — his feet and hands bound by plasi-cuff, and a large black hood was pulled tightly over his head. He was unceremoniously dumped into the boot and the lid was slammed shut. The man inside kicked and struggled; the larger of the two thugs ripped open the boot and rained down heavy blows on the man; his struggling ceased as he adopted a foetal position.

Poor fucker, thought Luka. His hands showed he was a white man. *Who the fuck is this?*

"Take him straight to the FOB."

Luka noted the military parlance. The whole situation wasn't looking good — the deeper in he got, the more helpless he felt.

"Who the fuck is this?" Luka demanded.

"A *Taghut*, just like you," spat the larger of the two men, now face-to-face with Luka. "Now get on your fucking way, Ibro is waiting." They turned and went back into the office. The shutter doors opened smoothly, and the outside world and a bright new day shone in. Luka stared out of the dirty windscreen, his mind racing.

PAUL TURNED TO DANNY, both men having been transfixed on the map and the commentary of the surveillance team follow over the radio.

"We cannot fuck this up, Danny." Paul Evans rarely swore and his whole demeanour had changed since he had come back inside from speaking to Julia Picton. The white Ford Mondeo had headed out of London via the Blackwall Tunnel and was heading towards the M25 motorway.

"That's off, off, off towards Maidstone. Team move up, Bravo One into filter lane, town centre." The operator in Heli 147 was concerned about keeping control of the target once inside a town.

"Griffin has Bravo One towards town centre; lane one of two."

Paul Allen turned to Danny. "That's Charley Holdaway, isn't it?"

"Yes."

"I hope her mind's on the job, Danny."

"I'm monitoring it; will sort it once this serial is over." Both men returned to silence, listening to the surveillance team's commentary. But something didn't add up. "Boss, I don't get Picton's involvement in this. At her level this is small fry, surely?" He waited.

His boss kept his focus on the screens to his front. "Nothing is as it seems. And that woman will haunt us until she gets what she wants."

"Boss?" They both looked round at the operator on the desk in front of them, the two radio handsets draped over his shoulders giving him the look of a city dealer on a trading floor. "The target vehicle stopped at a petrol station."

"Yeah, and?" Danny replied, somewhat nonplussed.

"Well, all these garages have CCTV and ANPR readers linked to the police due to drive-aways not paying for fuel, so the Alpha boys got the footage straightaway off the police Titan link."

"And?" Danny was getting annoyed.

"Look at this." The operator brought up the CCTV image of the garage, the white Mondeo clearly visible.

"The quality is outstanding. Good enough if it was called up in court."

"What exactly are we looking at here?" Paul Allen chipped in.

The operator was getting excited now. His unruly hair and bizarre dress sense gave him the look and feel of a student.

"Look at the Mondeo." He pointed to the car via an electronic cursor. "There, look, it's moving."

"Sorry, I'm lost here," Paul Allen said.

"Sir, look, that car is moving. I mean the suspension, *look*." Again, he pointed to the car. Both men moved closer to the screen. Sure enough, the vehicle could be seen bouncing on its suspension. "But both men are in the shop, and the front of the car is empty..." The operator paused. "There... there is definitely something — or rather *some*one — in the boot of that car."

Both men stood back in unison, letting the news sink in.

Danny broke the silence. "That could be our man in there."

Paul Allen nodded. "It's too much of a coincidence. Let me get onto this; we can have the SAS counter-terrorist team in the air within five minutes." He glanced up at the interactive map. "Where are they?"

"Just south of Maidstone in Kent."

"Thank you," he said and walked away, retrieving his mobile from his trouser pocket.

Danny noted that the back of his boss's shirt was drenched with sweat. The heat was getting to everyone. Danny felt for the poor fucker in the boot of that car. *Could it be Dom?* he pondered. His boss was likely correct: it was too much of a coincidence.

Danny moved back to his position just behind the operations desk, rather like a submarine commander perched slightly higher than his men, with a commanding view of the state-of-the-art operations hub.

"Where are we?" he asked.

"They're heading into deepest Kent, Boss, onto B roads in the area of Headcorn."

"How're we doing?" he asked.

"Good, Boss, Heli 147 is keeping it easy; the teams just have to shadow."

Danny glanced at the large electronic clock above the main screen: it read 1015. It had already been a long day, and it was only 1015.

Paul Allen returned to the room. Danny sensed a problem. Allen went over to the watercooler and drew a cup of water, taking a long drink. He turned to Danny. "We have to let it run; no hard stop authorised."

"What?" Danny could not believe his ears.

"That's the brief, categoric."

"Boss, that could be — in fact, most probably is — Dom in that car, one of us."

"She authorised SO19 to mount a raid on that industrial unit."

"When?" Danny inquired.

"She hasn't said."

"For fuck's sake, Boss."

Paul Allen turned to Danny, who immediately knew he'd overstepped the mark. "Less of the attitude, Danny. Like I said, she gets whatever the fuck she wants." With that, he walked back outside.

Danny turned back to the desk, then picking up his phone and punched\ in Charley's number.

Chapter 45

The man in the back had gone quiet. The heat of the day was building up inside the Mondeo, the air-con long since packed up. "I feel for that poor fucker in the boot," Luka said to his friend, who glanced sideways at him.

"You okay, Luka?" Ardian asked.

Luka gave his mate a pat on the shoulder. "You're a good man, Ardian. I'm so sorry to have gotten you involved in this."

Ardian looked at him with a look of compassion. "Don't worry about me. Sally is the one who needs us... and this poor fucker in the boot."

Luka focused back on the road; he recognised the orchard to his left with the large sign announcing the apple cider to be the "finest in Kent". "Left at the end of this hedgerow, then take it slow. It's a shitty road and we need to give our friend in the boot a steady journey." Luka turned to his mate. "When we drop our guest off, I must go straight to Merjem. If these bastards found Sally, they can certainly find her." He let out a long breath. He knew what he had to do, but he needed time to make sure his sister was safe before he acted.

Dom felt the panic wave again, starting in his legs, then surging up his body. He had never been claustrophobic, but the heat, the darkness, and the fact he was locked in the boot of a car had changed that. His heart was pounding, and he tried to control his breathing. He could hardly breathe and was gasping for air. He had long since lost the feeling in his hands. His whole body was screaming in agony and panic.

He felt the car slowing to a halt. *Could be another false alarm.* The smell of fuel and exhaust fumes was making him feel sick, but he had to avoid vomiting. It could choke him. This time he heard voices and a car door open. More raised voices. Dom was straining his senses. He was tensed, expecting another kicking or worse. He'd never faced a situation like this; everything in the Army was so much simpler: *kill or be killed.* This enemy was like a demonic ghost, never leaving your senses alone.

Since his incarceration, he'd had plenty of time to assess his life, or the car crash that was an excuse for a life. He missed his daughter so badly; he remembered her shouts of joy when she had opened her birthday present to find it was the toy horse she wanted; he felt her warmth as she lay asleep on his chest. Her blonde curls and large blue eyes would melt any heart. He feared that in a very short space of time they would be separated for ever: Daddy, just another statistic of the war on terror.

The car came to a halt again and relief surged through his body as he felt someone inserting a key into the boot lock. Light flooded into the car — he could make out daylight and the warmth of the sun. "Dirty bastard's pissed himself," someone said. They manhandled Dom out of the boot, smashing his knees and then his feet as they dragged him face-first out of the boot and across a rough gravel track. Dom felt metal steps hitting his shins, then a door opened, and they pushed him inside; he stumbled and fell. Dom stayed down, safer on the floor, curled up in a ball. He smelt cigarette smoke, strong coffee, and the unmistakable stench of unwashed bodies, with the sweet, ripe smell of body odour.

He was grabbed and pulled to his feet; the hood roughly

pulled off his head; the bright sunlight felt as if it would burst his eyeballs. His vision slowly cleared as he got a first sight of where he had been taken.

In front of him stood a male: average build, dark olive skin, short black hair, pointed features on a pock-marked face, and, *dressed in the khaki combat gear so loved by bad asses the globe over,* thought Dom. The overriding feature was his eyes, dark and sinister like a shark. They didn't move from Dom. Behind stood Buzzard and Tarek, both dressed like the others in the room in sandy-coloured combat trousers and camo pattern t-shirts. The silence lasted a long time. Buzzard stood to the rear, oozing hatred. He also didn't break his stare.

Ibro moved forward. "So, who the fuck are you?" He walked towards Dom, stopping an inch from his face. Without warning he screamed at Dom, "WHO THE FUCK ARE YOU?!"

Dom flinched, caught off guard. The room erupted into laughter. The man turned away and walked up to the long table that ran the length of the room. Dom noticed it was covered with maps and photographs, and a bank of monitors beaming CCTV images of the camp and surrounding areas. These were no amateurs.

Ibro picked up something off the desk and walked back towards Dom, oozing menace. He held up something in front of Dom's face, who struggled to focus on the object, his eyes still not able to fully handle daylight.

"Look!" the man screamed. Dom felt the icy chill of fear sweep down into his bowels. The object was the tracking device he had planted on the shitty Ford Fiesta he'd been in prior to being lifted. Dom knew the next few minutes would make the difference between life and death. A wrong move now, and it was over. "We first saw these in Aleppo." He paused, closely looking at the small black square of metal and plastic. "Tracking devices, very useful. The Russians used to strap them to the donkeys that pulled the carts delivering cooking gas to families wanting to simply feed themselves," he carried on calmly. "And then you know what they did? Once they found a large enough group of people in the ruins of their once-lovely city, they dropped laser-targeted bombs on them directed by these little boxes of death: true ethnic cleansing." He moved closer to Dom, too close. "But you wouldn't know what that is about, would you?" His voice rose. "But you will, you will know what it is like to get bombed, butchered and murdered whilst trying to look after your loved ones. Soon enough, you people will know. So, my army boy," he said through a smirk, "you are now of use to me, just like the donkey." The man turned away and moved to the back of the room with Buzzard and Tarek.

What the fuck does that mean? Dom tried to get a grip of exactly what was going on. *And where the fuck is my quick reaction force?* He felt the hood being pulled back over his head and then he was harshly dragged back out of the room, down the steps and back across the rough ground and into another building; it smelled of animals and decay. He was pushed into a sitting position, then they handcuffed his hands to a chain. He heard the door close, and then silence. He tried to get comfy as best as he could. He settled into his surroundings, getting used to the noises the old building made.

He drifted off to sleep; for how long he didn't know. But something woke him. He was confused and lost in the broken dreams of his daughter and her tears. He strained his ears. He wasn't mistaken; he could hear breathing, rhythmic human breathing. He wasn't alone. Someone else was in this dungeon.

Chapter 46

Luka entered the Portakabin, the air was heavy with cigarette smoke, a thick grey band of it hanging in the air. The atmosphere in the room was equally heavy with menace, the men in groups animated, and a variety of dialects were audible. Luka counted nine men in the room, two of whom he didn't recognise.

Ibro walked to the centre of the space and brought everyone to attention by slamming the table with his hands. Everyone fell silent.

"Brothers, it is time. We are now in the last stages of preparation. Soon we strike at the heart of the infidel mouthpiece of the great Satan."

The room erupted into chants of, "Allahu Akbar, Allahu Akbar."

Luka looked around the room: this crew was about to unleash some form of hell onto unsuspecting people. It was always the weak who suffered, never the people in power who actually made the decisions.

"Brothers, we shall begin our operation. I thank you all for the efforts you have put in. We are ready, and our leader is pleased."

Again, the room roused into "Allahu Akbar, Allahu Akbar."

Ibro Al Makki stood in the middle, intoxicated with the adoration he was receiving. Luka watched, animated by the scene; this bunch of desperadoes would stop at nothing. He feared for Sally Anne. He didn't know where she was being held but he suspected it was at this base. So near, and yet so far.

Why am I in this room? What is the reason? Luka was desperately trying to get some semblance of order into his mind. He was being involved too much, and it made little sense.

Ibro approached him, the ever-present lump that was Buzzard on his shoulder.

"So, Bosnian," he began.

"I have done what you asked. I'm done here," Luka spouted, somewhat angrily.

Ibro edged closer. Luka stood firm.

"You," he said, and prodded Luka in the chest, "are never finished. You know too much, but you cannot go telling stories again. We know you like that." He paused. Luka sensed the entire room was watching this unfold. "If you did, they would take you to some black site and torture you until you admitted what they wanted." He smirked. "And whilst they had their fun with you, we could have ours with your secret girlfriend." Luka felt a surge of red-fiery anger course through his veins.

Ibro saw it in his eyes. "You don't have the balls, you *Taghut*." He spat directly into Luka's face. Luka felt the warm, thick phlegm on his cheeks. It trickled towards his lips as he wiped his face. The room burst into noise again. Ibro turned and moved back to the table and the untidy array of maps and photos. Buzzard turned to follow Ibro, then turned back to Luka and passed him a tissue. Luka accepted it with a nod.

"Bosnian, come here." Luka walked over to the gathering around the table. He recognised the areas on the maps as south London. "The weapons are arriving tonight; you need to pick them up and bring them here, then assist these two men." He pointed to two Arab men wearing a uniform of blue trousers and blue shirts emblazoned with "Southern Water." Ibro continued. "Both are brothers from the mosque — but you never go, so you probably don't recognise them." Ibro's cutting remark got glib smiles from the group. "You need to meet the vehicle with our produce on at Gravesend Service Station. It will be on a vehicle with other produce but don't get involved — it's none of your business. Then take it to the designated handover with the Irish." He turned to the table, looking amongst the mass of papers and eventually retrieving a map. "We don't need any fuck-ups. Your little Bosnian smugglers need to help you. Before we offload our goods, we need to be one-hundred percent certain that no heat is around." Ibro spoke with menace, as always.

"Where do I meet the Irish?" Luka inquired.

"All in good time, Bosnian, all in good time." Ibro waved to one of the other members of the team. "Show Bosnian the van and the places to stow the goods."

Luka followed the man outside. The summer afternoon was sultry, the sky cloudless and deep blue. They moved across the car park. Inside the large hay barn, long empty, was a large white Mercedes Sprinter van. The man opened the rear doors and climbed inside. He took out a big tool and eventually pulled up a section of the floor to reveal a large concealment area. It ran the entire length of the vehicle and was lined with a thick rubber substance. The smell of glue was intoxicating in the heat.

"This is where you place the bags, then secure them with this tool. It's unique, and there is only one, so don't lose it." Luka recognised his accent now; it had a French lilt to it, probably North African. Luka accepted the tool off the guy, noticing the crescent-shaped tattoo the group all had in the gap between their thumbs and forefingers. "The keys are in the front and it's full of fuel. You will hand this over to the Irish and they will do the same with the van they bring the weapons in." With that, the man walked off.

Luka stood for a moment in contemplation: should he run and get the fuck out of there now? He was in a desperate situation; he knew that to run now would mean a life of running, never safe and permanently looking over his shoulder. And then there was Sally — she didn't deserve this. He wondered where she was now. He couldn't look for her. The place had a battery of technical cameras and surveillance devices.

The weight of the world was certainly on his shoulders, and he couldn't see any end. He went to look for the only friend he had in the world, who was sitting in the trashed Mondeo.

"My friend, I need your help once more," Luka said with an air of total dejection. Ardian's stare said it all to Luka. He knew his friend was in deep; being caught in possession of drugs or weapons would lead to years behind bars. "We need to use your counter-surveillance boys again." Luka let out a long breath of desperation. "We have to do another job for these fuckwits."

Ardian got out of the car and they both sat on the bonnet. "Luka, I know you're not to blame. It wasn't meant to be like this for any of us," Ardian said softly.

Luka grabbed him round the shoulder and pulled him into a brotherly embrace. "I know this, my friend. All we wanted was revenge for our families. But time has moved on and this bunch of bloodthirsty lunatics will not stop until they have put El Muz on the world map." He paused for a moment. "Can we really be part of it?"

"What can we do? They have Sally and I hate to think what they will do to her if we don't do as they say."

Ardian spoke in a whisper. "She must be here somewhere."

Luka looked at his friend, then glanced around the large complex of buildings that housed migrant fruit pickers. "But where, my friend? They could have put her anywhere, and my stomach is knotted permanently. Anything I touch is going to shit."

"Bosnian, here now," Ibro shouted from the door of the makeshift operations room.

"Here we go." Luka got up and started towards the building.

Chapter 47

The Omega operations room was a hive of activity, the bank of interactive screens on the wall all beaming images back to the assembled group, huddled together behind the operator manning the radio.

"Boss, that's Heli 147 back on task." Danny moved over to the images transmitted from the helicopter's powerful cameras. "This is called Bon Fleur: it's a migrant workers' camp for fruit pickers. Not been used for a season, due to issues with locals complaining," the operator continued. They all viewed the footage. "Of interest is the heat signature from these two buildings," he added, pointing to the interactive plan of the site.

"Meaning?" Danny asked.

"Well, Boss, basically these two areas are occupied by humans. This type of camera is sensitive, even in this summer heat, and can tell us if it's animals or humans."

"So, if Dom is in this camp, he is in one of these buildings." Danny moved closer to the screen.

"Boss, whoever's there is very surveillance-aware. Alpha projects are picking up no Wi-Fi, mobiles, nothing, and they seemed to be adopting anti-drone protocols. We have seen only two men sat by this car here which is the Mondeo we followed. We believe one of them is Avdic."

Paul Allen walked into the room with a tall, fit-looking man dressed in olive style walking trousers and a tight blue polo shirt. "Danny, this is Mal Perkins, Gold Commander of the SO19 Team." Danny shook the offered hand. "Well, it's not good news." Paul Allen turned to the tall police officer.

"Yeah, we hit the place about twenty-five minutes ago. Totally cleaned out, and looks brand new."

"Nothing at all?" Danny said in disbelief.

"Clean, probably too clean: they must have sanitised it prior to lifting off."

Danny turned around to the operations desk. "Get onto Alpha and see if we can get anything off those cameras by the industrial unit."

Paul Allen brought the proceedings to an end, sensing Danny's anger building. "Mal, pass on my thanks to your team for their efforts."

"No probs, sir. Anything else we can do, just shout." Mal Perkins nodded a cursory goodbye to Danny and left the room.

Danny stood looking at the live camera feeds. The camp was still in the haze of a scorching afternoon. His anger was indeed building. "Boss, why the fuck did we wait for over five hours before hitting that unit?"

Paul Allen stood quietly, deep in contemplation. "I doubt I will ever know the answer to that, Danny. But what I do know is that things are probably not what they seem and I'm just as fucking frustrated as you are," Allen replied, his voice angry.

Danny sensed that this battle wasn't for winning and returned to the operations desk to survey the images. He knew the Heli 147 was happy sat off by five kilometres; they weren't audible or visible to the people at the camp. He would have to wait until dark before sending in a CTR Team to infiltrate the camp and have a look around.

"Spoke to the guy manning the cameras on the Heli. He reckons this building has in excess of six bodies in it, and this one here, two, maybe three."

"Do we know what the buildings are?" Danny inquired.

"Yes, Alpha has got land registry online and this group here are semi-permanent — so Portacabins. And these two are farm buildings dating back to the sixties when it was still a farm."

"So, it's likely Dom is in here — but he isn't alone; possible a guard?' Danny said aloud.

"Stand by, stand by, that's a large white van manoeuvring," Heli 147 burst over the loudspeaker. "That's van out the farm and towards the main."

"Danny, are we taking this?" Charley's voice came over the surveillance net.

"Heli 147, I have white van onto the main and towards White Seven."

Danny was now in a predicament: did he follow the unknown vehicle and lose any cover on Dom's likely location, or follow the van in case Dom was being moved?

"Heli 147, can you get any heat signatures from the rear of the van?"

"Heli 147 copy: wait out... Nothing detected, rear looks clear."

"Copy that." Danny put down the headset on the desk, watching the image of the large white van as it sped down the narrow lanes of rural Kent. *Who the fuck are you?*

Paul Allen came level with Danny. "Let them go, Danny; we may have one of ours in there and I don't intend to let him rot."

"All call signs, we are staying put. Bon Fleur is our priority. Once we get into darkness the CROPS boys are going in. Charley, I'll brief you over other means."

"Copy." Charley sounded more upbeat, thought Danny. He knew he would have to take her off being team leader on this task — he was sure now there was a romantic link between her and Dom and he didn't want to make things any more complicated than they already were.

"Danny, we need to get an update ready; you know she'll come asking."

"Well, it's a lot of loose threads; but what I want to know is who they are, and what the people in that camp are up to. We *must* get in there tonight," Danny replied. "Boss, we need authority for a full CTR insertion and to the have the SAS counter-terrorist team on standby. I think this is bigger than we think."

"Okay, prepare me a brief for authorisation and I will get it signed off ready for last light tonight."

DOM STRAINED his senses to the maximum; he could have sworn he heard someone sobbing. The black hood blunted much of his sensory perception and the musty smell and the coarse material irritated his throat and nose. He was losing the feeling in his hands. Luckily for him he was in a sitting position, not a stress position which would have been excruciating by now. He was trying to keep a sense of time by singing the same Abba song in his head; "Dancing Queen". He wanted to know when it was night; he had only one option, and that was to try to escape. How much he had craved this life of special forces work — but now he had it and was deep in the shit. His mind wandered back to his lovely daughter. It all came home to roost: playing cowboys and Indians was great but this was reality now. Would he ever see those curly blonde locks again?

He heard it again. It was definitely a sob, no doubt. He had no idea of the building they housed him in, but it felt large, the air circulating freely.

"Hello? Are you okay?" Nothing. "Hey, my name's Dominic. I can't help us get out of here unless you can tell me you're okay, and who you are." Silence.

"I'm scared," came the broken voice of a woman, obviously petrified.

"Okay, okay — you'll be fine, but we need to help each other, okay?"

"Yes." Her sobbing was audible.

"Are you tied to anything?"

"Yes, I'm... tied to a chair by my hands and feet."

"Okay, good. Can you move the chair?"

"I'm not sure."

The door suddenly burst open and light flooded the floor beneath Dom's feet. He felt at least two people brush past him and then the scream of the girl followed. He heard the chair being dragged across the floor, the girl pleading with them.

"Please, no, don't hurt me, please."

Dom felt the approach of someone towards him, and tensed every sinew, expecting blows to rain down on him. Two sets of arms grabbed him on his arms and with strength and speed, they yanked him to his feet and frogmarched him forwards. He was spun around and pushed back; he tensed for a fall, but he hit a chair. His hands were untied, then retied to the chair. They removed his hood, his eyes struggling with the light.

He looked around; he was in a large barn, hay bales piled high to the ceiling at one end and farm machinery parked haphazardly around the large interior. Dom looked to his left at the girl; her hood was still on her head, which had slumped forward. He then suddenly realised she was dressed in an orange boiler suit. The men to the front were unloading kit for a large silver pelican case. As they assembled the equipment, it became apparent that they were preparing a camera rig.

Once they had finished with setting up the kit, they approached the woman and ripped off her hood. It took her eyes a while to get used to the light. Dom watched her; she was desperately trying to keep it all together. "You'll been fine." Dom hardly got his words out before the larger of the men hit him hard with the back of his hand. His head hit the floor first, followed by the chair they'd tied him to slamming to the floor with a loud crash. The girl screamed.

"Silence, bitch!" someone screamed back at her.

From his prone position on the floor, Dom saw that someone had hung a black flag behind where the girl was sitting. *This is a hostage video, like the ones I normally see on briefings and the TV.* The two men grabbed hold of the woman and lifted the chair to a position marked on the floor. They handed her a piece of paper. Dom knew that this would be a script. They were about to the tell the world their demands.

Chapter 48

Luka sat in the front of the van in silence. Darkness was descending over this godforsaken place, and it couldn't come quick enough. The Irish were switched on after years of paramilitary action; their drills were slick, down to the choice of handover location. This was the dark web equivalent of a secure base to do bad things. The service station on the A2 about thirty miles outside of London was mainly for lorries. The car park was situated around to the rear of the two buildings that made up the restaurant and garage. They hid it from view, and that's exactly why it was occupied by girls selling their bodies to fat, greasy truck drivers and drug dealers in large, high-powered saloon cars with music booming out of the open windows. The heat of the day had diminished to a sultry, heavy night. The smell of diesel, tarmac and urine was strong enough to make Luka's eyes water. This was a lawless hell hole and he wanted out of here as quickly as possible.

Luka's phone vibrated. It was a *Telegram* message: "Bosnian, after you handover with the Irish, await further orders."

The small Icom radio on Ardian's lap burst into life, the volume low but enough to hear it. "That's our boys into the services, and they're clean: nothing since junction two."

Ardian's team of tobacco smugglers were also well-drilled and had complete counter-surveillance on the Irish team.

The van slowly drove into the lorry park. It was two up, an almost identical white Sprinter van. They nose-parked next to Luka, and as planned, the men left the vehicle as if heading to use the services. Luka made sure the special device to unlock the concealment was in the glove box.

"Ardian, you're clear, no one paying any attention." The team in the carpark was keeping watch on the vehicles. The handover of the vehicle keys was to be done in Costa Coffee. Luka ordered two black coffees and moved to the milk and sugar area where a man stood, adding the extras to his drink. Next to him was his baseball cap, with a set of Merc keys inside. That was Luka's cue: he quickly grabbed the keys and left his next to the cap. Key changeover done, Luka and Ardian took a seat in the small seating area of the cafe. The table was filthy and piled high with crap, so Luka pushed it to one side and sat down.

"What now, Luka?"

"We wait for further orders." Luka let out a long breath. The whole situation was getting to him now; he was beside himself with worry about Sally Anne. He knew they wouldn't touch her whilst he was of use to them, but once that changed, she was in trouble. It would be a kill-or-be-killed situation for all involved, including his trusty friend next to him. They both fell silent for a moment, drinking the poor excuses for coffee. "How can you fuck up something as genuine as a coffee bean?" Luka said, looking at his cup. "Fucking awful." He got up and walked over to the bin and ceremonially threw the cup in. Ardian smiled, a rare moment of humour in this living nightmare.

Luka's phone beeped: "A lorry is arriving in thirty mins, collect what they give to you. I will tell you where to bring it."

Luka returned his iPhone to his pocket. Great, more contraband. The police would have a fucking field day. A vehicle full of weapons and fuck knows what else.

"We're clear," Ardian confirmed, and they got into the van. It was immaculate inside; the Irish hadn't left a thing out of place. The vehicle smelled of acetone as they had removed any fingerprints and DNA using a substance made famous by a serial killer — true pros.

Minutes passed like hours. Luka wasn't comfortable sat amongst these people. If they got turned over by some south London drug dealers, they would think Christmas had come early, with enough ordnance to start a proper turf war.

Luka's phone beeped again.

"White articulated lorry, Titan Haulage on the side; SM17 MEG. Pull up next to them once I tell you."

Ardian briefed his team, and they did the same counter-surveillance on the lorry.

Headlight beams illuminated the car park as the large lorry pulled in and the hiss of airbrakes filled the night. The blue lights under the trailer shed a blue-ish shadow onto the ground. The driver got out with a mobile phone to his ear, obviously looking for someone. Luka raised a hand to stop Ardian from moving. "Something's going on my friend. Check out that driver, he's not right. Look how agitated he is."

A black BMW X5 slowly pulled into the car park. The driver looked up from his phone towards the vehicle. It moved towards the lorry.

"That's a meet," Luka said

"What do we do?" Ardian sounded worried.

"Let's see what happens first," Luka replied.

"That's two vans into the services at speed," Ardian's team alerted them. Luka's heart pounded; surely not the police. The vans entered the car park, blue Ford Custom, brand new; hired for cash, no doubt. They both stopped at the rear of the vehicle, the driver moving round with the occupants of the BMW, heavy-set men with tight white t-shirts and bulging muscles.

"Fucking Albanian motherfuckers," Ardian spurted out.

Before Luka could reply, the drivers of the vans jumped into the back of the artic. The unmistakable sound of girls screaming resonated out the back. Luka watched as what looked to teenage girls were offloaded and then roughly thrown into the vans, the doors open, ready to receive their unwilling passengers. The girls looked in a bad way: unkempt, thin and totally panicked.

"People-smuggling cunts! Look, Luka, young kids. We can not let them fall into the hands of those bastards," Ardian growled.

Luka raised his hand. "We can do nothing, my friend, we have a van full of weapons and people we love are in danger. We have to let the poor girls go." Luka struggled with himself more as the days passed. This broke every moral rule in his book. He'd seen too much of this in his homeland. His mind went back to his sister — but she was safe, for now.

As quick as they'd arrived the BMW, followed by the two vans, sped away out the car park and onto the dual carriageway.

"I hope God blesses those girls Luka, because they will fucking need it," Ardian said.

Luka sat in silence. His moral compass was broken, and he knew it.

His phone beeped. "Move now."

"Okay, Ardian, old friend, it's our turn."

Ardian started the engine, and they crept across the car park to the rear of the artic. The driver stood to the rear. Now his live cargo was gone, he had a cocky edge to him.

"Well, well, more eastern Europeans. Your country is that shit then?" The driver's mocking tone niggled Luka.

Luka moved forward, ready to launch at the fat, dishevelled

driver with a huge belly straining his dirty white t-shirt. Ardian grabbed Luka's arm firmly. "Not the time."

The driver smirked. "In here. I'm not humping them for you." He disappeared into the rear of the artic. They both climbed in. The smell of human excrement was eye-watering. The artic was only half full once you pushed through the first lines of boxes. The middle of the trailer was clear. Thankfully, no lights illuminated the rear so they couldn't witness how the girls had been living during their hideous journey.

"Here." The driver pointed to a pallet containing nine large white containers. No labels or wording.

"Fuck this." Luka approached the driver. "I don't fucking care, just offload and fuck off."

"You will have to do it one-by-one; they are fucking heavy. And be careful, the blokes who loaded them at the Karameh Border Crossing said they were fucking lethal."

Great, thought Luka, *what the fuck is this?* It was a liquid of some sort.

It took a while to load the containers in the rear of the van. Both men, now dripping with sweat, sat in the front of the van watching the lorry exit the car park, the array of lights lining the trailer giving it the look of a weird Christmas tree.

He felt the dreaded beep of his iPhone. He read the message, then reread it.

"For fuck's sake."

Ardian looked at him. "What's wrong, Luka?"

"Fucking everything is wrong. It's all fucked."

Chapter 49

Danny Haigh turned as the door opened. Paul Allen walked back in, his phone still in his hands.

"Right, Danny, we have the green light: the team can infiltrate the site now, the authority is in place."

"Roger that, Boss. Get me the Recce team commander on the secure live feed," Danny directed the comms desk operator.

Both men stood in silent anticipation. It had taken an age to get the green light to send the cover recce team into the complex. Danny struggled with why; it seemed as if he was being hamstrung at every step. No doubt the old firm across the river and at MI5 were doing their best to scupper this new organisation with the big budget and new kit. However, he did know the law of the land had to be abided by.

"Boss, on feed now."

Both men turned to the bank of screens. A fresh-faced man appeared, with long blonde hair and an angular face; he looked like a surfer dude.

"Adam Vaudrey. Boss, how are you?"

"All good, Adam. You ready to deploy? We just got the green light off the Headshed here in London."

"Yeah man, all cool, be a two team insert. Once happy, I will do the master probe into the heart of the complex. First light is 0345 hours, so will be off target by 0300."

"Thanks Adam. Remember, get as much as you can but avoid detection at all costs. We don't need this blowing up in our faces." *Hopefully not literally,* Danny mused internally.

"Boss, we have top cover up. Alpha Projects have the Titan drone on circuit for us. Can be airborne for six hours, plenty for our task; has night vision and infra-red so you can track us, and we can also send you live feeds from our head cams."

"Copy all that, Adam. Good luck. Catch you on the airwaves." Danny ended the call. Paul smirked. "Yeah, Paul, he is a surfer-dude type — but an excellent operator." Danny defended his men with a passion.

"So they go in and skulk about to find something on what's inside that camp. Do we have any idea what the fuck this is all about?" Paul sounded exasperated and tired.

"Boss, all we know is that Buzzard is involved in something and it's of importance — but as yet we don't have a clue." He paused. "They had an interest in this Luka Avdic fellow and then it's all gone tits up, with Dom potentially being held hostage."

Paul Allen shuffled in the seat he had taken, his gaze towards the ceiling. "Danny, I know that this is bigger than we both understand. Have we been given this job to fail, or do they rate our chances of a result?" He paused, his chin perched on his finger which he joined to form a spire type formation. "Why do they not let us go in? We always have to wait."

"Well, the wait will soon be over." Both men looked at the clock on the wall; last light was fast approaching.

The room was now a hive of activity as the technicians from Project Alpha went about setting up a battery of screens and other technical gear. Another guy took his seat at the back of the room, wearing a mask like one you'd wear for a VR game.

"Who's he?" Danny asked the operator manning the desk.

"Drone pilot, Boss. He will fly the drone from here; the tech team have taken it to an airfield close to the target Headcorn," the guy replied whilst dialling in various numbers on the high-tech radio gear that surrounded him. "Boss, we're ready to go."

"Okay — everyone, quiet please." Danny brought the room to attention. "Alpha: you ready?" Nodding heads all round. "We good to go?" he asked the Omega operations team.

"All set."

Danny put on his hi-tech headset. "Sierra One One, move now."

"Copy," came the whispered reply.

Screens flickered as various hi-tech images appeared. Head cam footage showed ghostly green shapes from the team as they crawled and crept through the orchards that surrounded the camp.

"RV one."

"Copy."

"They're making good ground, Boss."

The screens for the drone footage burst into life, the camp clearly visible, the outlying village showing white-hot on the infra-red footage.

"Sierra One One, is the drone obvious?"

"Negative," came the muted reply.

Danny looked at his desk operator with a confused look.

"Just checking if the drone can be heard," the operator replied.

The images on the large screens from the drone stabilised and focused, four white dots visible against the green background.

"That's Sierra One One and his team approaching RV two."

The four dots separated and headed into the farm complex slowly, stopping regularly. The entire room went silent, just the hum of the various computer fans kicking in.

"Negative, Sierra One One, no signature from the building to your front."

"That's Sierra One One, about to enter building one," the drone operator announced.

The tension in the room was at fever pitch. Danny felt someone next to him; it was Paul Allen. "Is this wise? What happens if there are people in there?"

"The drone is up with thermal imaging and the teams carry sensitive listening devices that can pick up the breathing of a sleeping man at a hundred yards." Danny was struggling to keep his cool.

"Sierra One One, building checked and empty; moving to building two."

The pattern remained as the teams moved stealthily through the camp. They had reached the southern perimeter and gone firm. The situation report they sent back didn't make for a message Danny or Paul wanted to hear.

"Zero, this is Sierra One One; CTR complete, camp is empty, no one is here."

Paul and Danny sat outside in silence. The night was balmy and the road outside the base was still busy, the tyres of cars humming on the melting tarmac. A plane flew over, lights rhythmically flashing the engines slowly as it made its final approach into Heathrow.

"Heli 147 was offsite for thirty minutes to refuel, and in that time, they bugged out? Come on, Paul, this isn't right."

"What are you suggesting, Danny?"

"I don't know, but it seems we are chasing shadows."

"You look tired, Danny. Go home, get some sleep. We'll regroup in the morning, or in a few hours at least," Paul said, looking up at the sky as dawn broke. Another long night was ending, and tomorrow wouldn't be a good day, both men knew that. Danny wearily got up, finishing the dregs of his brew.

"I'm going to get my head down here, Paul. I want to make

sure the teams are all back to their staging posts safe, then get them reconfigured for the morning." Paul nodded his appreciation. "So, what's the plan?" Danny asked.

"The only tangible lead we have is Luka Avdic. Let's hope he goes home." Allen looked up as another plane flew overhead. "What about the girlfriend? Is it worth putting a team on her? We know her HA, don't we?"

"Yes, we do."

"Okay. Danny, get some sleep, you look out on your feet."

The door to the building opened, casting a long beam of white light onto the grass where Danny and Paul stood.

"Boss, got Adam on the secure line from the FOB, says it's urgent."

Danny picked up the secure phone and scrolled down the screen to find the number. "Adam? It's Danny."

"Alright, Boss, thought I'd give you a heads ups before my CTR report gets published on the Omega live ops link."

"Okay, what's the issue?"

"Well, during the after-action review, or in your language, when we cleared each building on the way out looking for evidence or anything of intelligence use, we came across a building that I would say was a bunkhouse for sleeping and admin. It smelled of food and unwashed bodies. Someone had sanitised the whole place to a high standard, Boss, but under one of the beds we found a packet of cigarettes."

Danny couldn't help himself; the tiredness and fatigue were wreaking havoc on his body and his rational mindset. "Well done for that," he replied, rather disingenuously.

"Boss, I know this sounds bone intel, but I have mates working for Special Reconnaissance Unit and Hereford, so when I found this, I got in touch and they confirmed it." Adam paused. "If you look on the Ops screen, I have an image for you; they are a brand called Al Hamra and look very similar to Marlboro, but this brand is Syrian and not available outside Syria." Adam paused.

Danny let the information sink in; *just as if it couldn't get any worse,* he thought.

"Boss, whoever was using this base was most probably from Syria or had links to that country, to the level they smoke their shitty own-brand cigarettes."

"Okay, Adam. Listen, sorry for being tetchy. Been a long day. But great work from your guys tonight, top job."

"Thanks Boss, quick beer whilst weapon cleaning, then bed for us. Night." The screen went blank.

Danny stood looking at the now-blank screens, his mood dark and the sense of defeat or failure all encompassing. He took stock of the situation: he had no teams on the ground, an operator missing, presumed kidnapped, and little else but the fear of a Syrian team operating on UK soil. He knew Paul had left to go home for a few hours' sleep and then a change of clothes into a suit and off to brief Picton; no doubt feeling like a premier league manager going to see the board after a string of poor results.

Danny laid on his camp cot, too hot to get into his sleeping bag. He was tired, but sleep evaded him. He had a niggling feeling, almost a sixth sense; surely this wasn't coincidence. The helicopter surveillance asset went off target for thirty minutes and they bugged out, sanitising the place so nothing tangible was found. Surely they didn't have a leak. He almost dismissed the theory as an irrational thought because of extreme fatigue. Then an image flashed across his brain: yesterday afternoon, Paul Allen coming back into the Operations Centre, putting his job mobile phone back in his pocket; but what Danny had etched onto his memory bank was the furtive look he had all over his face. Surely *he* wasn't passing information over. But if he was, then to who? For fuck's sake?

Danny lay staring at the ceiling, its metal beams and roof

engineered for a efficiency, grey but boring. *Okay,* Danny mused, *I have a theory so I'm going to test it. I will find out if he's a tout or not.* He knew sleep would evade him, but he needed a plan.

His phone beeped: "What's the plan?" A curt message from Charley. Danny put the phone back under his pillow. *I'll park that one for a few hours*, and with that a fitful sleep engulfed him.

Danny awoke with a start. The place he had set up to be his bedroom had been a storage area when the army had been in residence. He looked at the ceiling some more. *Fuck it, I can't sleep.* He swung his legs off the bed and walked barefooted into the large ops room that was quiet The only person awake the duty watchkeeper; the bank of radios were quiet, the screens blank. Danny got himself a coffee and walked over to his desk and wearily sat down.

"You okay, Boss? You look fucked," the watchkeeper said.

"I think we're all tired mate. Not good when one of us is missing."

The watchkeeper turned to face Danny. "Boss, with my old firm, if one of the guys on the ground went missing, they deployed every asset to get them back safely."

Danny mulled the reply over in his mind, and he didn't have an answer. He knew that they could do more, but he was told to wait or to let it run, or some other bollocks. He returned to his coffee and his thoughts.

Chapter 50

Luka sat alone in his flat. It was the first time he had been back for days, and the place smelled musty, not helped by the sour milk and overflowing bin in his small kitchen. His mood was verging on defeatist. At the very end of the dark road he had long wished he wouldn't have to journey down again.

He didn't understand why the Syrians had moved from Bon Fleur and were now holed up in an industrial unit in London. He had dropped off the weapons and four large blue containers holding what he believed to be a liquid substance. Now he was told to wait. He kept the large white van and, as usual, had parked it away from his flat.

He'd called his sister. She wasn't handling being away from the unit well, exacerbated by the re-emergence of Julia Picton after all those haunted, tortured years. His own mental health was now in question, and he blamed himself totally for the Sally Anne situation. He slept with the demons, if he managed any sleep at all, thoughts of what those savages would do to her if he didn't follow orders to the letter swirling around his mind all night.

He made himself coffee: strong, Turkish style with loads of sugar and a Marlboro red — the combination had become his staple diet. He hadn't eaten for what seemed like months. The only constant in his life was Ardian. Ardian knew nothing about Luka's time in the camp — or if he did, he'd never asked. Ardian had settled down with a family, but now, because of helping Luka out, that family was no longer safe.

Luka's thoughts returned to his own excuse for a life — it hurt that he had never settled down with a wife and children. Maybe Sally Anne had been the chink in his armour. The briefings at the camp had been to have no one in your life that you cannot leave in five seconds flat if you feel the heat around the corner. And he'd stuck to that by the letter. But, he'd never thought his calling would be to assist a psychotic attack on London by a bunch of bloodthirsty Syrian jihadists. He stared out the large old-fashioned sash window to where another day was dawning in the capital. The first red streaks of dawn were breaking through the dark; streetlights were still giving out their amber cones of light; the odd person was heading out for an honest day's work; decent people who didn't deserve random acts of violence in the name of Allah, or hitting back against the great Satan of the US of fucking A. His desire for revenge wasn't as strong as he'd thought, especially once the realism of who would get hurt the most became clear.

His phone woke him out of a deep, tormented sleep. He sat bolt upright, lost for a second, not knowing where he was. However, all too soon he knew exactly where he was; in a living hell.

"Go to the van, instructions are under the seat."

Someone must have placed that envelope in the van since he'd parked it, as he had sanitised it fully when he left it.

He went to the bathroom, and splashed some cold water on his face to wake himself up. The ghost looking back from the mirror was not a pleasant sight. His face was gaunt, eyes sunk deep into his head with dark blue bags beneath them, his pallor that of a washed up drug user. "Fuck me, I look like shit," he said back to the devastating reflection. He looked at the toilet cistern.

He had never expected to call any favours in from George Taylor, happy in the knowledge he was in credit with him. But he had been desperate. His sister was not a problem for Taylor, and she was now a guest at his large country estate perched on the South Downs overlooking the sea. He had only briefly outlined what had happened to her during the war.

Luka now was under no illusion: the time had come to kill or be killed. His life as a lone wolf waiting to avenge his kinsfolk would now have to wait; he had too many people in grave danger not to act. He checked the tell-tale sign he'd left on the cistern lid; it was still intact. He lifted the lid off and retrieved the thick plastic bag. He pulled out the short compact pistol and admired it for a brief moment. Typically Italian in design, and it felt good to hold a weapon again after years of being hidden. He pulled back the top cover to check inside, then placed in the magazine of nine-millimetre Parabellum rounds and let the slide go forward with a metallic clunk. He placed the spare magazine into his pocket and slid the pistol down the front of his jeans.

Casting an eye around his flat to ensure it was suitably sanitised, he exited, then replacing the small tell-tale sign in the door frame.

The morning air was warm and humid. Diesel fumes clung to every breath as the nearby bus stop received the endless flow of buses, transporting people into the city. He closed the main front door behind him.

"Get the feck back into your flat or I will blow your fucking liver and kidneys to shite." The Irish accent had menace to it, but Luka thought he recognised it; he felt the cold, snubbed metal point of a pistol. He now knew the voice but didn't turn around. He duly opened the communal front door, and both men stumbled into the tiny decrepit hallway of the Victorian town house.

Luka was roughly spun around to face the man: it was Kevin Donaldson, his glass eye weeping as ever, his good eye oozing menace. His face flushed red with rage, and he had an unkempt air about him.

"Ye fookin' cunt, your lot stitched me up." His anger got the better of him and he raised an arm to hit Luka with the pistol in his hand.

"For fuck's sake, not here. Anyone can walk out: my flat is up the stairs."

The Irishman nodded.

Luka led Donaldson up the stairs, turned the key, and once inside, closed the door behind them. He pointed to the tiny kitchen.

"Coffee?" Donaldson nodded. "Kevin, I don't have a clue what you're on about." Luka stirred sugar into the two cups of instant coffee he had hastily prepared and sat down at the small kitchen table opposite Donaldson. Donaldson placed the pistol on the table with a heavy clunk. He picked up his coffee and took a loud gulp. He never let up eye contact with Luka. "Honestly, you're going to have to tell me what you're annoyed at."

"Annoyed is an understatement." His voice rose. "The feckin' drugs are shite."

"How do you mean, 'shite'?"

"They're fucked up... not good, for feck's sake. We got them out to our suppliers and within days a kiddie died, and now the Feds are all over us."

"Died? What, an overdose?"

"Nay, not a fecking overdose! They're shit, man — all fucked up, dangerous, and now we've had to take 'em all back." Donaldson paused, taking a loud slurp of his coffee then absentmindedly lit a cigarette, drawing the smoke aggressively up through his nose.

Luka sat in silent dismay. This had huge ramifications for all involved. The Irish element would reap revenge, and after decades of practice they were very good at it.

"It rightly pissed my bosses off and they want this shite sorting."

"Okay, I appreciate the situation looks grim."

"Grim — you fecking what?" He was irate. "Do you know what my lot are capable of? And as it stands, I brokered the deal, so I need to sort it." He paused to light another cigarette.

"What are they proposing to you?" Luka tried to sound sympathetic, but it didn't really work.

"They want all the shite pills taken back, and either the hardware back or money with compensation for lost earnings."

"Any idea of figures?"

"How much? One large."

"What, a hundred grand?"

"Nah, you fecking eejit, a million."

"What? How on earth did they come to that figure?"

"I don't have a fecking clue but that's what's on the table."

Luka sat back in his chair, his mind spinning. What he needed was a plan: could he possibly use the Irish in his favour? He needed to get on with the task he'd been given by Ibro. "Listen, Kevin... I need to go on a task. Make yourself comfortable here and I'll be back as soon as I can, and we can start to work a way out of this mess."

Donaldson looked up from the table, his face craggy and enormous bags under his eyes; the weeping of his glass eye had now dried into a crust. He looked like a condemned man. Luka reckoned he probably was if things didn't change.

"Task? For who?"

"These Syrian cunts have me jumping through hoops." He

decided not to tell Donaldson about Sally Anne being held as a bargaining chip.

"Well, you need to tell them fookers that they're bang in the shit with some nasty wee bastards."

Would they really care? Not a chance. Luka knew this all too well.

Luka got up, placing a caring hand on the man's shoulder. "Grab a shower — there're towels in the bathroom— and help yourself to clothes in my wardrobe." Donaldson nodded in appreciation. Luka left the flat for the second time that morning.

He went a totally unnatural route to where the large van was parked; the route gave him long stretches of straight road, which enabled him to check for any surveillance teams attempting a foot follow. He got to the van and clicked the remote control from a suitable distance away; he didn't trust Ibro and an under-car booby trap would be a great way to announce the arrival of his team and also vaporise Luka in the process.

The indicators flashed orange twice. He entered the van and reached under his seat, pulling out an A4 sheet of printed dialogue. He read the first paragraph; the English was grammatically correct; no way Makki had written this. Luka read it, dreading each sentence as he read on.

"Go to the following address. They will give you some kit and protective clothes. Then go to the address at the bottom and pick up two brothers and bring them here. No deviation off the route entered in the satnav: if you disobey us, we will hurt her."

"Bastards!" Luka shouted. "Fucking cunts!" *My fingerprints are all over that house.* Why the fuck were they returning to Broadwater Farm? He slammed his hands down on the steering wheel. He was getting embroiled deeper with this shitshow, and he wanted blood on his hands from only one person: Ibro Maaki.

He gunned the engine; true to Ibro's twisted word, the satnav was programmed.

Luka waited outside the address for the two men to appear. The gear they had detailed him to collect had been left to collect under a false company name. Hazmat suits and specialist breathing apparatus designed for chemical spills and contamination emergencies, the packaging stated. Six sets. *Who the fuck were these for, and for what?*

This part of London hadn't succumbed to the urban sprawl that made areas like Hackney and Dalston trendy. It had its fair share of ethnic groups and had long since been forgotten about by the police. Drug paraphernalia was ever present, as were the people who drifted the streets, looking for their next fix and a brief respite from reality. For once, Luka could equate to them. The two men appeared from a door between shops selling fried chicken and dry cleaning. The flats above looked seedy from the outside, so the inside stood no hope. They both got in, uttered not a single word, and as Luka eased the large white van into the slow-moving traffic, they burst into animated conversation in a dialect Luka struggled to place but was some form of Arabic.

The journey was uneventful but fully uncomfortable. Luka sensed they were talking about him and wanted nothing more than to pull the vehicle over, drag them both out and give them a good kicking — but that wouldn't help anyone's situation.

Luka employed a couple of anti-surveillance manoeuvres and, when happy, turned into the one-way street to the industrial unit where he had picked up the random poor fucker he had taken in the boot of Ardian's car to the camp in Kent. This part of London had been unscaled since the urban riots of the 1980s, but all the urban regeneration was now gone and the modern concrete square monstrosity was a modern slum of the highest order.

He eased the large van into a space between a battered old van, long since abandoned, and a new-ish BMW, which sat empty. It didn't bode well, Luka thought, suspicious as ever. Luka brought up the rear as they left the van and made their way through the rear gate of the maisonette. The houses on either side looked uninhabited, and both gardens were overgrown and full of filth. The whole place stank and felt like somewhere no one would ever want to be, yet once there it would be impossible to escape.

The boarded-up rear door opened before they had a chance to knock. Luka recognised one of the Syrian team, in his stained green t-shirt, large sweat patches under his armpits, and the smell of body odour that hung in the room like a disgusting guest who wouldn't leave.

Luka had known they would search him, so his Beretta was taped to the underside of the driver's seat in the van. The ritual was the same: they forced him to the floor, foot firmly in the back, and he was roughly searched before being allowed to stand up and literally face the music.

Ibro came at Luka in his normal psychotic manner, his Glock held in his right hand. With the speed of a boxer, he brought the pistol up and rammed it between Luka's eyes at the bridge of his nose. Luka was tiring of this routine; and it had become just that. Routine. He would have liked nothing more than to spread this creature's brain over the filthy walls he was looking at now as he avoided eye contact.

"Bosnian, how do you explain how our base was compromised?"

"I have no idea what you're on about," Luka replied, his mind racing now. If they had left Bon Fleur, where the fuck was Sally?

Ibro pressed the Glock with more pressure into Luka's skull.

"You were one of a handful of people who knew the location." He spoke as if addressing a child.

"Do you fucking think I would do anything like that? From where I stand, you hold all the cards." This seemed to appease Ibro, and he slid the pistol down Luka's face before pushing it into his sternum.

"Yes, Bosnian — do not forget that, or you will pay dearly." He paused, smirking, a horrible evil look. "I hope your sister is enjoying her holiday."

That was the spark.

"You fucker." Luka lunged forward with a speed and aggression that took Ibro by surprise. A jab followed by a hook knocked the smaller man to the ground. Within seconds the tiny kitchen was a scene of chaos. Two men pinned Luka to the wall as Ibro got to his feet, his nose pumping out blood. Luka hoped it was broken for a fleeting second but then realised his momentary lack of self-control could cost him.

"You will live to regret that, you filthy *Taghut*." He turned his back on Luka. "Fuck off, Bosnian. When you're needed, I'll call you. I'll give Sally your best wishes," he said, and laughed as he left the filthy kitchen.

They manhandled Luka out the door, which was locked behind him.

He got into the van, reaching for the pistol and the reassurance it offered. There was no other option; if he didn't take the fight to Ibro and his desperadoes, Sally — and potentially his sister — would get hurt. Whatever these crazy fuckers were planning was going to happen soon.

His only option now was to form an alliance with the Irish, bring down retribution on these fuckers, and stop their crazy, ideological campaign of murder.

Chapter 51

"Charley, listen to me. I know we're all grown-ups, but you have a relationship with Dom and that will no doubt cloud your judgement." Danny was trying to be calm.

"So, you've dragged me over here to sack me?"

"No, but we think it best for you to come off this operation until such time as we can find Dom."

Charley was indignant. "I've done nothing wrong. All my strategic decisions have been sound, and the team have done well."

"Charley, like I said, this is not because of your performance. This is just the basics — that your judgement may become clouded if the Dom situation gets worse."

"Worse? What do you mean by that?"

An uneasy silence followed. Danny sensed Charley was just about holding it together; Dom had been missing for over seventy-two hours, and they'd heard nothing.

"So why are we doing fuck all about going out and finding him? Why aren't we kicking down a few doors? It fucking stinks at the moment."

Danny stood in silence; he had to agree, but couldn't and

wouldn't show it. He had his suspicions about the whole Phalanx situation: was it a large-scale setup of some sort?

A loud knock on the door brought proceedings back to the now. "Boss, you need to see this," the fresh-faced operator said with urgency.

"Okay, coming." He turned back to Charley. "It's for all our sakes, believe me; we could lose everything in a heartbeat. Believe me, please." Danny walked back into the operations centre. "What's up?"

"From the top, Alpha Projects have noticed a distinct reduction in the usual jihadist rhetoric on the dark web and also, known players have mysteriously gone off-grid, so to speak."

"And?" Danny replied.

"Well, this normally happens prior to a big spectacular. The Firm never picked up on this prior to 9/11, and the rest is history." He stopped and turned back to his keyboard and tapped away, his fingers covering the keyboard they way a musician taps the keys.

"So, are we taking this as a combat indicator that something is about to go off?"

"Erm... I think you need to watch this."

The large screen burst into life; the focus was out initially. A man of Middle Eastern appearance — black wispy beard and dark piercing eyes — sat cross-legged on the floor. He was dressed in American combat fatigues and perched on his head was a Gilgit cap. He cradled an AK-47 in his lap. Behind him was a black flag with Arabic writing, with a symbol of a Scimitar.

"Where's this, then? What's it got to do with us?"

"Boss, please watch."

"I am the leader of the El Muz Special Task Force, seeking vengeance at the very heart of the great Satan's plaything." The man on the video paused. "We have come to you to show you that you cannot get away with killing our innocent families, invading our countries and torturing our brothers, so today we fight back."

The camera panned around to two figures sat on chairs. As the camera focused, Charley was the first to let out a gasp, but it was echoed around the gathered operators watching the proceedings unfold. Sat tied to the chairs were two figures dressed in orange boiler suits: one was a woman, medium-length brown hair; the other was Dom Leigh, who sat with his head down, avoiding the camera.

"Oh God, please, no..." murmured Charley, her voice breaking.

"My name is Sally Anne Nixon. I work at the Savoy Hotel in London. I am innocent like so many of their country folk our government has murdered on their illegal crusades. I call on the UK Government to listen to this message, and God bless us all." The woman was clearly reading from a script.

"Check her out now," Danny ordered.

She was cut off by a loud barking voice. A hand grabbed Dom by the hair, yanking his head back. His face was bruised, both eyes blackened underneath.

"This man is a member of the infidels' secret army, who spy on us, kidnap and torture us, and plant these devices to guide bombs to our homes and families."

The man in the combat fatigues held a black square object up to the camera.

"Is that what I think it is?" Danny barked.

"Yes, Boss, it's our brand-new Discovery One tracker, the one Dom deployed."

"How the fuck did they find that?" he yelled. *Now this is no coincidence,* he thought.

The man on the video carried on holding Dom's hair, pulling it back further to reveal his neck. "WE HAVE NO TIME FOR SPIES!" he shouted.

"Allah Akbar," echoed around the room.

From underneath his combat jacket, he pulled out a large knife, a huge sparkling blade with a serrated edge.

"God, please, no!" Charley was hysterical now. "Turn this off now, for fuck's sake."

"Somebody take Charley outside and get her some water," Danny ordered. The room was in shock. The video on the screen paused at a sinister moment: the knife midway to Dom's throat. "Is this live on TV yet?"

Sky News channel was playing on a screen in the corner. "Nothing yet, Boss."

"Right, play it."

The video started again. Dom was tied securely to the chair, but he was frantically trying to move his head from side to side, his eyes side-stepping, trying to keep an eye on the blade.

The man released his grasp on Dom's hair and his head dropped forward once again. The man placed the knife back into his belt. From off camera he was passed a large pair of rubber gloves which he slid on with theatrical difficulty. He was then passed a glass jug of a clear liquid. He held it up to the camera.

"You tried to find this with your infidel armies from our brothers in Iraq, but you failed. This is Allah's poison, so now we can unleash hell on you."

He grabbed Dom by the hair again, viciously pulling his head back. Two men appeared, dressed in the same combat fatigues, though these two had their faces covered. Dom started to struggle, contorting his body in gyrating movements in a futile attempt to escape his fate. Three men were too much for Dom and they held his head in a vice-like grip. One of them grabbed Dom's cheeks and forced his mouth open, then pushed in a rag.

"Oh my fucking god." Danny couldn't take his eyes off the screen.

The man started to pour the clear liquid carefully onto the

rag jutting out of Dom's mouth; he was clearly struggling to breathe. The liquid sank into the rag.

Danny and the group in the operations room were transfixed on the screen, no one uttering a word.

Dom started to convulse, his eyes bulging, clearly unable to breathe; his whole body was now in the throes of a really violent seizure. The man ripped the rag out of Dom's mouth, his desperate battle for breath audible over the shouts of "Allahu Akbar" from the hidden crowds in the room. Blood appeared from the corner of his mouth and nose. Vomit, thick and red, erupted from his throat. The video operator moved the camera to Dom's lower body, where urine was clearly dripping onto the floor. His orange boiler suit darkened with his involuntary incontinence. The camera panned back onto the main poisoner: The Leader.

"This happens every day in Syria. You turn your gaze away and do nothing. Women and babies die like this pig will." He grabbed Dom's hair again, head now lifeless — his face a deep red colour, eyes bulging.

"So, as you did in 2001, you have slept whilst we have worked. And now we are here in your capital and we're going to unleash hell upon you."

A cacophony of sound erupted. "Allahu Akbar, Allahu Akbar, death to the great Satan." The chants got louder and louder as the camera zoomed into Dom's lifeless eyes, still open, frozen in eternity. His face — a vision of hell — had taken on a blueish tinge, swollen like a football, his eyes now blood red. Dominic was dead.

The video panned back to the large black flag and the two crossed AK-47 assault rifles perched below.

"Where the fuck was this posted?" Danny barked.

"Everywhere on social media, Boss. They seem to have a large social media footprint. Alpha Projects are working on voice and face recognition to see if any of them are known."

"Bit fucking late for that." Danny turned to walk out for some much-needed air.

"Boss."

Everyone's attention switched to the screen broadcasting Sky News as the video was about to be aired — but not all of it, as the entire video was too graphic, the newsreader announced.

Chapter 52

Paul Allen looked how Danny felt. They both sat opposite each other on the smart chesterfield sofas, both deep in their own tormented thoughts, the minutes passing like seconds as they awaited their fate.

Paul Allen broke the silence. "Could this be any worse?"

"No," Danny stated. Not only did he have the death of one of his operators to contend with, but also the fact that he'd sanctioned the operator to go undercover with little training.

"Danny — before we go in, just remember Picton is cut from a different cloth: she can leave her conscience at the door like her coat and umbrella. Be under no illusion. She is brutal, but ultimately effective. In fact, she's one of the best."

Julia Picton stuck her head around the heavy mahogany door. "Please, gentlemen."

They both got up wearily, neither wanting this meeting to start.

The office wasn't what Danny had expected of a Prime Minister; it was more like a doctor's surgery. Family pictures adorned the walls and were spread around her desk. She stood, offering her hand, a model of British decorum. Dressed in a smart business shirt and trousers, she looked an archetypal, modern female at the height of her career.

"Please, sit down. Can I offer you a drink? This heat is absolutely draining me." Her accent was educated, calculated. Picton took her seat at the opposite end of the sofa from the PM. "Gentlemen, to say this is a difficult time for us all is somewhat of an understatement, but it would be remiss of me not to do my homework before calling a COBRA meeting."

An uneasy silence settled on the Prime Minister's office, the only noise coming via the open windows, the traffic on the Mall as busy as ever.

"Okay, Ma'am, I'll start." Danny took the lead; he needed to. He felt he had to.

"Please, call me Helen."

"Thank you." Danny recognised the PM's attempt to normalise this break in protocol. Danny outlined the job for inception, not missing a detail; the PM sat animated, taking it all in, regularly checking the file of documents on her lap.

Danny paused, taking a nervous sip of the water in front of him on the large wooden coffee table. "It is my view that we have some form of leak within this operation."

The atmosphere in the room could be cut with a knife. Danny noted the looks between Picton and Allen, as if to say, "get your dog back on a lead," but Danny wasn't in the mood for politics. He had recently witnessed one of his team being killed by an as-yet-unknown person, broadcast live on global TV. So, fuck protocol.

"I really do, Prime Minister; look at the evidence: the factory unit, the camp in Kent, and, above all, the compromise of Dom Leigh." Danny paused, his anger receding.

Again, the room fell silent. The PM was deep in thought.

"Danny, you have a point here. Julia, Paul, anything to add? In fact, it would be nice for your input." Danny sensed the PM getting annoyed.

"Prime Minister, I find it incredulous that we are considering a leak within Tier One anti-terrorist operations," Picton retorted.

"I have to agree," Paul Allen piped up. *Fucking Judas,* thought Danny.

"So, you both seem to think it's a run of bad fucking luck, do you?" The PM's turn to get angry. Neither added anything. The PM stood, then walked back to her desk and took a seat. "Julia, Paul, I would like a moment on my own with Danny, please."

Both of them struggled to hide their feelings but knew better than to argue with the most powerful woman in the free world. They got up and left in silence.

"Danny, I have read up on you. You have walked a road similar to mine: I'm a woman in politics and you're a Black man at the heart of the Security Service. We have both battled against the same barriers, so I want it from the hip, so to speak. The floor is free, so go for it."

Danny left no stone unturned; he outlined the whole task, even his surprise at getting Buzzard as their first target and the job literally spiralling out of their control, as if guided by some unseen hand.

The PM looked confused. "Danny, to be honest, I'm not sure why you were given that target. I'll look into it, but Julia oversees our Tier One enhanced programme."

Tier one enhanced? What is all that about? Danny was confused. "Prime Minister, can I ask you a very frank question?"

"Of course."

"Why did you delay the authorisations for the strike on the warehouse in east London where we thought Leigh was being held?"

"I don't like what you're intimating here. I would never jeopardise one of my operatives: any authorisation across my desk got signed-off immediately."

"Well, the strike by SO19 was apparently delayed and went in at 1700, but we had surveillance footage that the targets had left the premises three hours previously."

"I have to go to the COBRA briefing shortly, Danny, then address the nation. As you know, we are in unprecedented times, but rest assured Phalanx will be at the forefront of the fight. Believe you me, that will not sit well with some of the people in that room." They both fell silent, and the PM got up from behind her desk. "Danny, we're both cut from the same cloth. Here — this is my personal mobile number. Few people have it. If you have any issues, call me... but never, ever let anyone know you have this."

"Helen, are we clear to go operational again? My teams are straining at the leash to get back to the fight."

"Yes, of course; get back out there, and you have my full backing to utilise any assets you need."

"Thank you."

"Use your chain of command — but Danny, if you feel you have no option then call me directly. I will be paying close attention to this until we get these men caught." She offered Danny her hand. Danny took it and shook, and it felt sincere. She held his gaze. "Danny, we *will* catch these bastards and dispose of them in some godforsaken pit. Trust me, I'm onto this."

Danny turned and walked to the door.

Chapter 53

Danny stood behind the lectern, looking out over the assembled teams that made up Phalanx. He paused, a moment of reflection, a moment of respect for Dom Leigh. The last time he'd briefed the team in this large colonial annexe room of Custom House, the situation had been very different.

"Team, these are sad times for us all. To lose a colleague so soon and in such circumstances is quite unbelievable." He paused, inhaling. "But it is the brutal reality of what we're fighting against every day, out of that window on those very streets that we see and hear. Those murderous bastards are here in this city." He pointed toward the floor-to-ceiling windows with their view over the City of London with its skyline of strange-shaped buildings. "It's our task to get back out there and hunt these people down." The assembled group grunted and nodded in approval. "I have met with the Prime Minister, and she has given us her blessing to front this operation and bring those who killed Dom to justice. To achieve that, she has promised us any resources we need."

The large screen behind Danny burst into life; he picked up the remote and started his briefing. He outlined the events so far leading up to the death of Dom and the direction they would take with the limited intelligence now available. He was very careful not to mention the chat he'd had with the Prime Minister; that would have to be kept very close to his chest. He would limit his dissemination of information to his senior command from now on.

The large door opened and one of the Custom House staff motioned to Danny that he had a call to take.

"Team, talk amongst yourselves. There's tea and coffee available. I'll be back as soon as I can."

As he left the room, it erupted into animated chatter, which was a good sign, Danny thought. He would have to elect a new team leader, as Charley Holdaway was now on compassionate leave with suspected PTSD.

Danny eventually found where he had to go in the maze of this huge old building. The door sign read "Target Team South"; it was the drugs intelligence team office. *Why has the person rung the landline here, and not my mobile?* The lady sitting behind the desk smiled politely and pointed to the phone on the empty desk opposite. Danny then realised it was a secure landline, similar to the one he had used whilst in Belfast.

"Any idea who it is?" he asked.

"Just asked for you," she replied.

Danny nodded. "Hello — Danny Haigh speaking."

"Danny, It's Andy Lothian, SIO of Alpha Projects."

"Hi Andy, how are you? Is something wrong? I hadn't expected a call via this means."

"Sorry, yes, I wanted to ensure we were totally secure. Can we meet?"

"Yes, once I've finished here. Should be about another hour."

"My office, if that's okay?"

Danny checked his watch. "Yeah, that's fine." He would need to get back to Whipps Cross ready for action soon. *I hope this is worth it.*

Danny enjoying being out in the open after a long afternoon stuck in the bowels of the large old building that had housed Her Majesty's Revenue and Customs since the 1500s. The air-con never worked, and the place always seemed to be stuck in a musty twilight zone. The streets around this part of the city were full of workers heading for the nearby train stations or standing on the pavements drinking cool pints of beer. Another hot day — now a record-breaking summer, boasted the headline on the *Evening Standard* that was being pushed into unsuspecting hands as they walked past the newsstand. Dom Leigh's story had been held by a court injunction and would be reviewed in forty-eight hours.

Project Alpha, the intelligence and cyber-warfare side of Phalanx, was housed in a nondescript office block just off Cheapside. The choice of location impressed Danny. No one would suspect this rather tired-looking office complex housed the most technically advanced intelligence team outside of Israel's Mossad. The men manning the security desk certainly weren't from RTS Security, as their uniform stated: all were ex-military. Danny could tell these guys knew their shit as they processed him with quiet confidence, then led him to the lift that stood in the middle of the glass atrium, together with a smattering of old sofas and dog-eared magazines untidily arranged on small coffee tables.

"Danny, welcome. Please come in," Andy Lothian said, welcoming Danny into the small office. It was clinically clean, with no photos or personal effects. "Sorry for the location but I know this room is secure and swept for devices every day." He paused, following Danny's gaze as he glanced around the room. "It's designed for debriefing our CHIS; totally secure with very limited access, hence why you were shadowed down here."

"Andy, what's all this cloak-and-dagger shit about? I'm very busy." Danny sensed an edge of uncertainty.

"Okay, I'll get straight to the point." Andy turned to the

large computer perched on the desk "Please bear with me. I just want to get this all aligned."

Danny took time to consider what to do next; the team were on their way back to Whipps Cross FOB and they would redeploy at first light back into Hackney to try to get hold of the only target they had left: Luka Avdic.

"Okay, Danny, here we go." Danny refocused his attention on the screen. "Right, this is CCTV and traffic camera footage that we have highest level access to with a free remit, which means we can do what we like, controlling cameras and traffic lights as we see fit." He paused again as he aligned to rows of images on top of each other. "Danny, since the hideous events of yesterday, I have taken personal control of our after-action review. I have been through literally dozens of hours of footage, initially to ensure we have stayed within our powers and to check we hadn't dropped the ball in anyway." He turned to the screens, getting visibly excited. "So, this is the industrial unit where we believe Dom was taken to prior to being moved to this location: Bon Fleur migrant camp." He pointed to Heli 147's aerial photo of the camp. "Firstly, the Industrial Unit, SO19 can be seen on this camera, turning off the A102 approximately five miles out."

Danny nodded. "Okay."

"Right, check this: we managed to get into the CCTV system of this double-glazing firm across the road from the unit." Danny watched as the shutters opened and the Ford Fiesta sped out of the unit and took the left turn. "If they had turned right, the most logical route, they would have driven into the four-car SO19 team holding off here."

Danny carried on watching as the SO19 team smashed through the shutters of the unit to find an empty location.

Danny sat back. "Could just be bad luck?"

"Well, I thought that too — but now watch this." The screen burst into infra-red footage. "So, this is Heli 147's last footage prior to heading off station to refuel. As you can see, clearly visible are the heat signatures of bodies, showing the camp is occupied." Andy brought up another screen. "These are traffic and police CCTV cameras in the local area around the camp."

Danny watched the footage; nothing out of order or to report about. Suddenly, they all went blank. "What the fuck?" Danny let out a long, exasperated breath.

"One camera out isn't strange, but all those going blank at once. I find that very strange." Andy pointed to the time on the screen. "This is exactly the time Heli 147 commenced refuelling. I checked the flight log; even if we had requested, he couldn't have taken off. Okay, finally, this is the drone footage as the CTR move onto target: no heat signatures, so the camp's empty. What I'm surmising, is that both locations were tipped off that we were about to hit them. I feel there's no other explanation; someone with access to the infrastructure we have enabled their escape. Not once but twice on the same day — and now Dom Leigh is dead. And furthermore, because of the danger to public life, Danny, this has to be signed off at Assistant Chief Level or above." Danny sat staring at the frozen image on the screen. "I wanted to put this to you first before taking it to Paul."

"Can I ask you not to tell anyone else, at least for a few hours? I have something I need to do." Danny's face painted a thousand words, worry lines creasing his brow.

Chapter 54

Luka parked the van on Cadogan Terrace on the opposite side of the park to his flat. He cut through the park using a more direct route than he would have normally chosen, but they knew where he lived so they wouldn't need to follow him.

He entered the communal hallway, the dank smell of wet carpet ever-present, and checked for mail in the letterbox marked with a 9. He found a letter from the Savoy Group, no doubt a disciplinary for not providing a doctor's note for his extended sickness. *At this rate I'll never go back to such normality.*

He gently walked up the creaky staircase to his first-floor flat; he placed the key in the Banham lock, but the door swung open. Luka pulled out his Beretta 900. He swept in, light on his feet, arms extended, pistol locked between his hands, clearing the rooms, the pistol always in the aim. Bedroom clear into the lounge. He sensed it before he heard anything, and swung around.

Donaldson was sitting on the chair, arms resting on the table, his hands cradling his head, his widow's peak prominent and his head covered in the scars of wars fought long ago.

"The fucking door was wide open," Donaldson said as Luka

carried on clearing the small flat, checking the bathroom, then returning to the kitchen.

"Take a look at this." Donaldson pointed to the small TV mounted flush to the wall of the kitchen.

Luka came into the kitchen holstering his pistol in the front of his jeans. Sky News was playing, a live feed with a reporter stood with the MI6 building as a backdrop. Luka sat down. Donaldson stared at him in silence. The image flashed to the video. Luka recognised Sally Anne, and the guy next to her was the one he had taken to the camp.

The video rolled until the point where Dom Leigh was forcibly made to drink the poison. The footage pixilated, then went off. The newsreader stated it was an unknown jihadist group associated with the El Muz front, but no demands had yet been made.

Luka sat in stunned silence; Donaldson broke it. "We are now involved in the biggest manhunt on UK soil, for feck's sake." The crude, guttural Irish accent sounded raw.

Luka smelled alcohol; he must have left to get booze from Mr Patel's shop on the corner. No sign of the bottle though. Luka decided to leave that subject for now, as the enormity of what he had just seen sunk in.

"You, my boy, are tied up to a murder now and, to make matters worse, it was most probably a cop or spy. You better hope them wee feckers on the other side of the river haven't got a bead on ye. Or Guantanamo is where you may end, my boy." Donaldson reckoned MI6's involvement, Luka observed.

Luka hadn't smoked for years, until recently, but he reached over to grab the Marlboro red packet, which sat next to the full ashtray on the kitchen table. He lit one and took a long drag, the smoke filling his mouth with a metallic taste. He drew the smoke further into his lungs. He coughed violently.

Donaldson laughed. "Not so quick, big man." Both men chuckled in a rare light-hearted moment.

"Give us a drop," Luka intimated, pointing at his empty teacup on the table. Donaldson reached into his jacket pocket and pulled out the half-bottle of Jameson whiskey.

"Nice drop." Luka picked up the cup. "Cheers."

They both tapped their cups together. Luka took a sip, and felt the harsh but smooth burning sensation of a quality whiskey descend into his throat. Then the heat hit his stomach; a delightful feeling. They both sat in silence, smoking and drinking whiskey like two old friends without a care in the world, if only for a moment.

Luka broke the quiet. "I'm going to have to sort this. If I don't, anyone I have left in my life — and that doesn't amount to many — will be dead, as well as me."

Donaldson nodded, his glass eye an ever-present wherever his other eye glanced. "For the likes of us poor wee feckers, the war will never end. We will take it to our graves." Donaldson finished the last of his whiskey and placed the cup down. "But these cunts need stopping. That shite was barbaric, the poor bastard."

Both men sat in silence for a while, the constant news feed regurgitating what was already known, and little else. They wouldn't name the victim, and would neither confirm nor deny whether he was an undercover operative of the security services. They replayed the footage again; the image of Sally was too much. Luka grabbed the remote, switched the channel off, and threw the remote onto the kitchen work surface, narrowly avoiding the mass of dirty plates now spilling out of the sink.

"I think we can stop these fuckers, but I need your help."

"Boy, let me tell ye, there is no fecking credit left on your account. Believe me, the only reason the Nutting Squad ain't tracked ye down yet is because they sent me to do their shitty work for them." Luka looked at Donaldson, his face stern, the glass eye seemingly more cold and deep than ever. He reached behind him and pulled out the Browning nine millimetre Hi-Power and placed it on the glass table with a loud clunk. "I was sent to slot you, boy; my bosses don't fuck around. The minute them pills were found to be shite, that was game over in their eyes." He paused, broke eye contact, and looked out of the large Victorian sash window over the rooftops of neighbouring houses. A normal world, a world these two men had never had and never would. "But first I needed to get our hardware back. They fear it's traceable to one of our big shipments from Libya back in the day. Since them feckers got turned over, many records have turned up and my bosses fear it may include what we got delivered off Uncle Gaddafi."

"Why didn't you play along and then slot me?" Luka asked.

Donaldson paused, lighting another cigarette and pouring himself a large shot of whiskey. He offered it to Luka who refused, placing his hand over the cup in front of him. "Because, Bosnian, I'm tired, fecking worn out." He raised his gnarly hands, the left one missing the fingers he'd lost making bombs. "These are blood red, and my mind is, too. Every night I sleep with the devil. This helps." He picked up the nearly empty bottle of Jameson.

"Well," Luka said, "I have a plan that I think may work."

Chapter 55

The hangar was a hive of activity as the team went about their pre-deployment prep with determined vigour. Five cars lined the back wall of the garage, doors open and boots up as they packed the vehicles full of gear. The on-duty paramedics had placed at the front of each vehicle oxygen bottles for med kits. No stone was being left unturned. The loss of a fellow operator dug deep into the flesh of any close-knit team, but to be murdered in such circumstances made it even more hideous.

The door to the operations centre opened. "Briefing in figs ten for everyone."

Danny sat in quiet contemplation at his desk. He hadn't been home for days and this had become his de facto home — and prison — of sorts. A diet of coffee and fast food had given him a bloated look; he felt like shit and had begun smoking again.

The battery of screens on the walls flickered into life, with interactive maps and live footage of today's target area. The bank of hi-tech secure communication systems was a myriad of flashing lights. The entire team was straining at the leash to get back out.

The team assembled into the room, taking their seats in surveillance car team order, expectant faces beaming back at Danny as he wearily mounted the podium.

"Team, it's a great feeling to go live again, and we must keep in the back of our minds that revenge is a dish best served cold." He gathered his thoughts, and to get breathing time, as he felt tears welling up and a burning sensation in his chest. "We only now have one lead, Luka Avdic. Of interest, it seems this lady—" An image flashed up onto the large screen behind the lectern of the woman and Dom, just before they killed him. "This is Sally Anne Nixon. We believe she is the secret girlfriend of Luka Avdic. Which leads to the question of why they have kidnapped her as well. The main train of thought is that she is being held to ensure Avdic does exactly as he should do."

"Why keep her secret, Boss?" came a voice from the crowd.

"Maybe because his Muslim faith won't allow it; or, more likely, he is the classic lone wolf, as they say, not allowing anything in your life that you cannot drop in five seconds flat when you feel the heat around the corner." The crowd murmured.

"Boss, phone," the duty watchkeeper said.

"Excuse me, please. Grab a brew, and I won't be long." He sat down at his desk. "Danny speaking."

"Danny, it's Helen."

"Sorry, who?"

"Helen Jones, the Prime Minister."

"Sorry, Ma'am, um, Helen, bit blindsided. Just giving a final brief to the team before they deploy onto Avdic."

"Well, I have an update for you, which I would like to give you face-to-face and which may affect your brief." She paused. "I've just had to call a COBRA meeting. As you can imagine, Saturday morning went down well."

"Is it really Saturday?" He'd lost total track of the days and times; he should have been on the football run, but that was a normal life and his was far from normal. Danny knew that for sure.

"My intention was to brief them about the tragic events and highlight my chosen response, but late last night I got a call from a scientist in Belfast." She again paused, shuffling papers. "It seems there may be a link between the Syrian ASU and Irish paramilitaries. To cut a long story short, a boy died of a drug overdose, or so they thought, but it wasn't that at all. A switched-on scientist at the NISIL lab tracked down the drug — it's Captagon, the drug of choice of jihadists, apparently." Both sat in their own spaces in silence, piecing together this fucked-up jigsaw. "Danny, you worked in Belfast for years; could it be possible these two sides would do business?"

"Possible, and probable, given the right circumstances."

"Go on," she encouraged.

"Well, the old school are bored and not very good at peace and want to re-engage, so to speak, but they don't have the funds they once had and all lines have dried up, especially the American and Libyan links. So, in my view, if the chance occurred, they'd do business."

"Business of what kind?"

"They would exchange weapons and expertise for a commodity they could sell for a huge profit. And that's drugs, for sure." Danny had a thought, a flashback to the video footage of Dom's murder. He opened up his silver MacBook, furiously tapping the keys. He brought up the video. He played it: the evil man with the wispy black beard and piercing piggy eyes sat cross-legged, cradling an AK-47. Danny paused the video. "Helen, if you look at the start of the video, the man speaking is seated in front of a black flag." A pause.

"Yes, I see it."

"He's holding an AK-47 Russian variant and in good condition; they'll have sourced these in the UK. They wouldn't have risked bringing these in, especially the route they'd have taken."

"So, your point?"

"My point is that only one group of people have access to this type of weapon on the mainland: Irish paramilitaries."

"Oh my God." Her voice tailed off. Silence filled the void for long moments.

"Helen, exactly that; this takes on a whole extra dimension. You know as well as anyone from your time as Home Secretary how proficient and murderous they are; and if they want to get their name back on the map, what better way?"

"Are they not ideologists, though?"

"Not anymore, just murderous thugs, very similar to the fuckers who murdered Dom. Excuse my language, Helen. Please."

"No problem, and I couldn't agree more. Danny, do you have any links back in the province? Be good to get a feel for the atmosphere over the water."

Danny smiled inwardly at the PM's use of operator level terminology. "Yes, Helen, I do. I know exactly the guy, and he'll be only too happy to help."

"Great, get onto it please. And Danny? These conversations are between us."

"Of course, Ma'am."

Chapter 56

Luka eased the large white Sprinter van into a space and turned off the engine. He checked his *Telegram* message again: "Wait outside garages at 29–58 Turpin Way, Holland Park Estate."

I'm in the right place. The estate was very similar to Broadwater Farm: square, brick-built maisonettes, two perched on top of each other. Beneath them, lines of garages with one communal entrance, an urban designer's bright idea to negate theft and vandalism. It turned out to be a criminal's paradise, creating excellent storage facilities for contraband goods — and worse.

Luka sent a simple message. "Outside."

The reply didn't take long: "Wait."

Luka took in his surroundings. A group of young adults walked past him, giving him the eye, all dressed the same, in low-slung jeans, chunky white trainers and black hoodies, with hoods up. Each carried a small man-bag slung diagonally across the chest. Luka stared back as they walked past, one of them knocking into the wing mirror in an act of defiance.

Two men turned the corner. They were older than the previous gang, dressed in green trousers and shirts with heavy work boots. As they got nearer, Luka noted the logo of Islington Council Gardening Department. Both looked Middle Eastern and had black beards and scowls. Luka kept eye contact with them: he didn't like the look of these two. One of them walked around to Luka's side of the car and, with a heavy hand, knocked on the window. Luka turned to face the man; a hand pointed into the underground garage area.

"Reverse into bay thirty-two," he said in heavily-accented English. Luka noticed the same small crescent-shaped tattoo on his hand that Ibro had.

Luka managed to manoeuvre the Sprinter van into the bay, a large space within a steel cage. All along this underground space were similar units.

"Open the doors." A loud slap rattled the side of the van.

Luka jumped out and came round to the rear of the vehicle. Both men were in the back of the lock-up, pulling on respirators and large gloves. Four large plastic barrels sat on a pallet. Between them they carefully picked up the barrels and loaded them into the back of the Sprinter. Luka looked on. *What the fuck is in those barrels?* They must be the ones he had collected off the lorry from Europe. He hadn't been offered any protective clothing when he handled them, and he wasn't offered any now.

"Take these back to Ibro."

"Where's my safety gear? And, actually, what am I carrying?"

The larger of the two squared up to Luka. "Fuck you, *Taghut*. We all hope you fucking die along with the infidels. You don't deserve any protection." He turned his head slightly and spat on the ground, pushing past Luka and returning into the lock-up.

Luka got in and drove away, taking it very slowly.

. . .

DANNY SAT BACK, assessing the gigantic map on the screen to his front. Islington wasn't the easiest area to mount covert surveillance, but the team had done well to get close to Avdic without a clear third-party interest. The Holland Park area was new ground to this operation, and Danny was keen to get into that underground lock-up to work out at why Avdic was there.

"Boss, footage is back from Alpha Projects."

"Get it on the screen." The images appeared; excellent quality, considering it was from a body-worn camera. "Have we got face recognition on these two yet?" Danny turned to his watch keeper.

"Alpha is on it."

What the fuck is this game of cat and mouse all about? He picked up his mobile and went outside the building into the cool of the shade, the overhanging trees providing cover from the baking heat. He hated anything political and didn't enjoy having to play his boss, but he was desperate to ensure Dom's death hadn't been totally in vain. He scrolled down his iPhone and found the number — under a fictitious name — and hit the red phone symbol.

"Hello — can you please give me ten minutes?" The PM sounded harassed.

Danny pocketed his phone and went back into the operations room. The banks of radios and interactive screens were busy and noisy as the surveillance team kept a covert hold on Luka Avdic. Danny walked up to the main watch-keeper.

"Where are we?" Danny looked up at the flashing dots on the screen; the luminous red dot was the all-important one.

"Boss, it seems he's heading back to Broadwater Farm; still one up, Avdic, two unknown IC3s, last seen at Holland Park Estate. We have assets ahead to receive him."

"How is it on the estate?"

"Pretty hostile, loads of third-party interest. Young gangs are the worst. The team regularly rotate; most of the team are on foot, and anyone sat in cars would get blown."

"Good, very impressive." Danny walked back to his desk. He had already written out the search warrant and would normally send it to Paul Allen for sign-off, but he was still suspicious. His phone vibrated. He dashed outside.

"Hello, Helen."

"Danny — sorry about that. I was hosting a Cabinet meeting, deflecting pressure from the media to lift the ban on reporting."

"I can imagine." Danny paused, gathering his thoughts. "Helen, we currently have Avdic under surveillance. He recently went to a lock-up in north London on a pretty dodgy estate. I believe he picked something up and I want to search the garage. But..."

"But what, Danny?"

"Well, normally Paul Allen would sign off the authorisation, but I'm not sure I trust him."

"You're making some big allegations, Danny. Paul's a Branch Head."

"Ma'am, I know, and it doesn't sit well with me. But I have a dead operator on my watch and someone leaked vital intel which led to his death."

"Okay, here's what's going to happen. I'm authorising a Section Eighteen search on grounds of national security. I'll prepare it now; you will tell no one in your chain of command, on my orders."

"Okay, thanks, Ma'am. I think whatever they're planning is imminent."

"Yes, so do I."

"One more thing: I plan to fly to Belfast later to meet with one of my old informants. The man who took my place has been putting pressure on him and apparently, he has something big for us. I'm hoping he can confirm the Captagon link."

"That's fine by me. But please be careful and trust no one."

"Thanks, Ma'am."

"Call me once you're back and let's hope we have something tangible to track these people down."

The call ended and Danny walked back into the ops room.

"Boss, Avdic has gone firm to the rear of a property in Broadwater Farm, a maisonette. Alpha are checking council records to see who the tenant is exactly."

Chapter 57

Danny Haigh and his trusted colleague, Andy Carr, left the safe haven of Palace Barracks and headed initially towards Belfast, then on onto the ring road towards the coast road and the town of Newcastle. A stream of red lights stretched away in front of him, glowing in the dusk as people made their way home. The covert earpiece he wore kept up a live commentary over the secure radio. Since the briefing from the professor from the NIFSIL lab, the pressure on the intelligence services had been huge; from the very top of the tree, they had been bluntly told to leave not a single stone unturned to find out why Captagon was being distributed in Belfast clubs and pubs. The man he was about to meet was not a decent human being in anyone's book, but no one would care if he could shed any light at all on this mystery.

Danny had flown in from London on the last evening flight and had made his way to Palace Barracks on the outskirts of Belfast on his own, with no covert collection from the military side of Belfast Airport anymore. He waxed lyrical that, since the so-called end to the Troubles, everything seemed to be in slow motion and not anything like the kinetic days of old, when three thousand troops were based in Northern Ireland. The

Province Tactical Communication Net was quiet, and the radio traffic was now much more mundane. His call sign Tango Seven would be annotated on the Route Sheet board and his vehicle tracked; ironic, he thought, as he was about to meet the most prolific informant of the nineties, and he was on his own.

Back in the day, he would have had the "Troop" (an SAS unit permanently based in Northern Ireland) supporting him in their upgraded Audi A6s, carrying enough ordnance to start a minor war. If he got hit now, it would be the police service of Northern Ireland's tactical support group who would react; that is, if they weren't too busy.

"That's Tango Seven at Blue Two towards Blue Three." His updated position would be constantly logged on the TSG ops board back at Palace Barracks.

Danny turned to Andy. "Do you believe the link between the gang we're chasing and the Irish?"

"Danny, you know the old boys are getting restless. They're hardly going to be happy stacking shelves at Tesco, are they?"

"It's a major step and a break from old rules."

"Those rules are long gone. The Loyalists used to be more involved, but now both sides see it as a commodity, and they're desperate for money. The organisation is penniless."

He liked to take the less obvious route to Silent Valley and the town of Newcastle, which afforded a couple of good back doubles he could use to see if he had tails, without letting the vehicle following knowing he was onto him, which might ultimately save his and his informants' lives.

The lights of the houses and shops illuminated the wet pavements and roads as night took its hold.

Danny left the confines of the town and headed deep into the country, his headlights burning into the rainy night, casting shadows deep into the darkness. The rain was so heavy that big droplets leapt back up off the road.

They'd built the Silent Valley Reservoir to gather water

from the Mourne Mountains, a remote location ringed by the natural security of those mountains. It also made for a great meeting point when an MI5 operative wanted to ensure he could meet his informant unnoticed.

He liked this venue and had used it before; it was far enough away from Belfast to ensure that even the most bone bloke could sanitise himself and ensure nobody was following him before entering the meeting.

Danny had taught Andy the covert art of handling the informants well. The drill never changed, always getting his rats to enter the location before them. Each informant was issued with an IR strobe light, unnoticeable to the naked eye but when viewed through NVGs it was like a beacon. The standard operating procedure was to place it on the dashboard if the meet was on.

They slowed and turned off Head Road and into the Silent Valley Park.

"Tango Seven complete, Bravo One." Danny's heart started to beat faster; it seemed like an age since he had been operating on the ground. His body tensed; if this was a setup, they would hit now.

The headlights allowed a full illuminating sweep of the car park as he manoeuvred the car into a vacant space.

Just two cars, Andy saw using the NVGs; he killed his lights, and saw the regular pulse of the strobe light, bright and true on the dashboard of the car opposite, putting a sinister shadowy grey glow into the car and silhouetting its occupant in a ghostly manner.

"That's our boy, Danny."

An innocuous Facebook page was used to communicate between them. A text message alerting to a new post beeped on his phone with the simple, coded message: "Having dinner with an old mate tonight." Using a pre-organised Facebook message, all the contact had to do was 'like' the post and Andy would know all was good for the meet. Social media had a use, after all.

The meet was on.

"We're good to go."

Andy broke the silence on the Province net. "Stand by, stand by," he said, the warning for all to keep the net clear as something was happening, or life was in danger.

Danny felt his hand gripping tight onto the Glock 19 pistol perched beneath his right bum cheek, his senses on over drive, especially his hearing.

They heard footsteps approaching the rear passenger side of his car. He reached back and checked on the rear seat for the G3 7.62mm assault rifle which was made ready, hidden under his trusted Barbour jacket, in case it went noisy. Andy took no chances; he couldn't afford to.

It seemed like an age. The night was pitch black, with just the sound of the rain battering onto the roof of the car.

A tap on the rear passenger window startled him; two taps with what might have been a wedding ring.

It was his man, so Andy broke the safety seal and hit the unlock button on the Toyota Averis. It looked like a family saloon but far from it, with its armour and upgraded engine and brakes.

The door opened and the man got in. Alpha Whiskey: the code name for Frank Mulhern, one-time member of South Armagh's best and most destructive ASU, and one of the best informants the British Army had ever nurtured. Andy hit the central locking: safe again.

"AW complete, Griffin."

Andy could smell the cigarettes on his breath and probably a few cans of Tennants lager. *Dutch courage. Drink driver as well; what a twat.*

"Hello, Frankie, how are you? Bit wet?" Danny said to begin

the conversation. "Thought all the money we paid you, you'd have a decent jacket for the occasion."

"What the fuck are you doing back here?"

"Nice to see you again, Frankie. How's tricks?" Danny replied sarcastically.

"Fuck off. Was great until you got in touch. I thought we were all done with this shite," he stated in his guttural Belfast accent.

Andy cut him dead. "Oi, you scumbag piece of shit, we're never done. You sold your soul to the devil years ago and that means when we call, you come running." He paused. "Because, one word from me to the boyos and you'll find yourself strapped to a fucking gas cooker in some shit hole farm in Dundalk until you tell the Nutting Squad everything you know. Then they'll feed you to the pigs, after they chop off your bollocks for good measure. You know how much they hate people like you." Andy shifted in his seat and stared long and hard at Frankie: it was the look of a man who was good to his word. "Anyway, how's Robbo?"

Frankie shot Danny a disdainful glance. "So, have you got me any info on what I asked, or what?"

Frankie Mulhern was not a pleasant person; his only god was money, and this was used to feed his other big addiction: gambling. Ironically, Frankie's sister was married to a member of the PIRA discipline unit known as the "Nutting Squad". James (Robbo) Robertson was a nasty man with no compassion and a psychopathic nature; the love of his sister was Frankie's golden ticket to protection. He had never made the big time as a member of an ASU, nor had he become a technical expert in bombs or anti-surveillance; he had merely been around the fringes doing low-grade courier and driving jobs. However, it didn't stop him big timing it in the pubs and betting shops where FRU (agent handlers) had approached him, offering him money to someway pay off the enormous gambling debts he had racked up. Now he was a low-level criminal, no doubt doing minor jobs for the PIRA command team that were still active and plying their trade throughout the province.

"Unfortunately, when you sell your soul to the devil, however long it may be, he will come calling," Danny said to no one in particular.

"I've been trying my hardest, believe me, but all I know is it's something big and involves the old school eighties crew, as they had a big meet on the mainland."

"Well, I'm fucking overwhelmed with that gem — are you taking the piss? Some senile old players, having a beer, watching the Old Firm game, discussing the old days. THAT'S BOLLOCKS," Andy screamed.

"Serious. I saw Ray Kennedy with my own eyes."

"Ray Kennedy?" Danny blurted, now suddenly interested.

Raymond Kennedy had been a member of the seven-man PIRA council during the height of the Troubles. He had single-handedly brought the organisation out of the dark era and was rumoured to be the main player behind the links with Gaddafi and Libya, allegedly instructing at their terror-training camps.

"All I know is that Robbo had to secure the venue with some of his boys, and that Ray and some others were discussing a major issue about future funding and new commodities to trade."

"You're sure it's funding, or is it another of your bullshit guesses?"

"Positive. You know Robbo speaks openly at home; he said it: big money for the launch of a new offensive. He mentioned they had re-opened some of the big weapons caches on the mainland." He paused. "He also mentioned it would be all ours, and that no other firm in Belfast or the province would have this."

"WHAT THE FUCK IS... THIS?" shouted Danny; he wasn't annoyed but was using an old school tactic. "Okay, enough," he snapped. "Now fuck off and find out what this is. Get back to your fellow creatures and put some meat on the bones. I want to know what the link is, and fast." Danny nodded towards the car door, a sign the meet had finished.

"T-Seven, that's AW complete, his Charlie and mobile, I'm backing."

"T-Seven complete and backing," came the reply.

Danny knew this was big. The jigsaw was slowly being pieced together; it seemed the weapons being used by the Syrians were supplied by the Irish dissident groups.

He was happy that AW was not being tailed so he dropped a gear, overtaking AW and heading back towards Belfast and a secure chat with London.

As the small houses and villages flashed past him in a blur of rain and mist, Danny went through a mental checklist of operational requests, number one being a RIPA request for the phone tap on Ray Kennedy to be re-instated asap. If that era of player was involved, this was a major swing in the province's situation.

His thoughts drifted as he passed lonely cottages with their lights on. Behind every window is a story, and how true that would prove.

Chapter 58

Luka sat alone in his flat. He'd been told to go away from the house in Broadwater Farm and come back later that night. He prepared strong coffee and sat back down in the kitchen. He waited, but he knew he didn't really have that luxury. He'd been deliberately lax on his anti-surveillance drills, in the event that he was being followed; he thought it best to let himself be caught than to allow the impending hell to be unleashed on London. He couldn't go to the police, as the gang had Sally Anne. Then again, he had no idea where she was now.

The buzzer to his flat rang. He went to the window, checking the street by using the long white voile curtain as cover. It reminded him of the sniper screens his father had put up in his house as the fighting had neared his town. He could make out a bald head and widow's peak, and the cheap red Lonsdale jacket. He pressed the door release; he heard footsteps, then a stumble and muted swearing. Donaldson blustered into the flat, and it was clear he was drunk.

"Aye, I'm a wee bit pissed, Bosnian." A total understatement: Luka could smell the alcohol on his breath from across the kitchen.

"For fuck's sake, this isn't going to help."

"Well, let me tell ye, my bosses have told you to go fuck yourself. They won't help, and they want the goods back."

"And what the fuck did you say to them?"

"It was a one-way conversation. These boys don't fuck about; they are seriously pissed off, and because I brokered this deal with Zac, now I'm in it up to my wee neck."

Luka sat back down and for the umpteenth time, contemplated his lot with another strong coffee. He knew he had to act, and fast. He'd be back out soon to do whatever Ibro dictated him to do. Donaldson sat opposite, staring at the wall, his glass eye an ever-present menace. The clock on the wall seemed to be moving out of sync with time; he only had an hour before Ardian and his tobacco-smuggling gang turned up to assist Luka on tonight's grim mission.

"So, you're positive your side will not offer any help to sort this out?"

"Correct, they won't give you fuck all. Like they said to me, they wouldn't give us the steam off their piss."

Charming, thought Luka. He was fast running out of options. He needed to sort out the Syrians and the only way to do that was to take the fight to them. But, as it stood, he only had a drunken, one-eyed Irishman and a bunch of middle-aged tobacco smugglers with no hardware and little knowledge of how to take out a jihadist active service unit. *Fuck it, I have one option left: George Taylor.*

Luka got up and went into the bathroom. He opened the airing cupboard and dropped to his knees. He untwisted the red cylinder that would normally hold a thermostat for a hot water tank, but this one was false. The bottom of the tank was false, and held a secure space for contraband. Luka reached in and pulled out his small burner phone; this was a real gamble, but what option did he have?

He found the number and pressed the green phone symbol

to connect. The phone rang out for longer than was normal, but didn't go to voicemail.

"Hello. A pleasant surprise." Taylor's voice was heavily accented.

"Mr Taylor, I need to see you. I have a business proposition for you."

"Really? Sounds interesting. Usual place, eleven o'clock."

"Many thanks, sir."

A man like George Taylor did nothing for free. On the face of it, he was a pleasant, self-made businessman from a tough background. In reality, he was a ruthless killer, instrumental in large-scale criminal activity, cross-border and with some thoroughly nasty business partners. Links to Irish paramilitary groups were never proven, but almost certainly true.

Luka had to make sure he knew where the large cash bundle was that Ibro had brought over to finance this trip and fill up the coffers of various movements within London. Luka had only seen the holdalls when he had taken them from the service station when he arrived, but from various *Telegram* messages he had received, they contained around a million dollars; no doubt American cash, stolen from the Sunni tribes in Iraq who had turned against the movement in favour of American greenbacks.

His phone rang. It was Ardian. "Stay outside, my friend, I'm coming down." He didn't want his friend seeing the drunk Irishman, who was now prostrate on the leather sofa in the minimalist lounge. *If he pisses himself, I'll be fuming.*

Luka closed the door quietly and made his way down the stairs. His phone beeped. "All clear."

Ardian is a top man. Luka knew he could rely on him and was confident he would assist in the plan. Luka only hoped he had until the morning.

"Where are we going, my friend?" Ardian turned to face

Luka. "You look like shit. When did you sleep last?" The comment didn't help, and anger surged through Luka.

"I'm fine, just drive." He immediately knew he was out of order. His friend kept quiet and simply drove. Luka remained silent a while. "Sorry Ardian, you're right," he finally said. "It's getting to me, the whole fucking situation. Sally really worries me. Those fuckers are animals, and she is so naïve to the world, as we both know only too well."

They both fell silent. The roads were less busy as people enjoyed an evening in the sun, drinking beer and eating barbecued food. They went through the Blackwall Tunnel, under the River Thames, large skyscrapers dominating Canary Wharf flashing red beacons to warn off the planes en route to the nearby London City Airport.

"What're we up to tonight? Why do my boys need to come out to play?"

"Pattern of life on some security guards. You bring the night vision and radios?"

"Yes, all in the boot and ready to go."

"Great." But all Luka could think about was his meeting tomorrow with George Taylor: his last chance, otherwise it would be nothing more than a suicide mission.

Chapter 59

Danny was awoken by the safety belt warning as the plane started its early morning approach into London Heathrow. He'd been away for less than thirty-six hours in Belfast and was keen to get back to the team as they carried on with the surveillance of Luka Avdic. Down below, the early morning traffic on the M25 was at a standstill, and the grass around the large reservoir on the edge of the runway was brown, scorched by the relentless sun.

Danny rubbed his eyes; his head ached slightly, courtesy of the beers he had shared with Andy Carr the previous evening. He settled back into his seat and watched as the ground approached him. The plane touched down with the smooth precision expected of British Airways and it didn't take long to taxi to the stand. As the sky bridge was being connected to the aircraft door, Danny turned on his phone. Messages came flooding in; mixed in with the operational chat, he had a message from Paul Allen: "Call me when you receive this" And another from the only number with a fictious name, the PM's private line: "Lock-up was clear, nothing, clinically clean as before."

Danny sat back in his seat and let out a long, slow breath. He'd cooked his goose with his boss now for sure, and he was nowhere nearer catching Dom's killers.

He got through passport control quickly, the airport quiet at this early hour, and made his way out to the taxi rank. A man in a high-vis vest hailed a black cab and Danny jumped in. For a fleeting moment, he thought about going home for a shower and breakfast with his family. But he soon dismissed the notion. "Cartwright Street, please." The driver nodded and eased the cab down the ramp and onto on the perimeter road. He eased back into the rear seat of the cab, the window down, blowing cool air into his face. *Different to the incessant rain in Northern Ireland.*

Danny was dozing in the back as the radio played a news station, but he only had one ear on it. He was fully focused on the shitshow that he faced once back in the office.

"Oh, fuck me, can you believe this?" the cab driver blurted out.

"Sorry, mate, what're you on about?"

"Listen, mate: another of those jihadist videos has been released. It's on Sky TV now."

"Turn it up, please."

The old cab driver obliged. The radio presenter was describing a newly-released video from the gang responsible for the death of Dominic Leigh, the undercover police officer.

Danny's phone rang. "Boss, you online?"

"Yeah but haven't got visual, only voice."

"It's that cunt again. He's saying the war is soon to begin and the pain his nation has felt will be coming to our doors soon." The watchkeeper paused. "Frank Gardiner's on the TV and he reckons they've released it at this time because families will be watching breakfast-time TV before the school run, maximising the fear factor."

Danny sat back, the back of his shirt damp with sweat. His phone vibrated. "Sorry mate, got to go... Hello, Danny speaking."

"It's Paul. Come straight to my office."

"Okay, be about twenty minutes."

Danny didn't get a goodbye from his boss. He thought of phoning the PM, but he reckoned she'd be busy; the city would now be in full panic mode.

Luka sat in his kitchen; he was dog-tired after a sleepless night watching guards patrol a large complex. *How fucking pointless, just to keep us occupied.* Donaldson was still on the sofa, talking loudly in his sleep; a haunted man, and Luka knew enough of those. He moved to the sink to refill the kettle. The TV, on as background noise, caught his eye.

He turned up the volume and sat down as Ibro Makki spoke, sitting cross-legged and dressed in combat gear, with the AK-47 cradled in his arms, the black El Mudžahid flag dominant behind him. Luka's heart sank; please — not Sally. "Please, no," he whispered.

"You have seen what we are capable of — so now is the time: we are here to gain revenge for the people of free Syria, and our leader and great fighter for the cause, Qasem Soleimani, who you murdered in cold blood. You are lapdogs to the infidel pigs. Innocent women and children, just like you, now sitting with your children eating breakfast, are slaughtered every day: bombed, shot and burned to death in cellars. My family has no food. My village has no clean water. A regime you have armed and supported in the past brutalises us. Now is the time for you to suffer. To be slaughtered in your homes, to have to give your children dirty water, to not be able to clean their wounds for fear of infection. Today the tables turn. You will know what it is like to live in Aleppo. We have brought you a present from our friends in Iraq. You tried to find it and couldn't. Now we have added something to make it even more special for your people."

Luka knew he had to act to stop these crazy psychos. He picked up the burner phone and scribbled a text: "Sir, can we meet early? Things have taken a turn for the worse."

"Okay, same place. My boys will keep watch."

Chapter 60

Danny paid the driver and told him to keep the change. His phone pinged nonstop as his team kept up the pace. He dodged through the slow-moving morning traffic crawling along Embankment towards the centre of London. The police were certainly out in force, and the traffic did seem lighter than usual.

Danny showed his pass to the security guard, who scanned it and opened the turnstile gate. He made his way up the corridor; it felt like a walk of shame. The corridor smelled of floor polish and potent wood varnish; it was dark and oppressive, a classical colonial building. The nondescript corridors had no name plates, just small blue squares with a number denoting the office location for emergencies. Room 389. Danny knocked.

"Enter," came a muffled voice from behind the door.

Danny walked into the large office, untidy in a busy way, the desk piled high with paperwork, and family photos adorned the wall behind the desk.

Paul Allen was sitting behind that desk, his head down, reading some correspondence. "Sit, please." He pointed to the sofas. Danny took his seat like a naughty schoolboy awaiting his punishment. The office was near-silent, the only sound the background hum from the busy Lower Thames Street and the methodical ticking of the large Customs clock that sat majestically behind the chief's desk.

The phone rang, breaking the quiet. "Hello — yes, we're both here... okay, we're en route." Allen pushed his chair back and retrieved his suit jacket and placed it neatly over his arm; far too hot for wear it. He motioned for Danny to follow him as they left his office in silence. Outside, heat reflected off the pavement and the huge concrete and glass buildings that surrounded them as they made their way to the meeting that had just been sprung on them both.

The pavements were quiet and the small tables that were squeezed onto them outside the coffee shops were also surprisingly empty. Danny reckoned people had stayed at home because of the latest El Muz video, that was now viral.

"Where are we going, Boss?" Danny asked.

"Picton has called a meeting," Allen almost spat, obviously pissed off with Danny.

Danny decided that discretion was the better part of valour and stayed silent for the rest of the walk. Both men were sweating profusely as they entered the modern building that housed Branch Eighteen in the heart of the financial district close to the Bank of England. Great cover: everyone in that area was looking for the richest banker with the largest entertainment budget, not spies. Danny was impressed again.

The interior of the building was cool and corporate. A uniformed guard sat smartly behind the reception. A huge gold logo adorned on the wall behind him, which declared "McM Consultants".

"It's their cover story," Allen grunted, collecting his things off the metal detector belt and heading for the lifts. Danny noted two men sitting in the reception and waiting area: no coffee, and the papers and magazines lay untouched. Danny eyed them and they avoided his stare; *who the fuck are they?*

Danny wasn't feeling the love at the moment; was he about to be sacked?

Allen led the way down the corridor, the door at the end looming large. He stopped and knocked sharply.

"Enter." Paul opened the door. "Come in, please." The office was larger than Danny had expected, with its own boardroom within behind frosted glass. Picton made her way toward the door to this inner sanctum. Danny noted a shadow of someone sitting inside. So, it was a set-up: he was now convinced he was getting fired.

Danny entered the room last. The large oval table was neatly laid out with notebooks and bottled water, and looked exactly as a corporate boardroom would.

"Hello Paul, Danny." The Prime Minister sat there as serene as ever, calm and calculated. *Fuck me, not expecting this.* Danny's mind was now racing. "Please, gentlemen, sit down. Grab some water, and a tea or coffee." Both men grabbed a bottle of the cold Evian, refusing the offer of a hot drink. Paul Allen sat as far away from Danny as was physically possible round the oval table; it wasn't lost on the PM, who gave Danny a raised eyebrow.

Picton appeared in the office, closing the door and moving to a position at the head of the table as a large plasma screen behind her burst into life. The recently-released video was replayed; the room remained silent, everyone's eyes fixed onto the screen. The diatribe finished, the screen went blank and the room fell quiet.

The PM cut the tension. "So, the Iranians basically want the West to allow them to legitimately start production of enriched uranium, and for all our monitoring teams to pull out. Best estimate is that they may now have enough to start production of a nuclear weapon. Israel for one are ready to act." The PM sat back in her seat. Her face was stony, fixated on Picton.

"Prime Minister, shall I begin?" The PM nodded. Picton inhaled, then commenced. "Gentlemen, I have to remind you that this briefing is classed as Tier One Deltext eyes only, so no notes, no recordings, and certainly no discussions with anyone outside this room." Picton started her brief, outlining the Iranian threat and the joint pact between the Americans, French and the British to maintain pressure on the regime and ensure they didn't get the necessary know-how to enrich their own uranium and thus the chance to create a nuclear arsenal. Pictures of bombed laboratories and bullet-riddled cars highlighted the covert fight being waged against this threat. "So, as you can see, this is a very dirty war and both sides are stopping at nothing to gain an upper hand." She paused as the screen came back to life, showing a scene of carnage, with both body and car parts spread over a motorway, still blazing away. "We had the upper hand, and then the Americans decide to do this." She turned to the screen.

The news footage was in Arabic. Danny struggled to understand the connection.

"This is the highway out of Baghdad Airport, and that mess is the remains of the convoy taking Qasem Soleimani. And in one move, it turned the whole Shia Middle East against the US and Her Majesty's Government, as the drone was flown from a base in Norfolk."

She let the info hang for a second.

"So, the point to Julia's excellent intelligence brief is that we needed to get ourselves back in the game and fast. All our human sources had dried up, no human intel or anything; the whole Shia Muslim world shut up shop. Then we got a chance, by sheer luck, to get someone on the inside."

"What, an undercover operator?" Danny asked.

"No, Danny, one of theirs, who we turned, so to speak," Julia replied. "We ran him for a while and he provided some excellent results; and then he got his big chance — a new organisation: El Mudzahid Front, a rekindling of an organisation that formed during the Bosnian war approached him."

"A very informative brief, Julia, but what relevance is this to the issues we have within our own organisation — in fact, within this room?" Allen gave Danny a death stare.

"Paul, all will become clear, so just stay calm and focus." The PM waved for Julia to carry on.

"So, I recruited this man, and he has been working and providing credible results since." Julia picked up her iPad and scrolled furiously, looking intently at the screen, then the large flat-screen flickered to life again. A grainy image appeared on the screen. Both men looked at the image.

Danny stared; he knew that face and kept looking at the screen. "That's Abu Talib Haleem: our call sign Buzzard. Omega's first target, given to us by you."

"Correct, Danny, and he is our source; he is our link to inside."

Allen and Danny, almost in unison, shifted their attention between the PM and Picton, each speechless.

Danny broke the silence. "Are you fucking serious?" he blurted,, almost shouting. Danny felt anger surge up his legs like a crazed panic attack. "I have one of my team laying on a mortuary slab cause of these fuckers, and now you tell me he is your source?"

"Danny, you need to understand this is bigger than the sum of all its parts. We're talking about nuclear war in the Middle East if we do nothing."

"But, Ma'am, why not brief us? In fact, why sanction Dom Leigh to go undercover?" Allen was shocked.

"So, you're telling me Buzzard is reporting back to you and he was tipped off about the raids on the locations I highlighted?"

"It's a dirty business Danny, but we planned the whole

scenario. We let it happen to cement Haleem's reputation with the gang."

"You fucking what?" Danny had now lost it. "You're telling me Dom was a plant?" The PM nodded. Picton stood staring at Danny, her face set, showing no emotion. "I even came to you with my fears, doubting my boss, and all along you were playing puppet master with me!" His anger erupted.

"Fucking unbelievable. Sorry Boss." Danny glanced across at his Allen who sat stony-faced, white as a ghost.

"It was the plan all along. We got him the place in the shelter. Branch Eighteen set up the whole thing," Picton said in a matter-of-fact tone and cast a glance over at the PM. "We knew the Iranians wanted to avenge the death of their hero; unfortunately, things got out of hand."

"Dom Leigh was unfortunate, but necessary for the benefit of the free world. His family will be looked after and he will get a full-service burial."

Danny sat staring at the ceiling, shaking his head. He felt as if he wanted to cry. He had never signed up to this dirty war bollocks, and now he had sent a man to his hideous death.

Fuck it, he thought, *I'm out of here right now.* He stood up and pulled a small black wallet out of his back pocket and threw it on the desk. The wallet opened, showing a shiny Phalanx badge and warrant card. "I'm off this gig right now. I feel people in this room are complicit in the manslaughter of a brave man and a loving father." His anger turned to raw emotion, his voice breaking, tears pouring down his checks.

Paul Allen spoke for the first time. "Danny, if you do this now, we'll have no chance of catching that bastard who did for Dom. And the whole of London is in danger — and on our watch."

Danny was halfway to the door. He stopped, still facing away them, realising he had his back to the Prime Minister of Great Britain, which was a balls-out move.

"How can you be sure this tout will play ball and not fuck us over again? The cunt has blood on her hands."

"Language, Danny, please. Believe me, we have this creature by the bollocks and I'm squeezing hard," Picton said, almost with pleasure.

"So, that's why my team is sitting on their arses doing the square root of fuck all while you play Tinker, Soldier, Fucking Spy with your asset?"

"Cut the sarcastic tone, Danny," Paul Allen prompted.

"Danny, we have a plan, and we cannot compromise it now. Furthermore, we need you and your team on the ground when the time's right. I want these bastards as much as you do." Julia sat down for the first time and opened up her iPad. The screen burst into life again with another grainy image. Danny glanced over at Paul, whose face said it all. How many more surprises? Branch Eighteen was like a Jason fucking Bourne movie.

Chapter 61

Luka arrived early. He had borrowed Ardian's trusted Ford Mondeo and driven himself out of London, going against the easy morning traffic, all heading the opposite way into the capital. The entire city seemed paranoid about the gang of cutthroat mercenaries running riot around London. If only they could see them cooked in that squalid flat, awaiting the go-ahead from Redbeard.

The traveller's site was on the edge of London; it was larger than he remembered, with a wide variety and size of caravans parked haphazardly, together with a comprehensive collection of vehicles, from modern, expensive saloon cars to battered old lorries covered in dirt and grime. Dogs roamed the site. It was untidy, even dirty, but had a jovial community spirit about it. It was safe, and Luka needed that now more than ever.

George Taylor appeared, not in his Savile Row suit, but a set of blue coveralls, his hands smeared in oil.

"Luka!" he bellowed, purposefully walking across the broken ground, kicking dogs out of the way as they raced around his feet. "Get these fucking jukuls from out of my feet, for fuck's sake. My boy, you look like shit — you okay? Not in the shit with that lovely girl of yours?"

How the fuck did he know about her?

"Sir, I can't lie; I'm in a terrible state."

"My boy, we can't have that. Come on, let's get some breakfast and see what I can do about it. Carry on with that trailer, boys, it's due to leave on the one o'clock ferry."

They sat drinking tea. While George Taylor listened in silence, his face stern, eyes staring into space, Luka had retold the complete story.

The larger-than-life figure seemed bemused by Luka's request for help. "Luka, what happens if the Feds are on the case, and we get caught up? That's my best boys doing a stretch, and some of my top ordnance in police hands. And they have done some work in the past, my boy, so we could be in a world of pain."

"It will be clinical, George, quick; in, then gone. I'll mop up the mess."

"And the money? How can you guarantee it's still there?"

"Because I'm their courier. I've done all their running around since they arrived; one of my jobs is to distribute the cash once they've completed their twisted mission."

The breakfast duly arrived; a pretty young girl distributed the food to the gathering of men cramped into the dining area of the caravan. The men never uttered a word of thanks to the girl. A male-dominated world, similar to his childhood, Luka mused, as he enjoyed the first decent food he had eaten in what seemed like years.

"How can we protect that wee girl of yours?"

"She will be here with your family," Luka replied, somewhat confused.

"No, you eejit, that girlfriend of yours."

Luka didn't have an answer; it hurt him to even think about her, and whether those bastards had touched her. It brought back too many memories of a life long-since past, but still with him every waking moment.

George gave Luka a fatherly hug, tight and long. "We'll sort this out for you. We can't have these types running roughshod over us. They'll muscle in next." Luka wound down the window of the car and George laughed. "You need a fucking pay rise, boy, what a shit heap." He laughed again, banging loudly on the roof with his fist. Luka eased past the large group of barking dogs, generally being a nuisance.

He eased out onto the A2 and back towards London, looming large on the horizon in the haze of yet another hot day. Whatever happened from now on in, it would be all over before he saw another dawn rise over the capital, that much was sure.

His phone vibrated, a *Telegram* message that could only be from one person. *Here we fucking go. Bring it on.*

Chapter 62

"Okay team, calm down please, and take your seats." Danny approached the lectern. Paul Allen sat next to him, shuffling through his papers, ready to give his part of the brief. The two of them had cleared the air over a beer and now were together on what had to be done. Paul Allen stepped forward to take the lead.

"Team: at last, we're going to take the fight back to them. I can't stress enough how this next twenty-four hours will dictate the future — or lack of — for the Phalanx organisation." He paused, and seemed to be searching for the right words. "The murder of Dom has affected us all, but we have been granted this one opportunity to avenge his death and also prove ourselves credible once and for all. Danny will give you the operational brief now. Godspeed, team; we're in this together. I will be here alongside Danny, ensuring you get all the assets you need. Thank you." He left the lectern and took a seat.

Danny began. "Our mission today is to impose covert surveillance on Luka Avdic and facilitate, when suitable, his arrest." He let it sink in; the team all looked shell-shocked.

"Yes, team, we're going to bring him in." He looked at the screen, the image of a sinister-looking Avdic. "He's been given the code name 'Diablos', and for those non-multilingual amongst you, it means 'devil' in Spanish." Danny continued with an in-depth briefing on Avdic, giving the team more about his training at the camp in Bosnia and his lone wolf status. The only location they had was his home address. Since the meeting with the PM and Picton things had moved; a search of his girlfriend's flat had revealed nothing and his office in the Savoy was being looked at now by a specialist search team. "So, guys, you know the orbat; Alpha projects, whilst we are speaking, are deploying into a house across the road from Avdic's flat so we have an electronic trigger. Be on your game, team; he's good, and will sniff you out. Questions?"

"Any intel from usual sources, Boss?"

"No, the whole thing has gone super quiet; probably gone into radio silence due to whatever this gang is planning. It's important to remember they are still on the loose with a hostage and we do not know where, as yet."

The room dispersed to prepare vehicles and kit. In fifteen minutes, the team would be deployed. Danny sat at his desk observing the operation coming to life, banks of radios being answered as cars and people checked their communications gear.

Paul pulled up a seat. "This is it: as an organisation, we live or die in the next few hours."

Danny turned to look at his boss. "I think it's more important than that; we need to stop these people before they do what they do best."

LUKA PULLED up at the rear of the maisonette. The estate had come to life and was busy, with young mothers pushing prams and gangs of youths aimlessly wandering their patch, looking for trouble or a tear-up with gangs from other parts of London trespassing on their turf; the whole place was territorial. It was a decaying concrete mess and the people inside it had little or no option to get out. The heat, and the smell from bins piled high to the rear of the maisonette, was overwhelming. Luka gently pushed open the gate to the backyard. Nothing had changed; the place looked empty and heavy curtains obscured the view. Luka felt naked; he'd left the pistol in the van. He knew the drill too well. They would humiliate him, make a show that Makki was boss, but he would handle it this time. He had an end plan, and that was all he needed.

He knocked on the door; it opened. The kitchen area was empty. Luka walked in, the man behind him deadlocking the door.

"Turn around," he was ordered, then searched. They pulled up his shirt checking for wires.

"I'm clean. Why do you need to check if I have a wire or plant on me?" The man hustled Luka away and stood staring at him. "Where's Ibro?"

"Next door, but be quiet."

Luka wandered into the large open-plan lounge/dining area, devoid of anything close to furniture.

Ibro was in the middle, flanked on either side by two people. It was a prayer session and Luka quickly realised this was a call for a blessing from Allah, almost asking permission to die. Luka now knew today was the day; he quickly did his maths: five people, the four in the Syrian team and Abu, but what role would he be playing? Luka watched as they went about their routine; it was impressive and inspiring to have such faith. Luka wished he possessed it.

He moved back to the kitchen. He hadn't noticed when he'd entered, but the place smelled of bleach. Everywhere was immaculate, a total transformation, a sure sign they weren't coming back. Along the back wall of the kitchen was a line of black body armour and AK-47 rifles, each with four curved magazines next to them in an orderly fashion.

Animated chatter came from the large living room. He heard footsteps going upstairs, and he wondered if Sally was here. The guilt of the situation hit him hard; he hated what he had done to her. She would be another person fucked for life for having got involved with Luka Avdic.

Ibro Makki appeared. He wore an olive-green t-shirt and combat pants. His angular, tanned face was different; the wispy black beard had been trimmed back and he looked smarter. A tight black bandana on his head gave him a resemblance to a young Mike Tyson, back when he had oozed aggression and violence, as the man in front of him did now.

"Okay, Bosnian, we go silent from now. Phone." He stuck out a hand.

Luka breathed heavily. "Is this necessary? How will you contact me?"

"Give it now." He jabbed Luka in the chest with just enough force to put Luka off balance, powerful for such a slight man. Luka handed over his phone, and it went into a heavy-looking case. "Now everything is done on timelines. You miss one, I will kill you and your *Taghut* slut will be thrown to my wolves."

Luka should now be immune to this intimidation, but his whole body tensed, and Ibro noticed. Invading Luka's aura, he said, "Yes, Bosnian? You got something to say?" He was so close Luka could smell his breath of coffee and cigarettes, but with something else pervading over the top, a pungent aroma. *Surely, they're not taking the drugs they're peddling.*

Ibro gave Luka a handwritten note, with all the day's events laid out. "So, Bosnian, we move from here at four o'clock to go to our mounting base; I'm sure you know it." Luka scanned down the list. It was his mosque in Walthamstow. He thought about telling Ibro about the drugs being dangerous, but that would only confuse things; he needed to have control of these guys at exactly the right time. "Take the goods in the van and this bag to the rear of the mosque, arrive just before morning prayer, and someone will be there to meet you." With that, Ibro pushed past Luka and left the kitchen. A man appeared and handed Luka a large black North Face holdall. Luka left the maisonette, for once happy to be outside, breathing in the pungent air of rotting rubbish. The caustic aroma in the house was overbearing. His eyes were streaming.

He climbed into the van, placing the holdall next to him on the bench seat. It was padlocked with a heavy-duty lock, but Luka managed to prise open a slight opening and, using the camera on his burner phone, he could see the green shades of dollar bills.

He typed in a message, checked it had been delivered, then gunned the engine of the large white Sprinter van. It had begun: the beginning of the end was underway.

Chapter 63

Danny sat just behind the watchkeeper, while two other men worked feverishly either side of him, answering requests on the radio and feeding down images of cars and people as the surveillance team requested them. The main screen showed the camera footage from the flat opposite Luka Avdic's. Danny reached over and checked the surveillance log: no movement had been recorded since the team had gone in this morning — Avdic must be out, or be a very heavy sleeper.

"Okay, let's go through our assets to see if we have all bases covered," Danny said.

"Okay, Boss — we have Heli 147 holding on top of the Royal London Hospital, out of sight on the large HLS they have on the roof. The counter-terrorist team with attachments for CBRN and SO19 has a team dedicated to us in case of hard stops or raids needed."

"Okay, and are all the relevant authorities in place?" Danny's attention went to the main screen as a man exited the flat and turned right towards the shops at the bottom of Brookfield Road. "Can you rewind on that system?"

"Yes, Boss."

"Get me an image of the man who just left." The camera

rewound as Danny got up and moved around in front of the screen. "Well, I'll be damned — if it isn't Kevin Donaldson," Danny said, laughing as he turned to the desk.

"You know him, Boss?" the watchkeeper inquired.

"Oh yes — Kevin Donaldson, one-time master bomber maker and a leading player in the New IRA. A genius at his deadly craft," Danny informed them.

Julia Picton took the call. She was in the Branch Eighteen gym; the harshness of physical exercise always eased her mood. She was alone and took a perch on the bench next to the stack of barely-used dumbbells. Few in Branch Eighteen had the fitness bug. She listened to Danny, her mind now in operational mode; this was going to be a day of small margins for sure, but nobody was going to jeopardise her asset.

"Danny, are you sure it was him?"

"It's him alright. I spent years of my life chasing him and his team. Julia, this is the definitive link we need; the Irish are one hundred percent mixed up with this."

Julia grabbed a towel and wiped the sweat off her face and neck. "Give me twenty minutes, Danny. I need to clean up, then we'll schedule a confirmatory brief before we go in and do the hard stop on Avdic."

"Julia, can your source help?"

"No, he fucking can't help. Leave him well out of this." She hung up, grabbed her things and rushed back to the secure sanctum of her office.

She got out her burner phone from the long slim drawer at the top of her huge ornate desk, then

sent a text: "I need her location; it's going to guns soon. Ensure you place the beacon to find."

Picton sat back, dressed in a smart trouser suit and blue business shirt. Power dressing was her thing, especially in a male-dominated environment. She'd used her good looks to her advantage throughout her stellar career to date and wasn't shy about jumping into bed with people if it made the difference. Luka's father had been different: that was love, and she'd never found that again, but exercise had replaced alcohol before it got hold of her.

"We left her at the old place, and need to go silent on these means; they have all dumped comms as of now, which means it's on."

Picton smiled to herself; this was the buzz she'd missed. *Right, let's go.*

She called for her driver. She wasn't going to miss this for the world.

Chapter 64

"All call signs, you have blue light clearance from the Blackwall Tunnel to Blue Five two, then police escorts down to the location. We need to move, team."

The whole A2 dual carriageway had been cleared to allow the strike team to get to Bon Fleur, as the last intelligence had Sally-Anne Nixon at that location.

"Griffin copy, I'm lead, lane two of two."

Danny watched the interactive screen as the four cars exited the Blackwall Tunnel. They had limited time to get to Bon Fleur camp. He watched as the dots made progress along the A2.

"Blue Fifty towards Blue Five One, speed one forty, lane two of two." The engine noise was audible over the radio.

The four cars had the A2 to themselves, police blocking all entries and exits. They had to make progress; Sally Anne needed to be safe before they could take out Luka and the Syrians.

"That's Kilo coming through, lane two of two, one mike out, speed one sixty." The roar of the wind and the engine noise let everyone listening on the loudspeakers know how fast the operator was going on his race-standard pursuit bike.

Danny looked back at Picton and the Prime Minister observing proceedings. "That's the motorbike, Ma'am; he will get ahead of the team."

"I should think so too, at those speeds," she said, laughing.

Danny turned his attention to the surveillance feeds. "Any movement?"

"No. The unknown male returned with shopping, but no sign of Diablos," the watchkeeper replied.

Danny walked to the rear of the operations room where the group stood drinking coffee out of paper cups.

"Ma'am, Julia, what about the Irish element? We know about Donaldson, but they could have a full active service unit on standby."

"They walk."

Danny looked bemused. "Sorry, what?"

"Danny, they walk, no questions. That's a fight for another day."

Danny walked away, head spinning. He'd spent years chasing those fuckers. He took his seat again. He picked up his headset and placed it over his head. "Any update on Diablo?"

"Negative; unknown male in the flat keeps checking out the window, but nothing else to report."

Time stood still in the operations room as the background commentary of the team heading to rescue the hostage continued. Those in the know were just praying she was alive. If not, they had no bargaining chips left.

"Stand by, stand by, that Sprinter van coming off the A102 towards Alpha One."

"Okay, strike team: if it's Diablos, it's a go." Danny alerted the SO19 team to get ready. None of the covert surveillance assets were to be involved: unseen, unheard, and that's how it should stay.

"That's Diablos manoeuvring, attempting to park; engine off, driver still in the vehicle."

Danny punched down on the pressel. “Go. Go. Go.”

The strike team, in two black Range Rovers, sped down Casland Road, both vehicles screaming to a halt and blocking the van in.

“Out of the van and lay in the road; keep your hands on your head,” a large man shouted as one of the occupants of the first Range Rover stood in the road, dressed in black with sinister-looking balaclavas, HK-53 rifles pointing at the now prone body of Luka Avdic laying in the road.

Chapter 65

Luka felt someone behind him. Plasticuffs were biting into his wrists. The blindfold was removed, and his eyes struggled to focus as the harsh lights blinded him. Slowly, he made out the shapes of people.

"Take your time," came a woman's voice, kind and compassionate. Luka knew to remain tight-lipped. He presumed the Security Service had lifted him. The woman came into view. He blinked his eyes in rapid succession, trying to clear his view. "Hi Luka. It's been a while." Julia Picton spoke first.

Luka thought his mind had gone; he stared at the woman for a long time. Silence filled the barren, empty room. They seemed alone; no sound permeated the silence.

Without warning he pushed against the bindings, every sinew in his neck and face bulging; he couldn't move in any direction other than to the floor, the chair bowling over backwards.

Unseen hands grabbed him and put him back upright.

"You are as dead to me now as the day you walked out on us so fuck off!"

"Now, Luka, you need me more than you could know. As it

stands your girlfriend is still a hostage and you're looking at life in prison for offences under the Terrorism Act."

Luka just kept staring with hatred at the woman for long moments, the woman who he'd spent years planning to kill.

Picton knew she could play the long game, but nobody had the benefit of time. She knew that once the Syrians got wind that he'd been arrested they would go underground, and as it stood, Abu Haleem was uncontactable.

She eventually broke the silence. "He was the best we ever had." No reply. "He loved his country, and he loved his family. He was more than an interpreter." She paused, and Luka's eyes fixed back on her.

"What, your fuck-buddy? Your plaything, you fucking whore," he spat back.

"No, Luka, your dad and I met through work, but he was working for us and he was the best intelligence gatherer we had. A true professional."

Now Luka was fully engaged, his anger still apparent. "What, he worked for you?"

"Not just me, but for the greater good. Some of the intel he gave us changed the course of the war."

"Didn't stop the massacre, though. You fuckers walked out on us."

Picton paused; she felt long-dormant emotions emerging from the bottom of a dark pond.

"Luka, I loved him, and not one day has passed since that I haven't thought of him. It fucking hurts me too. People may know me as a steel-cold bitch with no heart or morals, but I'm not that. This life has been my escape from the loss of your father." Luka's anger subsided as the room went quiet again. "You're the image of him, and if you're like him, you will have a strong moral compass. You aren't like those people, Luka. Yes, you want revenge, but for now humanity needs you."

"Where was humanity in ninety-five? You people let those bastards murder us."

"Yes, Luka, we did, and I have no reasoning why."

The phone rang and Picton walked to the back of the room, that looked like an army barracks.

Luka reckoned he was at a special forces base somewhere. He quickly glanced around the room; they were indeed alone.

"Luka, I have someone who wants to talk to you." The phone was passed to him.

Tears flooded down his face. "Did they hurt you? Are you okay?" He nodded, sobbing but smiling with mixed emotions.

Picton turned to Danny and Paul Allen, who had come into the room. "She's alive. They kept her in a fucking empty septic tank with no toilet facilities; she's in a right state, but alive. SAS medics are treating her en route to the secure ward at the Royal London."

"How did the CTR teams miss her? Heli 147 had thermal capability, as did the operators." Paul Allen sensed a fuck-up.

"Don't worry, Paul, the team missed nothing. They had lined it with material that counters thermal image cameras, technology they used in Syria against the regime and the Russians. Right, leave me. I need Luka buying into our plans and back on the streets asap. We only have three hours."

Chapter 66

The room was tense. The Prime Minister took her seat facing the bank of screens. Technicians worked with a renewed intensity to get everything ready. The assembled entourage chatted in hushed whispers.

"Ma'am, all set."

"Thank you." She nodded her appreciation. Once they had left she stood up. "Thanks, everyone, for being so prompt. The briefing packs you have been issued are very detailed, so please study the contents. Carry on please, Julia."

"Tonight, we have mounted an operation to negate the threat posed by the Syrian active service unit currently operating within our city." She paused, and a map flashed up on the screen. "Their intended target is the Honor Oak Water Treatment Plant with a plan to pollute the system with a hybrid toxin designed by Saddam Hussein's scientists and kept hidden from the world until now." Again, she paused. "We have an asset working within the team. He is briefed and will facilitate the plan to strike as they attempt to enter the plant via this back route here," she said and pointed to the map with an interactive laser pointer. "It's a golf course, which provides our strike team great cover and is also away from any public intrusion."

"Julia." She looked up, as did the PM, who flashed a look of disdain.

"Yes, David?"

The head of the Met Police had interrupted her brief. "Do we have a contingency if they actually get into the plant?"

"Yes, we do: a team from Hereford inserted about an hour ago into the actual plant to ensure it's secure."

"Julia, please carry on."

Julia continued on with her brief, outlining the plan to facilitate a hard stop using a joint SAS and SO19 team. "And we have CBRN teams supported by the HART teams from London Ambulance. The Army is also supplying a specialist EOD team." She paused, taking a sip of water, her hands shaking gently. "We shall secure the arrest area and contain any hazards in situ. We will take any captives to Paddington Green for initial questioning, and we have decontamination teams at the station. Finally, the media have agreed an embargo until 0900 tomorrow morning."

"Julia, thank you. I will now take any questions." The PM took over. None came.

Strange that, thought Julia. *Fucking cowards.*

"Okay — the time now is half past midnight. We set H hour for one thirty. There are refreshments at the back so please help yourselves." The room burst into animated chatter.

People had slowly drifted back to their seats around the large oval table. People initially started to mutter, then talk openly.

Picton looked at the clock: almost two thirty. She was now regretting not putting a covert follow on the gang. The surveillance shield started close to the plant. *Luka knew that,* she mused. *Fuck, he's not been turned, has he?* She suddenly doubted her rationale.

Chapter 67

Luka was leading the vehicle convoy in the trusted old Ford Mondeo with Abu, aka Buzzard, as a passenger. Buzzard was as yet unaware that Luka knew he was working for the security services. The Sprinter van was behind them, containing the Syrian ASU and their deadly chemical cargo. Luka had practised the route and knew every little shortcut they could take. With his senses on hyper-alert, all it took was one inquisitive police officer bored on night shift to pull the Sprinter van over. Then all hell would break loose. The Syrians were carrying some exceptional firepower and wouldn't think twice about using it.

The route took them into the heart of south London — not as hostile as Broadwater Farm, more suburbia; normal families trying to live normal lives, which made Luka's job even more vital. Honor Oak Water Treatment Plant was situated off Hichisson Road, backing onto a large, disused golf course. The plan was to use the main gate, which was left unsecured by friendlies working at the plant. But Luka had other ideas.

The small Icom radio burst into life. "Why are we going off route?" Ibro asked.

"Too risky to go in the main gate, overlooked by houses. I have sorted a more concealed route in," Luka lied.

The alternative route went to the rear of the large treatment plant and down a tree-lined road with no houses. The trees were heavy with foliage, branches struggling under the weight; it was perfect for the new plan.

The two vehicles eased off Brenchley Gardens onto a dirt track. Two-hundred metres down was a five-bar gate where Luka pulled up the car. He picked up the radio. "I have the keys to the gate. I'm getting out to unlock it, so stay tight."

"Okay, but fucking hurry up," came the curt reply.

Luka got out of the Mondeo. The woods were dark; even the nearby streetlights only managed to cast an amber edge to the darkness. The shadows in the depths of these woods held a menacing deepness. Luka walked to the gate and pulled on the rusty chain holding the padlock. The rattling sound filled the void.

He glanced around suddenly; he saw movement — no sound, just ghostly shadows.

Emerging stealthily from the darkness, four men appeared. Dressed in black and with their faces smeared with camouflage cream, they each held short Remington 870p pump-action shotguns. They moved in unison, two going to the side of the van, two moving to the rear, waiting to reach for the handle silently.

Luka braced himself.

The still of the night erupted into a cacophony of noise as the four men pumped round after round into the occupants of the van, glass shattering amid the deafening percussive sound of gunshots.

Luka raced to the side of the Mondeo. Abu sat in the brace position, head firmly in his lap, paralysed by the sudden eruption of noise.

Luka grabbed him. "Get out! Move, for fuck's sake!" He

grabbed him out of the car, putting his mouth to his ear. "Picton wants you to go to this address and stay put." Abu shot Luka a confused look; even in the semi-light Luka sensed fear in the man's face.

The four men stood at the rear of the vehicle.

"Job done?" Luka asked.

"Yeah, all done," came the reply.

Luka looked into the rear of the van. Even in the darkness, it smelled and looked like a scene from hell.

Paul Allen's phone rang. He turned away from the masses and took the call. He whispered in Picton's ear. A picture truly painted a thousand words.

"Ma'am, we have a development."

"Really?" The PM looked up from her notes, concerned.

"Can you please switch to the surveillance radio channel, and put the centre screen onto their live feed?"

The technician tapped commands into his laptop. "Sierra Three, you're on an open mic to COBRA briefing room; carry on, please." Allen sat down.

"Copy that. We got alerted to sounds of gunfire to the rear of the target location." The surveillance operator outlined what they had found down a track to the side of the golf course. "There are two dead IC4 males in the front of the van and two in the rear." The video images showed the carnage of the scene in a shadowy, spooky green glow.

Picton butted in. "Confirm four dead?"

"Copy, four dead, all wearing military gear and body armour. They have all been close-quarter assassinated with shotguns, multiple shots to the heads and torsos. No weapons found, but four clear plastic containers of liquid, as briefed, are accounted for. A note was left stuck to the windscreen giving a location for the rest of the liquid; specialised team are checking now."

"Thank God." The PM looked around the room.

"Get that team to the location asap," Picton ordered. "Not the way it was planned, but an excellent result," Picton whispered to Paul Allen. "Gentlemen, I want no stone unturned with the after-action review and assessment: full DNA matches, the full nine yards. I need to get the CIA at Langley onside with this and how it's panned out. The intelligence world will want answers." Picton turned to Allen. "This is all Luka, the devious bastard; he got his way, for sure, and a significant result for us. He's good — very fucking good." She smiled, a rare occurrence.

The PM walked over. "Julia, can I have a word please? We're going to blame the Irish, Julia, but let's be honest with each other — we know who orchestrated this, don't we?" The PM gave Julia a stern look, then she turned and left the room.

EPILOGUE

Luka pulled into the travellers' camp and was met by the same escort pack of feral dogs. It seemed like an age since he last had been here, but it had only been forty-eight hours. The plan had worked like clockwork. George's boys acted with a stealth and violence Luka had found surprisingly efficient; they executed the plan to the finest detail. They looked like gypsies, but you'd only fuck with them at your peril.

George appeared, a beaming smile on his face, and strode across to Luka. "Fuck me, boy, last night took me back twenty years."

"George, your boys were fucking awesome. I owe you big time."

"No, you don't, boy, you've looked after me in the past. Oh, and Merjem is fine — she's out in the paddock feeding the horses with Molly, one of my granddaughters. She's good as gold, that one."

Luka grabbed the bag out of the boot. "Here you go, George. Nice doing business with you." Luka smiled as he passed over a bag containing a million dollars of untraceable USA State Department money, once destined for Iraqi warlords and now in the hands of a unique type of warlord — but just as deadly.

"Would pay to see the Iman's face at the mosque when he opens the bag to find it full of paper towels," Luka said, and both men laughed.

"How did you manage that?"

"Swapped them over when I went to pick up the bottles of Botuline or whatever fucked-up stuff they had planned to use."

"Shame about that boy — the ex-para lad, though. What was their plan?" George asked with genuine compassion.

"To pour poison into the Honor Oak Treatment Plant. Would have fucked up the fresh water supply in London for years."

George grabbed Luka in a bear hug, and they embraced tightly. "You're like a son to me, boy."

"George, can you look after Merjem for another day or so? I have some business to attend to."

"Work can wait. Fancy a tea, or breakfast?" George offered.

"Not work. Something more important. I need to go."

DANNY HAIGH PARKED the car outside the idyllic thatched cottage and entered a well-tended garden via a small white gate. The rose bushes were in full bloom, and the lawn was trimmed to perfection. The owners of this property loved their garden, no doubt.

He paused for a moment, then knocked on the door. Dogs barked inside. A voice calmed them down. The door opened.

"Hello — um, you must be Charley's mum," Danny said politely.

"Yes, that's correct — and you?" she inquired.

This caught Danny offside. He thought Charley would have told her parents of his visit, but clearly not. "Sorry, my name is Danny Haigh, I'm Charley's manager." He paused for thought. The woman turned without a word and moved back down the hallway and into the kitchen. Danny followed without any prompting; he could almost taste the animosity.

The kitchen was deceptively big. Large stone floor tiles and oak cupboards gave it a farmhouse feel. It was immaculately tidy. Two dogs, English Pointers, shared a bed by the huge Aga stove.

"Sorry, I didn't get your name," Danny said.

The lady turned to face him. "I didn't give it to you, that's why." She stared through him. Danny felt uncomfortable. "Mr Haigh, my daughter is a wreck. She hasn't spoken two words since she came home. She either sits in her room, or at the bottom of the garden, not wanting company; she wants to be on her own. God only knows why she wanted to do what she did, but it's come back to haunt us all." The woman turned to face the large patio doors, which were opened onto the vast back garden. "You will find her at the far end of the garden. Be careful — you lot have done enough to her."

Danny walked down the gravel path between deep borders of flowers. Charley was sat on the grass hugging her knees into her chest. Danny was almost on top of her before she glanced round. She gave Danny a rudimentary smile and returned to her gazing. Danny took off his suit jacket, loosened his tie, and sat down next to her. He put an arm around her shoulder, and she nestled into him without a word. He could feel her sobbing before he heard it.

She looked into Danny's eyes. "I miss him so much. I loved him — he was so vulnerable, so caring. That fucking wife of his fucked his head up."

Danny nodded; he didn't know what else to say. They sat in silence for a long time until her sobbing abated.

"Excellent result," she finally said.

"Yeah, amazing really; we're pinning it to the Irish, but it was Avdic for sure. God knows how he pulled it off, but he did."

They both returned to silence, just a gentle breeze and the sound of birds.

"When will the funeral be?" Charley asked.

"Because Dom was murdered, it may take a while before he is released for burial. Will you go?" he asked.

She paused, looking up at the sky. "I want to, but I don't know if I can." She started to cry again.

"Well, the choice is yours. You have my support whatever you choose."

"Can I get you a drink? I'll get Mum to make us tea."

"No, thanks — your mother made it plain that I'm not welcome."

"Sorry," Charley said.

"I have some news for you. Paul Allen has resigned, and they have made me Branch Head. It seems Omega has a future."

Charley smiled. "Any chance I can come back? I need to get out of my own head and back to work."

Danny turned to her. "Charley, you're an excellent operator and I'd have you back in a heartbeat. So when you feel good to go, call me."

They hugged. *She looks better than when I arrived, like a weight's been taken off her shoulders; maybe work is what she needs.*

Danny left via the side gate; he didn't want to face Charley's mother again. Now he knew where Charley got her tenacity from.

THE LIFT OPENED at the 37th floor. A warning sign stated, "No entry. Floor not finished. Authorised people only".

The Shard building, with its unique glass fragment shape, dominated the skyline for miles around. The top of it was as-yet unfinished, and no workers were present on a weekend, so it was a perfect place for a covert rendezvous.

Luka walked out of the lift and towards the figure stood by the edge of the unfinished floor. It was totally wide open, with no windows, and definitely not for the faint-hearted or those scared of heights.

She was looking down onto the train lines that merged in and out of London Bridge station far below.

She turned, smartly dressed and elegant as ever.

"Hello, Luka."

"Hello, Julia." Picton put out her hand, and he took it.

"Well done." She turned to the vista of London that spread out before them. "Abu?" she inquired.

"At the safe house you told us to take him to. He's scared, Julia, shitting himself. Thinks you're going to rendition him or something."

Picton looked out over London without replying.

Ruthless bitch, Luka thought.

After a long pause she turned to Luka. "The millions of people out there will never know what you did for them. Same for my work, and indeed your father's work; people in our line of employment will always go unappreciated, but that's just how it is." They both stood observing the vast city in silence, looking out over the huge concrete metropolis. "Have you had time to think about my offer?" She turned, looking straight into the eyes that reminded her so much of a love she'd had and lost many years ago.

END

HAVE YOUR SAY

Did you enjoy *UNHOLY ALLIANCE*?
I hope you did.

If you have a moment, would you mind rating it, or leaving a review?

It would be hugely helpful.

Click here to rate this book!

And many thanks for your time.

Printed in Great Britain
by Amazon

30637689R00223